Some Are Sicker Than Others

ANDREW SEAWARD

To purchase this book online please visit:
http://www.amazon.com/dp/B007B7GJGE

For my parents who,
even after all the hell I put them through,
never gave up on me, not once, never.
Mom and Dad, if it weren't for you,
I wouldn't still be here. I love you both very much.
Thank you.

Table of Contents

Chapter 1

Monty

Tonight was the night, the night he'd ask her, the night he'd finally lay it all on the line. Monty felt sick and nervous, thrilled and excited, like a thousand butterflies were fluttering against his ribs. But, he had to do it. He had to go through with it. He'd been through too much already to just chicken out now. He'd get up on that stage and deliver his one-year speech at the podium then propose to Vicky in front of everyone at AA. If she said yes, then everything would be perfect—everything would be the way it was supposed to be.

He took a deep breath and felt the outside of his jeans pocket to make sure the little felt box holding the ring was still there. It was; pressed against his thigh, nestled in his pocket, a modest, one-carat diamond that he'd gotten from his mom.

As he picked up his pace, he made a left onto Thirteenth Street, being careful not to slip on the icy asphalt. It was a beautiful night. The moon was out and the stars were shining, like diamonds impregnated in a coal-black sky. What a wonderful night to be clean and sober. What a wonderful night to be alive. To think, all he had to do was quit drinking and he could've felt like this his entire life—no more shaking, no more seizing, no more getting up to puke in the middle of the night. If he'd just listened to his parents and stopped a little sooner, he could've avoided all those years of suffering and pain. All those nights of lying face down in a puddle of his own blood and urine, praying for God to come and take him away, his hands around a bottle, his head above the porcelain, and that sick, vile poison bubbling inside his veins. Those trips to the emergency room in some random state hospital just so he could get pumped full of fluids and strapped down to a bed, while nurses with bad breath, bad hair, and bad makeup stuck a tube down his dick just so he could pee. Christ, what a fucking nightmare. Thank god it was finally all over. Thank god he finally found a way to stay clean.

As he rounded the corner, the AA house appeared before him, all lit up and decorated like some grand, old hotel. It was a redbrick, renovated, four-story school building that the city had bought and transformed into an AA meeting hall. It was tucked inside the corner of York and Thirteenth Street, a few blocks off of Colfax, between the zoo and the park. And tonight it looked absolutely majestic covered with hundreds of twinkling, red, blue, and green Christmas lights. There were lights on the trees and wreaths on the doorway and a sign on the overhang that said, *Happy New Year!*

It was only seven-thirty, but the place was already busy, packed with people milling around on the front porch. They were laughing, talking, and slurping down cups of coffee, embers of cigarettes glowing red between their lips. Jesus, look at them all. In less than an hour, he was going to be up in front of them, standing at that podium, pouring out his guts. The very thought of it made him feel queasy and he wondered if maybe he should just take off and run. He could grab Vicky and get the hell out of here and take her some place where they could be alone. Some place quiet, like a candlelit restaurant or maybe that cute lodge up in Nederland—the one with the Jacuzzi and the view of the mountains, right there at the entrance of the Rocky Mountain National Park. If they started now, they could be up there in an hour, under the stars, alone in the dark—no meetings, no prayers, no counselors, no sponsors, just the two of them naked in each other's arms.

He smiled as he pictured the image of Vicky's naked body curled in his arms—her lips, her eyes, her soft, wet kisses, her face in his hands, her legs coiled tightly around his hips. Unfortunately, he knew that it was only wishful thinking, because there was no way in hell Vicky would let him back out now. She'd probably kick his ass just for even mentioning it. This AA crap was more serious to her than life itself. In fact, to her, it was life. She believed that if she missed even one measly meeting, then she'd be risking the chance of relapsing again. Monty, on the other hand, didn't take any of this crap seriously, and the only reason he went was because of her. He knew that if he didn't at least try, he might lose her, and that was something he couldn't risk.

He pushed open the iron gate and started up the porch staircase, one hand on the railing, the other over the ring. When he got to the top, he stood on his tiptoes, searching for Vicky through the busy crowd. But, he couldn't see her. There were too many people, and the haze of the cigarette smoke seemed to blur his sight. He leveled his heels and took a step backward then reached in his pocket and pulled out his phone. He scrolled to Vicky's name at the bottom of the directory then typed in a message that said, "Where are you?"

Just as he hit the send button, he could feel someone watching him, like the current of a riptide pulling him out to sea. He looked up and there he saw her, smiling like an angel from underneath the garland of a brightly lit Christmas wreath. She was dressed in jeans and a fuzzy, white sweater, her face blushed with winter, her smile so damn sweet. He put away his phone and moved towards her quickly, the snow on the porch crunching beneath his feet. When he got to her, he threw his arms around her, then kissed her lips and kissed her cheeks. She tasted sweet like cinnamon candy or one of those red and white striped peppermints.

"I missed you," he said, as he pulled her in close, her face in his hands, her arms around his neck.

"I missed you too, baby."

"You did?"

"Of course, I did."

Monty smiled and squeezed her tighter, feeling his face against the warmth of her skin. "Did you have a good Christmas?" he asked, looking down at her, at the thick, black curls falling over her forehead.

She nodded and smiled up at him, her chin resting against the base of his neck. "I sure did. I've been busy. Getting everything ready for next week."

"Oh yeah? You getting excited?"

"Oh Monty, I can't wait. I've been getting the house all set up. I've probably been to Bed, Bath, and Beyond like four times in the last week, just buying all sorts of stuff—stuff I didn't even know I needed. I got Tommy a new bed with cute blue and white, bear-imprinted bed sheets, matching pajamas and fuzzy bear slippers. It's going to be so great. I can't tell you how excited I am to be a mommy again."

"I'm happy for you, Vicky. I really am. That's so awesome."

"Thanks, baby. Only one more week and he's all mine—no grandparents, no supervisors, nothing—just me and him, like old times."

Monty leaned forward and gave her a deep kiss on the forehead, while caressing her cheek with his hand. "You're a good mom," he said. "I'm proud of you."

"Thanks baby, you're sweet. You've been a good friend to us. You're a big part of Tommy's life. He loves you, you know?"

"I love him too. He's a good kid."

They smiled at each other for a while as the Christmas lights twinkled all around them on the porch. Then Vicky took his hand and pulled it towards her and held it against the crease of her neck. "Hey, wait a minute," she said, as if she suddenly remembered something, her eyes widening to the size of two silver dollar coins. "What about you? We haven't even talked about you yet. How was your trip?"

Monty hesitated and looked away from her. Damn. He was hoping he wouldn't have to get into this just yet. "It was okay, I guess."

"Just okay? Didn't you get to spend some quality time with your parents?"

Monty snickered. "I don't know if I'd call it quality time."

"Aw, why not? Weren't they happy to see you?"

"Oh…I don't know. It's weird now. Different."

"How so?"

Monty sighed and turned away from her, moving his eyes out across the snow-covered park. He didn't want to think about it tonight, but all he could see was his mother and the look on her face when he first asked for the ring. She didn't laugh or cry or throw her arms around him. She didn't even break a smile as she handed over the ring. It was as if she was holding her breath, waiting for something bad to happen, waiting for the walls to crumble in again. And at that moment, he knew that things would never be better. He knew that he'd probably never get to hug her again. She'd always look at him like he was some kind of monster who could snap at any moment and hit her in the face again.

He shut his eyes and took a deep breath inward, rubbing his hands against the bridge of his nose.

"Monty?" Vicky whispered, moving in towards him, her hand rubbing against the back of his neck. "Are you okay?"

"No, not really."

"What's wrong?"

"It's just—" He shook his head and looked away from her. The words were like pieces of hot metal lodged in his throat.

"What is it, baby? Come on, you can tell me."

"It's my mom."

"What about her?"

"I don't know, it's like she's afraid of me or something— afraid I'm going to start drinking again. I mean, she couldn't even bring herself to hug me. She couldn't even look at me without bursting into tears. And anytime my dad got up and left us together, she'd always find an excuse to leave the room. She either had to do the dishes or fold the laundry—it was like she was afraid to be alone in the same room with me. I just wish I knew what I could do to make her trust me—what I could say to prove to her that I'm going to be okay."

"Well, I guess it's just going to take some time. I mean, it's only been a year. It's going to take some time to build up that trust again."

"Yeah, I guess. I just wish I knew how to make it go faster."

"Well, just keep working your program and going to your meetings and everything will eventually work itself out."

Monty scoffed. "You really believe that?"

"Of course, I do. It's the only thing that keeps me going. If I didn't believe that then what would be the point? You know?"

"Yeah, I guess."

"Hey, come on, baby. Cheer up. It'll get better. I promise. You remember what it says in the Big Book about promises, don't you?"

Monty just looked away and shrugged his shoulders. He really didn't want to hear this AA crap right now. "I don't know," he said.

"Yeah, you do. Come on, you remember." She started reciting the words slow and easy, as if she actually expected Monty to join in: "No matter how far down the scale we've gone, we will see how our experience can benefit others. That feeling of uselessness and self-pity will disappear. We will lose interest in selfish things and gain interest in our fellows, and our whole attitude and outlook upon life will change. Are these extravagant promises?" Vicky paused and looked up at Monty, waiting for him to say the verse.

"We think not," he said halfheartedly, not really believing it himself.

"They are being fulfilled among us, sometimes quickly, sometimes…"

"…slowly."

"And they will always materialize if we…what?"

"Work for them."

"That's it! You got it, baby!" Vicky squealed and wrapped her arms around him then leaned forward and gave him a big, wet kiss on the cheek. "See. Now, doesn't that make you feel better?"

"No. Not really."

"Uh! And just why not?"

"I don't know. I guess I just don't get it."

"Well, what don't you get?"

"I don't get how God is supposed to keep me sober."

"Well, it doesn't have to be God, Monty. You know that. It can be whatever you want it to be."

"Can it be you?"

"What?"

"Can it be you? Can you be my higher power?"

"No. Absolutely not."

"Why not?"

"Because it just doesn't work that way."

"It's worked pretty good so far. I mean, you're the only reason I quit drinking. You're probably the only reason I didn't kill myself."

"Please don't say that, Monty."

"Well it's true."

"I know, but—"

"—but what?"

"But you just can't say that to me."

"Why not?"

"Because it's not fair."

"To who?"

"To me! Look Monty, I don't want to be your only reason for living. I don't want to be your only hope of surviving this thing."

"Well, what do you want?"

"I want you to be happy. I want you to stop punishing yourself and start living your life again."

"That's a little easier said than done, don't you think?"

"No Monty. It's not. You just have to want it. You have to want it for yourself. Look, no one but you is going to keep you sober, and the quicker you realize that, the easier it's going to be. I mean, you say you want to speed things up and have a better relationship with your parents, right?"

"Yeah."

"So, what are you doing about it?"

"What do you mean?"

"I mean, it's already been a year and you're still on your fourth step, right?"

"Yeah. So?"

"So, I'm already on step twelve."

"Well, I like to take my time, I guess."

"Yeah, I guess so."

"Hey, come on, don't be nasty. I'm trying, aren't I? I mean, I'm doing this silly one-year speech tonight. Hell, if it was up to me, I'd skip the whole damn thing."

"You know I'd never let you get away with that."

"Yeah, I know. Why do you think I'm still here? Like I said, if it wasn't for you, I would've never gotten sober. I wouldn't have even made it through that first week. You may not want to hear it, but you saved me, Vicky. You're the only reason I didn't end up killing myself."

"I know, but I just wish you'd take this program a little more seriously. I wish you'd do it for yourself instead of for me. I mean, what would you do if something were to happen? What would you do if you were to lose me?"

"Oh come on. Don't talk like that. Nothing bad is going to happen. We've been through too much already to have some bullshit happen again. Besides, I'd never let anything bad happen to you. You're too damn important to me. I love you, Vicky."

"I love you too, Monty."

Monty smiled and stared at her for a while in the haze of the cigarette smoke as the snow floated off the overhang of the porch. Then, he leaned forward and kissed her forehead, kissed her nose, and kissed her lips. "Come on," he said, as he took her hand and pulled it forward, motioning towards the front of the house. "We better get going. We don't want to be late."

Chapter 2

Speaker Meeting

Monty and Vicky walked arm and arm through the crowd of people, across the porch, and through the front double doors. When they got inside, they headed towards the meeting hall, which was up two flights of stairs, on the second floor. However, when they got to the foot of the stairs, Vicky said she first wanted to find her sponsor, Susan, and asked if Monty would wait for her in the front room foyer. Monty nodded and stepped under the staircase, tucking himself into the little pocket between the stairs and the wall.

As he stood there waiting, he watched as people began to wander in from the outside porch area and get in line for fresh cups of coffee. They all seemed so happy, laughing, smiling, and carrying on with one another, as if nothing in the world could ever cause them any harm. It made him sick. He couldn't understand how they could be so cheery after all the horrible things they'd done. He'd seen these people before. He'd listened to their stories. He knew what kind of shit they'd pulled. These people committed crimes, they went to prison, they stole from their families, they abandoned their kids. But, it was like they had no remorse, like they were proud of it, like going to jail was a merit badge on their sleeve. What did they think? That they had no culpability? That they were free from guilt? Free from blame? That by joining this silly, little club and simply quitting drinking, they were suddenly absolved from all of their sins? That all they had to do was turn their will and their life over to some bullshit higher power and suddenly they were saints about to enter martyrdom? Ha. What a lie. What a cop out. What a bunch of Judeo-Christian horseshit.

Monty would never do that. He'd never be like them, unwilling to take responsibility for all the damage he did. It was his past and he had to live with it. He had to live with it every moment up to his dying day. No matter what he did and no matter where he went, he'd always be the son who punched his mother in the face and called her a cunt—the son who threw away his life and turned his back on his family so he could go live on the streets as a fucking drunk. Why? Why'd he do it? Why'd he put his mom through all of that pain? All he had to do was pick up the phone and let her know that he was okay. Three fucking years...that's what he wasted...three fucking years of nothing but pain. What was wrong with him? Why did he take so long to get clean? He could've been a doctor or a scientist or a professor, he could've been more than just a fucking dry drunk waste of a human being. If only he could go back to school and finish his doctorate—if only he could go back now and achieve his dream. But how? How could he go back after everything that's happened? How could he ever hope to be normal again? He was an alcoholic, plain and simple—a sick, demented person with an incurable disease. For the rest of his life, he would have to walk around on eggshells as if one misstep would knock him right back to his knees. Well, wasn't that what his sponsor taught him? Wasn't that the main message he got from AA? That no matter what he did or how long he stayed sober, he would never escape this disease? It was a part of him now—it lived deep inside his tissue, pumping from his heart, pulsing through his veins. He couldn't erase it, he couldn't hide from it—it was as much a part of him as was his DNA. All he could do was go to his meetings, call his sponsor, and pray to God for just one more day.

But why? Why did he have to live like that? Why did he have to live like such a fucking slave? Like a servant to some intangible infection—a victim of some abstract disease? Why couldn't he just be sober and be done with it already? Why did everything in his life now have to revolve around AA? For fuck's sake, all this talk about faith and higher powers and those endless lectures about spirituality and God. It was too much…too much to handle…too much for someone who didn't even like God. He was sick of God. He'd had enough of the bastard growing up in the South in a Catholic school and a Catholic family in a Christian country in a Christian town. All those people packed in the church on Sunday mornings, praying and singing to their precious God—a God who punished them if they sinned against him, who came from the clouds and struck them down, and that giant statue of Jesus hanging above the altar, the one with his hands and feet nailed to the cross, and all those people kneeling down in front of him with their eyes closed and their tongues rolled out. He didn't get it. He didn't get why people prayed and sang to him…why they killed and gave their lives for his love. Were they that impressionable? Didn't they have minds of their own?

He considered himself lucky that he got away when he did and went off to public college and was finally able to de-program himself of all that crap. But now, because he was in recovery, it was like he had to hear about it all over again—about how God was his only chance at redemption, how staying sober wasn't even possible without him. How was God going to keep him sober? How was God going to keep him from drinking again? He couldn't see him, he couldn't touch him—as far as he was concerned, God couldn't do a god damn thing. The only one that could was Vicky. She was the only one who could keep him from drinking again. But nooooo…what did these idiots in here say when he told them about Vicky…about how her love helped him to stay clean? The bastards said that it wasn't real love…that it was just codependence…that he was just using Vicky as a way to cope without alcohol…that if they continued seeing each other, they'd just end up relapsing. They said that they should wait a year and see what happened, wait until they were both recovered and then, and only then, could they start a relationship. Well, fuck that. Fuck their opinions. Who were they to tell him he couldn't have a relationship? Who were they to tell him he couldn't be in love? If it weren't for Vicky, he wouldn't even be here. He wouldn't have made it one week, let alone an entire year.

And tonight was the night that he was going to show them. Tonight was the night he was going to fuck up their little program. He'd prove to everyone, once and for all, that love was possible…even in AA…even in recovery.

He took a few deep breaths and felt the ring box in his pocket then closed his eyes and leaned back his head. Just as he started feeling settled, he felt a tug on his jacket and a sharp, country twang bellow in his ear. "Yo Monty! What's up man?"

Monty opened his eyes and peeled himself from against the wall. Oh great, speak of the devil—it was Robby, his twelve-step sponsor, probably the biggest AA fanatic in the whole world. He was grinning like a lunatic and chewing on his tobacco, the dip like a golf ball tucked between his lips and gums.

"Oh, hey Robby," Monty said, trying to sound delighted, while at the same time trying to move out from under that disgusting, minty dip smell.

"Hey Monty, where the hell you been, man? I ain't heard from you in what, like, a couple weeks now, right?"

"Oh yeah, sorry about that. I was actually in Florida visiting my parents."

"No shit? How'd that go?"

"It went."

"That bad, huh?"

"Yep."

"Well, you could've called me. What? They don't got phones in Florida?"

"Well, I was pretty busy. What with all the Christmas presents and dinner parties and stuff like that."

"That's no excuse man. You still gotta call your sponsor. Let me know how things are going. Shit, Vicky called Susan like everyday, twice on Christmas. You need to take after her man. She should be a shining example for you."

"I know, I know. Story of my life, right?"

"Damn skippy." Robby cleared his throat and spit into his spit cup then wiped the saliva from his chin. "So, how's that fourth step coming?"

"It's coming."

"Yeah, you've been working on that thing for like three months now, right?"

"Yeah, I'm still trying to get my head around it."

"Shit man. There ain't no trying. You just gotta sit down and do it. Write that shit out, you know?"

"Yeah, I know, I know."

"I know it can be overwhelming at first, having to write all that shit down; all the terrible things we did and said in our addiction; the people we harmed and pushed away; it's fucking humiliating. Nobody wants to have to relive all that bullshit and they sure as hell don't wanna confess it to someone they barely even know. But, trust me, dude, once you do it, you'll feel a million times better, like a weight has been lifted off your soul. You'll be able to breathe and put all that bad shit behind you and finally start living your life again. It's worth it." Robby smiled as he patted Monty on the shoulder, looking at him with pride as a father would a son. He cleared his throat and spit again into his spit cup, then checked the grandfather clock that was wedged up against the back wall. "Oh shit dude. It's almost time. You ready?"

"I guess so."

"Yeah? You nervous?"

"A little bit."

Robby snickered and took a step forward, slapping Monty open palm on the back. "Yeah I'll bet you are. Don't worry dude. You'll be fine. Just get up there and let them words flow through you—open your mind and open your heart. You'll be alright."

"I hope so."

"It's a special god damn night, boy. I'm real proud of you. I mean that."

"Thanks Robby."

"Ya'll doing anything later to celebrate?"

Monty looked down at his pocket, smiling at the bulge the ring box made against his thigh. He did a quick scan of the foyer to make sure Vicky was nowhere in sight. "Actually…" he said, with a slight hesitation, not too sure if he should tell Robby the news.

"What?" Robby said, in almost a whisper, his eyes darting between Monty and the foyer. "What is it? Is it something about Vicky?"

Oh great. Now he had to tell him. He already knew that something was up. "Well, it's just…"

"Yeah?"

"…I kinda have something big planned for tonight."

"Well, spit it out. Shit, you're keeping me on pins and needles here."

"Well, I was kinda thinking I might propose to Vicky tonight."

Robby's eyes lit up like a pair of Christmas luminaries and the dip in his mouth dribbled out like hot wax. "What? You're kidding me?"

Monty shook his head. "Nope."

"You're not just fucking with me right now?"

"No, I'm serious. I've never been more serious in my entire life. Here, I got the ring right here to prove it." Monty stuffed his hand into his pocket and pulled out the box that contained the ring. He positioned it in his palm then pulled it open, first checking the foyer to make sure Vicky wasn't around.

Robby looked at the ring then back at Monty like some kind of animated jack-o-lantern on Halloween. His eyes were swollen and his mouth was wide-open, dark spots on his gums from the dip tucked under his lip. "Holy shit," he said, as he tore off his Denver Broncos ball cap and scratched the thinning patch of hair on his head. "I don't believe it. When are you gonna do it?"

"Tonight. After my speech."

"Well, I'll be damned."

Monty smiled proudly as he snapped the box closed then stuffed it back into his jeans.

"Well, how do you feel?" Robby asked.

"Nervous."

"Well, no shit. I'd be sweating my balls off. I mean, this is big. This is bigger than big, this is huge. I mean marriage. Wow dude. You sure you know what you're getting yourself into? I mean, you guys have only known each other for what, a couple of months now, right?"

"A year, actually."

"Still, this is pretty huge. I mean, don't take this the wrong way—you're my sponsee and I'm real proud of all the great progress you've made so far, but…"

Oh great, here it comes—the part about him not being ready for a relationship.

"…you're not exactly what I would call a *recovered* addict. I mean, you've still got a lot of your own problems to figure out."

"Yeah, so?"

"So, are you sure you're ready to take hers on too?"

"Vicky doesn't need me to take on her problems. She can deal with them just fine on her own."

"No, I know, I know, but—"

"But what?"

"But, you're still so early in this program. I mean, I don't really think you're in a place where you can be making a decision like this."

"Well, I'm sorry you feel that way Robby, but I love Vicky—"

"Are you sure?"

"What?"

"That you love her?"

"Of course, I'm sure."

"You sure it's love and not something else?"

"What the hell else would it be?"

"Hey, you tell me. People in this program get into relationships for all sorts of reasons. Some are confused or just sad and lonely, looking for something to make them feel whole again. I can't tell you how many young guys I've seen come into this program and jump into relationships before they've had a chance to heal. I'll tell you this—they usually don't last too long. They usually end up relapsing and leaving the program together, going out in much worse shape than when they first came in."

"Yeah well, Vicky and I aren't like that."

"I'm not saying you are. I'm just saying that you need to be careful and really think about what you're doing. Never underestimate the power of this disease. Because it'll sneak up on you when you least expect it and tear a damn hole in your ass."

"Yeah, I know, Robby. You've told me a million times."

"Well, I'm telling you again. I mean, this is a big step."

"Yeah, I know. Look, if it hadn't been for Vicky, I would've never gotten sober and I sure as hell would've never come through those doors over there."

"I know, but that's exactly what scares me."

"Well, don't be scared. This is a good thing. Trust me. I love Vicky and this is what I'm doing and nothing you say or do is going to change my mind now. So, you can either be a part of it or get the hell out of here, because I have no problem finding another sponsor in here."

"Aw, come on Monty, don't be like that. You know I'm just looking out for you, right? I care about you, dude."

"Yeah, I know, but sometimes you just gotta back off a little. I mean, I only got"—Monty glanced at the grandfather clock ticking next to the stairs—"another ten minutes before I have to get up in front of a room full of people and profess my innermost secrets and fears. I really don't need you of all people telling me about the *"incomprehensible demoralization"* of this disease. I've heard it a million times already, and I really don't need to hear it right now, okay?"

"Okay, okay. No worries. I'm just trying to help."

"Well, go help somewhere else, because I really need to focus. I feel like I'm about to have a damn heart attack over here."

Robby laughed and stepped forward, slapping Monty again on the back. "Don't worry dude. You don't gotta be nervous. Everything's gonna be just fine. I promise."

"That's easy for you to say. You like giving speeches. In fact, I think attention should be your new drug of choice."

Robby chuckled and spit into his spit cup, his eyes moving towards the front door. "Uh-oh," he said, as he bent slightly forward, covering his mouth as if he had a secret to tell. "Don't look now, but here comes Vicky."

"Where?"

"Right there."

Monty looked to where Robby was pointing, over by the porch, near the front doors. Sure enough, there was Vicky, coming towards them, smiling and waving like the cutest girl in the whole world.

"Just act natural," Monty said as he stiffened his posture and ran his fingers through his still snow-damp hair.

"Hey Robby," Vicky said walking up to them, stopping just short of the winding staircase.

"Hey Vicky," Robby said. "How's it going?"

"Pretty good. How are you?"

"Oh, I'm okay. You ready for the big show tonight?"

"Heck yeah." She wrapped her arm around Monty's. "It's about time this slacker gets up on stage."

"I know it. I'm excited. It's gonna be a big night."

"It sure is."

"Well," Robby said, turning to Monty, a sly smirk on his tobacco-aged face, "you have fun up there tonight buddy. And try not to get too nervous."

"Yeah. I'll try."

"If you need me, I'll be right there in the front row, okay?"

"Yeah. Alright."

"See you up there?"

"Yeah. See you."

Once Robby left, Vicky turned to Monty and pulled him tightly against her chest. "You ready?" she said looking up at him, a smile in her eyes, a smirk on her lips.

"As ready as I'll ever be."

"Alright. Let's do it."

When they got to the second floor, they took a right along the banister towards the meeting room at the end of the hall. The room was quiet and still a bit empty with only a handful of people congregating around a coffee pot that was percolating against the back wall. The center of the room was filled with a sea of empty, folding chairs arranged in a horseshoe pattern around an old, dusty stage. On top of the stage sat a large, wooden podium, its paint chipped and cracked from probably more than fifty years of wear and tear. That's where he'll be, he thought, staring at the podium, his eyes a bit bleary from the smoke-saturated air—on that stage, in front of all these people, glaring up at him with their judgmental stares. Christ—what the hell did he get himself into? Why did he ever agree to do this thing?

"You okay?" Vicky said, looking back at him as she led him forward to the front row of chairs.

"Yeah, I'm okay. I'm just nervous, I guess."

"Do you want me to get you something? Maybe some water?"

"Sure."

"Okay. You go get seats and I'll get you some."

"Alright."

Monty nodded and made his way around the maze of folding chairs to the foot of the stage. He picked the two seats that had the easiest access to the podium then pulled off his jacket and draped it across the back of the chair. As he sat down, he focused on his breathing, his eyes on the floor, his elbows propped on his knees. Vicky came back and handed him his water, then pulled off her coat and took her seat.

As the minutes passed, the room grew more and more rowdy with people greeting one another and taking their seats. As they wandered in, so did the stench of stale cigarettes, following them in like a stray cat from the cold.

Monty just sat there, quietly staring at the podium, going over the speech in his head. Then, like a host for some kind of obnoxious game show, Robby appeared and jumped up on stage. He smiled and clapped as he ran towards the podium then grabbed the microphone and pulled it towards his face. "Welcome," he said, grinning like a maniac with that disgusting lump of dip still tucked under his lip. "Welcome to the Sunday night edition of Alcoholics Anonymous. I am your host, Robby, a grateful, recovering ex-*crack head*."

"*Hi Robby*," the room replied in unison like the congregation of some kind of twelve-step church.

"How's everybody feeling tonight?"

"*Good.*"

"Aw come on now. I know ya'll can do better than that. I said, how's everybody feeling!?"

"*Good!*"

"Isn't it great to be alive and sober!?"

"*Yes!*"

"Hell yeah it is!" Robby laughed and threw his head backward as he pounded the podium with his fist. "Boy, have we got a special meeting planned for ya'll tonight. One of my very own sponsees, probably my best buddy in the whole wide world, Monty Miller, is gonna get up here and share with ya'll his story of experience, strength, and hope. But, before we get into all of that, I need a volunteer to come up and read *How It Works.* Any takers?"

Vicky shot up and waved her hand around excitedly, so fast that she nearly fell out of her chair. "Oooh, Oooh, I'll do it, I'll do it!"

"Ah, yes," Robby said peering down at her, "Vicky, our very own Venezuelan beauty. Come on up here girl. Show us how it's done."

Vicky smiled and set down her coffee then, in one quick thrust, popped up to her feet. She hopped on the stage and strutted over to the podium as the people in the crowd whistled, clapped, and stomped their feet. "Hi everyone," she said, as she grabbed the microphone and pulled it so close that it almost touched her lips. "My name's Vicky and I am a grateful, recovering addict."

"*Hi Vicky!*"

"Hi everyone." Her cheeks turned red as she laughed with embarrassment, dropping her face into her hands. "Okay,"—she regained her composure and pulled her loose bangs back from her face—"so, this is *How It Works:*

Rarely have we seen a person fail who has thoroughly followed our path. Those who do not recover are people who cannot or will not completely give themselves to this simple program, usually men and women who are constitutionally incapable of being honest with themselves. There are such unfortunates. They are not at fault; they seem to have been born that way. They are naturally incapable of grasping and developing a manner of living which demands rigorous honesty. Their chances are less than average. There are those, too, who suffer from grave emotional and mental disorders, but many of them do recover if they have the capacity to be honest. Our stories disclose in a general way what we used to be like, what happened, and what we are like now. If you have decided you want what we have and are willing to go to any length to get it—then you are ready to take certain steps.

At some of these we balked. We thought we could find an easier, softer way. But we could not. With all the earnestness at our command, we beg of you to be fearless and thorough from the very start. Some of us have tried to hold on to our old ideas and the result was nil until we let go absolutely.

Remember that we deal with alcohol—cunning, baffling, powerful! Without help it is too much for us. But there is One who has all power— that One is God. May you find Him now!

Half measures availed us nothing. We stood at the turning point. We asked His protection and care with complete abandon.

Here are the steps we took, which are suggested as a program of recovery:

1. *We admitted we were powerless over alcohol—that our lives had become unmanageable.*

2. *Came to believe that a Power greater than ourselves could restore us to sanity.*

3. *Made a decision to turn our will and our lives over to the care of God as we understood Him.*

4. *Made a searching and fearless moral inventory of ourselves.*

5. *Admitted to God, to ourselves, and to another human being the exact nature of our wrongs.*

6. *Were entirely ready to have God remove all these defects of character.*

7. *Humbly asked Him to remove our shortcomings.*

8. *Made a list of all persons we had harmed, and became willing to make amends to them all.*

9. *Made direct amends to such people wherever possible, except when to do so would injure them or others.*

10. *Continued to take personal inventory and when we were wrong promptly admitted it.*

11. *Sought through prayer and meditation to improve our conscious contact with God as we understood Him, praying only for knowledge of His will for us and the power to carry that out.*

12. *Having had a spiritual awakening as the result of these steps, we tried to carry this message to alcoholics, and to practice these principles in all our affairs.*

Many of us exclaimed, "What an order! I can't go through with it." Do not be discouraged. No one among us has been able to maintain anything like perfect adherence to these principles. We are not saints. The point is, that we are willing to grow along spiritual lines. The principles we have set down are guides to progress. We claim spiritual progress rather than spiritual perfection.

Our description of the alcoholic, the chapter to the agnostic, and our personal adventures before and after make clear three pertinent ideas:

a. That we were alcoholic and could not manage our own lives.

b. That probably no human power could have relieved our alcoholism.

c. That could and would if He were sought."

Vicky smiled and turned toward Robby, as she brushed a thick, dark curl away from her face.

"Thank you," Robby said as he walked back to the podium. "That was wonderful. Wasn't that wonderful everybody?"

"*Yes!*"

"Thank you," Vicky said, then did a little curtsy and hopped down from the stage. When she got back to her seat, Monty put his arm around her and gave her a soft kiss on the cheek. "Good job. You rocked."

"I know."

"Alright," Robby said, as he winked at Monty. "You ready?"

"Yeah, I guess."

"Alright. Let's do this thing. Come on up here buddy boy."

Monty took a deep breath then put his hands on his kneecaps and slowly pushed himself up from his seat. When he got to the podium, Robby was there waiting for him, his arms extended out by his head. "I'm real proud of you," Robby said, as he threw his arms around him, wrapping him up in a bone-crushing bear hug. "Remember what I told you. Just open your mind and listen to your higher power, and I promise those words will pour right from your heart."

"Yeah right."

"Go get 'em."

Monty turned to face the podium and slowly looked out into the crowd. There were fifty of them, maybe a hundred, their heads like bobble-head dolls bobbing up and down. His hands were shaking, his heart was pounding, and everything inside of him told him to just turn around and run. But, where could he go? His family was afraid of him. His friends didn't want to talk to him. The only friend he had was sitting right here in this room. This was it. This was what he'd been waiting for. His life, his future, his only shot at redemption—it all came down to this one simple speech.

He grabbed the microphone and pulled it towards him then cleared his throat and parted his lips.

"Hi," he said, his voice a little shaky, his throat still parched from the dry, Colorado air. "My name's Monty and I'm an alcoholic."

"Hi Monty."

"Hi everybody." And just like that the nerves began to leave him, the butterflies in his stomach emerging from their cocoons. "You know, when Robby first asked me to do this I was like, you gotta be kidding me. You must be out of your mind. There's no way in hell you're going to get me up on that stage in front of all those people and make me open up about my life. But, after a few weeks of coaxing and threatening to keep me on my fourth step forever, he finally convinced me to quit being such a baby and get up here and share some of the lessons I've learned. Now, I don't really have anything written down or prepared, but Robby told me that if I just cleared my head and opened my heart that my higher power would grant me the words that I needed to say."

Monty paused for a moment and reached for his water, closed his eyes and took a long sip.

"Now, a lot of people, when they get up here, like to talk about where they're from and who their parents were and what their childhood was like and all of that. But I'm not going to spend a whole lot of time talking about that, simply because there's not much to tell. I had a very normal childhood. Nothing tragic ever really happened. My dad was a commercial pilot, my mom was a personal trainer, and I grew up with my little brother and older sister on an average street, in an average neighborhood, in a little suburban beach town on the panhandle of North Florida. My parents were great. They're still great. They got us everything we ever wanted—all the things that they never had growing up as kids. They sent us to the best private, Catholic schools in all of Northwest Florida and made damn sure that they were front and center at every single, trivial school function that we had going on in our insignificant, little lives. Whether it was basketball games, soccer practices, volleyball matches, swim meets...whatever it was, they were there. And they're still there, to this day. Even after all the bad shit I've done and the horrible, hurtful things I've said—things that no parent should ever have to hear come out of their child's mouth over the telephone in the eerie twilight of the early morning hours, after a hundred bottles of pills and a thousand cases of liquor when your mind is so fucked up you don't even know if you're running around or standing still. After all of that shit and all of that insanity, they never stopped loving me. Not once. Never."

Monty looked up amazed and with astonishment, as if he didn't believe the words he just said. He had to calm down. He was getting too excited. He didn't want them thinking he was losing his head. He paused for a moment to regain his composure, then closed his eyes and took a deep breath.

"So what happened? How does a sweet kid from a supportive family go from being a straight-A student and a star athlete in high school, to a crazed, drunken, suicidal waste of a human being? How does someone with every opportunity to be successful in life suddenly decide to just chuck it all away?"

"Well," he said, as if he was sighing, in one long, continuous breath, "if I knew the answer to that, I probably wouldn't be up here. I'd probably be at some convention in Geneva, Switzerland accepting the Nobel Prize for Chemistry and Medicine."

The room swelled with a sigh of laughter, as if they were relieved he didn't storm off the stage. Monty relaxed and began to laugh with them, rubbing his hands, and shaking his head.

"The truth is, I don't know why I did the things I did—why I gave up on life, gave up on my ambitions, gave up on my family, gave up on myself—why I couldn't just stop after a few

sips of bourbon or a couple shots of whiskey and just go to
bed—why I had to drink glass after glass and bottle after bottle
until I was so drunk, I couldn't even make it from the couch to
the bathroom without passing out in a puddle of my own piss. I
mean, it obviously didn't feel good, right? I didn't really enjoy
drinking by myself in some dark, university apartment trying to
work up the courage to put a bullet in my brain. So, why'd I do
it? Why did I keep going for that bottle, when I knew full well
with every fiber of my being that if I didn't stop and get some
help, I was going to end up dead?"

"Well, that's exactly what I was going to figure out. Me,
Monty Miller; a clinically depressed, twenty-three year old
alcoholic, with not even a second of sobriety or the physical
ability to even get out of bed and pee. I was going to figure out
what has eluded thousands of doctors all throughout the medical
community for the better part of the last century. I was going to
deduce the reason for the insanity—I was going to find a way to
beat this thing. The only problem was, I was so fucked up from
all those years of drinking that I couldn't even hold the fucking
steering wheel still let alone think with a straight head. But, I was
determined, you know? I was determined to drink like a normal
person—to live my life as a functional alcoholic. You see, I
wasn't ready to stop. I wasn't ready to be sober. I could outsmart
this stupid, little so-called disease. I had the brain, the
knowledge, and the determination to do it. I graduated first in
my class out of a total of fifty, in one of the toughest chemical
engineering programs in the entire South. There wasn't a
problem I couldn't solve, a riddle I couldn't unravel, and if
anyone was going to figure out the solution to addiction, it was
going to be me."

"So, I decided to do what any good research student would
do—I'd take a trip down to the local library and check out every
single book there was on the topic of addiction. Everything from
self-help books and psychological case studies, to detailed
pharmacological reports and articles in the New England Journal
of Medicine. But, I couldn't go to just any library. Oh no. I had

to go to the absolute best one around, which, as you all know, is on the CU campus out in Boulder, nearly forty-five minutes from my apartment in downtown. I remember that day very clearly. It was a little over a year ago, during the week of that terrible blizzard, the one that shut down the city for two whole days. Do you all remember which one I'm talking about?"

Monty paused and watched as the heads in the room all nodded; the bobble-head dolls gyrating up and down. He picked up his cup and took another sip of water then cleared his throat and eased it back down.

"All the roads were closed in and out of Denver and there was absolutely no way I was going to get to Boulder in my car. So, I laced up my boots, buttoned up my jacket, threw on my helmet, and hopped on my bike. Now, I know what you all are thinking. What about the snow? What about the blizzard? What if I slip and crack my head on the ice? Well, that was a risk I was willing to take. You see, I was so deluded that getting to that library became my only saving grace. I thought that if I could just get on my bike and make it out to Boulder, I'd prove to everyone that I was going to be okay. Even if I died along the way, I'd at least be a hero, and everyone would remember me as a martyred saint. But, here's the sick thing—before I went I had to make sure I packed enough provisions to keep me warm for the long trip. So, I took one of those Camelbaks—those little satchels that professional cyclists fill up with water—and I filled it up with an entire box of Franzia wine. I know, I know, pretty sick, right? Well, that's how fucked up I was. I figured all I needed was a little bit of Franzia to ward off the pesky symptoms of alcohol withdrawal. I mean, I couldn't very well risk hallucinating in the middle of the freeway and going into convulsions on the side of the road. I mean, that would be crazy. That would be absolutely absurd. I couldn't risk dying, I was about to come up with the addiction cure!"

"So, I took my Camelbak, slung it over my shoulder, hopped on my bike, and headed off down the road. I don't remember exactly what happened next, but somewhere between my apartment and downtown Denver, I must've slipped on the ice, hit my head, and lost consciousness and ended up passed out somewhere in about a foot of snow. The next thing I knew, I was being wheeled through the Denver county hospital, connected to a bunch of machines and those long, spaghetti-like, plastic tubes. And I was a mess too. My face was frozen, my lips were purple, and my fingertips were so frostbitten, they looked like pieces of black liquorice. When the doctor came in, he said they might have to amputate if the color in my fingers didn't come back soon. But I wasn't really too concerned about that. I didn't really care if they had to cut off all my fingers and leave me with nothing but two nubs for hands. As sick as it sounds, the only thing that I really cared about was getting the hell out of there and back to my apartment so I could polish off my box of Franzia wine. That's how sick I was. That's how fucked up I had become. I didn't give a shit about losing my fingers. I didn't even care if I died right then and there. Anything was better than the pain I was experiencing. Anything was better than the alcohol withdrawal. My head was on fire, my body was thawing, and I was shaking and heaving so much that I was willing to do anything for just one sip of alcohol. So, I did what I had to do. I got out of the bed, ripped out all of that tubing then marched out of the room and into the hall. Well, I didn't even make it three steps before a nurse saw me and started shouting, chasing after me like a wild boar down the hall. Two seconds later, a stampede of security guards jumped on top of me and dragged me back to my bed, kicking and screaming, while nurses with latex gloves and giant sized needles strapped restraints to my wrists and ankles to hold me down. And they basically left me like that—strapped to a bed, sweating and seizing, staring up at a fucking wet spot on the wall. I pulled against those straps until my wrists became bloody and cried out constantly for someone to come let me out. But, no one ever came. I was stuck there, alone in the dark with my hallucinations, seeing things move that weren't moving, watching things crawl around the corners of the ceiling. The feeling that at any moment, someone could come into that room and do whatever the hell they wanted to me and I wouldn't be able to do a god damn thing, was without a doubt, the most terrifying experience of my entire life. To have your freedom and your liberty taken away like that is the worst fucking feeling in the whole world. I'll tell you this much…I would rather put a gun in my mouth and pull the fucking trigger than ever have to go through that experience again."

Monty shook his head as he stared down at the podium, breathing slowly in and out through his nose. He could actually feel the straps getting tighter and tighter, cutting into the soft flesh on his ankles and wrists. He looked up at Vicky whose hands were folded, her fingertips touching the bottom of her chin. She nodded once for encouragement. Monty nodded in return and took another deep breath.

"So what happened?" he said, shaking off the memory. "How did I escape all of that madness? How did I find a way to end all that suffering and pain?" He looked once more at Vicky, closed his eyes, and blew her a kiss. She smiled and mouthed the words, "I love you," then folded her hands against her chest.

"Well, it's simple really," he said, as he moved his hand against his pocket and felt the ring box that he knew was still there. "I finally found a reason worth living. I finally found someone who made it all okay. All that guilt, all that suffering, when Vicky smiled she took it all away. Now, a lot of you in here said that it could never happen…that rushing into a relationship would only make matters worse…that after a month, we'd be out of the program, relapsing together, getting high and getting drunk. You told me to wait a year and see what happened, wait a year and see if I was still in love. Well, if I'd listened to you guys, I wouldn't still be here. I wouldn't have made it one day, let alone an entire year. Vicky gave me something that no God could ever give me—she made me feel that I deserved to be loved. And all that crap about twelve steps and higher powers…well, it's all a bunch of bullshit if you don't have love." Monty paused and looked directly at Robby, at the look of betrayal on his knotted face. His arms were folded tightly across his chest and his eyes were filled with a deep, disapproving rage.

Monty stepped off the stage and moved towards Vicky in the front row. "Vicky," he said, as he knelt down before her, the thousands of butterflies flying from his throat. "You are my heart, my soul, my reason for living…without you, I know I would've never made it this far." He paused for a moment then reached into his pocket and pulled out the box that contained the ring. "Vicky," he said as he pulled it open, "will you do me the honor of accepting this ring?"

Vicky's eyes lit up and her mouth fell open as the entire room gasped in complete disbelief. She looked at the ring then back at Monty, then at the ring and back again.

"Well," Monty said, scooting closer, trying to balance the ring on his quivering knee. "What do you say, baby? Will you marry me?"

"Yes!" Vicky shot up and crashed into Monty, throwing her arms around his neck.

"You will?" Monty said, as though he didn't believe her. "You'll marry me?"

"Yes, of course! Of course I will!"

Monty got to his feet and wrapped his arms around her then pressed his mouth against her lips. He held her there for what felt like an eternity, caressing her face, and tasting her peppermint kiss. The room went wild with whistling and shouting, people clapping their hands and stomping their feet. But, Monty didn't care, because he couldn't see them—all he could see was Vicky's face—her perfect smile, her perfect cheekbones, her perfect eyes, her perfect lips. She was everything in the entire world to him and now the moment was finally his.

Chapter 3

Vicky

The next half hour or so was like a dream. The clouds rolled in and the sky grew heavy, sinking lower and lower until it seemed it was almost touching the roof of Monty's red Isuzu Rodeo. As they got on the interstate, the light from downtown became dimmer, until, all at once, it was gone. The mountains loomed in the darkness like granite apparitions, their peaks pointed and their faces completely flat. It was just Monty and Vicky, alone on the highway, heading north for Boulder, towards the jagged peaks of the Flatiron Park.

It was already ten by the time they pulled into Boulder, and Monty decided to take a little short cut. He got off the main drag and turned left on Canyon and slowly ascended the winding mountain road. As they climbed higher and higher, the air became thinner, and the snow shifted from flakes into a flurry of clumps. It looked like feathers from the entrails of a gutted pillow, kissing off the windshield and floating off into the dark. Monty squinted his eyes and leaned as far as he could forward, both hands on the wheel, one foot on the brake. He flipped on his brights and hit the windshield wipers, which began to screech against the glass like the teeth of an aluminum rake.

"Wow," Vicky said, leaning forward. "It's really coming down now, isn't it?" She sighed and turned toward Monty, a hint of concern in her eyes. "You sure you still want to go all the way up there?"

"Yeah," Monty said, surprised, as if she was kidding. "Don't you?"

"Yeah, I do. But look at this. You can barely see, baby. Maybe we should just stop and wait until it quits. We can always spend the night and go up there tomorrow."

"What? Here? In Boulder?"

"Yeah. Why not?"

Monty groaned. He didn't want to wait until tomorrow. He wanted to get up there right now.

"I think it'll be okay," he said, as he twisted the lever on the wipers, cranking them up to full speed.

"I don't know," Vicky said, peering out the windshield, wringing her hands in her lap.

Monty reached over and reassuringly placed his hand on her hand. "It'll be okay. I won't let anything happen, alright?"

"Alright."

Another twenty minutes and they were at the top of the canyon, snaking along slowly under a now starless, black sky. As the air became thinner so did the vegetation and, all at once, the road seemed to open into a desolate tundra of snow and ice. What was it? Monty thought, peering out the windshield, rubbing the sleep away from his eyes. Was it the Barker reservoir? Could they have already gotten this far? But, it was all frozen over. It looked nothing like how he remembered it in the summer. What was once brilliantly blue and surrounded by green, lush forests, was now nothing more than a thick layer of impermeable ice. The trees along the shore looked like bulimic cheerleaders, completely stripped of their once thick, full-figured leaves. Even the highway seemed to be getting skinnier, squeezed on both sides by an embankment of snow. Monty had to hug the center lane just to keep from sliding off it, down into the icy reservoir below. This sucks, he thought, as he eased off the gas pedal and changed the wipers from high to low. Maybe he should've just stopped and spent the night in Boulder. By now, he could've been in bed curled up next to Vicky, her legs wrapped around him, her warm breasts pressed up against him, the smell of her hair, the taste of her body, the touch of her fingers running up and down his skin. Damn. It gave him goose bumps just thinking about it, but he had to hold on, another forty minutes and they'd be there.

He turned and smiled at Vicky, when something snatched his attention up in the road ahead. It was a pair of headlights, piercing through the snowfall, barreling towards them on the wrong side of the road. Vicky screamed, clutching the sides of the car seat, as Monty slammed on the brake pedal and cut the wheel left as hard he could go. But, he cut too hard and the Rodeo started sliding, its right back bumper twisting outward towards the oncoming lights. The other car caught them on the end of their right fender and sent them spinning across the midline towards the other side of the road. They hit the guardrail and flipped over it and started tumbling down the mountain like a fractured stone. Shards of glass slung out from the windows as cold metal crunched between the rocks and the trees. When they got to the bottom, the car was turned over, spinning on the ice like a beetle on its back. They spun several more times and the car finally halted somewhere in the middle of the frozen reservoir.

Somewhere between stupor and awareness, Monty began to hear the echo of a strange sounding song. It was an old song, with a twangy guitar rhythm, and what sounded like the banging of sticks against a metal pole. He recognized it, but couldn't quite place it. Was it real? Or was he just imagining it? And why would that song be playing right now?

As he lifted his head, he forced his eyelids open and let out a deep, labored moan. But he couldn't see—his vision was blurry, distorted by something warm and wet flowing over his eyes. He lifted his hand and touched his fingers to his forehead, feeling the gash that was just above his right eye. The cut was deep and somewhat jagged by the pieces of glass sticking out of his skin. When he turned his head, he saw that Vicky wasn't moving, and tried calling out her name but she didn't respond. She just hung there, upside down, as lifeless as a rag doll, her arms above her head, her hair covering her eyes. "Vicky, wake up."

He tried to reach for her, but was restrained by the seat belt that was still locked from impact. "Vicky! Wake up! Wake up!"

He reached across his lap and unbuckled the seat belt, but lost all his leverage and crashed into the roof. He whimpered in pain as he moved his hands out from under him and, in one quick thrust, he tried to push himself up. It took all his strength, but somehow he managed to turn his entire body over, such that the ceiling was now down at his butt. He crawled towards Vicky underneath the center console and brushed her hair back away from her face.

"Vicky, wake up!" he screamed, as he shook her shoulders. "Wake up! Please, baby, don't do this to me! Wake up! Wake up!"

He lifted his hand and forced her eyelids open and positioned his ear close to her lips. She was alive. He could feel her breathing, a warm whisper of life blowing against the hairs on his neck. "Vicky?" he said, as he got closer, moving his lips right next to her ear. She groaned and her eyelids began to flutter like the wings of a moth caught in a spider's web.

"Vicky? Can you hear me? Are you okay?"

She said nothing and just stared up at him, her face covered with blood, her eyes locked in a daze.

"Don't worry, I'm going to get you out of here baby. I'm going to get you out."

He reached across her lap and unbuckled her seat belt, then grabbed her shoulders and tried to pull her out. But, she wouldn't budge. Her legs were stuck between the dash and the floorboard that had been forged together from the impact of the crash. No, no, this couldn't be happening. She was stuck. She was trapped. He grabbed her arms and began to pull harder, but Vicky screamed in pain and pleaded with him to stop.

"What baby? What's the matter?"

"It hurts."

"I know, I'm sorry, but I have to get you out. You'll bleed to death if I don't get you out."

"No, Monty, don't. Please don't."

"I'm sorry, baby. I have to." He leaned forward and kissed her forehead then grabbed her again and pulled with all his strength. Then, something happened. He heard something cracking, like the sound of lightning splitting through the trees. It was the ice. It was cracking all around them, splitting open from the weight of the car.

"Oh God, no! Please don't do this to me! Please God don't fucking do this to me!"

"What is it Monty? What's happening?"

"We don't have time baby. We have to get out of here. I have to get you the fuck out of here!"

"Why? What is it? What's happening?"

Monty leaned as far as he could forward, wrapping his arms around Vicky's waist. "Here. I want you to put your arms around me. Okay?"

Vicky nodded and wrapped her arms around him, locking her hands tightly around his neck.

"Alright, now, I'm going to count to three and I want you to hold on to me as tight as you can, okay?"

"Okay."

"Alright. You ready?"

"Yeah."

"One…"

"Two…"

"Three!"

Monty snapped as hard as he could backward, shifting all his weight towards the driver's seat. But, as he pulled, the car shuddered and began to slide forward, angling into the crevice, first the front then the back. It floated there for a moment, bobbing up and down in the water, until the last shelf of ice cracked and the car began to sink. The water poured in through the pockets in the floorboard, flooding first the engine block then the air conditioning vents. It was so cold that it felt like a wall of concrete crashing down on him, stealing the air right from his chest. He gasped as the water overtook him, pouring over his legs and filling up to his neck. He turned toward Vicky. Her head was already submerged under water, filling up fast past her shoulders and her chest. He took a deep breath then put his head under the water and grabbed hold of the metal that was trapping her legs. He tugged and pulled, trying to pry away the wreckage, but the metal was too slick and he couldn't get a good grip. So, he picked up his foot and brought it down against it, over and over, trying to weaken the forge. But, he couldn't do it. He'd become too exhausted and he had to go up for another breath. But there was nowhere to go. The car was now completely filled with water, plummeting towards the bottom like a cinderblock.

Monty panicked and turned back towards the wreckage and started tugging and pulling as hard as he could. Vicky stopped him and grabbed him by the collar and pulled his face up towards her lips. Her face was a blur in the watery darkness, a small trickle of light coming from the dome lamp overhead. She looked in his eyes and mouthed the words, "I love you," then brought his hand against her chest. As she opened her mouth, her grip became tighter, her nails digging deeper and deeper into his flesh. Then she stopped struggling and her mouth dropped open. Her head fell limp against his chest. Monty screamed out in a distorted murmur, as a frenzy of bubbles dispersed from his lips. He grabbed her hair and pulled her head upward and emptied his lungs into her mouth. But, it was too late. Her lungs were flooded. There was no room for air left in her lungs.

In a last ditch effort, he grabbed a hold of the twisted metal and pulled and pulled until his hands became bloodied and raw. But it was useless. The metal was fixed like dried cement. He couldn't do it. He had to leave her. He was about to run out of breath.

He turned and took one last look at Vicky then rolled down the window and swam through the small slit. He kicked and pulled his way towards the surface, the beams from the headlights guiding his path. One last thrust and he breached the surface, punching his way through the glassy ice. He reached his hands out for something to grab onto, but there was nothing there so he just floated in the dark, his eyes turned up towards the starless atmosphere, his breath like smoke signals spiraling from his lungs.

Chapter 4

Coach Dave

Dave was awakened by the sound of dishes clanging against the steel of the kitchen sink. He opened his right eye first, painfully and slowly, peering around the room like a one-eyed snake. It was only partially light out—the sun was just rising, trickling through the windows and creeping across the lower half of the house. It took him a few moments to recognize his surroundings. It seemed he was downstairs on the living room couch. What was he doing down here? Did Cheryl kick him out of the bedroom last night?

He took a deep breath and turned himself over, peeling his face from the sticky leather of the couch. With his elbows on his knees and his shoulders hunched slightly forward, he started rubbing his face as if he was trying to rub it off. Jesus Christ, he felt fucking horrible. His neck was throbbing…his head was splitting…it felt like he'd been in a head-on collision.

As he uncovered his face, he looked down the line of his body and noticed that he still had on his clothes from yesterday—a pair of pepperoni-encrusted khakis, his green and gold Catholic High Crusaders warm-up jacket, and his yellow and black bumblebee running shoes. What the hell? Didn't he even take a shower? Or did he just come home last night and pass out?

He shook off the sleep and pressed his palms into the cushions, then straightened his legs and slowly stood up. But, the walls of the living room started to spin around him like the Tilt-a-Whirl ride at an amusement park. He swayed for a few minutes, like an inflatable doll outside of a used car lot, then leveled his vision and straightened himself out. With his eyes on the floor and his hands out in front of him, he staggered across the living room towards the stairs.

When he got upstairs, he went straight for the bathroom, flipped on the light switch, and locked the door. He leaned inside the shower and cranked on the water, turning the knob up as hot as it would go. Sitting on the toilet cover, he untied his shoelaces, kicked off his shoes, and pulled off his pants. As he unzipped his jacket, he felt something bulgy in the pit of his side pocket. He reached inside and pulled it out. It was his pipe, lighter, and a red, plastic pill bottle, like little chess pieces, all in a row. He unscrewed the cap and turned the bottle over, but nothing came out except for some white, chalky residue. Damn. He must've polished off the entire bottle. It looked like he was gonna have to make another trip down to Aurora. He couldn't start the week without any motivation. He'd never make it, especially not in this condition.

He stuffed the chess pieces back into his pocket then carefully folded his jacket and laid it beside his pants. He stripped off the rest of his clothes and stepped into the shower then began lathering his chest, legs, and butt. About half way into it, he began to get that feeling, like something slimy sloshing around in his gut. He put down the soap and crouched into a squatting position, his knees against his chest, his palms flat against the sides of the tub. With his eyes closed and his mouth wide open, he lurched repeatedly forward until the vomit churned out. It was pale yellow, like freshly squeezed lemon juice with chunks of something acidic spinning around like pulp. It mixed with the water raining down from the shower and danced

its way down the drain of the tub. He stayed in that position for
a little while longer then rinsed out his mouth and stood back
up.

The rest of his routine went along without too much
difficulty. He always felt better after his morning throw-up.

After he got dressed, he staggered downstairs into the
kitchen and went right for the coffee maker, which, thankfully,
had a fresh pot. His wife, Cheryl, was standing barefoot at the
sink, hand-washing dishes and loading them into the machine
for another unnecessary run.

"Good morning," she said, turning towards him, holding a
handful of soapy silverware.

"Morning," Dave groaned as he opened the cupboard and
pulled down his favorite #1 Dad coffee mug.

"How'd you sleep?"

"Fine."

"Yeah, I'll bet you did."

Dave rolled his eyes as he grabbed the coffee decanter and
emptied it out until there was nothing left but sludge at the
bottom. He knew that Cheryl was just trying to pick a fight with
him and that really wasn't what he needed, at least not until he
had his morning cup of joe. He set the decanter back on the
burner then went to the refrigerator and pulled out a bagel and
some cream cheese. He put the bagel on a plate and grabbed a
knife and napkin then took everything back with him to the
kitchen table. His son, Larry, was sitting there at the table,
happily coloring in his Blue's Clues coloring book. His tongue
was out and his head was turned sideways, and he was making a
noise that sounded like a high-powered motorboat.

"Hey daddy," the kid said, looking up at him, little drops of
drool glistening the corners of his cheeks.

"Hey kiddo," Dave said, as he sat down at the table then set
down his coffee, bagel, and cream cheese. "Watch ya working
on?"

The kid set down his crayon and held up the coloring book, proudly displaying his current masterpiece.

"Wow," Dave said, without really looking at it, concentrating more on smearing his cream cheese. "What is it?"

"Ith uh twee bwanch."

"A tree branch? Really? Wow, that's…super."

"Yeah, I know." The kid placed the book back down on the table then grabbed his crayon and went back to scribbling.

Dave let out a long sigh and put his elbows on the table then started rubbing his forehead in long, counterclockwise circles. The pain in his neck was unbearable. It felt like someone was taking an aluminum bat to his vertebrae. He glanced at the clock on the kitchen microwave. It was only six-thirty. Damn, he still had another hour. His dealer told him to never call before seven-thirty. Bastard. What was he doing, still sleeping? Didn't he know people actually had to work for a living? He had to be up at the high school in less than two hours. He had to grade Earth Science exams then pack up the school bus. His girls had a big volleyball match tonight up in Estes Park. How was he supposed to coach if he was feeling this shitty? How could even drive a school bus if he was coming down this bad?

He lifted his mug and took a long slurp of coffee, feeling as the caffeine diffused into his blood. Ahh…that felt good. Just what he needed. A couple more sips and maybe he'd be ready to go.

As he set down the mug, he heard a loud crash echo from the upstairs hallway. It was the girls, Megan and Mary, probably getting ready for another day of middle school. What were they doing up there? Why were they stomping? Did they really have to be so god damn loud? It was bad enough he had a migraine the size of Connecticut. Now, he had to put up with a bunch of stomping teenagers and slamming doors? And to make matters worse, Cheryl was still banging away with the dishes. It was like she knew he had a headache and was trying to annoy him, seeing how far she could push him before going over the edge. At least Larry, the little angel, was sitting somewhat quietly beside him and not running around screaming like he usually did in the mornings. It probably had something to do with that coloring book he bought him. The kid seemed to be completely engrossed.

Dave lifted his mug and blew across the surface of the coffee, while studying the kid as he scribbled with his blue crayon. It was funny. The kid looked just like Dave, only chubbier—same curly red hair, same droopy eyelids, same freckled complexion, and same flat, two-by-four forehead. He probably even weighed about the same as Dave, even though he was only eleven. Of course, he still had the reading level of a first grader. Poor kid. The doctor said it was some kind of abnormality in his chromosomal makeup, something called Klinefelter's syndrome or forty-seven XXY. Whatever the hell that meant. Back when he was growing up, they just called it retarded. Of course, you weren't supposed to say that anymore. It was insensitive. Nowadays everything had to have its own politically correct terminology. Black people weren't black, Mexicans weren't Mexican, and retards weren't retarded—they were mentally challenged or developmentally disabled or someone with special needs. Ha. Yeah right. Special needs. That was one way of putting it. If that meant screaming at the top of your lungs and marching around banging a wooden spoon against a metal pot on your head, then fine, he could go with that one—that was certainly a special need. He loved the little shit and would do anything for him and all of that, but sometimes it just got to be too much—too much work, too much hassle, too much struggle, too much stress. It wasn't fair. It wasn't fair to Dave, it wasn't fair to Cheryl, and it sure as hell wasn't fair to that poor kid. Larry would probably never get to experience any of the things that normal kids experience—things like driving, dating, college, sex. Jesus—sex! The poor little bastard would probably never get to experience anything even remotely close to sex. The closest he'd come is watching monkeys at the zoo jerking off on one another. He'd always be a second rate individual, a prisoner to his own mental handicap.

He'd have to go through the rest of his life wondering why God made him special and why he couldn't do things that other people could...like why he couldn't just hop on a plane without a legal guardian...why he couldn't belly up to a bar and order a cold beer...why instead of having his own car and driving to work in the morning, he had to sit on a bus with all the degenerates and scum of the earth. It just wasn't fair. Why him? Why Larry? Why not some other person's kid?

Dave sighed as he grabbed the newspaper and flipped it to the Local Boulder page. It seemed there was a big accident last night up around Nederland—two kids drove their car out onto the ice of the Barker reservoir. Idiots. What were they thinking? Didn't they know that ice was too thin?

He tossed the Local page aside and fished out the Sports section, checking to see if the Broncos had won. As he read through the scores, the banging of dishes seemed to be getting louder and louder, each sharp clang causing him to flinch and gnash his teeth. He set down the paper and looked up at Cheryl, examining her swollen, sweat-streaked face; from her double chin to her droopy eyelids and the wild tangle of dirty blond hair that made her look like a refugee of some viral outbreak. What happened to her? Was this the same girl he knew in college? That tall, sexy pre-law student who would ditch all her classes and drive five hours just so she could be on the sidelines, cheering for him as he finished his runs. The one with those cherry-red, sand dollar shaped nipples and an ass so tight that it made him quiver. The one he would take to the motel after the races, and squeeze and kiss and fuck all night long. No, it couldn't be her. It couldn't be his Cheryl. This couldn't be the same girl he knew back then. This woman was fifteen years older and a hundred pounds heavier with a series of moles on the fat of her neck. Her butt was a beanbag and her thighs were sofa cushions and she looked like one of those mythical trolls he'd read about in Larry's storybooks—the ones with the big elf like ears and frumpy bodies who lived under bridges and terrorized kids. How was he supposed to make love to that? How was he supposed to get an erection? And Viagra? Please. What the hell was she talking about? He didn't need any god damn Viagra. It wasn't his fault he couldn't get hard. She needed to lose a couple hundred pounds first then maybe she could talk about Viagra. And what the hell was she thinking anyway? Another baby? Was she fucking crazy? Larry was more than they could handle. Hell, it took a superhuman effort just to get the little shit to school on time.

Dave sighed and glanced under the table, looking at the sorry excuse for an appendage attached to his hip. He propped his foot on the chair beside him and rolled his pant leg up to his knee. Christ, look at this thing. It was all scrawny, twisted, and contorted. It looked more like a piece of rotted driftwood than an actual human leg. There was a long, red scar running from his thigh to his shin bone from where the doctors cut him open and gave him a new knee—some damn, metal contraption they said would help relieve the inflammation, the only problem being he'd never get to run again. The most he'd be able to do is walk and climb a staircase and maybe...*maybe* take in some light biking. Bastards. What the hell was Cheryl thinking letting Larry behind the wheel of that golf cart? What was she doing thinking a mentally challenged kid could drive a four-wheeled cart? She wasn't thinking—that was the problem. She was so caught up with her stupid little Blackberry that she couldn't even shut up for two seconds, let alone keep an eye on the damn kid. If she would've just shut the thing off and watched him like she was supposed to, the kid would've never put that thing in drive and smashed into his hip. He'd still be able to compete for the qualifiers in January. He'd still have a shot at making the final cut for the Boston marathon. But now look at him. He was nothing...he was nobody...he could barely even make it down the stairs, let alone run a four-minute mile. Everything he'd worked for; all those meets and competitions, all that training and preparation gone; gone, because of his wife's stupidity; gone, because she didn't care about anyone but herself.

He shook his head and looked over at Larry, at the look of concentration in the kid's happy, little eyes. The page of his coloring book was nearly all finished—a mad swirl of greens, blues, and magenta, none of which stayed within the solid, black lines. Oh well, at least he was staying on the page of the coloring book and not on the table or the kitchen tile.

He grabbed his knife and smeared some more cream cheese on his bagel then shoved it in his mouth and took a giant-sized bite. As he chomped it down, Cheryl flipped on the garbage disposal, which felt like an oil derrick pumping into his brain. He couldn't put up with this. He had to say something. Anymore of this shit and he was gonna have a nervous breakdown. He put down his knife and looked up at Cheryl, pushing his plate aside.

"Do you mind?" he asked, as nicely as possible, hoping this wouldn't turn into an all out bitch-fest.

Cheryl pretended like she didn't hear him and continued stacking her dishes into a neat little pile.

"What's the point of having a dishwasher if you're just going to wash them in the sink?"

Cheryl hesitated for just a split second then turned on the faucet and started rinsing the plates.

"Fine," Dave said, "pretend like I'm not here. All I'm asking for is a little god damn peace and quiet."

Cheryl grabbed a handful of silverware and slammed it down into the sink. She ripped off her gloves, rolled them into a tight ball of yellow latex, and hurled them through the air right at Dave's face. Dave flinched as an afterthought, jerked his hand forward, and the cup of coffee went flying all over Larry's freshly colored page. The kid paused for a moment to process what was happening, then looked down at the table and then back up Dave. His lips curled up into his nostrils and his face scrunched together like the face of a puppy St. Bernard. He started to wail and beat his chubby fists against the table as the coffee dripped from the table onto the floor.

"Oh that's just great," Dave said, as he shot up from the table and grabbed a wad of napkins from the silver napkin holder. "Now, look what you did."

"What I did?" Cheryl said, stepping away from the counter. "You're the one who started it."

Dave knelt beside Larry, put his hand on the kid's shoulder, and started sopping up the coffee from the page of his book. "It's alright Larry," he said, "everything's gonna be okay. It's just a little coffee. It'll come out. See?" He held up the wad of napkins to show Larry, but the kid continued to bawl his eyes out. "God damnit!" Dave slammed his fist down against the table so hard that it shook the family portrait hanging on the wall. "Can you please do something?" he said, looking up at Cheryl, the coffee from the napkin dripping onto the floor. "It's too early for this shit. I can't take it."

Cheryl sighed and came out from behind the counter then went over to Larry and helped the kid up from his chair. "It's alright, baby," she said, as she grabbed a fresh wad of napkins and started wiping coffee from the kid's jean shorts. "It's going to be okay. Mommy's here now. Mommy's here, baby."

Dave snarled and pushed himself up from the table then took the wet ball of napkins over to the trashcan. "And you want another one of those?" he said, motioning to Larry, who had his face buried against his mother's belly. "Are you out of your damn mind?"

"If you'd just give me a hand once in a while, we wouldn't have to go through this every morning. I have to do everything around here."

Dave laughed as he opened the trashcan and tossed the dripping ball of napkins into the bag. "Oh please, don't give me that bullshit. I do plenty around here."

"Oh really? Then why is it that whenever I come home, Larry's not in bed, the kitchen is a disaster, and you're passed out in your underwear on the god damn couch?"

"I was not passed out."

"I couldn't even get you up last night. You were out cold."

"I told you, Cheryl, it's the medication. It makes me drowsy."

"Yeah right. You expect me to believe that? You think I don't know what you're up to? You have a history with this shit, Dave. You're sick. You need help. Rehab, something, anything."

Dave laughed and took a step backward, looking at Cheryl as if she was insane. "Rehab? Are you kidding me? I don't need rehab. I'm not some bum living under a bridge. I can quit whenever the hell I want."

"Then why don't you?"

"Why should I? It's all I have now. I can't run. I can't compete."

"There are more important things than your running career, Dave."

"Like what?"

"Like your children! Jesus, are you so busy feeling sorry for yourself that you forgot about your own kids? Don't you even love them anymore?"

"What the hell kind of question is that? Of course, I love them. I love them more than anything in this whole godforsaken world."

"Do you love them more than you love your dope?"

"What?"

"It's a simple question, Dave. Do you love them more than you love your dope? Because if you spent as much time with your kids as you do getting high then we wouldn't—"

"I spend plenty of time with those kids."

"Oh really? When was the last time you helped Megan with her homework? And what about Mary? I mean, where were you last week? You knew how important that meet was to her. She finally did a full back tuck in her floor routine and you weren't even there to see it. You used to love being with your children, but now we don't even see you. You spend all your time out driving around doing God knows what."

"I don't have time to listen to this shit. I have to get to school. I'm gonna be late."

Dave turned away and walked back to the kitchen table, picked up the newspaper and wedged it underneath his arm. He hobbled towards the front foyer, his bad leg dragging behind him like a ball and chain. But Cheryl wasn't finished and came marching in after him, her bare feet slapping against the marble floor.

"Yeah, keep running," she said. "Keep running away to your dope and see what happens. See what happens, Dave. This might be the last time you ever get to see your son again. Have you thought about that? Has that thought ever crept into your sick head?"

Dave rolled his eyes as he zipped up his green and gold jacket then bent over and scooped his blue gym bag off of the floor. "Cheryl, I told you, I don't have time for this. I got a million things to do before our match tonight. I can't stand here with you all morning and argue." He stood up and slung the bag over his shoulder then turned away from her and walked across the foyer. But, just as he reached for the front door, Cheryl grabbed him, her fingers digging into the flesh of his forearm.

"Don't do this," she said, basically begging him, trying a new tactic since shouting didn't work. "You shouldn't even be driving around in your condition. What if something happens? What if you flip that bus?"

"Nothing's gonna happen, Cheryl. I'm fine. Everything's fine."

"You are not fine. Look at you. You can't even walk straight."

Dave whirled around, pulling his arm away from her, his fists clenched, shaking by his sides. "Of course I can't walk straight! I'm a god damn cripple! I'll never walk right again thanks to you."

"It wasn't my fault. It was an accident."

"Yeah right. If you'd been watching Larry like you were supposed to, he never would've run into me with that god damn golf cart." Dave glanced at the kid. His face was buried underneath his mother's nightgown like a frightened ostrich hiding its head underneath the sand. "Do you realize what you took away from me, Cheryl? What I could have been? What I could have done? I could've gone to the Olympics. I could've competed in front of the world."

"The Olympics? Please, Dave, don't be delusional. You weren't even fast enough to make it when you were in college. You rode the bench most of the year."

"That's because I was too young and inexperienced."

"But you never even won a race."

"What about all those records I set in the 10,000 meter?"

"You were in high school."

"What about that half marathon I won a few years back in Denver?"

"That was for charity."

"So?"

"So, you were the only one in your heat!"

Dave snorted and turned away from her, then grabbed the knob and pulled open the front door. He didn't have time for this shit. He had to get down to Aurora. It was almost seven-thirty. It was time to call Juarez.

"You're sick, Dave," Cheryl said. "You're delusional. You need help."

Dave rolled his eyes and turned away from her, then stepped out onto the patio while pulling the front door closed.

Chapter 5

The Score

Dave stood on the porch for a moment trying to regain his focus, staring out at the lawn that was covered with a fresh layer of snowfall. Jesus, what a morning. What a horrible way to start the week. All that bitching and moaning was completely unnecessary especially for a Monday morning. Rehab? Please. What the hell was Cheryl talking about? He didn't need no god damn rehab. It wasn't like he was some junkie living out of a shopping cart, standing by the highway, holding up a sign. He was an Olympic runner for Christ's sake. The best god damn middle and long distance runner on this side of the Mississippi. He'd set records in everything from the two to ten thousand meter. How did she think he set all those records? It wasn't talent. It had nothing to do with talent. In fact, he didn't even have the right genetics to be a great runner. His legs were too short, his upper body was too bulky, but he had one thing those fuckers in Ethiopia would never have—heart. He had more will and more drive in his little pinky finger than those bulimic fuckers had in their entire undernourished bodies. If he wanted something bad enough, he'd just go out there and take it. It didn't matter what it was. The junior's two thousand meter Colorado record? Please. He crushed that when he was only a teenager. And what about district 3A Cross Country Championship? How did three straight, back-to-back five thousand-meter titles sound? See, he didn't need no god damn rehab. If he wanted to quit, he'd just do it. He'd do it on sheer willpower. But why should he? Why should he quit? It felt too good. It was the best feeling he'd had in a long time. It gave him that rush, that high he hadn't had since high school when he was winning medals, running races, and leaving everyone in his heat a hundred yards behind. If he couldn't have that, he had to have something—he had to have something to replace that feeling. Those pain pills the doctor gave him weren't worth a damn. They were about as strong as Larry's cough medicine. One measly bottle wouldn't even get him through an entire day. But a few hits off that pipe—shit, that was all he needed. The only problem was getting it. It was quite a hike.

He adjusted his blue gym bag higher up on his shoulder then stepped down from the patio and stumbled across the front lawn. His little blue Volkswagen was parked out in the driveway, the back and rear windshields frosted with a thick layer of ice. Oh great, just what he needed. It was gonna take at least ten minutes to scrape off all this ice. Maybe he could just do the front driver side windshield. There wasn't enough time to do both sides and the back.

He went to the trunk and pulled out the ice scraper then brought it back with him to the front of the car. As he came around the side, he noticed that the passenger side mirror was missing—in fact, it looked like it had been completely knocked off. What the hell? He crouched next to the tire for a closer inspection and noticed that the mirror wasn't the only thing that was all messed up. The headlight was cracked, the front bumper was crumpled, and there were etchings of what looked like red paint all along the passenger side door.

He froze for a moment, staring at the damage, trying to remember what in the hell happened. But he couldn't think, he couldn't remember, everything from last night was all fragmented—a disjointed series of snapshots and voices, a blur of lights, colors, and music. He remembered going to Cosmo's to pick up the pizza, but that was early in the day, like around one-thirty. What about after that? And what about Larry? Did he even pick the kid up from his Morningstar program? He must have, because Cheryl couldn't have done it. She was up at the courthouse all day preparing for cases. Then what the hell happened? Did he hit something? Did he run something over?

He cursed to himself as he stood up from where he was crouching then looked up at the house then back at the car. He'd better get the hell out of here before Cheryl saw all this damage. He'd never hear the end of it, especially if she found out he didn't even remember how it happened. But, what was he gonna do? How was he gonna fix it? How was he gonna find time to take it to a mechanic?

He bent back down and picked up the scraper, then rapidly chipped away the ice from the rest of the windshield. When he was finished, he opened the door and tossed in the scraper then picked up his gym bag and threw it on the passenger seat. He hopped in the car and turned over the ignition then threw it in reverse and sailed down the driveway.

Twenty minutes later, he was off the interstate heading west down Colfax towards Aurora, or as the natives liked to call it, Saudi-Aurora. It got its nickname on account of the fact it was all the way out in the boonies, about fifteen miles east of Denver, somewhere between the beltway and I-70. Because of its remote location, it was a city that seemed to have been forgotten, as if time and technology had gone on without it. In fact, every time Dave came here, he felt like he was going through some kind of time portal. The place looked like it was straight out of 1950. The buildings were all old, dirty, and dilapidated, and some even still had that retro 1950's architecture; diners that looked like space ships had landed on top of them with bright, neon *Welcome* signs written in cursive...bowling alleys with pins the size of Volkswagens sitting on top of their wing-tipped entries. There was even an old drive-in somewhere around Havana. It wasn't showing pictures, but it still had the original supporting structure that held up the movie screen. It was kind of neat, if you liked going backwards. Unfortunately, the farther west you got down Colfax, the more the city began to look like a slummy ghetto; hotels became motels that charged by the hour and bowling alleys became strip clubs that reeked of cum and stale whiskey sours. English turned to Spanish, burgers became tacos, and banks with glass windows became iron-barred pawnshops. Jesus, what a neighborhood. Every time he came down here, he thought he was gonna catch dysentery.

He eased on the brake as he pulled up to a stoplight then gently pressed down the door locks and peered out the window. A woman with wild, wiry hair was pushing a shopping cart, staring at Dave as she staggered into the crosswalk. Her cart was filled to the brim with aluminum cans and boxes, ratty blankets and torn up newspaper. Dave tried not to make eye contact as she walked out in front of him. She was muttering something at the pavement in a language that was definitely not English. On the opposite side of the street stood a bunch of Mexicans, waiting for the bus that would take them into the city. Their hands looked more like claws, clutching their grocery bags, shivering and waiting in the merciless Colorado winter. Poor bastards. Look at their fingers. They were all split and frozen like hot dogs with freezer burn. What a horrible life. What a miserable existence. Thank god he would never have to end up like them.

Finally, the light turned green and Dave stomped on the gas pedal, then put on his blinker and turned left at the next corner. He went about a quarter of a mile down the street then made a quick U-turn and pulled to a stop in front of a horribly plain brick building. The building was five stories high with microscopic slits for windows that made it look more like a prison tower than an actual apartment. In front of the building was a patch of dirt no bigger than the size of a pitcher's mound that Dave figured was supposed to serve as the building's front garden. Around the dirt stood a six-foot tall, chain-link rectangle that looked strangely familiar to the kind of fence you'd put around a prison yard. The only thing that was missing was some razor wire, a couple of free weights, and maybe some basketball hoops. Even the name of the place made Dave chuckle. It was called, *Casa Grande—The Big House*. How ominous.

He laughed to himself as he scanned the grounds of the building, but his temperament quickly sobered when he locked eyes with a short, angry-looking Hispanic. He was just a kid, nineteen maybe twenty, with a black baseball cap on his head that said *Colorado Rockies*. It was hard to make him out from underneath the building's shadow, but Dave knew it had to be Juarez, because who else would be up this early on a Monday morning?

Dave tapped the horn once as a sign of identification then reached across the center console and rolled down the passenger side window. The kid nodded and put down his still-burning cigarette then trotted down the steps of the front porch patio. Before he got to the street, the kid stopped and looked down both ends of the corner. Once he was satisfied that there were no cops around, he opened the gate and walked towards Dave's passenger side window. "What's up?" he said, leaning in the window, one hand on the hood, the other dug deep into his jacket pocket.

"Hey, what's up Juarez?" Dave said, unable to stop grinning, half because he was nervous and half because the glands in his mouth were burning with salivation. "How's business?"

"Business is business. What you want man?"

Dave nodded and quickly reached into his back pocket and produced five crisp twenties from his brown, chewed up wallet. "I guess the usual," he said, as he held out the money, his hands trembling from utter anticipation.

"The usual huh?"

"Yep."

The kid smiled a smile of arrogance, probably because he thought he had Dave wrapped around his little finger. But Dave didn't care, because he knew something this little punk didn't; if he really wanted, he could quit tomorrow; no detox, no rehab, no counseling, no therapists; he could drop this shit right now on sheer willpower. Then, who'd be laughing? Who'd be smiling? Who'd be paying this kid's rent and buying his groceries? Not Dave. That was for damn sure.

Dave smiled right back as he handed the kid the money, who inspected it and stuffed it inside his pocket. The kid disappeared from the view of the window, but returned a few seconds later holding a small, red plastic pill bottle. He unscrewed the cap and turned it over, counting off the rocks as they slid into his palm.

"Alright, that's ten," he said, as he funneled the rocks back in the bottle then handed it to Dave through the car window. "Ten fat ones."

At the sight of the rocks, Dave's heart began to flutter. He felt like a kid on Prom night who was about to get lucky. He snatched up the bottle and took a swift inspection of the product, then pulled open the center console and placed it under the cover of a couple McDonald's hamburgers wrappers. Alright. Now, he was set. Now, he was ready. He was ready to cook this shit and get on with his Monday.

He shifted from park and buckled his seat belt then looked back up at Juarez through the passenger side window. "We good?" he said, as he tapped the dashboard, his fingers twitching like he was playing an imaginary piano.

"Yeah, we good," Juarez said. "We good."

"Alright. I'll see you later then."

"I know you will." The kid smiled then turned away from the window and trotted back through the gate of his trashy, little prison yard.

A few minutes later, Dave was back on Colfax heading east towards the Capitol Hill neighborhood. He decided to stop off at the park for a couple quick ones. He was gonna need something in his system to keep him moving. That coffee and bagel he had for breakfast wasn't nearly enough energy for him.

He took a left onto York towards Cheesman, driving past a four-story brick house that someone had once told him was an AA meeting hall. As he came to the light, he glanced out the window and saw a bunch of people standing around on a porch smoking cigarettes. Jesus, look at them all…the sick bastards…standing around in the cold looking miserable. Thank god he wasn't an addict. It had to suck being sober.

He shook his head and put on his turn signal then took a right off of York onto Thirteenth Street. When he got to the park, he drove around a few times to make sure there were no cops lurking in the shadows. The pigs were notorious for hiding out in this neighborhood. Once he was satisfied that the place was empty, he drove to a small, secluded parking lot next to some big, blue Porta-Potties. The things were nasty looking, but they were well hidden, underneath the shade of some monstrous, snow-glazed evergreens.

He pulled to a stop then opened the center console and removed the red plastic bottle from underneath the McDonald's hamburger wrappers. He reached into his jacket pocket and pulled out his cheap, plastic, Bic lighter along with his trusty glass pipe that he unwrapped from some toilet paper. He twisted his body and looked out the back window then took a deep breath and reached into the pill bottle. He dumped out a rock and held it up between his fingers, studying it in the light as if he was appraising a diamond. The rock wasn't as fat as the kid made it out to be. It was small, about the size of a kid's molar, Larry's molar. He brought it to his nose and took a deep whiff inward then touched it with the tip of his tongue—it tasted bitter and metallic, almost inky.

He grabbed his pipe and held it eye line then carefully placed the rock on the end near the filter. His hands shook, his lips quivered, and tiny beads of sweat were dripping onto his crotch from his forehead. He took a deep breath then sparked up the lighter. The flame was like a torch glowing inside the little Volkswagen. He lowered the flame underneath the pipe's glass bottom. The glass turned black and the tooth sublimed to vapor. He wrapped his lips around the pipe's mouthpiece then took a deep breath in and held it for a few seconds.

Almost immediately, it came to him—the feeling of strength and power crashing into his blood stream. He felt like he did when he was winning races; the ecstasy, the euphoria, the in-fucking-vincibility. He could do anything. He could be anybody. All he needed was a couple hits and he could finally feel normal. No more insecurity…no more inadequacy…he was ten feet tall and fucking bulletproof.

He took another hit, but this time held it longer then let the smoke slowly curl away from his lips. His throat became numb and his heart rate became rapid, and a surge of adrenaline began to pump through his ventricles. Yeah, bring it on, he thought, as he looked up in the rearview mirror, his pupils dilating to the size of black marbles. Bring on the pain, bring on the suffering, bring on anything you can throw at this motherfucker…because he's armed, he's ready, he's un-fucking-touchable…you can't hurt him, you can't even see him…he's a ghost, a phantom, a mother-fucking ninja…he'll fuck your daughters and eat your children.

"Ha, ha, ha…yeah."

Dave closed his eyes and sank back against the headrest, feeling as every muscle in his body oozed into the seat cushion. His arms went limp and his head became weightless, and if only for a moment, he felt absolutely nothing—no more pain, no more tightening, no more aching, no more throbbing. As he opened his eyes again, he glanced at the clock on the dashboard—it was almost nine-thirty, but he didn't care—he didn't care about anything. Nothing mattered right now. There was nothing—no Cheryl, no Larry, no fucking responsibilities…it was just him in this park in this moment…just him and his crack, the way it should be.

Chapter 6

The Office

It was a brisk walk across the snow-slick parking lot to Dave's office in the bowels of the Boulder high school gymnasium. He used the back gate in between the football field and the weight room, reeling like an escaped mental patient along the side of the chain link fence. He could see the blurry outline of the gym's entrance before him, like the gates of heaven calling his name. His ears were ice and his snot was crystal, freezing just above the cleft of his upper lip.

One final push and he was through the doorway into the safety of the high school gymnasium. It was nice inside, warm and quiet, only the soft humming of the pale overhead lights filling the muggy, sweat-saturated air. He shut the door and made his way down the sidelines of the basketball court, his tennis shoes squeaking across the freshly waxed floor. When he got behind the stage, he opened the door to the basement then descended the dark and winding stairwell. As always, it was muggy down there—the boiler was in full throttle, causing the walls to drip like an old woman with hot flashes. But, Dave didn't mind it. He liked the peace and quiet. It was completely cut off from the rest of the universe. If only he could stay down here, he could finally have a chance to think for a minute and figure out what he was gonna do with the rest of his life. At the rate he was going, he wouldn't make it; he wouldn't last one more month doing this shit, coaching girls' volleyball at a second rate high school, listening to Cheryl bitch every morning about every minuscule detail. It wasn't him. It wasn't his destiny. It wasn't how things were supposed to be. He was supposed to be rich and famous with his own book deals, corporate sponsors, and a mansion in Malibu. He was supposed to do to running what Lance Armstrong did to cycling, and make it accessible to the rest of the country. But how could he do that now with this fucking kneecap? He could barely even walk down these steps let alone win a marathon. He just had to accept the fact that he would never amount to anything and for the rest of his life he'd be a complete nobody.

When he got to the bottom, he turned the corner and stopped in front of his flimsy, wooden office door. He unlocked the door and pushed it open, feeling for the light switch that was mounted somewhere along the wall. When he found it, he flipped it upward, then limped over to his desk and collapsed backward into his swivel style office chair. He closed his eyes and tried relaxing, but it was pretty much impossible to do with all this anxiety. It felt like a gorilla had its hands wrapped around his larynx, the big, fat, hairy fingers digging into the muscles of his neck. His head was pounding, his face was sweating, and it felt like his heart was about to rip wide open. In retrospect, he probably should've gone a little easier at Cheesman and not have finished off that first rock. Oh well, he knew how to solve that; it didn't take a degree in pharmacy to know how to get balanced out.

He bent forward and flung the bottom drawer open looking for the only thing he knew that would take off the edge. There it was—hiding beneath a stack of his students' ungraded earth science midterms—a big, brown, beautiful bottle of Jim Beam's Kentucky Bourbon. He reached in and pulled out the bottle, unscrewed the cap and brought it to his lips. The alcohol burned as it slid down his throat, making him lurch forward and cough and cringe, but it felt so damn good inside his stomach that he lifted the bottle and went again, then again and again until his heart rate became steady and again and again until his entire body turned to jelly.

Once he was satisfied, he returned the bottle, tucking it safely back inside his bottom desk drawer. Then he reached into his pocket and pulled out the little red pill bottle and held it up between his forefinger and thumb. One down, nine to go. Hopefully, that would be enough to last him a couple days, maybe a week if he could keep it all under control. He'd better. He had that match tonight all the way up in Estes. If those girls knew anything was up, they'd probably tell their parents and he'd be out of a job faster than he could count to four. Then what would he do? How would he pay for his medicine? He'd have to steal money from Cheryl and hope she didn't catch him, because if she did, she'd probably want to divorce him or worse, send him to some silly rehab. No, no, no, no, he couldn't let that happen. He had to be careful. Maybe tomorrow, after the game, he could afford to be a little more reckless.

He took the bottle and shoved it back into his pocket then got up from the desk and walked towards the door. But, just as he was about to leave, something stopped him, like the tentacles of an octopus wrapping around his throat. All of a sudden, he couldn't breathe and he began to feel dizzy, as the razor sharp suction cups dug into his spinal cord. He looked down at his hands. Jesus, they were trembling, and the pain in his knee was now shooting up through his pelvis. He locked the door. This was ridiculous. How could he drive a school bus if he was hurting this bad? He had to have something to quell the throbbing. He had to have something for his knee. If he didn't, he could get into an accident. He could drive that bus right off a mountain. Christ, look at him...he looked like a Parkinson's patient... god damn Michael J. Fox on crack cocaine. How could he be expected to hold down the gear shifter? How could he be expected to push down the brakes?

He turned away from the door and marched back across the office then plopped himself back down into his chair. Just a couple more hits…that was all he needed…just enough to calm him down and ease the throbbing.

He reached into his pocket and pulled out the bottle then set it on the desk right beneath his little, green banker's lamp. Then, he pulled out his glass pipe and cheap, plastic lighter and took out one of the rocks and placed it on the end. As he mashed down the flint, the flame began to flicker and the rock started to sizzle like canola oil on a frying pan. He leaned forward and sucked in the vapors and almost immediately, the pain just melted away. His hands stopped shaking, his knee stopped throbbing, and the tentacles around his neck uncoiled their grip. Yes, that's it…that was all he needed…just one good, solid hit.

He set down the pipe and folded his hands behind him then leaned back in his chair and stared out at the *Sports Illustrated* swimsuit calendar hanging on the wall by the doorway. The model in the picture was tall and blonde with a pair of diamond hard nipples piercing through the fabric of her skinny string bikini. She held a slight resemblance to his middle blocker, Sarah, who was only eighteen, but looked like she was in her late twenties, with juicy breasts the size of watermelons and an ass so tight you could break your dick off in it.

He closed his eyes and thought about Sarah bouncing up to the net in that tight, black spandex. Damn, she was so strong, so tall and powerful…abs so tight you could actually see the muscles flexing. He began to feel movement down in his crotch area as the blood in his head drained down to his dick. He had a brilliant idea. He opened his eyes and pulled his chair forward then hit the power button on his computer. The monitor flashed blue and the processor began groaning as the little windows icon started running across the screen. A couple seconds later, his desktop appeared before him, a picture of Larry and his two daughters as the background on his screen. God damnit, he needed to change that. He couldn't deal with them looking at him right now.

He quickly grabbed the mouse and double-clicked *My Documents*, which brought up a folder filled with all sorts of files. He scrolled to the bottom to a file titled *Game Videos* and double-clicked it. "Alright, let's see what we got here." He scrolled through the selection and eventually landed on the one that he was looking for—*Crusaders vs Spartans_2000*. Ah yes, this was a good one. He double-clicked the file, which brought up the media player, then hit the play button and turned up the volume. As the video came on, he stood up from the chair and pushed down his khakis. Alright, let's go...let's get this party started...come on you little cock tease...smile at the fucking camera.

He sat back down and hunched forward, pulled out his dick and stared at the monitor. The camera was zoomed in on Sarah's nipples, which were poking through her sweat-soaked green and gold Catholic High Crusader's uniform. She was almost six feet tall with a long, blond, braided ponytail that swung wildly like a whip as she dove for the volleyball. Her shirt was tied up just above her belly button so that every time she lifted her arms to block you could actually see the outline of her ribs. "Jesus," Dave mumbled, as he hunched forward, pumping and pulling his now fully erect member. What he'd do for ten minutes alone with her. He'd give up his house, his car, all his savings, just to get in between those legs and wrap them around his torso.

He grabbed the desk and pulled himself closer, then got rid of the glare by tilting the monitor. He took the mouse and pushed up the little green volume button until it sounded like the girls were right there in the room, grunting in his eardrum. "Yeah...come on you bitch...give it to me...make me cum you filthy little animal." He clenched his teeth and hunched as far as he could forward as he thought about jamming his dick in between those young, perky titties. Yeah, he was almost there. He could feel it coming, like a fucking torpedo being shot from his dick hole. He grunted and gasped, pulling harder and harder, sweat like a sprinkler splashing down on the keyboard. "Yeah, come on you dirty whore. Give it to me. Make me cum you fucking cock tease."

Then it came, like a New Year's Eve party popper—a wad of cum shot out all over the screen. "Ah fuck." He closed his eyes and curled his toes inward, his body shaking and convulsing like he was having a seizure. "Ahh. Jesus Christ."

Once he was done, he just sat there for a moment, taking in deep swallows of the crack-laden oxygen. As he opened his eyes, he glanced up at the monitor—his cum looked like vanilla yogurt dripping down Sarah's body. He laughed to himself and nodded. Take that you fucking cock tease. Then, he got up from the desk and looked around the office for something that he could wipe his hands off with. But, there was nothing there so he reached down and pulled off his sock and used it as a jizz rag to wipe off the monitor. The cum was sticky and wet against his fingers and unfortunately, it didn't make for very good absorption. He soaked up as much as he could then tossed the sock into the wastebasket and reached down by his ankles and pulled up his khakis.

As he zipped up his zipper and buttoned his button, he felt his cell phone vibrating in his pocket. What the hell? He reached down and jammed his hand into his pocket, then pulled out the phone and looked at the display. It was Cheryl. What the hell did she want? He thought he was done with her today. Guess not.

He set the phone down on the desk then tucked in his shirt and buckled his buckle and sat back in the chair. He hit the stop button on the media player, closed out all his folders, and hit the power button on the monitor. Just then, the phone started buzzing again, vibrating on his desk like one of those table pagers they give you at a Ruby Tuesday's. "God damnit." He grabbed the phone and flipped it open and jammed the receiver against his ear. "Hello?"

"Dave?"

"Yes?"

"Where are you?"

"I'm at school. Where do you think?"

"Please don't be mouthy."

"I'm not being mouthy."

"Yes you are."

"Jesus Christ Cheryl, what do you want? I'm really busy here."

"I need you to do me a favor."

"Aw Christ, what now?"

"I need you to pick Larry up from Morningstar."

"What? Why?"

"Because I can't do it today. I got an emergency call from one of my clients and I have to run down to Denver for a couple of hours."

"Cheryl, I can't take off work. I got like a million things to do before the match tonight."

"Please Dave, don't argue with me. I really need your help on this one."

Dave wedged the phone between his ear and shoulder then bent down and began tying his shoelaces. "Well, what am I supposed to do with him? I can't watch him."

"You don't have to. My sister's going to watch him. You can drop him off there."

"Your sister's? What? Out in Broomfield?"

"Yes."

"Jesus, Cheryl. I don't have time for that. I gotta pack up the school bus."

"Please Dave, it won't take long. He gets out early today. You can do it on your lunch break."

"Aw for Christ's sake."

"Please Dave, I never ask you for anything."

Dave slammed his elbows on the desk and started rubbing his forehead. "Alright, well what if I just take him up there with me?"

"Where? To the volleyball game?"

"Yeah, it'd be good for him. Get him out of the house for a change."

"No, Dave, absolutely not."

"Why not?"

"Because I don't want him riding around with you in that school bus."

"Why not?"

"Because it's not safe, alright?"

"Aw for Christ's sake, Cheryl. He's not a little kid anymore. He's almost a teenager. When are you gonna stop babying him?"

"It's not him I'm worried about."

"Oh this again?"

"I don't trust you, Dave. I don't trust you behind the wheel of that school bus. You're not well. You're sick."

"I'm not sick, Cheryl. I'm perfectly fine."

"You are definitely not fine, Dave. Something is very wrong with you."

"Well, then why even call me? Huh? Why not have your sister pick him up?"

"She can't. She's stuck at the house waiting for the carpet people."

"Carpet people? What? Is she getting her carpets cleaned?"

"Yes."

"That figures."

"Look Dave, just promise me you'll take him directly to my sister's. That means no stopping for hamburgers or ice cream."

"Yeah, yeah, yeah."

"Do you promise?"

"Yes, I promise. Jesus!"

He hit the end button and shoved the phone back into his pocket then stood up from the desk and pulled on his jacket. He checked the clock. Shit, it was almost eleven-thirty. By the time he got back from Broomfield it would almost be twelve-thirty. How was he gonna do this? How was he gonna find time to load up the school bus? He still had to pack up the balls and pack up the coolers, fill up the gas and check the tires. God damn her. She always did this. She always treated him like he was an idiot. If she'd just trust him for once and let Larry come with him then there wouldn't be a god damn problem. There was no way he was gonna make it. He'd be lucky if he even got a chance to sit down and eat a fucking sandwich.

He reached across the desk and grabbed his pipe, lighter, and little plastic bottle and, in one sweeping motion, brushed them all into the bottom desk drawer on top of the ungraded earth science midterms. Alright, he could do this. He was gonna have to drive like a maniac and hope he didn't get pulled over. He took a deep breath and rubbed his forehead then walked across the office and flipped off the light switch.

Chapter 7

Larry

A half hour later, Dave was in his Volkswagen flying down Broadway, heading south towards Larry's school on Table Mesa Drive in South Boulder. He had the windows rolled down and the radio blaring and was singing along to *Crazy Train* by Ozzy Osbourne. But he was starting to get hungry. He hadn't had anything to eat all day except that bagel and coffee. He reached across the passenger seat and dug into his little blue gym bag then pulled out the bottle of Kentucky straight bourbon. He looked out both windows to make sure there was no one beside him then twisted off the cap and turned up the bottle. He coughed and gagged as the bourbon slithered into his stomach, causing his throat to pulsate and his eyes to water, but it felt so damn good that he wiped his mouth and took another, then another and another and another and another. When he was satisfied, he twisted the cap back on the bottle and safely tucked it back inside his little, blue gym bag. He pulled a shirt over it to hide the label then closed the bag and zipped up the zipper. Alright, good, great, grand, wonderful…he was ready to pick up Larry and finish off this nightmare. He flipped on his turn signal and swerved across the highway, almost colliding with a minivan that was hiding in his right blind spot. The woman in the van laid on the horn and threw up her hands in a "what the fuck?" gesture, mouthing something at Dave as he flew right by her.

"Woops. Sorry." Dave said, sticking his hand out the window, waving and laughing at just how close he came to hitting her. "Sorry you're such a bitch. Ha ha ha." He pulled his hand back in the window then eased on the brake and took a left onto Table Mesa.

Larry's school was on the corner of Table Mesa and Tantra safely tucked away inside a boutique shopping center. There was a crowd of children and teachers waiting on the curb of a brick-lined, semi-circle driveway that was jam-packed with a procession of Jaguars and Mercedes. Christ, look at these people, a bunch of rich assholes sipping on their lattes and chatting on their cell phones. Bet they never thought their kids would end up at this place—an overpriced, under-resourced daycare for the mentally challenged. Probably thought little Johnny was gonna grow up to be a stock broker, just like daddy. Sorry folks, guess that wasn't what the universe had in store for little Johnny. Hell, the kid would be lucky if he got a job as a fucking bus boy.

Dave shook his head in disgust as he put on his turn signal then got behind the last car in the line. It took an eternity, but he finally got to the front of the driveway, then turned down the volume and strained his eyeballs. Come on, where in the hell was he? Where was this kid? Where was he hiding? Oh wait—was that him, behind the flag pole, standing next to that big black kid that looked like fat Albert? Yeah, it was, but what the hell was he wearing? Black jean shorts and a tie-dye t-shirt with bright yellow socks pulled all the way up to his kneecaps? Jesus, why did Cheryl dress him like that? Was she *trying* to make him look like a retard?

Dave leaned across the center console, honked the horn a few times, and waved out the window. "Yo Larry! Over here!"

The kid cocked his head and bent his neck forward, like a confused moose standing at the intersection of a busy highway.

He honked a few more times. "Larry! Come on! It's me, daddy!"

"Daddy?"

"Yes, it's me. Get your ass over here. Come on, we're late."

The kid bent down and grabbed his Blue's Clues book bag then slung it over his shoulder and waved goodbye to his friends. He lowered his head and bent his body forward and took off running like a rhinoceros charging a safari van. A teacher shouted after him, "slow down Larry!" to which the kid slammed on the brakes and curled his mouth into a menacing grin. He power-walked the last couple of yards with his hands pinned by his kneecaps like a kid at a swimming pool who'd just gotten the whistle blown at him by the lifeguard. When he got to the car, he flung the passenger door open then threw his book bag in the back and hopped in the passenger seat.

"Daddy!" he screamed, as he threw his pudgy arms around his father and buried his forehead against his shoulder. "Where's mommy?"

"Mommy's not here today. It's just gonna be you and me kiddo."

"Weally?"

"Yep. Really."

"Hooway!"

"Hooray," Dave said, as he checked his rearview mirror and slowly edged back out into the procession of vehicles. "Hey Larry, would you mind buckling your seat belt for me, buddy?"

The kid nodded and pulled the belt over his chubby belly then quickly snapped it into the buckle. "I did it," he said, smiling up at his father, drool dripping onto his tie-dye t-shirt.

"Good job."

"What about you, daddy?"

"What about me?"

"You don't have your buckle."

Dave sighed as he flipped on his turn signal then took a right towards the ramp for the freeway. "I don't need one," he said.

"How come?"

"Because."

"Because why?"

"Because I just don't god damnit!"

The kid frowned as though the answer didn't suffice him, but then shrugged his shoulders and unzipped his book bag. "Where we going?" he said, as he dug into his book bag and pulled out a couple crayons and his Blue's Clues coloring book.

Dave checked the clock. It was nearly twelve-thirty. There was no way in hell they could make it out to Cheryl's sister's. Fuck it. If she was gonna make him drive all around town running errands then he was gonna do it on his terms, not hers. She couldn't tell him what to do. She didn't own him. He was Larry's parent too. He knew what the kid needed better than she did. And what the kid didn't need was to be stuck in some dingy house in Broomfield watching Cheryl's slutty sister flirt with the carpet people. What he needed was to spend some quality time with his father and be outdoors—have a god damn adventure. Just because the kid was mentally challenged didn't mean he also had to be a lazy, couch potato. If Dave had his way, he'd transform Larry into a runner. Three years time, he could have the kid in a good enough shape to compete in the Special Olympics.

Dave smiled and turned towards Larry. "Say kiddo, how'd you like to come with daddy up to the mountains?"

The kid slammed down his crayons and looked up at his father, a grin so wide it seemed to stretch from earlobe to earlobe. "Weally?"

"Yeah. Really."

"Oh. That would be awesome."

"Alright then." Dave switched lanes and made a quick u-turn then took a right onto Broadway back towards the high school. "It looks like that's what we're doing."

"Hooway!" The kid threw up his hands and started clapping, his fat belly bouncing up and down across his seat belt. "Are we gonna go to O'Weilley's?"

O'Reilley's? That was a shitty pub up around Nederland, near the banks of the Barker Reservoir. But how did Larry know about that? He never took him there, did he?

"Larry, how do you know about O'Reilley's?"

The kid looked up at Dave with a confused expression. "Lath night…we did O'Weilley's."

"We did?"

"Yeah. We pwayed chuckle board."

"Chuckle board? You mean shuffle board?"

"Yeah. Chuckle board." The kid threw up his hand and started cheering, pumping his fist in a repetitive motion. "Chuckle board! Chuckle board! Chuckle board!"

Dave looked at the kid. What the hell was he talking about? They didn't play shuffleboard last night, did they? Shit—why couldn't he remember? Why was everything last night so damn blurry? If that's where they were then how'd they get there? He didn't remember driving. Did they take the Volkswagen? How long were they there? "Shit." He clenched his fist and pounded against the steering wheel, making the pennies in the ashtray bounce around like Mexican jumping beans.

"Daddy?" Larry said, looking up at him with a look of concern on his chubby moon pie of a face.

"What?"

"Are you okay?"

"Yes, Larry, I'm fine, just—no more talking, okay? It's quiet time. Daddy needs to concentrate."

The kid shrugged and went back to his coloring book, as Dave slammed down the accelerator and shifted into the outer left lane. He didn't have time to think about yesterday. Whatever happened last night happened, and there was nothing he could do about it now. It was best to just keep calm and try to stay focused. There were still a million things to do to get ready for the big match tonight.

He checked his mirror and flipped on his blinker then turned left onto Arapahoe from Broadway.

A few minutes later, they were back at the high school. Dave parked in his space behind the track shed. He reached into the back and grabbed his blue gym bag then opened the door and cut off the ignition. "Come on," he said as he crawled out of the Volkswagen, pulling his bad leg out from underneath the steering wheel. "Let's go. We don't have time to dick around. I got a lot of shit to do."

Larry nodded and folded up his coloring book then stuffed it back into his blue book bag. He got out of the car and shut the door behind him then walked around to his father and clutched his hand. Together, they walked across the icy parking lot, their feet slipping and sliding like a pair of drunken penguins.

When they got inside the gym, Larry squealed and took off running, his arms out to the side like he was an airplane. He flew down the sidelines along the wooden bleachers, then made a sharp turn at the water fountains and spun around in circles underneath the basketball goal.

"Larry, what are you doing?" Dave said in a restrained whisper, trying as best he could to shout without making any sound.

"I'm fwying daddy, I'm fwying."

"God damnit, I told you we don't have time for this shit. Now, get your ass over here and down these stairs."

"Okay daddy, here I come!" Larry squealed then dipped his right arm sideways and made a wide left turn towards center court. As he straightened out, he began to gain momentum, fluttering his lips together making a propeller sound. When he got to the other end, he crashed belly first against the stage's green padding, waving his hands and feet in the air, laughing, like a beached orca.

"God damnit, Larry, will you get down from there?"

Larry laughed a little longer then hopped down from the stage's padding and ran over to his father.

"Come on, let's go." Dave squeezed the kid's hand and yanked him forward. He opened the door to the basement and descended the dark stairwell.

When they got to the bottom, he halted the kid in front of his office, fished his keys from his pocket, and unlocked the door.

"Alright Larry," he said, as he guided the kid into the office. "Daddy's gonna need a few minutes of quiet time. Do you have something to keep you busy?"

The kid nodded, sat down on the carpet, pulled out his crayons and coloring book and laid them all out in a neat little line on the floor.

Dave limped across the office and collapsed into his office chair. He kicked off his shoes and reclined backward, feeling as the blood drained down to his legs. Damn, he was tired. His leg was really aching. It felt like he had a bear trap clamped around his ankle. He closed his eyes and took a few deep breaths inward, seeing if he could try and breathe the pain away. But, it wasn't working. The knee was really throbbing, probably because of all the god damn running around today. Fucking Cheryl—why'd she always do this? Why'd she always spring this shit on him at the last minute? If she was gonna be working today, she should've planned for it. She should've told her sister about it last week. Didn't she realize the stress he was under? Didn't she understand the fucking pain he was in? The doctor was very specific—he said no overexertion, nothing that will cause the muscles to be overtly flexed. Not only did that mean no more running, it also meant no more chasing Larry all over the god damn city.

"Shit!" He slammed his fist down against the desk, which shook the mouse and caused the computer screen to flicker on. The clock at the bottom of the screen said it was almost one-thirty. That meant he only had another hour before the last period bell rang. What would one rock set him back, about fifteen minutes? That should leave him plenty of time to finish packing up the school bus. Yeah, it was a no brainer, and with a stronger knee, he could easily make up the fifteen minutes.

He grabbed the edge of the desk and rolled himself forward, opened the bottom drawer and reached inside. Like a surgeon preparing for a complicated procedure, he pulled out his pipe, lighter, and red, plastic pill bottle then set them all up in a straight line. He took a deep breath and wiped his forehead, pulled out a rock and set it on the end of the pipe. His hands were shaking, his leg was throbbing, but it didn't matter, because in a few seconds, it would all subside. All the worry, all the frustration, all the agony, all the pain—it would all be obliterated like a sand dollar in a tsunami, drowned by a surge of adrenaline and joy.

He took a few hits and reclined backward feeling as the pain began to dissolve. When he opened them back up, he saw Larry staring at him, his curious eyes fixed on the pipe and the red pill bottle. "What's that?" the kid asked, crawling towards him, stretching his neck upward like a curious giraffe.

"What...this?" Dave said, as he picked up the pill bottle, dangling it like it was his lucky rabbit's foot.

The kid smiled and nodded, his eyes transfixed as if he was hypnotized.

"This is daddy's special medicine."

"What's it for?"

"My leg."

"Does it hurt?"

"What?" Dave chuckled and set down the bottle. "No, silly. It's good for me. Makes daddy big and strong. See." Dave pulled up his sleeve and flexed his bicep, grunting like he was a weight lifter doing a curl.

"Wow."

"Pretty neat, huh?"

"Yeah. Can I try some?"

"No you can't try some. This is for grownups only."

"Pwease."

"No."

"Pwetty pwease."

"I said no, Larry. End of discussion."

The kid started pouting like a puppy that had just been punished for peeing on an expensive rug.

Dave did a couple more hits until the rock was finished then checked the clock—he only had another forty-five minutes. He gathered up the pipe, lighter, and plastic medicine bottle and swept them all into his bottom desk drawer. Then, he got up from the desk, went around to Larry, and crouched down so that he was eye level with the kid's stubby nose. "Alright, Larry, I want you to stay in here while I get some stuff ready, and I don't want you leaving until I get back—that means no exploring or playing around in the gym. Okay?"

The kid didn't respond, just nodded. He was still upset for getting scolded.

"Larry, I need you to answer me. Yes or no. Do you understand?"

"Yes."

"Alright then." Dave stood up and snatched the bus keys off the silver file cabinet then shoved them in his pocket and walked to the door. "I'll only be a few minutes, and when I get back I want you to be ready to get on that bus, okay?"

"Okay."

"Alright, I'll see you soon. Be good. No screwing around in here."

"Alwight."

"Bye Larry."

"Bye daddy."

Chapter 8

The Magic Bus

Dave was finished. It took him an hour, but he finally did it. He'd washed out the coolers, packed up the volleyballs, and even brought the bus around to the front of the gym. Now, all he had to do was get Larry and they might just make it back out there before the last period bell rang. He hoped to God the kid was ready. He didn't have enough time to mess around with him.

He took a deep breath and wiped his forehead then pulled open the doors and stepped inside the gym. Thank God. The place was still empty, but he better hurry, because it wouldn't be for long. Any moment now, this place was gonna be crawling with those annoying basketball players hooting, hollering, and bouncing off the walls.

He turned and walked as fast as he could down the sidelines, the pain in his knee now shooting up his hip. When he got to the locker room, he stopped at the basement, then pulled open the door and descended the steps. As he got to the bottom, he began to smell the stench of crack burning in the air. It was strong—stronger than usual. It didn't smell this bad when he left, did it? Huh. Guess he was just gonna have to pull out the old air freshener. He sure as hell couldn't leave it smelling like this.

He shook his head and dug into his pocket then pulled out the key and shoved it into the lock. As he turned the knob and pushed the door open, he nearly swallowed his tongue at what he saw—Larry standing on top of the file cabinet, furiously scribbling his blue crayon all along the office walls.

"Larry! What the hell are you doing? What are you doing to my god damn walls?"

The kid stopped scribbling and turned his head slowly, drool dripping from his mouth and out onto the floor.

"Larry?"

The kid's pupils were shaped like two flying saucers and he had alien green snot slithering down from his nose. "Hi dad," he said in a robotic monotone, like that creepy girl from *The Exorcist* film. "I did the walls. Do you like it?"

Dave stood there in complete astonishment, his eyes locked on the mad swirl of blue crayon. He couldn't believe it. He couldn't believe what he was seeing. It looked like a gang of Smurfs had an orgy with the Blue's Clues television dog.

He glanced behind him to make sure there was no one in the hallway then hurried into the office and shut the door. Why? Why was this happening? Why here? Why now? But things only got worse as he hobbled into the office and moved his eyes across the top of his desk. The pipe was out and so was the lighter and little rocks of crack were scattered all across the office floor. He looked back up at Larry—the kid was grinning, like he'd just been caught with an empty box of doughnuts. "No Larry, please tell me you didn't. Please tell me you didn't do this to me."

The kid nodded and started giggling then threw his hands up over his head. "I had the medicine daddy!"

Immediately, Dave began to feel woozy as if the carpet was sliding out from underneath his feet. He looked up at the walls—they were spinning, swirls of blue crayon crashing down on top of his head. No, no, no...this wasn't happening...it couldn't be real...it was just a dream. He looked back up at Larry—the kid was still giggling, his fat belly bouncing up and down through his tie-dye shirt. "God damnit Larry! What did I tell you? That stuff wasn't for you, it was only for me!"

He dropped to the carpet like a drunken paraplegic and started crawling around, picking the rocks up off of the floor. There were six of 'em left, but they were now covered with brown carpet boogers. He had to blow them off just to get them clean. Jesus, he didn't have time for this. Any moment now that bell was gonna ring. Then it did, like an ambulance siren, splitting through the walls of his fragile head. "Shit!"

He picked up the rest of the rocks and placed them back in the medicine bottle, then gathered up his pipe and lighter and stuffed them into his jacket pocket. He grabbed his gym bag, pulled out the bottle of bourbon, twisted off the cap, and took a quick swig. "Come on Larry," he said, as he put the cap back on the bourbon then stuffed the bottle inside his bottom desk drawer. "Let's go. We gotta go. We gotta get out to that bus before those girls do." He put up his hand and did a quick breath check—not too bad, he couldn't smell a thing. He marched over to the file cabinet and grabbed Larry's forearm and, in a surge of adrenaline, yanked him off the cabinet. The kid went wild and started screaming, pounding his fists and feet into the floor. "God damnit Larry, get up. We don't have time for this. We gotta get out there. We're gonna be late." Dave leaned over and tried picking him up by the armpits, but the kid just went limp and fell back to the floor. "Please Larry, don't do this to me. Please stop crying and get your ass up." He tried grabbing the kid's hands and dragging him across the carpet but the little shit was so heavy that he could only move him an inch. "Fuck!"

He dropped the kid's hands, went around to the file cabinet, and pulled a box from the top drawer. The box was filled with an assortment of goodies—power bars, protein bars, and bright fluorescent energy drinks. He pulled out the protein bar that most resembled a Hershey's milk chocolate and dangled it in front of Larry like he was waving a dog bone. "Oh Larry, look at what I got here."

The kid stopped crying and rolled over off his stomach. He wiped his eyes and looked up at his dad.

"You want some of this?" Dave said, as he peeled open the wrapper, opened his mouth, and took a big bite.

The kid nodded and pushed himself up from the carpet then walked over to Dave and held out his hand.

"Uh-uh, not so fast," Dave said, pulling the bar away from him. "I'll give you some, but you gotta promise that you're gonna be a good boy today. That means no crying and fussing while we're on this trip. Okay?"

The kid nodded. Dave had him. Larry's mouth was already salivating just at the sight of the bar. Dave broke off a piece and gave it to him. The kid smiled and shoved the whole thing in his mouth. "Alright," Dave said, as he stuffed the rest in his pocket. "I'll give you some more when we get on the bus. Oh, and one other thing. That stuff you took—daddy's medicine—that's just between you and me. I don't want you running off and telling mom, okay?"

"Okay, daddy."

"That's a good boy." Dave patted the kid's curly red mop top then turned away and opened the door. "Come on," he said, holding his hand out to Larry. "Let's get going. We got a game to win tonight."

When they got outside, the girls were already lined up by the school bus, bouncing up and down, trying to stay warm. They were dressed head to toe in their bright green and gold Catholic High Crusaders warm-ups, knee pads around their ankles, and gym bags by their feet.

"Hurry up coach," one of 'em shouted. "We're freezing our butts off out here."

"I'm coming, I'm coming," Dave said back to them, trying as best he could not to slip on the ice. "Hold your damn horses."

When he got up to the bus, he stopped beside them then swung Larry around to the front of the line. "Alright everybody, listen up. This is my son. He's gonna be joining us on the trip up to Estes Park."

All at once the girls stopped talking. They cocked their heads and cooed and cawed: *"Aw, he's so cute."*

Sarah, the team's middle blocker, walked over and bent down in front of Larry, and, as she did, Dave got an eyeful of those perky, young titties that he was jacking off to earlier. "What's his name?" she said, smiling at Larry like a doting mother.

"It's Larry. He's gifted, so please don't get him excited."

"Larry, huh? Well, aren't you just the cutest?" She was about to pinch Larry's cheeks when the kid lurched forward and puked all over the ground.

"Oooohhh…gross!" the girls all exclaimed, herding backwards, covering their mouths, and pinching their noses.

"Aw for Christ's sake," Dave said then snagged Larry by the collar and pulled him away from the puddle of puke. "What'd you have to do that for?" The kid looked up at his dad and started crying, the tears mixing with the chocolate-colored vomit. "Well, don't cry about it. It's nothing to cry about." Dave cursed under his breath as he reached into his gym bag, looking for something he could use to wipe Larry's face. But there was nothing in there, so he untied his shoelaces, pulled off his last sock, and used it as a puke rag. The kid squirmed and squealed as Dave cleaned off the vomit. "Stop moving, Larry. You're only gonna make it worse."

"Oh my God," Sarah said, looking at them in horror. "What's wrong with him? Is he sick?"

"Yeah, he's got a touch of flu, I think."

"Oh no. Poor thing."

"Yeah, poor thing."

Dave finished wiping off all the vomit then flung the sock onto the yard. He had to clench his jaw to keep from losing it. What was this kid trying to do, get him fired?

He pulled the keys from his pocket, but lost his grip and dropped them to the ground. "God damnit." He bent over to get them, but nearly lost his footing on the icy asphalt. Luckily, he grabbed hold of the bus's side mirror and used it as leverage to regain his balance.

"Whoa careful coach," Sarah said, jumping towards him, her hands out to the side like she was gonna try and catch him.

"I got it, I got it," Dave said, holding his hand up to her. "I'm fine, I'm fine."

"You sure?"

"Yeah, I'm just a little dizzy. I think I probably have what Larry has."

"Oh no. Are you sure you're going to be okay to drive?"

"Oh yeah, no problem." Dave nodded his head reassuringly then crouched to the ground and snagged the keys. "See," he said, as he jammed the keys into the lock and swung open the doors. "It's no problem. I'm a professional."

Sarah nodded somewhat suspiciously. "Well, let me know if you need anything."

"Actually, would you mind counting the girls and making sure we're all here?"

"I already did that coach. They're all here. We're good to go."

"Well alright then, what are we waiting for? Let's get this show on the road."

Before Sarah could say anything else, Dave jumped on board, cranked on the ignition, turned up the heat, and revved up the engine. "Come on, Larry," he said, holding his hand out to him. "I want you sitting up here with daddy." The kid nodded and climbed on the school bus then took his seat just behind his dad in the front row. "Alright, let's go girls. Hustle, hustle. We got a big game to win tonight."

As the girls piled on, Dave pulled his seat forward and adjusted the mirror so he could see Larry's eyeballs. Once the last girl was on, he released the emergency brake then pulled the long, metal lever that shut the doors. "Alright," he said, as he looked into the rear of the school bus. "Is everyone on?"

"*Yes,*" the girls replied.

"Okay then. Let's blow this taco stand."

He released the clutch and slammed down the gas pedal and the bus took off roaring down the road.

It took them twenty minutes just to get through downtown Boulder—rush hour traffic was horrible this time of day—but they finally made it and were flying up the foothills highway towards thirty-six then onto Lyons.

As Dave shifted into third and checked the speedometer, he felt his phone vibrate against his leg. He pulled it out and flipped it open. Cheryl's name appeared like a death threat flashing across the display. Oh great, just as he suspected. He figured it was only a matter of time before she called. She was probably freaking out, looking for Larry, wondering why he didn't show up at her sister's house. Good. Let her worry. About time she thought of someone other than herself.

He flipped the phone closed and shoved it back in his pocket then looked at Larry sitting Indian style beside him on the floor. The kid was picking his nose and playing with the buttons on the cassette player, trying to shove in some old beat-up tape. "You better not break that thing," Dave said as he checked his mirrors and shifted into second.

"I'm not gonna break it, daddy. I'm juth twying to git to my favit thong."

"Oh yeah and what's that?"

"*Magic Bus.*"

"*Magic Bus?*"

"Yeah."

"Who sings that?"

"*Who.*"

"What?"

"*Who* things it."

"I don't know who sings it. That's why I'm asking you god damnit."

The kid wagged his head and started laughing. "No, daddy...*Who* things it."

"God damnit Larry, what the fuck is wrong with you? I just told you I don't know who sings it. I'm asking you who sings it."

"Thath what I'm trying da tell you daddy. Ith *The Who*. Thath da name othuh band. *The Who*."

"*The Who?*"

"Yeah."

"What the hell kind a name is *The Who?*"

"You know *The Who*."

"No, I don't know no damn *Who*."

"But we pwayed it afta da chuckle board."

"Aw for Christ's sake, Larry would you please stop it with the god damn chuckle board? We didn't play any fucking chuckle board."

"Yeth we did."

"No we didn't."

"Yeth we did."

"NO WE DIDN'T!" Dave slammed his hands against the steering wheel so hard that it shook the driver side doors. "God damnit Larry, just stop talking! I can't play games with you right now! You're driving me nuts!"

The kid shrugged and pushed the tape into the cassette player then hit the play button and cranked up the volume. The song began with a strange arrangement of percussions. It sounded like wooden sticks being banged against a basketball pole. Then, along came the guitar and the singer's high-pitched vocals that made Dave cringe because they were so obnoxiously nasal. To make matters worse, Larry started screeching along with the lyrics as he strummed away on his air guitar.

"You wanna turn that thing down?" Dave said, as he flipped on his high beams, peering like an owl out through the windshield.

"Come on, Daddy. Thith ith da beth part."

"It's too loud. I can't hear myself think."

Dave glanced into the rearview mirror trying to keep an eye on the back of the bus. It was a circus back there. The girls were up and dancing in the aisle, their tight green shirts rolled up and tied at the waist. Every time they lifted their arms, Dave got an eyeful of those tight, young abdominals. Their belly buttons seemed to wink at him as they arched their backs.

"Hey girls," he said, glancing behind him. "You wanna save some of that energy for the match tonight?"

The girls ignored him and continued dancing, their muscular, volleyball player legs grinding against the backs of the seats.

"God damn," Dave muttered as he turned back towards the windshield. What he'd do to those girls if they were just a little older. He'd take those legs and wrap 'em around him and bury his nose into those young, curly muffs. He got goose bumps just thinking about it. If only they weren't so fucking young.

He shook off the goose bumps then flipped on the wipers as light flakes of snow began to float against the windshield. Christ, look at this shit. What a disaster. Thought they said it wasn't supposed to snow until tomorrow. Idiots. Fucking meteorologists. They wouldn't know a snow storm if it hit 'em in the dick.

He leaned forward and strained his eyeballs, trying to figure out how far they were along. Just then, Sarah came running up behind him, her soft, sweet breath blowing against the back of his neck.

"Hey coach, can we stop for a pee break?"

"What?" Dave turned around and looked at her—her nipples were like little strawberries poking through her tight, green uniform.

"Can we stop? I have to pee."

"Already? We just got on the road."

"I know coach, but I have to go."

"Can't you hold it?"

"No, coach." She crossed her legs and began gyrating up and down in an "I gotta go pee" dance. "Please coach," she said, her voice soft and raspy, like a child prostitute trying to sell a hand job. "Pretty please, I'll do anything you say." She reached up, put her hands around Dave's shoulders, and began to dig her fingers into his neck muscles.

"What are you doing, Sarah?"

"I'm giving you a massage. Doesn't it feel good?"

Almost immediately, Dave felt a tingling sensation move from the back of his head down to his nuts. His muscles went limp, his eyes rolled backward, and his dick got hard and pressed up against his zipper. "Please stop that Sarah," he said mumbling, one eye closed, his tongue hanging out. "I can't concentrate with you doing that."

"Only if you promise to stop."

Dave looked down. His dick was enormous. It looked a zucchini was shoved down his pants. "Alright, alright," he said, trying to push the zucchini downward, "but only if you go back and sit down with the rest of the girls. I can't have you up here while I'm trying to drive."

Sarah squealed then wrapped her arms around Dave's shoulders, hugged his neck, and gave him a wet kiss on the cheek. Then, she spun around, whipping her long, blond hair outward, adjusted her bra and strutted back to her seat. As she went, Dave took a peak in the rearview mirror, watching as that tight, little ass wagged back and forth. "God damn," he muttered, trying to flatten out his penis. These fucking girls were gonna be the death of him.

He exhaled deeply and shook off the tingling then moved his eyes to the clock on the dash. Christ, it was almost five-thirty. At this rate, they'd be lucky if they made it up there before the end of the JV game. But, did it really matter? What would the referees do? Forfeit the game? Please. They'd be doing him a favor. At least then, he'd get to go home early and curl up in bed. He needed some sleep. He felt like a fucking zombie. He could barely keep his eyes open let alone coach a god damn volleyball game. Maybe he *should* stop, just for a few minutes. He could sneak a couple quick hits somewhere while the girls were off taking their pee break. Why not? What's the worst that could happen? Hell, a few hits would probably be good for him.

He eased on the brake and put on his turn signal then pulled off at the next exit on the side of the highway. There was a gas station there, an old Citgo, with a couple self-service pumps and some vending machines.

He pulled into the lot beside a semi that was packed with tree logs covered with a layer of slick snow. He lifted the emergency brake, cut the ignition, and turned his head towards the back of the bus. "Alright girls," he said, as he pulled himself upward, "we're gonna stop for just a few minutes. This is your last chance before we get up to Estes, so make it count."

The girls all got up, pulled on their jackets, and filed out of the bus and into the parking lot. Larry just sat there in his seat smirking, watching as the girls brushed by him. He had a look on his face of deep concentration as if he was counting the number of boobs he saw go by.

"Larry," Dave said, snapping his fingers. "Stop staring. And put your damn tongue back in your mouth. You're drooling all over the place."

Larry quickly put his hands up over his eyeballs, but snuck a peek through the little slit between his fingers.

Once the last girl was out, Dave zipped up his jacket then tugged on his wool beanie and pulled on his gloves. "Alright," he said, as he peered out the windshield, looking for a good place where he could sneak away and smoke. "You gotta pee, Larry?"

The kid nodded.

"Me too. Let's go."

He grabbed the kid's hand and pulled him out into the parking lot, and together they walked around the front of the bus towards the opposite side of the road. There was a little, white shack back there, what looked like an old restaurant, and lucky for him, the place was closed for the winter. It was perfect—the perfect cover, tucked underneath an umbrella of snow covered Douglas Firs. "Okay," Dave said, looking back towards the gas station, "I'd say we got about ten minutes to go pee."

"Ten?" Larry said.

"Yeah. Here." Dave guided the kid over to some bushes. "You go over there by those bushes and I'll go over here by the shack."

The kid looked back at him with a confused expression. It was obvious he didn't want to be left alone. "But daddy—"

"Don't argue with me, Larry. There's no time. Just go."

The kid scowled then slunk away behind the bushes, his pudgy ankles disappearing into about a foot of snow.

Once he was gone, Dave pulled out his pipe, lighter, and red plastic pill bottle, first checking to make sure no one was around. He did a couple quick hits then tilted his head backward, feeling as the crack surged through his blood. He did a couple more just for good measure, but came to a sudden stop when he felt his phone vibrating against his leg. "Are you fucking kidding me?" He pulled it out and flipped it open. Big fucking surprise, it was Cheryl. What was her deal? Was she stupid? Didn't she understand he didn't have time to talk?

"Christ almighty." He mashed his thumb against the power button, waited for it to turn off then shoved it in his pocket. There. Now, try and call him. See how fucking far you get with the power turned off.

He chuckled to himself and returned to his lighter, lit up again, and went for another hit. But, before he could suck in the smoke, he felt someone's presence, their feet crunching behind him in the snow. He snapped his head around. Oh Jesus, it was just Larry, the kid looking up at him with a curious grin. "God damnit, Larry, you scared the shit out of me. What are you doing sneaking up on your daddy like that?"

"I'm finished," the kid said, with proud assurance as if he'd just accomplished something really profound. "And I did it all by mythelf."

"Well, good for you."

Dave wrapped his lips around the cylinder then did another quick hit and looked back across the road. The girls were getting back from their pee break forming a line by the bus's front doors. "Alright," he said, turning to Larry. "Guess we should get back over there. You ready?"

"Yeah."

"Alright, let's do it." He took the instruments, shoved them back in his pocket then grabbed Larry's hand, and headed off across the road.

When they got back to the bus, Dave's head was swimming. In fact, he was so loaded, it felt like his feet weren't even touching the ground. He was floating—floating across the pavement, like one of those floats in the Macy's Day parade. He felt fast, loose, free, and giddy, no twisting in his stomach, no pain in his knee. He could do anything. He could be anybody. Watch out motherfuckers, 'cause he was coming, and he was about to turn this shit up a notch.

"Alright," he said, as he moonwalked across the parking lot and hopped his way up the steps of the bus. "Let's go girls. Vamonos!"

Most of the girls were still hanging out in the parking lot, twirling their hair, and playing with their cell phones.

"Come on," Dave shouted down to them, his hands cupped around his mouth. "What are you waiting for? Let's go! Chop, chop! I don't got all damn day."

The girls all just looked up at him with utter annoyance then rolled their eyes and flipped back their hair. They formed a line at the base of the steps and, one by one, climbed back on the bus. "That's it," Dave said, as they brushed by him, his eyes focused on the clefts of their butts. "One, two, four, eight...who do we appreciate?" He waited for the answer but no one said anything, so he decided to answer it himself: "Dave! Dave! Dave!

Yeah! Whoohoo!" He raised his hand up to one of the players who just glared at it with a look of disgust. "Come on Lacy," he said, acting offended. "Don't leave me hanging girlfriend."

"My name's not Lacy, coach. It's Virginia."

"Oh shit, I knew that. Well gimme some skin anyway."

Dave stretched his hand up even higher, but the girl just crinkled her nose and crossed her arms. "What's the matter with you, coach? Are you alright?"

"Yeah. I'm fine. I'm just excited. This is a big game. It's the biggest. The best. We're gonna win. We're gonna kill 'em. We're gonna squash 'em. Right? Right?" He clenched his fist and started pounding it against the steering wheel. "Come on Lacy— I mean Virginia. Shit. Sorry. Come on, don't leave me hanging."

The girl slowly uncrossed her arms and tentatively touched her hand up to Dave's palm.

"Yeah!" Dave bellowed. "That's the spirit! That's what I like to fucking see! Way to go! Alright, keep it moving…one, two, Lacy, Jenny."

He kept his hand up as the girls moved by him, getting dirty looks from most, but sympathy high fives from some. Once the last girl was on, he stood up, cupped his hands together, and shouted back to the rear of the bus: "Yo Sarah. You back there? Where you at girl?"

Sarah raised her hand and stood up slowly. "Uh…right here, coach."

"Oh, there you are. Can you do a head count for me to make sure we're not missing anybody?"

"Sure coach." Sarah stood up and started counting, mumbling to herself as she pointed her finger in the air. "…eleven, twelve, thirteen, fourteen. Fourteen coach. Looks like we're all here."

"Alright. Good, great, grand, wonderful…hold on tight 'cause here we fucking go!"

Dave spun around and jumped back behind the steering wheel, then cranked on the ignition and pulled the doors closed. "You ready?" he said, looking beside him at Larry who was sitting Indian style on the floor. The kid nodded. "Alright. Hold on. Here we go!"

Dave wrenched into first and slammed down the accelerator. The bus reared forward, fishtailing through the snow. He didn't even bother to check in his rearview mirror. Just put the pedal to the metal and merged back onto the road. The girls in the back all began to cheer and whistle as a black cloud of exhaust plumed over the gas pumps.

"Alright, we're really moving now," he shouted down to Larry who had his pinky finger jammed up his left nostril. "Hey Larry, why don't you play that song you like?"

"Weally?"

"Yeah, Come on...play it, play it, play it. I wanna hear it. It's my favorite song now. Play it, play it, play it."

"Okay."

The kid reached forward and hit the play button then jumped to his feet and strapped on his air guitar. As the high-pitched vocals came howling out of the speakers, Dave began counting off the numbers on the speedometer. "Forty-five...fifty-five...sixty-five...seventy-five." He turned around towards the back of the school bus, pumping his fist like he was at a horse race. "Seventy-five miles an hour everybody! Whoohoo!" His body seemed to shift with the turns in the highway as he slammed down the clutch and wrenched into second. He felt like Dale Earnhardt at the Daytona Five hundred going for the prestigious Harley J. Earl trophy.

"This old banana can really cook, can't it Larry?"

"Yeah."

"We're really sailing now, aren't we?"

"Yeah."

"Whoohoo!"

"Whoohoo!" Larry started pounding his fists against the back of the seat cushions, drumming along to the beat of the song. He leaned over Dave and stuck his head out the window, his butt crack hanging out the back of his jean shorts. Dave laughed maniacally as he flipped on his high beams and pushed the pedal all the way down to the floorboard. "We're gonna murder those little pukes, right?"

"Yeah!" Larry screamed out the window.

"We're gonna kill 'em, right?"

"Yeah!"

"We're gonna destroy 'em. We're gonna show those stuck up mountain brats how we grow 'em down in the 'burbs. Right Larry? Right?"

"Right dad!" Larry pulled his head back in from the window then cranked up the volume as high as it would go. Then, he started shouting along to the song's chorus, something about having a magic school bus.

"Hey," Dave said, pointing at the stereo, his eyes enlarged to the size of grapefruits. "That's what we have. We have a magic school bus."

"Yeah, we sure do, daddy."

"Yeah. Fucking magic school bus." Dave nodded along, waiting for the chorus, then he joined in with Larry singing along to the magic school bus. *Too much Magic Bus...Too much Magic Bus.*"

As Dave joined in, Larry raised his own volume, and started marching up and down the aisle like a midget Nazi. Even Sarah ran up to the front and joined in the mayhem, tugging at Dave's sleeve, egging him on. "Coach! Coach!" she said, nearly screaming, a look of exhilaration in her young, wild eyes. "Stop it! You're going to get us killed. Slow down."

"Yeah Sarah. We're really cooking now, aren't we? *Too much Magic Bus...Too much Magic Bus!*"

"Whoohoo!" Larry added, now doing his own version of the funky chicken.

Dave looked down at the speedometer—they were almost up to eighty-five. He turned back towards Sarah—the girl was having so much fun that she was actually crying. "Yeah Sarah, that's the spirit. Come on, give me a high five." He lifted his hand up to the ceiling, but Sarah was too busy wiping the tears of joy from her eyes. "Come on Sarah," he said. "Don't leave me hanging. Slap me some skin. Give me five."

Sarah just looked at him as if he was crazy. "Please coach, slow down. You're going to get us all killed."

"What?"

"I said, slow down. You're going to get us all killed."

Before Dave had a chance to process what she was saying, a swirl of red and blue lights caught his attention. What the fuck? He sat up and looked in the rearview mirror. Oh shit. There was a patrol car behind him blaring its siren. Was it for them? Were they trying to pull him over? Or were they just trying to get around?

He instinctively removed his foot from the accelerator and brought the bus down to fifty-five. "Come on, go around," he mumbled, looking up in the rearview mirror, his heart thumping from the sheer adrenaline. "Don't pull us over. Please God, I won't ask for anything else, just go around." But they didn't go around—they stayed close behind him, the red and blue swirl reflecting in his mirror. "Fuck! Fuck! Fuck!" He started punching his fist against the steering wheel, his knuckles driving against the vinyl.

"What's wrong daddy?"

"We're being pulled over, Larry."

"Weally? Where?" The kid spun around and glanced behind him then started to cheer when he heard the siren. "Oh wow! Look daddy, a cop car. Awesome daddy awesome."

"No Larry, it is not awesome. It is definitely not awesome."

Dave eased on the brake, put on his blinker, and slowly veered the bus off onto the shoulder.

"Do they have guns? Daddy, do you think they have guns?"

"God damnit Larry, just shut up and don't say anything. If we're lucky, they'll probably just give us a warning."

"I doubt it," Sarah said, looking behind them, at the flash of blue and red shining through the back window.

"You can go back to your seat and sit your little ass down."

"But coach, I'm—"

"Don't argue with me, Sarah. Just do it. I'll handle this."

Sarah snarled and flipped her hair outward then strutted back to her seat and sat down.

Dave took a deep breath and waited for everyone to settle then cut the engine and peered out the back window. The lights were still going, but nothing was happening. No one was getting out. The cop was just sitting there. What the hell? What was he doing? Why wasn't he getting out of the fucking car? No, no, wait a minute...he had to calm down...he had to get a hold of himself...everything was fine...nothing was wrong. He'd just explain to him that he was sorry he was speeding, but he was in a hurry because they had a big match tonight up in Estes Park...and they were already late by about thirty minutes and if they didn't get there in time then they'd have to forfeit...and the girls worked too hard to just have to forfeit—hell, if they lost tonight, they'd lose their chance at a state playoff. He could appreciate that, couldn't he? How sometimes you had to make sacrifices for the good of the children? Yeah, of course he could. Hell, the guy was probably a dad. He probably had a couple rug rats of his own. He knew how demanding they could be sometimes, but that's why you did it, you did it for them. You sacrificed yourself for the good of your kids. You broke the law so that they could get what they want. Yeah. See? There was no need to worry. Everything was gonna be fine. Everything was gonna work out. He'd just write him a ticket, give him a stern warning, and send them off on their merry, little way.

"Alright." Dave took a deep breath and pulled himself together then turned his attention to the rear of the bus. "Alright, everybody listen up."

But, the girls didn't look up. They weren't paying any attention. They were too busy ogling the two officers now getting out of the patrol car. "Hey!" Dave shouted, clapping his hands together. "God damnit, listen up." But, the girls still weren't paying attention, so he put two fingers in his mouth and blew as hard as he could. The whistle was so deafening it caused the bus to immediately go still. "Alright you little brats, I want all of you to shut the fuck up and don't say another fucking word. I'm going to take care of this."

"Oooohhhh," the girls all said in unison, as if that was the first time they'd ever heard him swear.

Dave straightened his collar and turned towards Larry. It looked like the kid was doing an impression of a pile of dirty clothes. He was all curled up, his knees pulled up against his chest, his head buried beneath the collar of his t-shirt.

"Larry," Dave said, snapping his fingers. "Larry, Larry!"

The kid slowly popped his head from the t-shirt, like a gopher poking out of its tunnel.

"Larry, listen to me. I need you to sit here and don't say anything. Daddy's gonna go outside and straighten this whole thing out. Okay?"

The kid nodded his understanding then tucked his head back into his shirt.

"Alright, okay." Dave spit on his hands and exhaled deeply then patted down his hair and wrenched open the doors. "Please God," he mumbled, as he stepped out onto the shoulder, "just let me get through this. I promise, I'll never ask for anything ever again."

There were two of 'em. They looked like assholes, their shiny badges glistening in the taillights of the bus. They had on blue starch-stiff shirts buttoned all the way up to their collars with those ridiculous floppy hats and black leather boots. One of 'em pointed his finger in Dave's direction, beckoning him to the rear of the bus.

"Me?" Dave mumbled, looking behind him as if he was pointing at someone else. "You want me?"

The officer smiled and nodded, his hat like a decoy hunting duck bobbing up and down in a lake.

Dave took another deep breath and began to walk towards him, trying as best he could to walk in a straight line. When he got to the rear of the bus, the cop was just staring at him, his arms folded across his chest, his feet wide apart. "You some kind of sports team?" the officer said, flatly, glaring at the whistle dangling around Dave's neck.

"Uh, yes sir. Girl's volleyball."

"Uh huh. And where ya'll coming from?"

"Uh…Boulder."

"Boulder?"

"Yes sir."

The officer moved his eyes to the bus's back window—the girls were all crowded around it, their breath fogging up the glass. "And where ya'll headed?"

"Estes Park."

"You the one in charge?"

"Yes sir, I'm the head coach…Coach Bell." Dave extended his hand for the cop to shake it, but the cop just looked at it, snorted, then spit on the ground.

"Coach Bell, huh?"

"Yes sir."

"Your name wouldn't happen to be Dave, would it?"

"Uh…yes…yes it is. How'd you know that?"

The cop just smiled and let go another loogie. "You know what the speed limit is on this highway, Dave?"

"No sir. Eighty-five, is it?"

"Nope. More like fifty-five."

"Oh."

"Yeah. Oh." The cop cocked his head and took a step forward, squinting at Dave like he was trying to catch the whites of his eyes. "You wanna do me a favor?" he said, as he lifted his middle finger and touched it to the center rim of his big, floppy hat. "You wanna look right here for me?"

Dave lifted his chin and turned his eyes upward trying to focus on that ridiculous hat. He was shaking so bad that he could barely control his muscles and he started to sweat like some kind of farm animal. His hands shook, his legs quivered, and it felt like the gorilla fingers were back slowly closing around his neck. But, he had to stay calm…he had to focus…he had to keep his eyes on that god damn hat.

"You know what you look like to me, Dave?" the cop said, inching closer, the smell of dip and coffee thick on his breath.

"No sir."

"You look to me like one of those Colfax crack roaches. Is that you, Dave? Huh? Are you a Colfax crack roach?"

Dave clenched his jaw and shook his head nervously, casting his eyes down towards the pavement. "No sir."

Just then, the other officer appeared behind them, holding what looked like a long, black billy club. "What's up Donny?" he said, as he walked towards them, his black boots crunching on the shoulder's dirt infused snow.

"Looks like we got ourselves a DUI, Jimmy."

"Really? With all these kids on board?"

"Yep. Looks that way."

"Wow. That's not good."

"Nope."

All of a sudden, the one called Donny grabbed Dave's collar and, in one quick thrust, slammed him face first against the hood of the patrol car. "Spread your legs dickwad!" he screamed as he kicked Dave's legs out from under him and mashed his cheek against the hot metal of the hood.

"Hey, what are you doing?" Dave shouted, squirming, the heat from the engine searing his cheek.

"Stop that whining or I'll give you something to cry about asshole."

Dave tried to move, but he was paralyzed—the cop had him laid out like a fly on a wall. He was able to turn his head just enough to see the one called Jimmy, strapping on a pair of black leather gloves. "You got anything on you we should know about?" Jimmy said as he began running the gloves down Dave's torso, across his hips, and back up his arms. "Weapons, drugs, needles, anything like that?"

"No," Dave whimpered, his voice cracking like a fourteen-year-old boy.

"You sure? I'm gonna be real upset if something sticks me. You sure you don't got nothing down there you wanna tell me about?"

"No, I don't have anything. I swear."

"Alright, you better not be lying to me." He shoved his hands inside Dave's jacket pockets and turned them inside out then moved onto his jeans. He hesitated for a moment when he grabbed hold of something bulky then leaned forward so that his lips were just above Dave's ear. "Well, what do we have here?" he said, as he pulled it out slowly then tossed it on the hood beside Dave's head. "What's this coach? Hmm?"

Dave grunted and turned his head slowly. Aw shit. He forgot to take out the pill bottle and pipe.

"That looks like a crack pipe to me, coach. What about you, Donny? Is that what it looks like to you?"

"Yep. That's exactly what it looks like."

"Better call it in, huh?"

"Yep."

The one called Jimmy went around to the driver side window, leaned inside, and picked up the radio. "Yeah we're going to need some back up out here. We got a 23152. Girls' volleyball team on their way to Estes Park. Bus full of kids. Coach is all strung out. Better bring the paddy wagon."

Donny bent down and got within an inch from Dave's ear: "You hear that Dave? Backup's coming. You're fucked. Hope you like prison shit head, because that's where you're headed."

Jimmy leaned in the window and hung up the radio then marched back around the car and bent down by Dave's face. "You think it's fun driving around all fucked up with a bunch of high school girls? You realize what could've happened if you lost control of that bus? Do you?"

The one called Donny grabbed Dave by the back of his collar then jerked him up away from the patrol car. Then, he reached into his holster, produced a set of handcuffs, and tightly secured them around Dave's wrists. As he read Dave his rights, he grabbed him by the bicep and marched him around towards

the back of the car. Just as he opened the door, something
caught Dave's attention, something large and blurry, charging
from the front of the bus. Dave turned his head. Holy shit. It
was Larry, charging through the snow like some kind of crazed
rhino, screaming, "Daddy!" at the top of his lungs.

The cop released Dave and went for his holster and whirled
around with his hand on the gun. But, Larry was too quick for
him and plowed right into his stomach, sending the cop
backward and hydroplaning through the snow. But, Larry didn't
stop there. He ran up to the cop and jumped on top of him and
started flailing his fists against his nose. Dave was frozen with
shock. He couldn't believe what he was seeing. He'd never seen
Larry this violent before. "Larry!" he screamed. "What are you
doing? Stop it. Get off of him."

But, before Dave could even blink, the altercation was over,
as the other officer came out from behind the patrol car and
shot Larry with a set of cylindrical probes. Larry immediately
stopped moving—his body went rigid then he rolled off the cop
and went into convulsions.

"No!" Dave screamed, watching in horror as Larry thrashed
around like a shark on the deck of a boat. "Stop it. You're killing
him."

The cop smiled as he squeezed the trigger, sending a current
of electricity through Larry's skull.

"Stop it. It's not his fault. He doesn't know any better."

The one named Donny stood up and brushed the snow off
of him then wiped the blood trickling down his face. He picked
up his baton and walked over to the patrol car, grabbed Dave by
the arms and yanked him to his feet. "Who the fuck is that? Huh
Dave? Why didn't you tell me you had a god damn psychopath
in there?"

"He's not a psychopath. He's my son. He doesn't know any
better."

"Your son? You expect me to believe that?" Donny pulled
his pistol from his holster then lodged it into the small of Dave's
back. "March dickwad."

"You god damn bastards, stop it. You're killing him."

"I said march asshole!"

As the cop opened the door, Dave looked back at Larry, at his son's now motionless body, face down in the ground. He tried calling to him, but Larry didn't answer. He was a lifeless lump of flesh steaming in the snow.

Chapter 9

The Apartment

Monty awoke in the early morning twilight, slimy leeches of sweat slithering down from his head. His teeth chattered, his entire body trembled, and every bone in his body ached with a sharp, cold, pulsating pain. As he rolled himself over, he pressed his nose into the mattress. The stench of sweat and stale urine emanated into the damp, alcohol-saturated air. His mouth was dry, his lips were blistered, and chunks of vomit burned like acid on the top of his tongue.

He flipped over onto his back and kicked off the blankets then opened his mouth and tried gasping for breath. But his throat was restricted and he couldn't get enough oxygen. He felt like a fish slowly drowning in air. Instinctively, he lifted his hand and reached for the bottle on the nightstand, but the bottle was empty, not a single drop left. Shit. He was going to have to get up. He was going to have to make it into the kitchen. A couple more swigs and he could go right back to bed.

Clenching his teeth, he forced his eyelids open then pulled himself up against the headboard of the bed. The room was dark, the walls washed with blackness, no trace of light except for the blinking, blue glow coming from the power button on his computer screen. He twisted to his side and leaned over the edge of the mattress, straining for the digital alarm clock on the floor beside the bed. He grabbed it by the power cord, yanked it upward, and read the numbers from the green digital display. It said 3:05, but was it day or night?

He dropped the clock and looked towards the windows, but the glass was shrouded with clippings of newspaper secured with duct tape and spray painted black. What the hell? When did that happen? It must've been recently, because he could still smell the spray paint's strong, chemical stench.

He shook his head and scooted to the edge of the mattress then dangled his legs out over the bed. After a few deep breaths, he shut his eyes and rolled his shoulders then tilted his head back and popped his neck. It made a sound like someone stepping on bubble wrap as the bones in his back crunched against the muscles in his neck.

He let out a groan and planted his feet into the carpet then pushed himself up from the bed. But he got up way too fast and his vision became tunneled, his legs turned to liquid, and his head became a balloon. He swatted the air for something to grab onto, like a conductor directing a symphony in the dark. But his fingers found nothing and his knees buckled and he smacked his chin on the nightstand on his way to the floor. The pain was like lightning rippling from his cheekbone, splitting down his jaw line, and exploding in his head. He opened his mouth and let out a soft whimper as he flexed his jaw and cradled it with his right hand. Something warm and wet began to ooze through his fingers, across his palm, and down his wrist. He laid there for a while, breathing in the fibers of the carpet, as the blood dribbled out from the cut in his chin. Then everything went dark and silence consumed him and his eyes slowly rolled into the back of his head.

After about an hour of lying in the darkness, Monty awoke to the sound of voices penetrating the apartment walls. He opened his eyes and pulled himself up against the bedpost then looked towards the sliver of light between the door and the floor. The voices seemed to be coming from the living room and it looked like there were feet moving on the other side of the door. He rolled over, pressed his hands into the carpet, and slowly began to crawl towards the bedroom door. As he approached the light, the voices grew louder, like fluttering moths trapped inside a porch lamp. What were they? Who were they? Were they real? Or were they just a hallucination?

He reached up and turned the doorknob then nudged the door open with the top of his head. As he crawled through the doorway, he glanced towards the living room and noticed a strange light splashing colors against the wall. He strained his eyes and crawled a little farther, and noticed that the television was off its stand and sitting sideways on the living room floor. Jesus—what the hell happened? Did he do that? He must have.

He stooped to the floor and cocked his head sideways and stared at the infomercial that was flashing across the screen. There was a short, spiky-haired guy holding a mop handle over what looked like a puddle of dark brown shit. He said that the mop head was equipped with new, exciting space age fibers that NASA had developed when designing their rockets.

He redirected his eyes across the dining room and crawled towards the bathroom at the end of the hall. Once he got inside, he flipped on the light switch. The bathroom fan kicked on, revving up to a soothing hum. He leaned forward, his head hovering above the porcelain, both palms resting flat on the bathroom floor. He relaxed his jaw, shut his eyelids, and waited for the acidic fury to come. The first heave was dry. It felt like sandpaper ripping away the soft tissue lining the larynx wall. Then his eyes bugged out and his entire body tightened as snot bubbles the size of grapes respired from his nose. But nothing came out—it was all just saliva, pouring from his cheeks, dripping from his tongue. What he was really after was that hot, potent poison, bubbling in his liver, diffusing into his blood. If he could just get at that then everything would be better—his body would relax and his head would calm. He waited a few seconds, breathing steadily, letting the oxygen fill up his lungs. Then he clutched the rug and curled his toes inward, relaxed his esophagus and reached deep into his gut. The poison began to rise within his belly, crawling up his ribs and into his throat. It reached his mouth and slithered from his esophagus like some kind of putrid, alien bug. As it splashed into the water, it disseminated slowly like long, yellow tentacles descending towards the bottom of the bowl.

He laid his head down, curling next to the toilet, pressing his cheek firmly into the linoleum floor. His muscles relaxed and his body stopped shaking, and, all at once, a wave of calm seemed to swallow him whole. He stayed there for a while, breathing in and out deeply, listening to the fan whisper its long, droning hum.

Then there was that sound again, the sound of cracking, like teeth getting crunched between a pair of pliers. He opened his eyes and looked all around him. The floor was giving way like ice cracking beneath his legs. He shut his eyes and tried to block out the images, but the harder he tried, the clearer they became— shards of glass raining down from the ceiling, buckets of blood-tinged water pouring in through the dash. Vicky just sitting there as lifeless as a puppet, her eyes unblinking, her hands limp in her lap. No, he couldn't do this. He couldn't just lay here. He had to do something. He had to get up. A couple drinks, that's all he needed, a couple more drinks and he could crawl back into bed. He didn't want to think, he didn't want to dream, he just wanted to be sedated, no memories, no thoughts, nothing in his head.

He reached up and grabbed the towel rack, and using it for balance, he straightened his legs. He opened the door and spilled out into the hallway, staggering through the dining room across the carpeted floor. When he got to the kitchen, he stopped at the threshold, his body frozen by what he saw. The place was a disaster, a spectacle of ruin, like something out of a Hitchcockian film. There were shards of glass strewn across the counters and blots of dried blood spattered along the walls. The faucet was still running and the freezer door was wide open, a gash in the plaster from where the handle must've smashed into the wall. He sighed and looked down at his knuckles, noticing that the flesh was torn to the bone. Jesus—what the hell happened? Did he do all this? Was that his blood?

He cursed to himself and stepped into the kitchen then carefully tiptoed his way through the maze of glass shards. When he got to the sink, he shut off the faucet and crouched down until his knees were touching the floor. He opened the cabinets and peered into the darkness, searching for that one thing that would make him whole. But there was nothing there except for a bottle of blue dish detergent and a couple of ratty, mildew-ridden dish cloths. Where was it? Where did he put it? He hoped to God it wasn't already gone.

He jerked his body back, scooted across the linoleum, and started opening and closing every single cabinet door. But still, he found nothing—nothing but a couple of red Dixie cups and some empty pickle jars. Christ. Where the fuck was it? Where in God's name did he put that thing?

He pulled himself up then reeled towards the refrigerator, grabbed hold of the handle and wrenched open the door. There was nothing inside but some bottles of Gatorade, a carton of milk, and half-eaten wrappers of American cheese. He slammed it closed and looked up into the freezer, but there was nothing in there either, except an empty ice tray and a bag of frozen peas. "Fuck!"

He slammed the freezer shut then stumbled into the living room, empty bottles of liquor ricocheting off his toes. He knelt to the floor and picked up every single bottle, turning them over one by one. Fifths of scotch, pints of whiskey, quarts of vodka, handles of gin—every single one was completely empty, not even one measly drop left on the rim. No, no, no, this couldn't be happening, not now, not again.

He stood up and put his hands to his forehead, grabbed his hair and pulled it out from his skull. He felt like screaming, he felt like crying, he felt like punching a hole in the fucking wall. Just one drink…that was all he needed…just one fucking drink to make him feel calm. He grabbed the couch and flipped it over then tore away the cushions and flung them against the wall. But there was nothing underneath them either, except a box of pizza and roaches the size of pigeons crawling around on the cardboard. "God damnit! Please don't do this to me! Please God, don't fucking do this to me!"

He staggered back into the kitchen and stopped at the oven and read the numbers off the green digital clock: 5:05. But was it day or night? He still had no fucking clue. He spun around and stormed back through the living room, nearly tripping over the television's power cord. When he got to the front door, he flung it open, the doorknob smashing into the wall. The sun was coming up and some birds were chirping, the click-clack of sprinklers reverberating through the morning fog. Fuck. Just what he was afraid of—it was still morning, which meant the liquor store wouldn't be open until nine.

He slammed the door shut and staggered back into the living room, collapsed on the sofa, and dropped his head into his hands. He could feel the sickness slithering around inside him, clawing at his stomach, bubbling inside his veins. His legs were shaking, his hands were trembling, and it felt like his skin was engulfed in flames. He threw his head back and looked up at the ceiling, as cold beads of sweat poured down his face. How could he do this? How could he be so stupid? How could he forget to fucking stock up?

Suddenly, he had a moment of clarity—everything became so perfectly clear. His head stopped pounding, his legs stopped twitching, and it was as if God himself had reached out from heaven and kissed his forehead. Of course, he thought, as he turned his eyes towards the bathroom. How could he be so stupid? How could he forget he had that shit?

He shot up from the sofa and marched towards the bathroom, flipped on the light and knelt to the floor. He took a moment to regain his composure, said a quick prayer then opened the cabinet doors. And there it was, sitting straight up like a big, beautiful angel, wedged between the drain pipe and the cabinet's side wall—a brand new, unopened bottle of that minty fresh wintergreen Listerine.

He didn't waste any time and snatched up the mouthwash, bit into the wrapping, and ripped it away with his two front teeth. He unscrewed the cap, lifted the bottle, and pressed the plastic mouthpiece against his lips. The mouthwash was warm, but sweet and syrupy, like getting kissed on the mouth by a chemically infused peppermint. He lowered the bottle and let the first sip settle, smooth and warm as it fanned out through his chest. Then he went again and lifted the bottle, and again and again, in between short breaths. When he was finished, he set down the bottle, then shut his eyes and leaned back his head.

Just a few more weeks, he thought, and he'd finally be finished. He'd finally accomplish the impossible task—a mission so pure, so beautiful, so simple that no one would ever be able to comprehend it but him. He'd drink himself to death alone in this apartment, until his organs were bloody, until he breathed his last breath. He just hoped to God he had enough courage to go through with it. He hoped to God he didn't end up in some hospital bed. If worse came to worst, he always had his sleeping pills that he'd been hoarding away for the last couple months. Ninety pills of Trazodone…that ought to do it…that should be more than enough to shut down his brain. He smiled to himself as he glanced up at the medicine cabinet, at the red bottles of pills he knew were behind the glass. Good thing he never terminated the prescription. Deep down, he always knew that this day might come. There was always a chance that he might have to start drinking again. He just never thought it would happen so soon.

He closed his eyes and curled up against the toilet, letting his head sink against the bathroom rug. As his breathing slowed, his heart rate became steady, and Vicky's screams from that night became a distant blur, and all he could hear was the sound of his own breathing whispering softly with the humming of the overhead fan.

Chapter 10

The Store

Argonaut Wine & Liquor. It was two stories high with a dull, red brick exterior and immense plate glass windows that gave it the look of an international bank. It was on the corner of Colfax and Washington, a few blocks from Monty's apartment, across the street from the Fillmore Auditorium. It had been Monty's stomping ground for the past two weeks since the accident. In fact, he'd been there so many times, he now knew the store's layout by heart. He knew that the gin was in the back by the vodka—Seagram's, specifically, about a quarter of the way down the aisle. Then, there was the scotch on the opposite side of the store by the whiskey, his preferred blend, Cutty Sark, sitting on the middle shelf, about half the way down. Ah Cutty. He could almost feel it metabolizing inside his stomach, the calm, warming sensation pumping through his blood.

He took a deep breath and rubbed his forehead then glanced at the clock mounted on the dash. It was nine o'clock, but the *Sorry…We're Closed* sign hanging in the store's window had not yet been turned over, and all the lights were out except for a faint flicker from the office in the back.

"Come on," he muttered, peering through the windshield, chomping on his thumbnail with his two front teeth. "Hurry the fuck up people."

He peered down at his hands. Jesus, they wouldn't stop shaking. They looked like catfish flopping around on the sand. The alcohol from the mouthwash was losing its effectiveness. A couple more sips and he'd be ready to go.

He reached into the passenger seat and grabbed hold of the Listerine bottle then lifted it to his lips and took a long, deliberate sip. As he swallowed it down, he began to gag involuntarily as goose bumps the size of beetles crawled up and down his arms. Damn, he was freezing. His hair was still damp from this morning's shower and his skin was cold and clammy against his long sleeve shirt.

After he cranked up the thermostat, he pulled down the sun visor so he could get a better look at himself in the vanity mirror. He looked awful. His eyes were all bloodshot, his lips a shade of purple, and he had dribbles of snot crystallized just beneath his nose. His once sun-bleached, blond hair was now a disheveled mess of urine-encrusted yellow that looked like a mop head that had been left out in the summer sun. And the splotchy patches of growth on his neck and cheeks looked more like furry, brown lesions than a healthy, trim, beard. And what the hell was that? He tilted his head as far as he could backward to get a better look at the serration underneath his chin. Jesus—was that from this morning? It must've been from when he fell and hit it on the nightstand. It was pretty bad—black and blue around the outer edges and bright pink in the middle from where it was still bleeding. One look at this and the clerk inside was likely to call an ambulance, or at least turn him away for looking like a bum. He couldn't risk that. He needed his liquor. He was likely to have a seizure if he didn't get it soon. Maybe he could get something to cover it up with. But what? What could he use?

He looked around the rental car for something adhesive, anything that could potentially stick to his chin. He looked towards the floorboards, then in between the seat cushions, into the glove box, and back behind the seats. But there was nothing—the car was spotless, nothing but some loose change and a crumpled up car rental receipt. "Shit."

He twisted in his seat and peered out the back window. There was a gas station next door—but what good would that do? Even if they did have Band-Aids he'd still have to deal with the clerk at the counter. Fuck it. He'd better just stick to the plan, grab what he needed, and get out of there as quickly as he could. If anyone asked, he could just tell them he did it shaving or ran into a tree branch while out on a jog. They'd believe him, right? Why wouldn't they? What fucking business was it of theirs anyhow?

He took a deep breath and turned his attention back towards the liquor store, but it still didn't look like there was any movement inside. God damnit—what the hell were they doing? Why weren't they open? It was almost five after nine.

He bent his head forward and started rubbing his eyelids, digging away the mucus that was crusted in the corners of his eyes. As he brought his hands down, he caught a whiff of something strong and chemical, fanning from his fingertips and out beneath his nose. He knew what it was. It was the acetaldehyde, a byproduct of the dehydrogenation of alcohol in the blood. For a normal drinker, it hung out for only a matter of minutes before being broken down by a substance in the liver called glutathione. But for alcoholics, the chemical hung around almost indefinitely, because there wasn't enough glutathione to combat the massive amounts of alcohol entering the blood. The result was a stench not unlike that of vinegar or nail polish remover, emanating from the sweat pores like a bad case of B.O. It was so strong that people would often comment on it, but Monty usually just told them that he was trying out a new cologne. Funny. It had been such a long time since he'd smelled it that only now did he realize how much he missed it. Now, that it was back, it was almost reassuring, like the sweet, apple scent of his childhood home. He laid his right hand out flat in front of him then took a deep breath in, his knuckle pressed against his nose. Ahh. It was sharp, strong, pungent, and bitter...the smell of death like a spirit unfurling from his skin. He smiled as he sank back against the headrest, his eyes focused on the front entrance of the liquor store. Just then, he saw a hand move through the front store window and flip the *Sorry, We're Closed* sign to *Yes, We're Open*. Thank God. It was about fucking time.

He opened the door and cut the ignition then stepped out into the cold, merciless Colorado wind. The sun was out, but the air was blistering...so cold, in fact, that it felt like razors were cutting into his dry, alcohol-softened skin. He pulled up his hood, zipped up his jacket, and narrowed his eyes towards front of the store. He moved forward slowly, one foot after the other, his knees quivering with each unbearable step. It felt like he was moving in slow motion, as if he was wading out into the unforgiving sea.

When he reached the front entrance, he pushed the door inward. A set of bells tied to the handle clanged sharply against the glass. He looked around. The place was deserted. Soft murmurs of what sounded like Spanish radio oozed out over a set of speakers that hung somewhere towards the back. The music immediately reminded him of Victoria. She used to love singing along to songs Monty could never begin to understand. He could see her there, dancing in the gazebo, as little glimmers of light reflected off the pool. Her eyes were closed, her body swaying, her dark, curly hair floating in the gentle breeze. No, no, wait, he couldn't think about her. He had to stay focused. He had to do what he came here to do.

He shook off the images and stepped in a little farther when his eyes spotted a rogue shopping cart parked at an angle near the wall of red table wine. He moved towards it quickly, but carefully, making sure to plant each trembling foot firmly into the floor. When he got to the cart, he put all his weight against the handle, and used it as a kind of crutch to move across the glossy tile. The wheels squeaked, the metal basket rattled, as the sounds of a Mexican mariachi band echoed throughout the store. When he got to the end of the aisle, he swung a hard right at the Tequila then went a few more rows down toward the four-level-tiered shelf of gin. There they were, sitting on the top level; crystal clear bottles of Seagram's Extra Dry Gin. Its sweet, botanical taste always reminded him of April—the buzzing of bees, the sprouting of flowers, the mad frenzy of life coming anew. He reached up and grabbed two handles then pulled them down gently into the cart. Wait—was that enough? No, he needed reinforcements. He grabbed two more for good measure then pushed onward down the aisle.

Okay…next up was the Vodka. It wasn't his favorite, but he liked the smooth, easy taste. It was perfect for those shaky, dry-mouthed mornings, and mixed well with orange juice or lemon-lime Gatorade. He squatted down, scanned through the labels, and spotted something called Popov in clear, one and a half liter, plastic bottles. He picked one up and read off the price tag. It was his lucky day. They were on sale…two for twenty dollars. He grabbed four and stacked them neatly into the shopping cart then hung a left at the whiskey and went right for the Cutty. He didn't waste any time looking at the price tags—there was really only one brand of scotch that could satisfy his appetite—good ole Cutty Sark. His dad used to drink it when he was in the Navy and introduced it to Monty when he became a teenager. It was so rich and smooth it could be taken without club soda. Cracked ice and a little water—that was really all he needed.

He reached up and grabbed two handles then sat them in the cart next to the Vodka. Looking down into the cart, he took stock of his selection. Okay, let's see, was there anything else he needed? No, this was probably good enough. Anymore and he might look suspicious. Of course, he'd hate to leave here without getting everything. He didn't want to have to go through another ordeal like he had this morning. But what should he get? Bourbon? Whiskey? Nah, that stuff was too sweet. Then what?

He looked around the store, straining his eyeballs. God damnit—why couldn't he see? Didn't he have his contacts in? He wiped his eyes on his shirt and pushed the cart down a little farther, then saw what he was looking for, sitting right there next to the whiskey. He picked up a bottle and read off the label...ah yes...Seagram's Seven...the perfect drink for a bright, shiny Colorado morning. He picked up four and tossed them into the shopping cart. Alright, now all he needed was some Seven-Up, and if he remembered right, they were in the front by the cash registers. He walked towards them, picked up two twelve packs of diet seven-up, and stacked them side by side in the wire holder on the bottom of the cart. As he stood back up, he heard someone sneeze directly in front of him. It was the cashier—a Hispanic guy, short and chubby, with a set of light brown eyes and a couple thin strands of hair.

Monty gripped the handle and pushed slowly towards him, trying not to look directly in his eyes. His heart was pounding, his hands were shaking, and his feet felt like rubber melting to the tile. When he got to the register, he moved around to the front of the shopping cart then reached inside and began stacking the bottles on the rubber conveyor.

"All set?" the clerk said.

Monty didn't say anything and just nodded, trying as best he could to not drop any of the bottles. His muscles were so weak that he could barely grip the handles and he was disoriented that one abrupt move and he felt like he might fall over.

The cashier flipped a switch on the side of the counter and the bottles began to move forward, the glass clinking together.

Monty grabbed the last bottle and placed it on the rubber then took a step back and wiped the sweat from his forehead. He crouched to the floor and grabbed the two boxes of diet soda, lifted them up and placed them on the conveyor. As he straightened his back, he went for his wallet, but his hands were shaking so much that he could barely pull it from his back pocket.

"You need a box?" the cashier said, looking at him blankly, his eyelids blinking like flashing stoplights.

"Uh, what?"

"A box?" The cashier lifted up a cardboard box. "Do you need a box?"

"Oh, yeah, yeah, sure, thanks."

The cashier nodded and began grabbing the bottles and loading them into the little cardboard dividers.

Monty waited, his hands shaking, his mouth twitching, tiny beads of sweat dripping from his nose and splashing onto the counter. Jesus Christ, he had to stop shaking. It wasn't just his hands anymore, his entire body was trembling—his legs, his arms, his head, his eyelids, even his god damn cheeks were beginning to spasm.

He folded his arms tightly around him and squeezed as if he was giving himself an imaginary hug.

"You okay?" the cashier said, looking at him quizzically.

"Huh?" Monty relaxed and stopped squeezing then looked up at the cashier, who was pointing to the wound on his chin.

"Your face...it's bleeding."

"Oh yeah." Monty touched his finger to the laceration. "I had an accident. Sliced it while I was jogging."

"Jogging? How the hell you do that jogging?"

What was this, an interrogation? Who did he think he was, the CIA?

"I uh...I ran into a tree branch."

"A tree branch?"

"Yep."

The cashier shook his head and made a sound like he was sniffing, then picked up the last bottle of Cutty and stuffed it into the final divider. "You should get that checked out. It looks pretty bad."

What was he, a doctor now?

"Yeah, thanks. I've been meaning to go to the hospital."

The cashier nodded then turned towards the register, pushed a button on the keyboard and squinted at the computer screen. "Okay, it looks like it's gonna be two forty-one sixty-seven."

Monty nodded and pulled out his credit card, swiped it through the machine and took a step back.

The cashier looked at the computer screen, then back at Monty, then back at the computer screen and shook his head. "Nope, sorry. Didn't go through."

"What?"

"It didn't go through. You got another?"

Shit, the bastards must've frozen his credit. Wait—what about his health savings card? Would that work?

"Yeah, hold on, let me look."

He dug through his wallet and pulled out all his credit cards and laid them out on the counter like he was playing a game of poker. His health savings debit card was at the very bottom, underneath his license and his old student ID. He held it up and looked at the numbers. This ought to work, right? Yeah, there should be at least a couple thousand left on it. "Here," he said as he handed it over. "Try this one."

The cashier took it and slid it through the reader.

Please work, please work.

The screen flashed and a receipt started to print from the computer.

"Did it go through?"

"Yep."

Thank God.

The cashier handed the card back to Monty, tore off the receipt and set it flat on the counter. "Sign please."

Monty grabbed a pen from the paper cup on the counter. He didn't even bother trying to sign his name. His hands were shaking so much all he could muster was a small, crooked squiggly. "Thanks," he said, as he stuffed the receipt into his pocket then pushed the empty cart to the end of the counter. "You mind if I borrow this cart real quick?"

"Nah, just bring it back when you're through."

"Okay."

But before Monty could pick up the boxes, the cashier put his hand on Monty's shoulder. "Seriously man," he said. "You should really go to the hospital. You don't look good at all."

"Yeah, I'll do that. Thanks again." Monty pulled away from him and lifted the boxes and set them in the cart, one on top of the other. He grabbed the handle and pushed away from the register, the glass bottles clinking together like wind chimes in the summer.

When he got outside, he went straight for the rental car, unlocked the back door and unloaded the boxes onto the back seat cushions. Once he was finished, he wheeled the cart back towards the entrance, but when he got inside, he noticed that the cashier was missing. Oh no. Where did he go? What happened to him? What if he was calling the cops? What if he was going to have him arrested? "Shit." Monty's skin turned cold and his heart began pounding. He had to get out of here and get back to his apartment.

In a surge of adrenaline, he propelled the cart forward, which sailed across the store and slammed right into the register. "Double-shit."

He turned away and walked swiftly through the exit then unlocked the driver side door and jumped behind the steering wheel. He reached into his pocket and dug out his keychain, but he lost his grip and the keys dropped between his knees. "Fuck! Fuck! Fuck!" He reached between his legs and snatched them off the floor mat then jammed them into the ignition and cranked on the engine. His mouth was twitching, his teeth were chattering, and his hands were shaking so much that he could barely grip the steering wheel. But he managed to calm down just enough to get out of the parking lot and down the narrow driveway and back out onto Colfax.

As he made his way down the busy four-lane stretch of highway, his eyes bounced back and forth between the speedometer and the rearview mirror. Any moment, he expected a dozen police cars to come flying up beside him, flashing their lights and screaming their sirens. But they never came and Monty made it safe and sound back to his apartment.

Chapter 11

The Call

Monty was armed. He was ready. He had his liquor. Now, all he had to do was finish what he started. He drew all the shades and secured the deadbolt then went over to the kitchen and pulled open the cabinet. There wasn't much to choose from— some plates, some bowls, a tall, glass tumbler, a couple of coffee mugs, and a stack of those red plastic Dixie cups. He reached inside and went for the tumbler then took it over to the freezer and filled it with a couple ice cubes. After he set it down on top of the kitchen counter, he reached into the box and pulled out a handle of Cutty. Ah Cutty. He twisted off the cap, lifted the bottle, and filled the tumbler with about three fourths of Cutty. He took the tumbler over to the kitchen faucet and filled it with a little splash of tap water.

He took a deep breath, lifted the tumbler, closed his eyes, and took a long, deep swallow. The alcohol burned as it spread through his stomach, diffused into his veins, and bubbled through his blood stream. Yes, it was working. He could feel it already. It was like a warm, safe cocoon being spun around him.

He took the drink back with him into the living room, then kicked off his shoes, and collapsed on the sofa. He could feel his body dissolving into the fabric, like he was a wax candle being melted with a blow torch. He took another sip then dug the remote out from in between the cushions, hit the power button, and cranked up the volume. Alright, let's see what we got here. He went to the movie channels and scrolled through the selection, hopping back and forth between HBO and Showtime. But he couldn't find anything good, so he went to his own personal selection and popped in his favorite movie, *The Deer Hunter*.

He lifted his glass and took another deep swallow, draining the tumbler all the way down to its ice cubes. Then he got up and went into the kitchen, grabbed the bottle of *Cutty* and took it back with him into the living room. He pulled off the cap and lifted the bottle, listening to the glug-glug sound as the scotch splashed into the tumbler. When he got it up to the brim, he set the bottle down next to his feet beside the sofa. There. Now, he didn't have to worry about going back and forth to the kitchen. He could just reach down and freshen his drink whenever he needed. He snatched the DVD remote from off of the cushion, hit the play button, and fast-forwarded through the previews. The credits rolled, the music started, and Monty sank back with his scotch sitting on top of his kneecap.

About halfway through the movie and halfway through the bottle of Cutty, Monty saw something green flashing in his peripheral vision. He lowered his head and looked down at the sofa. His cell phone was going off in the crevice of the cushions. He dug it out and read the name off of the display: *Robby R.*

He sat there frozen, staring at the phone's green LCD screen as something sharp and hot shifted inside his stomach. Great. He could actually feel the anxiety moving around his stomach, like a giant tapeworm coiling around his intestine. After a few seconds, the phone stopped buzzing and Monty put it down and threw back the last gulp of Cutty. When he glanced down in his glass, he saw that he was out of ice cubes. He needed to get some more, so he put the movie on pause and made his way into the kitchen. But just as he got to the freezer, the phone started to make that awful buzzing sound again. God damnit. What the fuck did he want from him?

In a fit of rage, he grabbed the freezer door and flung it open, so hard that a piece of the handle broke off and ricocheted against the counter. He shoved his hand into the ice tray—a few cubes made it into the glass, but most rattled out like dice onto the linoleum. "Jesus Christ." He went to the box and pulled out a bottle of Seagram's, twisted off the cap and filled up the tumbler. In just three gulps, he drained the entire tumbler then slammed it down against the kitchen counter. He refilled it again, took another swallow, then again and again until he felt like he might vomit. He stormed back into the living room. The phone was still buzzing, so he flipped it open and jammed it against his ear. "Hello?" he said, abruptly, the gin in his glass sloshing out over the rim.

"Monty? Is that you?"

"Yes. This is Monty. And just who the hell are you?"

"It's me, Monty. It's Robby."

"Robby? Who the fuck is Robby? I don't know no Robby."

"Come on, man, quit playing games. You know who I am."

Monty laughed as he walked back into the kitchen and poured himself another tall glass of gin. He took a deep breath then threw it back, but half of it came back up out of his nose and spilled out onto the floor. "Whoops!" He cupped his hand over his mouth, the gin like bee stingers piercing the inside of his nostrils.

"Monty? Are you still there? Talk to me man. Are you okay? What are you doing?"

"Yeah, I'm still here. What do you want? Speak motherfucker. Speak now or forever hold your peace!"

"Jesus Monty, where have you been? Why haven't you returned any of my phone calls? Why weren't you at the funeral?"

"Hey Robby, what do you call a million alcoholics stuck in a blender?"

"What?"

"A good start! Ha ha ha!"

"What is wrong with you? Are you drinking again?"

Monty looked at the phone then down at the gin bottle, then back at the phone and back at the gin. "Uh…I don't know. Why? Are you? Ha ha ha!"

"God damnit. I am not interested in playing games with you right now. I wanna help you."

"You wanna help me? You wanna fucking help me? Fuck you, Robby. You can't help me. No one can help me. I'm fucking dead, Robby."

"Don't say that, Monty. You are not dead."

"Yes, I am. I'm a fucking ghost, Robby. A fucking dead man walking."

"No, you're not. Quit saying that. You have people who love you, man."

"Oh really? Who? Who loves me? Come on, Robby, tell me who loves me."

"Your dad loves you, your mom loves you, Susan loves you, I love you! You think that by drinking yourself to death you're gonna end all your problems? Do you realize how fucking selfish that is? What about all those people who love you? You're just gonna turn your back on them? Is that it?"

Monty grimaced as he lifted the tumbler, then closed his eyes and took another long sip. "Go to hell, Robby."

"I don't have to. I've been there, remember? I lived through that shit. And so have you. Do you really want to go through it all over again? I mean, how much more misery do you have to put yourself through?"

"As much as it takes."

"As much as it takes for what?"

"You know damn well what."

"Don't do this, Monty. You don't have to do this."

"Yes I do."

"Why?"

"Because."

"Because why?"

"Because it's my fault! I'm responsible! I killed her!"

"Monty."

"She knew it wasn't safe, but I made her do it. I didn't stop. I didn't pull over."

"What about the other car? What about the other driver? He came into your lane. He forced you into that reservoir."

"They never found him. No one ever came forward."

"So?"

"So, maybe it didn't happen. Maybe it was just my imagination."

"You're drunk, Monty. You don't know what you're saying."

"Yes, I do. I know exactly what I'm fucking saying. She should've never been with me. If we hadn't met, none of this would've ever happened. She'd still be alive. That kid would still have his mother."

"It was an accident, Monty. Plain and simple. Shit happens. Life on life's terms. Remember?"

"Don't you quote that AA bullshit to me, Robby. You should know better than that. Save that shit for your little lackeys. Not me, man. I'm done with all that shit. I'm gone. Four more weeks and I'll be as good as dead."

"You don't mean that."

"Oh no? You think I'm just fucking around? Is that it? You think I'm just playing games?"

"You're not going to kill yourself, Monty. You and I both know that. That's just the alcohol talking. You don't know what you're saying."

"Is that so?"

"Yeah, that's so."

"Okay, okay, alright. You wanna see some games, Robby? You wanna see who's playing? Alright, okay, I'll show you some fucking games. I'll show you who's fucking playing."

In one swift turn, Monty hurled the phone across the kitchen. It bounced off the wall and shattered into two pieces. He grabbed the gin bottle and turned it up towards the ceiling— the gin streamed down his cheeks and spilled out across the linoleum. Wiping his mouth, he charged across the dining room, his hand around the bottle, his eyes aimed on the bathroom. When he got inside, he flipped on the light switch then laid his hands flat on the counter and stared into the mirror. "Look at you. You're pathetic, you're disgusting, you're a fucking coward. You took the one thing good in your life and you fucking destroyed it."

He lifted the bottle and took another swallow then cocked his elbow and drove his fist into the mirror. Shards of glass rained down on the counters. He brought his hand out in front of him. His fingers were bleeding, the flesh torn wide open. He clenched his teeth, shook off the throbbing, then lifted the bottle, and took another swallow. He opened the medicine cabinet, reached for the pill bottles, and grabbed one of six that were lined up against the paisley patterned wallpaper. This ought to do the trick, he thought, as he popped open the bottle, dumped the pills into his mouth, some of which spilled out onto the counter. Keeping his jaw relaxed, he reached for the gin bottle, and holding it with both hands, he turned it upward. The first gulp nearly made him vomit, but he was able to choke it back just enough to get about half of the pills in one swallow. As he took another sip, he shut his eyes, breathing slowly in and out through his nostrils. He could feel the pills rubbing against his larynx, sharp and obtrusive scraping against the soft and fleshy tissue. But he worked them all down, inch by inch, swallow by swallow, pill by pill until they were all settled inside his stomach. He opened his eyes, went back to the medicine cabinet, and grabbed the next bottle in line...the Zoloft. He wasn't sure if it would even do anything. It was just an antidepressant. Wouldn't it just be like swallowing Tylenol? He didn't know, but it didn't matter, because he was too far gone to really care about anything. So, he tore off the cap and lifted the bottle, dumped the pills and started to swallow. Some of the pills fell out and danced around the sink basin then disappeared down the drain, never to be seen again. But it must've done the trick, because his shoulders went limp and his knees buckled. He slumped back against the wall and down towards the toilet. Everything became dark and he could feel his breath shortening, as if someone was stepping on his throat and slowly squeezing the air out of him. He tried to move his head but couldn't—it was like something was holding him down, like an elephant was sitting on top of his abdomen. He moved his eyes around, but he couldn't see anything; the walls of the bathroom had completely closed in on him. All he could see was Vicky screaming, her legs trapped under the dashboard as the icy water rushed in on top of her.

Chapter 12

Angie

Angie lay motionless on the grimy twin-size mattress, eyes wide open, following the blades of the fan as they slowly rotated around and around. She was completely naked, except for a pair of pink, fuzzy bunny slippers that were hanging precariously off the ends of her feet. Her bones ached, her muscles were tender, and the stench of stale smoke emanated from her skin. Where was she? And how long had she been here? Had it been days? Maybe weeks?

She sat up on the mattress and looked towards the window. The soft glow of sunlight was seeping in through the shades. Cradling the back of her head with one hand, she thrust her chin up with the other. "Ah." The cartilage in her neck made a grinding sound like a fork lodged in a garbage disposal's blades. As she shrugged off the pain, she moved her eyes across the floor of the bedroom. It looked like a garbage truck had driven right through the place. There were playing cards and aluminum foil scattered all over the brown shag carpet. Empty mason jars and two liter Pepsi bottles stained with a reddish brown residue, lay nearby. The mattress was speckled with splotches of red, brown, and yellow that made it resemble the back of a toad. As she breathed through her nose, she got a whiff of something strong and chemical, like some kind of cleaning fluid, maybe acetone.

Just as she was about to get up, she felt something stirring beside her, tickling the flesh of her left knee. When she looked down, she saw a lump of bare flesh underneath the bed covers, rising and falling, twitching and churning—was it an arm? Or maybe it was a leg. She leaned over and carefully peeled off the blankets. Oh, it was just Rick. His eyes were shut, but his mouth was wide open—he looked like an overgrown baby breathing in short, shallow breaths.

She leaned over him and put her lips within an inch from his ear. "Rick sweetie, time to get up."

Rick just groaned and rolled over, revealing his pasty-white butt cheeks. She sighed and reached over him, her breasts like pink udders draping across his back. She grabbed the remote and powered on the television, cranking up the volume and sitting back against the bed. "Hey Rick," she said as she flipped through the channels, trying to find the one with the list of shows.

Rick's legs twitched underneath the covers. He let out another deep groan.

"Rick, please wake up." She grabbed the sheets and ripped off the covers, exposing his scrawny, hair-covered legs.

His eyes shot open. He looked up at Angie. "Jesus Christ, what the fuck are you doing?"

"Where's the menu channel?"

"The what?"

"The menu channel."

"What in the world is the menu channel?"

"You know, the thing that tells you the time of shows and stuff."

"You mean the channel guide?"

"Yeah, whatever it's called. What channel is it on?"

Rick sat up and rubbed his eyelids while taking in a long, persistent yawn. "Crap, I don't know, Angie. Try fifteen."

Angie punched in the numbers, but the screen just turned completely blue. "What the heck?" She looked down at the remote and slapped it against her thigh. The fat jiggled like a dropped carton of cottage cheese. "I don't think there is a fifteen."

"Well then try thirty-three."

She hit the channel button up a couple times and unlocked it from the blue screen. "Oh wait. Never mind. I found it." Straining her eyes, she leaned forward and read the time from the bottom of the screen. "Hey Rick?"

"What do you want now?"

"Is this right? The TV's saying its Thursday, but that can't be right, can it? I thought we went to bed on Tuesday? Didn't we go to bed on Tuesday?"

"Jesus, I don't know Angie. If it says Thursday then it must be Thursday."

"You mean to tell me we slept through the entire day yesterday?"

"I guess so."

"Oh no." The remote slid out of Angie's hands and clunked on the floor. "That can't be right. That just can't be right." She straddled Rick and reached for his cell phone from the nightstand beside the bed.

"Ouch," Rick shouted. "Watch the nuts, Angie. Jesus."

"It can't be. It just can't be."

Angie opened the cell phone and read off the numbers. Her stomach began to tighten. She was gonna be sick. "I can't believe it. I can't frickin' believe it."

"What?"

"It is Thursday."

"So?"

She slammed the phone down against the mattress. "I was supposed to go to Sarah's volleyball game last night."

"Who?"

"Sarah."

"Who in the hell's Sarah?"

"Don't be an asshole, Rick. You know damn well who I'm talking about. Sarah, my daughter, the girl you used to date."

Rick smirked coyly. "Oh right. That Sarah. Sorry, I forgot for a minute."

"You didn't forget. You're just trying to be a prick." Angie picked up a pillow and hurled it at Rick's face.

"Well shit Angie, don't get mad at me. I'm not the one who made you miss her damn game."

"Screw you Rick. If you didn't get me so god damn high I wouldn't have missed it."

Rick laughed and sat up against the headboard. He pulled his hair back into a ponytail and grabbed his cigarettes from the nightstand. "That's hardly my fault. I didn't force you to smoke."

"I can't believe I missed it. I told her I'd be there. I made a promise."

"Just call her up and apologize. I'm sure she'd understand."

"Oh yeah right. I'm sure that would go over real well"—Angie lifted her hand like she was placing an imaginary phone call—"Hi Sarah, I'm sorry I missed your volleyball game, but I was too busy getting high with your old boyfriend, Rick." After she put the phone in its imaginary cradle, she turned to Rick and said, "Yeah, right, I'm sure she'd understand."

"Well shit Angie, don't tell her you were with me. Just make up some bullshit story. Tell her you had a doctor's appointment or something."

"I'm not gonna lie to my own kid."

Rick laughed and reached for his lighter. "A little too late for that, don't you think?"

"You're such an asshole."

"Oh, come on now baby, I'm just teasing you." Rick scooted forward and wrapped his arms around Angie's soft belly, but his breath was so vile it made her cringe. "Hey," he said, as he inched in closer, one hand in between her legs, the other massaging her left breast. "Since you're not gonna be doing anything today, maybe you can give me a hand with a few things."

She sighed and removed his hand from her nipple then got up from the bed and pulled on her robe. "Just tell me what you want me to get. And write it down this time. I'm not a frickin' mind reader, you know."

"Don't worry baby, I will." Rick leaned back, playing with himself underneath the covers, a sly smirk on his twenty-nine year old acne-scarred face. "Hey Angie."

"What?"

"You know I love you right?"

"Uh." Angie made a gagging sound as she tied the robe around her waist. "You make me sick."

"That's not what you were saying the other night."

"Yeah, well I was high."

Angie pulled back her hair and stomped through the hallway, her steps sounding hollow against the trailer's cheap, fake wood floor. When she got to the kitchen, she had to plug her nostrils. The smell was so revolting it nearly made her puke. The sink was piled high with empty mason jars and plastic bottles, covered with that reddish-brown residue and lumps of uncooked meth. There were half eaten pizza slices, rotten banana peels, and pieces of bread covered in a thick layer of furry black mold.

Angie took a deep breath and put her hands on the sink counter. The coffee decanter was wedged underneath a frying pan at the bottom of the sink. That's what she needed—a cup of steaming hot coffee to warm her insides and revive her soul. She reached in and pulled out the decanter then opened the overhead cabinet and stood on her toes. She pulled down the can of Folgers and set it on the counter. It looked like there was just enough for a few fresh cups. She scooped up the grounds and threw them into the little paper basket, poured in some water, and hit the power button on the bottom of the percolator.

After a few minutes, she pulled out the decanter and poured herself a fresh cup. She took a small sip and walked over to the kitchen table, stopping at the counter to grab her cell phone from the wall charger. She flipped the phone open. Damn, no missed calls. Should she try and call Sarah? Would she even pick up?

She took another sip and sat down at the table, staring at the phone's display glowing green in her palm. Screw it. What did she have to lose? She punched in the numbers and brought the receiver to her ear. It went right to Sarah's voicemail. Shit. Should she leave a message or should she just hang up? Sarah's message ended and the phone went beep.

Angie cleared her throat and set down her coffee. "Hi sweetie, it's me, uh…it's mom. I'm sorry I missed your game last night. I know I said I'd come, but I uh…I had a doctor's appointment in the city and by the time I got out, it was too late to drive all the way up to Estes Park. Anyway, I hope you girls had a good time. Give me a call back when you can. I love you sweetie. Bye."

Angie put down the phone and began to sob softly. What the hell was wrong with her? How could she do that? How could she lie to her only daughter? She only had one thing to do this week and that was to make it to that frickin' volleyball game so she could show her ex-husband, Bill, that she was capable of staying clean. But she couldn't even do that, could she? She couldn't even go one day without Rick and his meth and this godforsaken trailer. What the hell was wrong with her? Why couldn't she just stay clean? Now, there was no way Bill was going to let her visit Sarah. She'd be lucky if she could get him to drop that restraining order.

A few minutes later, Rick stomped into the kitchen. His hair was wet from the shower and his skin reeked of cheap aftershave. He grabbed a ballpoint pen and tore off a sheet of yellow notepad paper, then sat down next to Angie and began to scribble. "Alright, you know the drill. No more than three boxes per store. Spread it out. Hit the Walgreens on Broadway, the CVS on Speer, and the Super Target in Glendale. And make sure you get the right stuff this time. Not that crap that says *PE* on the label. Make sure it says *Pseudoephedrine*, not *Phenylephrine*. Got it?"

"Yeah I got it. I know what to do."

"You sure? Because you didn't know last time."

"It was one time, alright? I was in a hurry."

"Yeah, well, because of you, I wasted an entire day on a batch of shit."

"Look. I'll get the right stuff this time."

"You better." Once Rick was finished scribbling, he dropped the pen, folded the sheet of paper then looked up at Angie and said, "What's the matter with you?"

Angie sniffled, wiping the tears from her eyes. "I'm fine."

"You sure? You don't look fine."

"I said, I'm fine."

Rick snorted. His eyes moved from Angie to underneath the kitchen table. "Well, take off those slippers and wash your damn face. You look like a meth head."

"Screw you!"

Angie went to get up, but Rick grabbed her wrist and pulled her in close to his face. "Hey, do you want to end up in jail? You remember what happened to Greg don't you? Ten years up in Cañon City. They don't joke around with this shit."

"You think I don't know that? Just give me the list." Angie pulled away and snatched the grocery list from Rick's hand. She unfolded the paper and laid it flat on the table. "What the hell's all this other stuff?"

"We need to restock."

"Lantern fuel?"

"Yeah. Make sure you get the Coleman brand. It's the best."

"Where the heck am I supposed to find that?"

"It should be in the camping section with all the sleeping bags and tents and shit."

"What about this?" She pointed to the next item on the list. "Drain cleaner?"

"Yeah. Be sure to get the kind with the skull and cross bones on it."

"How much should I get?"

"Christ Angie, I don't know, like two bottles a piece, whatever we can afford."

"Well, what are *you* gonna be doing?"

"I'm gonna be busy doing the batteries. Look, do you wanna cook this stuff or not?"

Angie nodded.

"Well then stop asking so many jack-assy questions and hit the road, would ya?"

"I hate you Rick." Angie flicked him the bird and shoved the piece of paper into her pocket then walked to the bathroom and began washing her face.

"You better not be taking a bath back there!" Rick shouted from the kitchen. "I told you to wash your face, not your damn ass."

"Stop bullying me. I'm not a punching bag, you know."

"Yeah, yeah, yeah. Just hurry up. We're losing daylight."

When she was done rinsing her face, she dried it off with a bright yellow Coppertone beach towel then went into the bedroom and took off her robe. She threw on some jeans and one of Rick's flannel, long-sleeve hunting shirts, then exchanged her slippers for a pair of snow boots. She stomped back into the kitchen and grabbed the keys from the bowl on the table then stuffed them into her pocket along with her cell phone.

"Better get going sweetie," Rick said, as he laid out a box cutter and a couple packets of lithium batteries.

Angie stuck out her tongue and headed towards the front doorway, stopping to grab her white and red candy cane striped ski jacket from the living room floor.

"You sure that jacket goes with your boots honey?"

"Go to hell, Rick."

When she got outside, she stomped across the yard towards Rick's old, blue Chevy Camaro then unlocked the door and hopped inside. The seats were wet and rotting with mildew and the icy water shot like thorns through her jeans. That idiot. He forgot to roll up the frickin' window. What kind of moron was she dealing with here?

She sighed and stuck the keys into the ignition then cranked on the engine, but realized she couldn't see out the front or the back. As she slid on the defroster, she reached beneath the seat cushion, and pulled the little lever that popped open the trunk. She got out, walked to the back, and pulled open the trunk. All she saw was a bunch of empty mason jars and two liter bottles of Pepsi stained with a chalky white crust. Oh real frickin' smart, Rick. Makin' her drive around with a bunch of bottles caked with meth residue—what the hell was he thinking? Was he a frickin' idiot?

She shut the trunk and jumped back behind the steering wheel, reached behind the seat and felt around in the back. Her fingers wrapped around the ice scraper's plastic handle. She pulled it out and inspected both ends. There was a metal scraper on one end and a thistle brush on the other. This oughta do the trick.

She got out of the car and leaned across the windshield. The ice was about an inch thick, but was already starting to melt from the defroster. She finished the windshield, did both side windows, and a little of the back. That was good enough. Hopefully, it would melt by the time she got on the highway. The last thing she needed was to get into a frickin' car wreck.

She hopped back behind the steering wheel and chucked the scraper into the backseat behind her then took a moment to catch her breath. As she pulled down the sun visor, she happened to glance into the vanity mirror and was completely horrified by the skin on her face. Her forehead was freckled with little red lesions that were bright in the center from droplets of blood. What the heck? She took off her gloves and lightly felt them with the tips of her fingers, but quickly pulled away when they began burning to the touch. "Ouch." What the hell were they? Were they mosquito bites? Was it an allergic reaction? Did Rick do this? What the hell was going on?

She reached into her jacket pocket and pulled out a little, wool beanie, then carefully fitted it around the circumference of her head. She checked the mirror to make sure the sores were hidden. They were. She looked almost normal, except for a bloody blotch in the corner of her left eye. Good God. What the hell was happening to her? Was it from the meth? Did she have some kind of disease?

She shut the mirror and began sobbing, the tears dripping down onto her jeans. No, wait, she couldn't cry. She had to be stronger. The sooner she got the supplies, the sooner she wouldn't have to feel any more pain. She wiped away the tears and put on her seat belt then threw the car in reverse and stepped on the gas.

Chapter 13

The Ingredients

As Angie merged onto Highway 6, the tall buildings of downtown Denver began to appear in the distance, her daughter's favorite towering above them all. It was the one that was shaped like an old-time cash register, curved at the top, and dropping down to a flat façade. Sarah had drawn a picture of it when she was in kindergarten. They had it up on the fridge for the longest time. Wonder what happened to that picture? It probably got thrown out after the divorce along with everything else.

She shook her head as she popped in the cigarette lighter then pulled out a cigarette and wedged it in between her lips. As she looked in the rearview mirror, she caught a glimpse of the mountains behind her. They looked like giant vanilla ice cream cones, their peaks covered with a layer of fresh, milky-white snow. Aw the mountains. She couldn't remember the last time she went up to Breckenridge, or Aspen, or Copper, or even Vail. She was always trying to get Rick to go up there with her, but that lazy bastard never wanted to go anywhere. All he cared about were those god damn fertilizer tanks. He was obsessed with those frickin' things, totally paranoid, scared that if he left them for just one second, they wouldn't be there when he got back. What a jerk.

Bill used to take her up there all the time, her and the kids. That was back when she was young and beautiful...back when she had a tight butt and big, full tits...before all the shrinks, the lawyers, and doctors...the booze, the meth, and that loser, Rick. Back when life was simple...back when it was just her, Bill, the kids, and nothing else.

The cigarette lighter popped out and Angie grabbed it, then lit the end of her cigarette and took a deep drag. As the nicotine flooded her lungs, her mind began to wander back to that flicker of happiness, that perfect memory, that perfect place. The deeper she inhaled, the stronger the memories came back to her, as bright and warm as the Colorado sun shining down on her face.

It was summer. She was barefoot and walking down the pier at Lake Dillon, Bill's strong arms wrapped tightly around her, and his chin nuzzled against her neck. He was such a gorgeous man—those sparkling blue eyes, that strong jaw line, and hair that turned blond in the summer like bales of golden wheat underneath a cloudless sky.

They pinched each other and giggled, as they trotted down the rickety, wood pier towards their boat, *Pegasus*—a twenty-five foot schooner, with a beautiful blue and gold sail and deep, cherry wood trim. It was Bill's tenth anniversary present to her and cost him nearly an entire year's salary. But, God was it worth it. It was such a gorgeous boat. It made all the other members at the sailing club jealous. They took it out almost every Saturday in the summer, early in the evening, just as the sun was beginning to set behind the peaks of the continental divide.

But this particular Saturday, the one that stuck with her all this time, was more special than all the others. It was the 4th of July, and the *Rocky Mountain Post* had promised a fireworks display more spectacular, more dazzling than any other in history. The kids were young then and they scampered out ahead down the dock like little raccoons crawling onto the bow of the boat. Their smiles were big and their eyes were bright as they gazed out towards the underbrush of the shore, hoping to catch a glimpse of a moose, or a beaver, or a wild coyote. The scent was sweet from the aroma of wildflowers growing in thousands along the banks of the lake. There were rows and rows of yellow alpine parsley, their purple bracelets reclining in the setting sun. Tangles and tangles of soft lavender blue stars curled over one another in a florid orgasm as manes of rusty orange mountain dandelions erupted into rivers of carrot colored molten magma. And the sky was magnificent. Dark purple clouds loomed in the distance, their fluffy dollops streaked with sharp ribbons of crimson and violet. Crowds of people assembled on the banks of the lake, preparing for the show, laying out their trays of hamburgers and hot dogs, containers of potato salad and coleslaw, baskets of biscuits, chocolate chip cookies, and apple pies.

Angie cradled her bag of goodies close to her chest. When she got to the end of the dock, Bill put his strong hands around her and lifted her effortlessly up onto the deck. He jumped up on board then began to untie the lines and cast them into the water, while Angie whisked her way down the steps of the galley, her little white boat shoes squeaking on the water slick wood. She placed her grocery bag down and began pulling out all her goodies, laying them out on the cherry wood bar. She called to the kids, announcing that dinner was ready, but the kids were too busy dangling their feet over the edge of the bow.

Once Bill was finished with the lines, he cranked on the engine and they pushed off from the shore. Angie put her hand to her brow and looked out towards the center of the lake. A cluster of boats had already gathered in their special spot. Bill pointed the bow towards the boats and inched the throttle forward. They picked up some speed and cut through the water. The waves splashed against the sides of the little schooner, sending a fine mist into the air. She came over to the helm where Bill was steering and stood in front of him, leaned back against his chest, and gazed out at the orange glow of campfires flickering throughout the park. He wrapped his arms tightly around her waist, so tight, it was almost difficult to breathe. But she felt safe and calm, like nothing in the world could harm her.

As they approached the little cluster of boats, Angie heard the first bang ring out through the park, echoing off the sides of the mountains. The crowd of people turned their heads upward, their eyes gazing out towards the abysmal darkness of the nighttime sky. They waited in anticipation for the next sparkle of light to illuminate their faces. Then it came. Three loud thunderous roars followed by a shower of red, blue, and green. They blossomed in the sky and rained down on the boats like thousands of tiny fireflies. Everyone in the crowd, including the kids let out a resounding "Oooohhh- Ahhhhh" followed by clapping and a demand for more. And more came, in all different patterns and colors. Blues that burst like bombs, reds that rained down like rose petals, and violets that vanquished the darkness, and lit up the kids' eyes with wonder and awe.

After the grand finale, some of the boats headed back in for a night of eating, drinking, and dancing at the yacht club, but Bill, Angie, and the kids had their dinner by lantern light in the still calm of the lake. The air was cool and the water was quiet. They could see the reflection of the yellow crescent moon rippling across the surface. A gentle breeze blew through the forest. The trees swayed back and forth, and danced to a symphony of bullfrogs and crickets playing gently along the edge of the effervescent lake.

It was perfect. A perfect memory. A perfect time. A perfect place. What had happened? How did it vanish? Where did it all go so terribly wrong? How did she end up here in this shitty Camaro, driving around in the blistering cold, wet and tired, covered in lesions, her skin barely clinging to her face. And for what—some Sudafed and lantern fuel, so her idiot boyfriend could cook up some meth? Why? Why did this happen? She was a good mom and a good wife. She did everything for Bill and those children. She waited on them hand and foot for twenty years. She picked them up from school, took them to soccer practice, chauffeured them around to all their little dates—boy scouts, swim practice, gymnastics, everything. And where were they now? Why had they abandoned her? How could Bill do this to her? How could he be so selfish? What did that little slut have that she didn't? A tight butt and big tits? So what? She was the mother of his children. Didn't that count for anything?

She sighed and took a deep breath inward. She'll never forget that sight as long as she lives. Bill on his back, eyes closed, tongue licking the tops of his lips, a small head bobbing up and down above the covers, long, dark strands of hair fanned out over his crotch. She could never exactly remember what happened after that. She must have had what they call an out of body experience. Her senses went limp, her skin turned ice cold, and the next thing she knew she was standing in the doorway with a butcher knife in her hand, watching Bill, one pant leg in, the other out, hopping around pathetically like a one legged kangaroo. The intern was on the bed, frozen with fear, her naked body curled up in a bundle of quilts. Angie lunged forward, the knife raised above her towards the intern who was shrieking at the top of her lungs. But, Bill flew across the bed before she could get to her, hurling her backwards against the wall. She swung the knife wildly in a downward motion, catching the side of Bill's arm. He grabbed her wrist before she could do any more damage and hammered it as hard as he could until the knife came loose and dropped to the floor. After he kicked it out into the hallway, he wrestled Angie to the carpet and pinned her hands behind her head. She remembered tasting his blood as he straddled her, all two hundred pounds of him crushing down on top of her chest. She kicked and writhed, screaming at him to get off of her, foaming at the mouth, trying to break free.

The intern grabbed the knife and darted into the kitchen, picked up the phone and called the police. They arrived moments later in a swirl of blue and red flashing lights. They kicked down the door and trampled into the bedroom, their pistols drawn, their shiny badges gleaming off the bedside lamp. They rolled Angie over and slapped the cuffs on her then picked her up and marched her out the front door. By that time, all the neighbors had assembled outside in their driveways, watching as the cops shoved her against the patrol car. They patted her down in front of everybody then flung her into the back seat like a piece of white trash. And Bill just stood there, his head hung in embarrassment, his eyes on the ground, not saying a damn word. What a coward. What a spineless piece of trash.

What was she supposed to have done? Just sit there and do nothing, while that little tramp sucked on her husband's cock? She wished Bill hadn't stopped her when he had. She wished she could've sliced off a chunk of that whore's flesh. Maybe an ear or a finger or possibly a nipple. Yeah, a nipple. That would have been good. She would have been justified too.

It was a shame the courts didn't see it that way. They gave Bill everything—the house, the cars...even the boat. All she got was a monthly alimony payment and a year's worth of mandatory therapy. The kids stayed with their dad. Angie wasn't even allowed to see them without a chaperone and a set date and time. She felt like a stranger sitting out there in the driveway of her own house, that imposter inside, sleeping in her bed, watching her TV, screwing her husband.

Angie sighed and put on her right blinker then got off on the downtown exit and made a right turn at Broadway and Sixth. She turned into the parking lot next to the theater, threw the car in park, and finished her cigarette. Once she was done, she chucked it out the window then checked herself in the mirror, making sure her wool cap was pulled down over her sores. Then, she got out and made her way across the icy parking lot, her hands dug deep into her jacket pockets.

When she got to the entrance, the automatic doors slid open and a rush of warm air swallowed her whole. Mind-numbing elevator music played out over the speakers as she made her way over to the cough medicine aisle. She paced up and down, inspecting the products, squinting under the strain of the bright fluorescent lights. But it wasn't easy—there were so many to choose from—cough-gels, liquid-gels, extra strength, maximum strength, pills, capsules, caplets, red liquids, green liquids, boxes, rubs, sprays, gels, nighttime, daytime, cough and cold, cold and cough, sinus and allergy, congestion and pain, sore throat, drowsy, non-drowsy, PM, AM, all day, all night, double action, triple action, quadruple action. "Shit." She only needed one kind. Where the hell was it? There were hundreds and hundreds of different brand names to choose from. Advil, Afrin, Alavert, Aleve, Alka Seltzer, Anacin…and that was only the A's. There was also Bayer, Benadryl, Benefiber, Breatheright, Cepacol, Claritin, Chloraseptic, Ibuprofen, Metamucil, Motrin, Mucinex, Mylanta, Rite Aid, Robitussin, Theraflu, Tylenol, Tums, Vicks and finally Sudafed. But which one? There were more than a dozen types of Sudafed. She picked up the first one she saw, which was in a purple box. It read, *Sudafed PE Sinus and Headache. Contains: Acetaminophen and Phenylephrine.*

Was this the right one? No. Rick said not to get the stuff with PE on the front. It stood for Phenylephrine, which wasn't what she wanted. She needed ephedrine. She put the box back. She picked up the one that said *Maximum Strength Nasal Decongestant, Main Ingredient: Pseudoephedrine HCl tablets.*

Jackpot. This was the one. She remembered the bright red box and the picture of the head with the molten lava sinus cavity. But remember what Rick said—no more than three at a time. She picked up four and walked to the register. There was a short, Indian girl standing behind the counter, flipping through the pages of a Cosmopolitan magazine. The girl popped purple bubble gum and wore a pair of heavy looking hoop earrings that tugged at her earlobes and stretched out her flesh. Angie laid the boxes down on the counter. The girl folded her magazine and picked up the scanner. She scanned the boxes one by one and placed them into a plastic bag.

"Is that all?" she asked in a thick Indian accent then popped a purple bubble right in Angie's face.

"Yes, that's it."

"Flu?"

"Excuse me?"

"I said, do you have flu?"

"Oh yes, yes, I do, I do."

"Your kids have it too?"

"What?"

"I said your kids must have it too. Four boxes. One, two, three, four. That's a lot. You must have much sickness in your household."

"Oh yes, yes, I do. We are all very, very sick."

"Oh you poor thing. You look horrible. You should go lie down."

"Oh thank you. Yes, I will."

"Okay. So, total is fifty-eight dollars and thirty-five cents."

Angie pulled out her credit card and swiped the machine. It felt like an eternity for the transaction to go through. She clutched her arms and tugged at the sleeves of her jacket, the Indian girl looking at her with a pleasant smile.

What was she looking at? Was she looking at her forehead? She couldn't see her sores, could she? Weren't they covered up?

The receipt finally finished printing out. The girl ripped it off and slapped it on the counter. "Sign please."

Angie took a pen from a red plastic cup and went to scribble her name, but the pen was out of ink, so she smashed the ballpoint down on the counter and tried again, but still, no ink.

"Here," said the girl, "You try mine." The Indian girl pulled a pen from her front shirt pocket.

"Thanks," Angie said, as she took the pen and scribbled her name.

"You're welcome."

Angie gathered her bag and headed for the exit, but the Indian girl stopped her and said, "Wait mam, you forgot your receipt."

Angie whirled around and marched back to the counter and said, "thank you," as she snatched the receipt.

"You're welcome. Be sure to get plenty of rest today."

"Yes, I will. Thanks again."

"Okay. Bye, bye now."

Angie nodded then headed for the exit, clutching her bag close to her chest. When she got outside, she buttoned up her jacket and pulled her hood up around her head. She unlocked the door and climbed behind the wheel. After turning the keys to crank on the engine, she hit the windshield wipers to wipe off the snow. She threw the car into reverse and back out of the parking lot then made a right onto Broadway and headed north towards Speer. Okay, one down, two more to go. Next up was the CVS on Speer, and after that, the Super Target in Glendale. Everything was going to be okay. She could do this. She just had to hold it together for a few more stores.

Chapter 14

The Tanks

Angie stomped her way into the trailer, a half dozen grocery bags hanging from her arms. "Hello? Could use a little help here."

"Not now," Rick said, sitting at the kitchen table, a line of batteries beneath his nose. "I'm doing the batteries. I'll help in a minute."

Angie blew her hair back from her eyes and trudged in her snow boots across the trailer's hollow floor. "Well, where should I put these?" she said, stopping next to kitchen table.

"Jesus Angie. It doesn't matter. Anywhere's fine."

Angie dropped the bags right where she was standing. They thudded like cement blocks onto the kitchen floor.

"Jesus Christ. Be careful, would ya? You're acting like a two year old."

"Well, you said anywhere." She bent over, picked up her McDonald's bag, and carried it over with her to the living room futon. As she sat down, a cloud of dust exploded from the fabric and hovered above her head. "Oooh…gross!"

"What's wrong now?"

"This dust. It's filthy in here."

"Well then clean it."

"You clean it. It's your place."

"You live here too Angie."

"Please don't start with me Rick. I am not in the mood." She dug into the paper bag and pulled out her quarter pounder then unwrapped the paper wrapping and took a big bite. The meat melted in her mouth like a stick of butter and the cheese stuck to her lips in long, stringy strands. "Hmm. So good."

Rick looked up from the table, holding a pair of needle nose pliers. "Did you get any for me?" he said.

Angie looked at him with a mouthful of burger, half-smiling, half-choking on the cheese. "I didn't know you wanted any sweetie."

"That figures. You know, you are so selfish Angie."

"What?"

"It's always about you isn't it?"

"You should've told me you wanted some."

"I shouldn't have to. You should just know."

"I'm not a mind reader."

Rick made a snorting sound then bent over and started rifling through the plastic grocery bags on the kitchen floor. "Where is it?" he said, as he tore through the plastic, packets of Sudafed flying out of the bags. "Where the hell is it?"

"Where's what?"

"The lantern fuel. Where's the god damn lantern fuel?"

Angie froze and swallowed her last bite of burger. "Uh-oh."

Rick stood up slowly, a look of crazed apprehension in his eyes. "Uh-oh? What do you mean uh-oh?"

Angie shrugged and slumped down against the futon. "Sorry."

"Sorry? Sorry?" Rick flipped his long hair back and drove his fists down onto the kitchen table. "Jesus Christ! How could you forget?"

"Please don't yell at me, Rick."

"I can't believe you, Angie. Just how dense are you?"

"Stop yelling at me you jerk. It's not my fault. You had a gazillion damn things on that stupid grocery list. I can't remember everything, you know."

Rick turned away and laughed an insane, little laugh. "For God's sake, I ask you to do one simple thing and you can't even do it. Can you? How do you expect me to cook this shit without any lantern fuel? Huh? What am I suppose to put over the lithium I just spent an hour gutting from these fucking batteries?"

"Why can't we just use water?"

Rick stepped back, dropping his hands to his sides, looking at Angie as if she was out of her mind. "Water? Are you kidding me? Please say you're just joking around."

"What's the big deal?"

"Lithium and water are reactive. They'll explode. Christ, didn't you ever take chemistry when you were in high school? Oh wait. That's right. I forgot. You were probably too busy shaking your pompoms, sucking Bill's dick to even crack open a textbook. Weren't you? Weren't you?"

"Well, what do you want me to do? You want me to go back to Glendale and get it?"

"No, no, no. There's no time. We need to get out to those tanks before it starts snowing again. Shit. We'll just have to make due without it." Rick sat back down and started stacking the Sudafed boxes into neat little rows in front of the batteries. "You wanna help me with these?"

"Not if you're gonna be a jerk about it."

Rick rolled his eyes. "Let me rephrase. Honey, sweetie, it would sure would be swell if you helped me empty these Sudafed boxes so we can make the mud and get out to those tanks before the god damn blizzard of the century blows in."

"Alright, alright. I'm coming." Angie grabbed her McDonald's bag and walked over to the kitchen, shoving a fistful of fries into her mouth as she walked. "What do you want me to do?"

"Help me pop these things out."

"Alright."

She picked up a box and tore it open with her teeth. The Sudafed was encased in a plastic covering with perforated foil on the back. Angie dug her fingernails into the foil and started popping the small, red tablets out of their packaging. They bounced around like red M&M's on the table.

"Okay," Rick said, as he got up and walked to the sink, "you keep going on those and I'll get the blender ready."

"Don't strain yourself."

"Fuck you." Rick walked over to the cabinets and crouched beneath the sink. He pulled out the blender and set it up next to the table on the kitchen counter. It was a dinky looking thing, an Oster with four speeds and probably not more than a hundred watts. He unwound the cord and plugged it into the outlet. He removed the glass pitcher from its cradle, held it beneath the table, and brushed Angie's pile of pills into the pitcher.

"Hold on," Angie said. "I'm not done yet."

"Well hurry up. Shit. How many more you got?"

"One more box. Hold your damn horses."

Angie finished the last box. She slammed the Sudafed box down on the table. "There. Have at it big boy."

"Finally. Jesus." Rick brushed the pills into the pitcher then screwed it back into its cradle and secured the top. He hit the power button and the blender began wailing, the pills dancing around in a frenzy of red and white dust. After about thirty seconds, the pills turned into a fine red, chalky powder. Rick released the button and the blades came to a rest. He removed the top and lifted the pitcher. Angie held a little plastic baggy open while Rick carefully dumped the powder into the bag. A few clumps stuck to the sides.

"Hold on," Angie said. She put the bag down, walked to the drawer, and pulled out a long, skinny, wooden spoon. "Here, use this."

Rick smiled and grabbed the spoon. "Thank you sweetie."

"You're welcome. Now you see, that wasn't so hard was it? It's a whole heck of a lot better than fighting all the time, isn't it?"

Rick nodded and dug into the blender. He broke up the clumps into smaller, more manageable chunks.

Angie held the bag open as Rick scooped up the remaining pieces and shoveled them in. "Alright," he said, as he shook the bag and sealed it tight. "That should do it." He held the bag up to the light and gave it a few flicks with his finger. "We're good to go. Just gotta get the propane tank." He grabbed his jacket hanging on the door, slipped it over his shoulders, and stuffed the little baggy into his side pocket. He disappeared into the backroom and banged and clanged around for about a minute. When he came back out, he was carrying one of those white, cylindrical propane tanks, like the kind that connects to the bottom of a gas grill.

Angie looked at the tank then back at Rick. "We're not using the cooler?"

"No, not today. I'm tired of having to lug that thing around. If we fill this bad boy up, it should last us a couple days…maybe even a few weeks, if we're careful." Rick looked around the kitchen, readjusting the tank against his chest. "Okay, you got the keys?"

Angie nodded and patted her side jacket pocket. "Yep, got 'em right here."

"Alright, you ready?"

Angie put up her arms and flexed her biceps. "I was born ready."

Rick laughed. "Alright then, let's do it."

Angie went to the front door and pushed it open. She held it for Rick as he waddled through. "Can you grab that red thermos from the table?" he said, as he eased down the front steps of the trailer.

Angie nodded and ran back into the kitchen. "Where is it?" she shouted.

"On the table."

"Where?"

"On the table!"

"Oh never mind, I found it! It was on the table!" She picked it up and stopped for a pack of cigarettes, stuffed them inside her jacket pocket and looked around the kitchen for anything else. "Okay," she said to herself as she zipped up her jacket and moved towards the front door. "It's go time."

She closed the front door and locked the bottom lock. Rick was outside leaning against the back of the Camaro, his arms wrapped around the big, white tank. "You coming?" he yelled out.

"Yeah, yeah, I'm coming." Angie got around to the back of the Camaro, jammed the keys into the lock, and flung open the trunk.

Rick set the tank next to the box of residue-covered bottles.

"Where do you want this?" Angie said, holding up the red thermos.

"I'll take it."

Angie handed him the red thermos then went around the car and hopped in the front seat. She waited for Rick to get in then cranked on the engine, threw the car in reverse, and peeled out.

"Not so fast," Rick said, gripping the red thermos tightly between his knees. "You wanna get us killed?"

"Oh quit your crying. I was driving back when you were still picking bubble gum out of the braces between your teeth." Angie popped in the cigarette lighter and reached into her pocket for her pack of cigarettes. She knocked the pack against her knuckles and flipped one between her lips. "You want one?" she said.

"Are you kidding me?"

"What?"

"You wanna set us on fire? I have a homemade bomb between my knees for crying out loud."

Angie snickered and put down the cigarette. "Oh right. I forgot."

"Oh yeah, that's real funny Angie. You're going to kill us one day, you know that? And slow down will ya? You're driving like a damn maniac. You wanna get us pulled over?"

"Calm down. I was just out here. There's no one around."

"Just slow down please. For me?"

"Alright, alright." Angie eased on the brake and brought the speedometer down to twenty.

Rick put on his sunglasses and adjusted his wool cap down over his ears. He opened up the glove compartment and pulled out a pair of yellow latex gloves. He snapped them on over his hands as he peered out the window. "Okay, okay, slow down. Pull over."

"Right here?"

"Yeah, right here, right here."

Angie pulled over onto the snow-covered shoulder. She threw the car into park and peered out the window.

"I don't know," Rick said, looking out the window, rubbing the latex nervously between his hands. "I don't know about this."

"Don't worry, I was just out here, there's no one around. Trust me, they're all inside, probably plucking their chickens, cleaning their guns, or doing whatever it is farm people do on a Tuesday morning."

"I don't know, Angie. I don't think we've ever done it in broad daylight like this before."

"Oh quit being such a baby. This is the best time to do it— when no one's expecting it."

"What if they see us?"

"Who? I just told you no one's out here. They're all at the house, a mile down the road."

"I don't know."

"Look, I didn't just spend all morning driving around to every damn drug store in Denver just so you could wimp out now. I need to smoke, do you understand me? I need it. It's all I have right now. My daughter hates me, my husband hates me...I hate me."

"Your husband? You mean your ex-husband don't you?"

"Whatever. Look, let's just do this thing and get it over with." Angie ripped off her glove and dug her hand in between Rick's thighs. "If you do this for me, I promise I'll make it worth your while."

"A blow job?" Rick said.

Angie licked the top of her lips. "Whatever you want, baby."

"In the shower?"

"Yep. It's your choice."

Rick nodded, adjusted his sunglasses, clapped his hands together, and flung open the door.

"Alright, let's do it."

"That a boy! Now we're talking!" Angie slapped his butt as he hopped out of the Camaro.

Rick handed Angie the red thermos, which she took and wedged in between her knees. She bent forward and reached down beneath the steering wheel and pulled the little lever that popped the trunk. Then, she strapped on her gloves, got out of the car, and walked around to the wire fence on the side of the road. The big green tanks were about two hundred yards out, in the middle of the field, which was completely white, covered with a fresh layer of snow. There was a red barn another hundred yards out to the left of the tanks. "You ready yet?" she said bouncing up and down, trying to stay warm.

Rick shut the trunk and lugged the propane tank over, setting it down by Angie on the side of the road. His eyes darted from Angie to the barn and back to the tanks. "I don't know if this is such a good idea. Something just doesn't feel right."

"Come on, quit being such a baby. We're running out of time."

Rick nodded. "Okay," he said, as he bent down and picked up the tank. "Get the fence."

"Alright."

Angie grabbed the wire fence and held it apart. Rick stuck the tank through the opening and set it down on the other side.

He took the wire from Angie and held it for her. "Alright, you go first."

Angie crouched down and crawled through, one leg after the other, holding the red thermos against her chest. Rick followed. He bent over, grabbed the tank, and lifted it up to his chin. "Alright," he said. "Let's go."

Angie nodded and walked forward. She got about two feet when the ground gave way and sank all around them. "Holy crap." The snow was up to her knees. It was so high she could almost reach out and touch it with her fingertips. She turned and looked back at Rick. "How the hell are we supposed to get out there?"

Rick looked down at her knees then shrugged, shifting the tank higher against his chest. "We're just going to have to suck it up. Come on, let's go."

"Are you crazy? I can't walk through this."

"Oh, who's being the little baby now?"

"This crap must be two feet deep, Rick. There's no way we can make it all the way out there."

"Just shut up and walk. We'll make it just fine." Rick plunged forward through the snow.

Angie followed, pouting as she pulled up the rear. "I think I have frost bite. I can't feel my toes."

"Shut up and keep walking. We're almost there."

They got about a hundred yards out when Angie turned and looked down at the footprints leading back to the car. "They're gonna know we were out here."

"What?"

"They're gonna know we were out here. Look. Look at the footprints."

Rick set the tank down, turned around, and studied the snow. "Ah shit. That's just great."

"See, I told you."

Rick took off his wool cap and wiped the sweat from his brow. Steam radiated from his head as he looked up towards the cloud-covered sky. "Maybe we'll get that snow shower later."

"Yeah, but what if we don't? They're gonna know we were out here."

"Well, so what? So what if they see our footprints? I mean, what are they gonna do?"

"Call the cops, you idiot."

"Well, it's too late now. I mean, you've already got me out here freezing my ass off. There's a fucking breadcrumb trail right to the tanks. We may as well get what we need and hit the road." Rick looked around and scanned the field. "Look." He pointed over to the red barn. "You go over there and look for something to cover up our tracks with, while I go and fill up the tank."

Angie's eyes moved across the field towards the red barn. "What the hell am I supposed to get?"

"Christ Angie, I don't know. A broom, a shovel, anything. Use your fucking imagination."

"Don't yell at me Rick!" Angie put her head down and stuffed her hands into her pockets. She started to shake and shiver and snivel into her jacket.

"Oh god, what's the matter now? Are you crying? Aw for Christ's sake."

"I don't wanna go over there by myself, Rick. What if something happens? What if we get caught?"

Rick rolled his eyes and put down the propane tank. He walked over to Angie, took off his glove, and put his warm hand on the back of her neck. He leaned in and pressed his soft lips against her cheek. "It's okay Angie, everything's gonna be fine. We've done this a hundred times, right? Just think how good it's gonna feel once we get it over with. You can go back, take a nice, long, hot shower, put on your robe and cuddle up in bed. I'll get the first batch started and before you know it, you'll be on cloud nine. I promise. No more Bill, no more Sarah, and no more sneaking around in the freezing, cold snow. Just you and me cuddled up together with enough meth to last us a whole month. Now, what do you say? Can you do this for me? Can you go to that barn and find a broom or something to cover up our tracks?"

Angie nodded, wiping the snot from her nose. "Yeah."

Rick kissed her on the cheek and squeezed her tight. "That a girl. That's my brave girl." He let her go then went back and knelt beside the propane tank. "Okay Angie, go over there and see what you can find. But whatever you do, don't yell out if you need help with something. We don't wanna call any attention to ourselves. Okay?"

"Alright."

"Okay."

"Here. Take your thermos." Angie handed Rick the thermos then turned and trudged off towards the barn.

It was a painful, ten minute walk through freezing cold tundra—she couldn't feel a frickin' thing from her waist down. When she finally got to the barn, she went around to the back, but the back door was fastened with a metal chain and a Masterlock. "Oh great, now what am I supposed to do?"

Just then, she heard Rick screaming, calling her name over and over again. She dropped the lock and ran as quick as she could around to the front of the barn. "Rick! What's the matter? I thought we weren't supposed to scream?"

As she looked out across the field, she saw Rick standing rigid, his hands stuck straight in the air above his head. There was a figure of a man approaching from the highway, a rifle pointed squarely at Rick's head. "Oh no, Rick, get down!"

The first shot rang out like thunder. Rick ducked, covered, and dove to the ground. Angie screamed and ran towards him, shouting, "don't shoot! Don't shoot! Rick, get behind the tanks!"

Rick crawled on his belly and hid behind the pair of massive, green metal tanks.

The man took a moment to reload his rifle then brought it back up and fired again. But, the bullet hit the tank and pierced through the metal and a bath of ammonia came spewing from the puncture. A few seconds later, the tank exploded, erupting into a ball of smoke and flames. The shock wave from the blast was so powerful that it knocked Angie onto her back. She lay there stunned and trembling, whimpering a soft cry as the fire roared and crackled, clouds of black smoke billowing off into the now ashen sky. She lifted her head and rolled onto her stomach, her eyes desperately searching for Rick, but he was nowhere in sight. All she saw before her was a pile of twisted metal, burning furiously, the orange glow of the fire reflecting off an endless stretch of pallid white.

Chapter 15

The Four Points

At first, the beeping was only a murmur off in some distant, dream-like surrounding. But then, it began to grow louder, like the screaming of a train charging through a tunnel. Monty was on the tracks, his wrists and ankles bound to the rails. He knew he had to get out of the way or the train would run him over, but he couldn't move his body. He couldn't even turn over. Then, he saw it through the black, oval-shaped darkness—the single light of the train, whistling, as it charged through the tunnel. He kicked and pulled against the ropes that were binding him, screaming for Vicky, calling out her name. But, it was too late. The train was upon him. He could actually feel the vibration of the rails against his bones. But, just as the train came plunging from the darkness, Monty opened his eyes and suddenly awoke. The train had vanished, replaced by a hazy, white vapor, like the heat from the asphalt rising up after a summer rainstorm. He opened his mouth and let out a soft whimper, as the pain from being conscious slowly crept into his muscles. He lifted his head and looked down the line of his body—a thin, white sheet covered him from his toes to his neck. Where was he? What was happening? Was he alive or was he dead?

He tried to sit up and roll over onto his stomach, but something kept his hands pinned by his knees. He looked down. There were bright orange straps secured around his wrists and ankles, fastened to metallic bars lining the side of a bed. He tried lifting his hands and pulling up on the bindings, but they were on so tight that the fabric cut into his flesh.

Panic settled in. He started to struggle harder and harder, panting and pulling, moaning and groaning, his head floundering from side to side. But he was too weak, his body too exhausted, and he could feel his eyes rolling into the back of his head. The walls closed in, the light started to tunnel, and everything light began to turn dark again. No, no, he had to stay calm, he had to stop struggling, or he was going to pass out. He immediately relaxed and allowed his body to sink back into the bedding, breathing slowly in and out with the pulse of his heart.

There was a noise at the door, something squeaky, like the sound of tennis shoes against a wet, tile floor. He looked up. A full-figured woman dressed in a green, baggy uniform, walked with purpose to the side of his bed. As she reached up, she pulled down a plastic clipboard that was inside a cubby mounted to the wall behind his head. "Okay sweetie," she said without even looking at him, "do you know where you are?"

Who was she talking to? Was there someone else in the room? Was she talking to him?

"You're at the Denver County General Hospital. Do you know how you got here?"

Hospital? Why was he at the hospital? He didn't ask to be taken here.

"You arrived in an ambulance with your friend, uh"—she paused and flipped through the pages of the clipboard—"Robby...Robby Collins. Do you remember a Mr. Collins?"

Monty felt a chill as the memories came back to him—the store, the call, the booze, the pills. No, this couldn't be happening. He wasn't supposed to be here. He was supposed to be dead.

"Now Mr. Miller," the nurse said, leaning over him, her sour breath blowing against the front of his neck. "It is very important you tell us if there was anything else you swallowed besides the Zoloft and Trazodone. Can you remember if there was anything else? Anything at all?"

Monty tried to open his mouth, but it felt like his lips were Super-Glued, cemented shut by a seal of dried mucus.

"Please answer the question, Mr. Miller. Was there anything else? Anything at all?"

Monty turned away and let out a soft whimper. He shut his eyes and shook his head.

"Are you sure?"

Monty nodded. He could feel tears coming, pounding against his eyelids like an unwelcome guest pounding at the door.

"Drugs, pills...anything like that?"

"No!" Monty finally shouted, the tears from his eyes now dripping down his cheeks. "I didn't take anything! Nothing!"

"Alright Mr. Miller, just calm down. There's no need to get excited. Now, can I get you anything? Water? An extra blanket?"

Monty looked down at the straps secured around his wrists and ankles then tugged on them slightly and tried to lift his head. "Why am I tied down like this?"

"It's for your own protection, sweetie. You were in pretty bad shape when they brought you in. The doctor didn't want you trying to get up and hurting yourself."

"But I can't move."

"I know honey."

"How am I supposed to go to the bathroom? I can't move."

"I know sweetie."

Monty began to tug and pull against the bindings, kicking and writhing like a rabid squirrel. "I can't fucking move," he shouted, as globs of spit went flying onto his chin. "Why are you doing this to me? I didn't do anything."

"Please don't raise your voice Mr. Monty. We have other patients on this floor besides you who are trying to rest."

"Fuck your patients. I want out of this. Let me the fuck out of this." He kicked and pulled harder and harder, the straps like sandpaper chafing his wrists. "Let me out of here. Let me the fuck out of here. I don't deserve to be treated like this. I didn't do anything wrong."

The nurse tried to restrain him. She put one hand on his chest and the other on his head. "Monty, stop it, stop fighting. You're going to hurt yourself."

"Take your fucking hands off me! You bitch! You cunt! Let me out of here! Let me the fuck out of here!"

"Monty, stop it. Just stop it."

"I am not resisting arrest! I am not resisting arrest! Victoria! Victoria!"

"Fine," the nurse said, backing away from him. "If you're going to act like a crazy person then we're going to treat you like one." She took the clipboard and shoved it back in the cubby then turned away from Monty and moved towards the door.

"Wait. Where are you going?" Monty said.

She stopped at the doorway then flipped off the light switch. "Try to get some sleep. The doctor will be in to check on you later."

"Wait. Don't leave me like this. Please, don't leave me."

She exited the room and pulled the door closed.

Monty lay there, scared, confused, utterly helpless, as his eyes darted around the now pitch-black room. They couldn't do this, could they? Wasn't it illegal? Wasn't it a violation of his civil rights? He wasn't a threat to them. He wasn't a criminal. He wasn't some sick schizophrenic waving a gun. He was a good kid, first in his class, Phi Kappa Phi honor society, those gold colored cords tied to his cap and gown. Why were they doing this? Why was this happening? What the fuck did he do wrong?

He tugged and pulled against the fabric bindings, panting and groaning, thrashing and squirming, sucking in a barrage of shallow, labored breaths. No, no, he had to calm down, he couldn't get excited. No sudden movements, no frenetic thoughts, just cool, calm, and under control. He stopped struggling and focused on his breathing, letting his heart catch up to his breath. Okay, okay, that's it. He could do this...he had to stay calm...nice and easy now.

He lifted his head and looked down at his forearms and noticed that the strap on his right wrist was looser than the one on his left. He shifted his body toward the looser binding and lifted his right hand as far as it would go. If he could just reach the strap with his mouth, he might be able to unbuckle it with his teeth. He strained his neck and inched closer and closer until his chin was nearly touching his chest. He touched the strap with the tip of his tongue and somehow managed to get it inside his mouth. As he closed his eyes, he bit down on the fabric. The strap tasted foul and bitter like a pair of sweat-soaked socks. Using his tongue as a sort of conveyor, he gathered the loose fabric into tight spools inside his mouth. Then he took a deep breath and jerked his head backward, heaving and hauling like a dog playing tug-of-war. With each additional pull, the strap got looser, until he could hear the Velcro beginning to come undone. Yes, it was working. The strap was breaking. It was beginning to come apart.

He bit down harder and tugged more rapidly, the Velcro hissing, popping, and pulling apart. But, his tongue became tired and his jaw started aching and tears of pain began to roll from his eyes. Shit, he was losing his grip. The strap was slipping and he was finding it more and more difficult to catch his breath. He had to rest for a minute and let his mouth recuperate. If the strap fell to the floor, he'd never be able to get it back. He stopped pulling and just lay there quietly, breathing slowly in and out through his nose.

After a few minutes, he regained his composure then shifted into position for one last go. He was almost there. He almost had it. A couple more inches and it would break for sure. He closed his eyes and clenched down on the fabric then reared his head back as hard as he could. The Velcro gave way and the strap unfastened, slipping through the buckle and falling to the floor. Yes, it worked. His right arm was free. Okay, okay, now the left. He turned his head, shifted his body, and reached his hand across his chest. But he couldn't reach his arm. The left strap was too tightly fastened—it had his hand pinned all the way down by his knee. But he couldn't give up. He had to get to it. He was almost there. He was almost free.

He dug his heels into the mattress and lifted his butt completely off the bed. In one quick turn, he thrust his pelvis upward and turned his entire body in mid air. He came crashing back down onto the mattress and reached over across his hip. It was just enough. He could feel the strap with his fingers. He grabbed a hold of it and began to peel it away. Once he found the right angle, the strap came off easily. He pulled and pulled until finally it unraveled and the strap broke free and fell to the floor.

He grabbed his knees, pulled himself upright, and started on the ankle straps as quickly as he could. But he heard something out in the hallway, the sound of feet moving past the door. He froze, his mouth open, his eyes fixed on the door. He lay back down, pressed his head into the pillow, and pulled the sheet up over his neck.

Out of the corner of his eye, he saw a head poke in through the doorframe—it floated there for a minute then went away. He waited a few moments for the footsteps to become distant, then sat up and went to work on his ankles. Now that he had both hands, it was much easier, and he was able to free his ankles in about ten seconds flat. He swung his legs out around the side of the mattress then went to stand up, but quickly realized he was still attached. There were a bunch of tubes connected to small, metallic nipples protruding from blue pieces of circular tape attached to his stomach and chest.

He began ripping them off, but they didn't come off easily. In fact, it felt like he was tearing off a piece of his skin. He finally got off all twelve of them, but when he went to stand up, he realized he was still attached. Now what? He looked down at his arm. There was a tube running out from the vein in his forearm up to a plastic bag hanging from a hook on something that looked like a glorified coat rack. Damn, it was the IV.

He took a deep breath and started digging away the tape from his forearm, but it was even stickier than the pieces that were stuck to his chest. He'd never get it off at this rate. But wait. The IV was connected to a plastic adapter sticking outside of the tape. If he could remove the tube from the adapter then maybe he wouldn't have to pull the needle out. He grabbed the adapter and twisted it carefully, then pulled out the tube and freed his arm.

He scanned the room and began moving forward, but he was so sore that he could barely walk. It felt like he'd been dropped from the top floor of a twenty-story building then trampled by a marching band and run over with a car. He put one wobbly foot in front of the other until he got to the end of the bed, when he realized that something was wrong. He was still attached. Something still had him, pulling at the tip of his dick. He lifted his gown and looked down at his boxers—there was a tube running out from underneath his crotch.

He grabbed the tube and gently pulled it downward, but it was stuck on the inside. What the hell was going on? He tried pulling it again, only this time harder, but it felt like he was going to pull off his dick. He released the tension and sat down on the mattress, the panic beginning to bubble inside his head. Okay, okay, calm down, calm down, he had to think, he had to concentrate. It went in, right? So, somehow it had to come out.

He stood back up and pulled a little harder, but the pain was excruciating. It felt like a knife tearing into his nuts. But he had to do it. He had to get rid of it. He had to pull it out. Who knew what they might do to him if he stayed here any longer? They might put him in an institution where he'd be strapped down to a bed for more than a month. No, no, he couldn't do that. He couldn't allow that to happen. He needed his alcohol. He had to get home.

He wrapped his fingers around the plastic tubing then began to pull down as hard as he could. The tube gradually slid out, but his palms were so damp with perspiration that he couldn't seem to keep a good enough grip. So, he wrapped a piece of his gown around the tubing then wiped it dry and gathered up the slack. Okay, one last tug. No time to be a pussy. He closed his eyes and pulled it down. The tears welled inside his eyes and he began to let out a high-pitched moan. The tube slid out farther and farther, until finally it came out completely and dropped to the floor.

He stood there trembling, looking down at the tubing that was coiled in a small puddle of tears and blood. He lifted his gown and brought his hand against his boxers. His crotch was numb and damp with blood. He opened the fly to make sure he wasn't hemorrhaging. He wasn't, but his dick had shrunk to the size of a snail. Would he have permanent damage? Would he ever be able to use the bathroom again? Fuck it. Who cared? It didn't really matter. The only thing that mattered was getting the hell out of here.

He dropped his gown and tiptoed towards the doorway, then pushed open the door and peered down the hall. His eyes locked with a nurse who was sitting behind a large rectangular console that was filled with computers and stacks of brown files. The nurse stood up and started shouting, waving her hands and calling for help.

Monty turned and bolted down the hallway, his bare feet slapping against the cold, tile floor. Where was he going? What was he doing? He didn't know, but wherever it was, he had to get there as quick as he could. His legs were water, his head was oatmeal, and he had to slide his hands along the edge of the walls so he wouldn't spill out into the middle of the hall. A thunderous roar materialized behind him. It was the sound of jiggling keys and heavy black boots stampeding across squeaky, clean hospital floors. He could see something ahead. It was an exit, the door lit up by a sign with a red neon glow. When he got to it, he lowered his shoulder and smashed into the heavy wooden doors. But nothing happened. The doors didn't open and so he tried searching for the doorknobs, but there were none. He took a step back and planted his foot into the center of the door, his bare flesh slapping against the wood. Nothing happened. The doors were solid. They wouldn't open. He stepped back again and winded up to plant another, but just then, he felt a crushing blow to his lower back. His knees folded, his legs crumbled, and his entire body went flying into the door. He tried to recover and push himself upward, but was held down by an overwhelming force. He turned his head and look behind him. It was the weight of three men in blue polyester, starch-stiff shirts, and heavy black boots. One had his knee pressed in between Monty's shoulder blades, one hand gripping his head, the other squeezing his neck. Another had Monty's hands bound behind him, his fat knee driving into the small of Monty's back. Monty kicked and squirmed, screaming at them to get the hell off of him, but they only pressed harder until he was completely immobile.

In one sudden sweeping motion, they flipped him over and lifted him up by his ankles and wrists. Like a hog on a stick, they carried him down the fluorescent-lit hallway, Monty kicking and screaming, bullets of spit shooting from his lips. When they got him back to the room, they tossed him like a rag doll through the air and on top of the bed. As they swarmed in on him like a pack of hyenas, their sharp fingernails and elbows dug into his flesh. One grabbed his wrists and pinned them by his earlobes while another planted his knee in the center of his chest. The third went to the foot of the bed and forced his legs wide open, while a pair of nurses fastened the straps efficiently around his ankles. When they were done with his legs, they went around to his forearms, and with the help of the security guards, pinned his hands by his hips. Monty tried to resist, but they were too strong for him. He was completely helpless, his arms by his side, his legs secured to the bed. The wound on his chin was now wide open and he could feel the blood trickling down his neck. But the nurses didn't stop. They crouched to the floor and picked up the bindings, then fastened the straps around both of his wrists.

"Alright," one of them said, stepping away from him. "He's secure."

The men in blue polyester eased their weight off of him then slowly stepped away from the bed. They all just stood there for a moment with looks of disgust on their faces, folding their arms and shaking their heads. He felt like a freak in some circus sideshow, pulling at the straps and writhing around in the bed. Why were they doing this? Why was this happening? Why were they treating him like he was a fucking animal?

He kicked and pulled harder and harder, the fabric of the straps cutting into his skin. All of a sudden, it became too much for him; his breath began to shorten and his muscles went limp. It felt like he was being sucked down into the bedding, his body disappearing into a bottomless pit. He couldn't even keep his eyes open, he was so damn exhausted. He just gave up and quit trying to resist. As he slowly drifted in and out of consciousness, he could hear the conversation between the guards and the nurse.

"He's been here before," the nurse said, looking down at him. "He's some kind of engineer."

"What's wrong with him? He on drugs or something?"

"No. Alcoholic."

"That's a shame. That's a god damn shame."

"Yeah. We get all kinds in here."

Chapter 16

The Morning After

Monty could feel the presence of someone beside him, the cadence of their breathing dueling with the heart monitor machine beeping by his head. He opened his eyes and craned his neck forward and saw the silhouette of a man sitting beside his bed. The man was slumped over in a chair, his head tilted slightly forward, his hands folded together like he was deep in prayer.

Monty tried to say something, but his mouth was so dehydrated that he couldn't get enough saliva to even move his tongue. So he let out a moan that sounded more like a whimper, a soft, pathetic cry for help.

The man stirred. His posture straightened. He lifted his head and moved into the light. "Monty," he said, "are you awake?"

Monty recognized the man's voice. It belonged to his father. But it couldn't be his dad, could it? Why would he be here?

Monty turned his head as far as he could sideways and let the light come to his blood-pooled eyes. "Dad, is that you?"

"Yes Monty, it's me."

Monty blinked. He couldn't believe what he was seeing. Where was he? Was he at home? He looked down at the white blanket covering his body, at the series of plastic tubes and wires running out from underneath his blue hospital gown. "Where am I?" he said, his voice a bit shaky.

"You're in the hospital, Monty."

"Where? In Florida?"

His dad dropped his head and removed his glasses, wiping the tears from his tired, jet-lagged eyes. "No Monty, no son. You're in Denver, at the General Hospital."

"What am I doing here?"

"Don't you remember? Don't you remember talking to Robby?"

Monty looked away and moved his eyes towards the ceiling, focusing on a fly that was circling just below the corner of the wall. His stomach began to turn as the images flashed across his consciousness like the pieces of a puzzle that he didn't want to solve—the accident, the liquor store, the phone call with Robby, the pills, the booze, the straps, the catheter, the men in blue polyester uniforms. He lifted his arms and pulled against the straps that were binding him—the corners of the fabric had now cut red lines into his skin. This couldn't be real. This couldn't be happening. Why was he still here? Why was he still strapped down?

He turned towards his dad, his lips quivering, his body shaking, the pain from the straps shooting down his arms. "Dad?"

"Yes? What is it?"

"What are you doing here?"

"I'm here for you, Monty."

"But why—I mean, when? When did you get here?"

"Early this morning. Your mother and I came as soon as we could."

"What? Mom's here? Why? I don't understand."

His dad turned away and put back on his glasses, his thin, sun-dried lips quivering like a frightened child's. "Well," he said, trying to maintain his composure, trying to be the man Monty knew as a kid—the man who never showed any emotion, who believed that crying was a sign of weakness. "Robby called us and told us what happened. We got out here as quick as we could."

"Why am I still strapped down like this? What's going on?"

"I don't know, Monty. I don't know."

"I can't move, dad."

"I know, son. I know."

"I can't move."

"It's okay." His dad stood up and moved towards the doorway, his brown dress shoes scuffing against the hospital floor. "Let me see if I can get someone."

"Wait—where are you going? Don't leave me here, please."

"I'll be right back. Let me just see if I can get the nurse, okay?"

"Please don't leave me."

"I'll be right back, I promise."

His dad turned away, shuffled through the doorway, and left Monty alone, alone with his thoughts. He tried not to think about the straps around his wrists and ankles, but it was impossible to do when they were on so tight. They were like barbed wire, their sharp, serrated edges cutting into the flesh of his wrists and ankles, digging deeper and deeper with every slight tug.

He could hear his dad's voice in the hallway, talking to a woman with a high-pitched, nasal whine. Gradually, the voices became louder, until it seemed they were right inside the room. Then, Monty caught a whiff of an oppressively strong perfume that smelled like one of those rose-scented Glade Plug-ins. He opened his eyes. A woman was standing beside him, a nurse, but a different one from the night before. This one was Latino, short and stubby, with thick globs of eyeliner like the legs of a tarantula jutting out from her eyelids. She moved beside Monty and adjusted the bag of fluids hanging from the metal stand parked behind his head. "Good morning Mr. Monty," she said, without acknowledging him, inspecting the series of tubes running out from underneath his gown. "And how are we feeling today?"

What? Was she kidding? How did she think he was feeling? He was strapped down to a bed.

"Do you know where you are Mr. Monty?"

"Yes, my dad said—"

"You're at the Denver County General Hospital. Do you remember how you got here?" She hobbled to other side of the bed and punched in some buttons on the machine that was beeping by his head. "You came in an ambulance, Mr. Monty. Your blood alcohol level was at a 0.5."

"Is that high?" his dad said, moving in from the doorway, his hair-covered arms crossed tightly over his chest.

The nurse laughed as if something was funny, as if this was all one big, fucking joke. "Yes, Mr. Miller. The lethal limit is 0.4. Your son is lucky to be alive."

Lucky? What the hell was she talking about? He wasn't lucky to be alive. He was supposed to be dead.

"How much longer does he have to stay in those restraints?" his dad asked.

The nurse picked up the clipboard from the little plastic cubby, then licked the tip of her finger, and started flipping through the pages. "Let's see, it looks like we did two blood tests—one last night and one this morning—around five." She checked her watch and mulled over the numbers. "That means we should be getting the lab results back within the hour."

"And then what?" his dad said.

She popped the clipboard back into the cubby then moved back to the machine beeping beside his head. "And then, if his alcohol levels are low enough, we should be able to get the keys to the restraints and have Mr. Monty ready for discharge."

"Discharge? Really? So soon?"

"Yes sir."

"Don't you think he needs to stay here for a couple more days for monitoring?"

What? Monty looked up at his dad. A couple more days? What was he talking about? Was he insane?

The nurse chuckled. "I'm sorry Mr. Miller, but this is a hospital, not a hotel."

"Excuse me?" his dad said, uncrossing his forearms, a green vein the size of an extension cord protruding from his leathered forehead. "What did you just say to me?"

The nurse took one look at his dad and her silly grin quickly vanished and her posture stiffened like a frightened cat. "I'm sorry Mr. Miller, I didn't—"

"How dare you. How dare you say that to me. You see that kid right there? Huh?" He shot out his arm and pointed at Monty. "You see him?"

The nurse glanced back behind her and solemnly nodded. "Yes sir, I see him."

"That's my son, alright? He's a human being for Christ's sake. Not some number on your god damn chart."

"Yes Mr. Miller, I understand, I'm very—"

"He deserves to be treated with a little respect."

"Mr. Miller, please lower your voice. We have other patients on this floor besides your son who are trying to rest."

His dad threw his head back and let out an insane, little chuckle. "Oh, I'm sorry, but are those other patients strapped down like my son is? Huh?"

"No sir, they are not, but—"

"But what? Why do you have him locked down like this? He's my son for Christ's sake. He's not a god damn criminal."

"Mr. Miller, if you just lower your voice, then I'll explain."

His dad withdrew and unbowed his shoulders, folding his arms back across his chest. "Okay, fine, explain."

The nurse let out a deep sigh and pinched the bridge of her nose. "Mr. Miller..."

"Yes? I'm waiting."

"Mr. Miller, your son was out of control last night. He was a danger to himself and to the employees of this hospital. We had to take immediate action. It was either the restraints or we call the police and let them deal with him, which I know is not what you or your son wanted. Is it?"

His dad didn't say anything and just snorted. His nose was turned up so high it looked like it might disappear into his forehead.

"Now, like I said, I will go and check with the lab and if Monty's alcohol levels are down, which I believe they will be since we've been flushing saline through him all night long, I will talk with the doctor and see if we can't get him out of those restraints. Okay?"

His dad said nothing and just scowled at the floor.

"Mr. Miller?"

"What?"

"Is that alright?"

"Yeah, yeah, fine."

She turned toward Monty and batted her tarantula-covered eyelids. "Is that alright with you Mr. Monty?"

Monty nodded.

"Okay then, you just sit tight and we'll have you out of here in no time."

She forced a smile then shuffled towards the doorway, stopping just short in front of Monty's dad. His dad looked down at her in disgust then moved in from the doorway, allowing her to get through.

"Dad?" Monty said, pulling on the bindings, lifting his head up as far as he could.

"Yes, Monty?"

"I'm cold."

His dad's face immediately softened—all the rage just melted away. He let out a deep sigh and moved in from the doorway, his shoulders slumped over, his head bowed to the floor. He grabbed the bedding at Monty's ankles and pulled it up just below his chin. "Is that okay?" he said, looking down at Monty, with a weak, uneasy smile.

"Yeah, thanks."

Monty quickly looked away and turned his eyes back towards the ceiling. He couldn't bear having his dad see him like this.

After a few minutes of awkward silence, his dad reached into his pocket and pulled out his phone. "I need to make a phone call," he said. "Will you be alright in here by yourself?"

Monty didn't look at him and just nodded. He could feel the tears pooling in the corners of his eyes.

"Okay, just yell out if you need anything."

"Alright."

His dad turned away and walked towards the doorway, but just as he was about to leave, Monty stopped him and said, "Wait, dad?"

His dad turned around, holding his cell phone, his eyes moistening like he was about to cry. "What is it?"

"Please get me out of here."

"I will, Monty. I will."

Chapter 17

Discharged

His dad kept his promise and got him discharged from the hospital around noon. The car ride back to the apartment was eerily quiet, neither Monty nor his dad uttered a single word. Monty kept his eyes shut and his breathing steady, trying not to think about the pain he'd just endured. Every now and then, he'd open his eyes, peer out the window, and watch the snow that was floating to the ground. It was a bleak day. The sun was hidden behind a curtain of hazy, white snow clouds. But it wasn't dark out—actually, it was just the opposite. The little bit of sunlight seemed to be amplified by the reflection of the snow on the ground. It made his eyes tear just to look at it, like looking through a pair of binoculars directly at the sun. He grabbed his hood and pulled it down over his eyelids, retreating like a gopher into its hole.

About ten minutes later, the car stopped and the engine halted. Monty pulled off his hood and began to look around. Where were they? They weren't at the apartment. It looked like they were in a parking lot somewhere downtown. "Where are we?" he said, looking out the window at the tall buildings cutting into the sky.

"We're at the hotel," his dad said as he cut the engine.

"What are we doing here?"

"I have to get some things."

"Right now?"

"Yeah, right now. Come on, we're going in."

"Can I just sit here until you get back?"

"No. I need you to come in with me. Are you okay to walk?"

Monty grimaced and peeled his head from the headrest then grabbed the door handle and pushed it open. As he pulled himself out of the car, he began to feel woozy, the blood in his head draining down to his toes. Then something rose inside him, something hot and chunky surging into his throat. He fell to his knees and pressed his hands into the pavement, bucking forward like a mad bull. The bile came, sharp and acidic, like a stream of yellow jackets spewing from his throat. He coughed and gagged and lurched repeatedly forward, every vein in his neck about to explode.

His dad rushed around the car and crouched beside him, placing his hand on the back of his head. "Monty, are you okay? Are you alright?"

Monty couldn't respond. He was right in the middle of it. He couldn't speak. He couldn't breathe. All he could do was bend forward with his mouth open, the bile forming a small pool just beneath his nose. He did a couple more heaves until there was nothing left to vomit—no bile, no mucus, no water, no food. Then, using his dad as support, he pushed himself up, holding his stomach like he was a pregnant woman in labor.

"Monty, are you sure you can walk?"

"Yeah, I can manage."

"Okay, just take it easy. One step at a time."

Together, he and his dad walked across the hotel parking lot, Monty hobbling along like an eighty-year-old man. His face twitched, his legs trembled, and the bile began to crust inside the corners of his mouth. A group of valets working under the hotel's check-in canopy immediately stopped working when they saw Monty and his dad approach. He must look pretty bad, he thought, wearing nothing but bloodstained boxers underneath a vomit-splattered hospital gown. But what was he supposed to do? His dad wanted him to come in with him. Why didn't he just let him stay in the god damn car?

As they walked under the canopy, the valets started whispering to one another out of the sides of their mouths. But Monty didn't look at them. He kept his head down and his eyes forward, concentrating as he made his way through a set of automatic revolving doors. Once inside, he followed his dad down a wide, marble-floored lobby towards a bank of gold-painted elevators at the end of the hall.

"You doing alright?" his dad asked, glancing behind him.

"Yeah."

"Okay, we're almost there."

They got to the end of the hall and his dad hit the elevator button, while Monty took a quick breather, resting his forehead up against the wall. The elevator beeped and the doors slid open. Monty stepped in first and his dad followed. Just as the doors were about to close, a group of businessmen came up behind them, smiling, laughing, and telling crude jokes. His dad stuck his hand out in front of the sensors, keeping the elevators doors from closing. "Going up?" he asked.

They were about to get in until they saw Monty, at which point, they shook their heads and said, "No thanks, we'll take the next one up."

"Suit yourself." His dad moved his hand away from the sensors then took a step back as the elevator doors shut.

The ride to the fifteenth floor was unbearably quiet. Monty's dad looked like a marine standing at attention, his feet pressed together, his hands folded behind his back. Something was wrong. Something was definitely shady. What were they even doing here? What was so important that his dad had to get right now?

The elevator beeped and the doors slid open. Monty followed his dad down a long, dimly lit hall. They came to a door, number 1520. His dad pulled out a key card and shoved it into the metal slot. The red light turned green and his dad removed the key card then turned the knob and opened the door. As they walked into the room, Monty began to get that feeling, like everything in his life was about to come crashing down. And then it did, like a fucking earthquake bringing down a building right on top of his head. They were all there, sitting in the room, waiting for him—Robby, Susan, his mom, and some woman he'd never even seen. Bastards. He should've known. It was a fucking ambush. His dad must've had this planned the entire time.

Instincts took over and Monty turned for the doorway, but before he could get there, his dad grabbed him by the collar and spun back him around. "Monty!" he shouted. "What are you doing?"

"Fuck you," Monty screamed as he plunged his forearm forward, snapping his dad's head back against the wall. "Fuck all of you."

He went again for the door, but Robby was already on him. Like a linebacker, he tackled him, driving him down into the floor.

"Get off of me," Monty screamed, writhing beneath him, trying to reclaim his arms.

"Come on Monty," Robby said. "Don't do this. Calm down. Just calm down."

"Get the fuck off me."

"Monty, stop it. Just stop it."

Robby pressed his knee against Monty's cheekbone, driving his face down into the floor. Monty tried to break free but he couldn't—he was too depleted from being strapped down all night long. The more he struggled, the more his body began to wither, like an earthworm shriveling under the scorching, summer sun. Like the air being let out of an air mattress, he completely deflated and sunk down into the floor.

"Are you done?" Robby said, leaning over him, his fat knee pressing against Monty's ear. "Are you finished?"

Monty nodded his submission. He was so tired, he could no longer move.

"If I let you up, are you going to cooperate?"

He nodded once more.

"Alright then."

Robby slowly peeled his weight off of him, allowing Monty to roll over on his back. He lay for a few seconds just staring up at the ceiling, taking in long, deliberate swallows of breath. Once he caught his breath, he rolled over onto his stomach then, using the wall as leverage, he pushed himself up.

"You okay?" Robby said, looking at him suspiciously, his body positioned between Monty and the door.

"Yeah."

"You ready to get this over with?"

"No."

"Well too bad, 'cause we're doing it anyway."

"Whatever."

Chapter 18

The Intervention

His mom was sitting on a couch beneath a window that had a panoramic view of the mountains and downtown. She was crying softly and clutching a crumpled-up piece of tissue that was trembling between her wrinkled hands. Monty did his best not to look at her. He couldn't bear seeing her like this. Her face was worn, her skin was sallow, and she had deep indentations under both eyes. If Monty didn't know any better, he'd say she was a junkie, just another hopeless addict looking for the next high. And the worst thing was, he knew he did that to her—he was the reason she looked the way she did. If only he could apologize and tell her that he loved her—tell her he was sorry for all the horrible things he did, then maybe, just maybe she'd stop blaming herself for all of his depravity, maybe she could forget about him and move on with her life. Why was she doing this…trying to make him feel guilty…sitting there, crying, and feeling sorry for herself? This wasn't her choice. It had nothing to do with her. Why did she always have to make everything her fault?

He clenched his fists and walked towards the sofa keeping his eyes focused squarely on the floor. When he got about halfway into the room, someone called to him with a thick,

Texan twang that reminded him of Laura Bush. He turned to his right. A chubby woman with freckles was standing beside him wearing a red, poufy perm and a bright, phony smile. "You must be Monty," she said with her hand extended, the freckles like leaches sucking on her skin. "My name's Deborah. How do you do?"

Monty took her hand and gently squeezed it. "Nice to meet you," he said, his eyes turning away. That was a lie. It wasn't nice to meet her. Everything about this woman was infuriating—her perfume, her clothes, that phony fucking smile. He wasn't an idiot. He knew where this was going. He'd been through this exercise at least once before. The woman was an interventionist, a so-called facilitator, a bearer of false hope and counterfeit hugs. Her job was to get Monty out of the room and into rehab, and if successful, she'd take home for herself a nice little fare; something on the order of five thousand dollars, which, including the first class flight and free hotel room, made this a nice little trip. The only problem was, she didn't know Monty. She didn't know he'd already made up his mind. The only way he was going back was if he was in a straight jacket. There was no chance in hell he'd go back on his own accord.

Deborah put her hand on Monty's shoulder and slowly guided him to the couch. "Why don't you have a seat and we'll go ahead and get started?"

Monty conceded and walked towards the sofa then sat down on the cushion between his dad and his mom. At this point, he figured it was better to cooperate than to try to put up a fight. In less than an hour, this charade would be over and he could get back to his apartment and back to his scotch.

"You going to be alright?" Deborah said, still smiling, positioning an armchair right in front of the couch.

Monty nodded and bent forward at the torso, cradling his head with both hands. He couldn't understand why his parents were doing this. Didn't they know any better by now? Did they really think he was going back to rehab after everything that's happened? They were smarter than that, weren't they? Why would they go through all this trouble just so he could turn them down?

He looked across the room and saw Robby staring at him, a wad of dip tucked under his lower lip. It had to be him. It had to be Robby. He must've put them up to this ridiculous charade. He probably gave his parents some line from the Big Book, some stupid cliché about hope and faith. Bastard. Who did he think he was, some kind of martyr? Why'd he always have to get in the fucking way?

As Deborah eased her fat ass into the armchair, it made an obnoxious stretching sound against the leather. "I suppose you know why we're all here today, Monty. I'm what you'd call a professional interventionist. My job is to help people in situations such as yourself find and accept the treatment that they so desperately deserve. Your family is very concerned about your well being and they want to do everything in their power to get you feeling healthy again." She paused and folded her hands neatly in front of her, making a disgusting gurgling sound with her throat. "You are a very, very sick young man, Monty. Do you realize that? Do you realize how close you are to dying?"

"Well, that's kind of the whole point, isn't it?" Monty said flatly.

"What? What's the point?"

"Dying—that's the whole point. What do you think I've been trying to do?"

The tension in the room immediately tightened. Monty could feel the glare of his dad's eyes. "Don't say that," his dad said, stiffening his posture. "You don't mean that."

"Of course I mean it."

Deborah crossed her legs at the ankles and leaned forward in her chair. "Monty, drinking yourself to death is no way to die. It is a slow and painful death, and could take years, even decades to do."

"I disagree," Monty said academically, like a professor lecturing on alcoholic affairs. "I think all I need is another month or two."

Monty could feel his mom's body trembling next to him, her faint sobbing escalating into a shrill, heart-twisting cry. "Why are you saying this?" she said, looking up at him, dabbing the tissue underneath her eyes. "Why are you doing this to yourself?"

"Because."

"Because why, Monty? Why?"

"Because I have to, mom. I just have to."

"But why?"

"Because I deserve it! Can't you understand that? I deserve to die!"

The room grew still and uncomfortably quiet. The glare of ten, angry eyes were upon him now.

"You know, Monty," Deborah said, leaning forward, folding her hands just beneath her chin, "by killing yourself, you're not just ending your own life, but you're ending the lives of everyone around you. Everyone who loves you, who cares for you, who wants nothing but to see you get better, will be devastated, just devastated by your selfish actions. Do you understand that? Do you realize what you are putting your parents through?"

Monty said nothing. He just focused on a horseshoe coffee stain on the table in front of him.

"Monty, look at me," Deborah said. "Please look at me."

Monty lifted his head to meet his inquisitor's eyes. "What?"

"You don't have to live like this. You don't have to do this anymore. You still have a chance—a way out from under the maliciousness of this disease. There are people out there who can teach you. They can show you the steps to heal your mind, body, and soul. They can show you how to abandon your fears and insecurities and turn your will and life over to the care of God."

Oh for fuck's sake. Not this higher power crap again. Didn't she realize this wasn't his first time at the rodeo? Didn't she realize how long he'd been in the program? He probably knew more about this bullshit than she did.

"Now, I want you to trust me, Monty. Can you do that for me? Please open your heart, your mind, and your spirit and listen carefully to what I have to say. There is a place high in the foothills of the Rocky Mountains, a place for people caught in the vicious spiral of addiction and despair. And at this place, people such as yourself, who have lost their way and are drowning in the insidiousness of their own addictions, are able to restore their lives and bring back some semblance of sanity. It is a place of hope and redemption, a safe haven for those tormented by the brutality of their afflictions. It is a place called Sanctuary."

"You mean rehab?" Monty said, unimpressed.

"Yes, but it is not just any rehab. It is what we in the mental health care business call a dual diagnosis facility—a place that treats not only the addiction, but the source of the addiction. They can help you, Monty. They can help you find peace and understanding. They can help you regain your life again. Hundreds and hundreds of people have gone through the doors of Sanctuary and come out on the other end revitalized, renewed, rejuvenated. You can be one of those people, Monty. I just know you can."

Monty snickered at the notion. A dual diagnosis facility? Was that her offer? She was going to have to do a lot better than that.

"Now before you say anything, Monty, I want you to hear from your mother and father. And I want you to listen very carefully to the message they are trying to convey. Once they are finished, I want you to think long and hard about the choices you are making and the impact they have on the people in your life."

Deborah's eyes disengaged from Monty's. She sat back in her chair and looked around the room. "Okay, so who wants to go first? Mr. Miller, are you ready to go?"

His dad looked up from the paper he was holding. He took his glasses out from his front shirt pocket then pushed them up to the bridge of his nose.

"Alright Mr. Miller," Deborah said. "Just take your time and whenever you're ready, you can begin."

His dad cleared his throat and wiped his forehead, peering down at the paper trembling in his hand. "Monty," he began somewhat flatly, like a politician reading from a script. "It has been nearly four years since the first time you called in the middle of the night threatening suicide. Since then, I have been through the deepest, darkest corners of hell with you and this disease. Every night your mother and I wait for the call from the coroner's office to tell us that our son's body was found dead on the side of the road. Do you know what that is like? To get up every day wondering if today is the day that your child is going to die? You have to know what that does to us. You are killing us, Monty—both your mother and I. We just can't take it anymore. Our bodies can no longer handle the stress. We're too old and too damn tired and this is the last time we're going to offer you any help. After this, there will be no more second chances. If you do not take this offer we are giving you today, you will be cut off completely from the family and you will no longer be welcome in my home. That means no more Christmas vacations, Thanksgiving dinners, credit card payments, or student loans. No more money period. It will all disappear. There will be nothing left but you and your liquor. You will become nothing more than a bum on the street."

His dad looked up from his paper, and for the first time in the entire monologue, it actually sounded like he was talking to him. "Is that what you want, Monty? To become one of those people living in the underpass, scrounging for food, begging for change? Because that's where you're headed if you keep going like this. That's where you'll end up if you don't stop now."

He relaxed his face and sank back against the cushions, his eyes returning to the script in his lap. "I'm sorry to be doing this, but you've forced me into it. I can't allow you to pull this family down. If we continue to let you and this disease ruin our lives, we will have no chance of survival. Please take this offer, Monty. Go to rehab. Go to Sanctuary. Find the reason behind your addiction. Find out the reason why you can't quit."

"You know the reason. Don't try and pretend like you don't."

"No, I don't, Monty. Please, tell me. I want to understand."

"You, of all people, should know better. You should know how impossible it is to quit. Like father like son, right?"

"What are you saying?"

"How many drinks did you have before you came here? How many cocktails did you have on the plane?"

His dad scoffed. "Oh please Monty, don't try and change this thing around. You're the one who needs help, not me."

"Oh really? What about that time you got pulled over, had to spend the night in the drunk tank?" His dad's posture immediately stiffened and his face flushed as red as a garden beet. "Yeah, I bet you thought I didn't know about that. I bet you thought that was just between you and mom. What do you guys think, I'm stupid or something?"

"You're right, Monty. I made a mistake. I shouldn't have been out driving around. But that was ten years ago. I learned my lesson and I haven't since drank and gotten behind the wheel of a car."

"Yeah right. You expect me to believe that?"

"It's the truth."

"You mean to tell me you don't drive around the block a few times after work sucking down one of those two liter bottles of wine?"

"No, of course not."

"Bullshit."

"Hey!" His dad shot up from the sofa, jamming an accusatory finger in Monty's face. "I'm not the one who just got out of the hospital. I'm not the one trying to kill myself. Look at you. Look at what you're wearing. You're in a god damn hospital gown."

"Alright," Deborah said, standing up from the armchair and waving her hand in a calming motion. "I need everyone to take a few deep breaths and just try and calm down." She walked over to where his dad was standing and placed her hand on his shoulder. "Dad, that means you too. Can you sit down for me?"

His dad shot her a look of exasperation that seemed to say, *why are you telling me to calm down?*

"It's okay," she said reassuringly, as if she could read his mind. "Everything's going to be okay. Just have a seat."

His dad threw his hands up in frustration then returned to his seat on the couch. Monty scooted as far as he could away from him. He could feel his anger permeating the room.

"That's right," Deborah said, returning to her armchair, breathing deeply in and out through her nose. "Everyone just relax. Breathe in and out, in and out. There. Does everyone feel better? Are we all ready to continue?"

"Are we done yet?" Monty blurted.

"No, Monty, we are not done. I still need you to hear from your mother. Can you do that for me? Can you listen to what your mother has to say?"

Monty let out a groan of irritation. How much more of this shit did he have to take?

"Alright, Cindy," Deborah said. "Are you ready?"

"I don't think I can," his mom said quivering, her frail, veiny hands trembling in her lap.

"Just take your time, Cindy. Focus on the words in front of you."

"I can't, I just can't."

Monty's dad leaned forward, reached across the couch, and grabbed her hand. "Come on honey," he said, "you can do it. Just read the words, please."

Monty could feel his mother's entire body trembling. Her sobbing was so unbearable it made him want to open the window and jump.

"Monty," she began, her voice shaky, barely audible. "You have no idea what you've done to me and your father. Your actions the past five years have been incomprehensible. The horrible things you've said to me on the phone are unforgivable. You have completely torn this family apart. If you do not accept this wonderful offer we are giving you, I will have no other choice but to turn my back on you. I will no longer accept you as my son. I know deep down inside your corroded soul, there is still a little piece of that sweet boy that I nurtured and cared for as a child. I know a little part of him is still in there just screaming to get out. Please for the sake of your soul and for the sake of our sanity, go to this facility in the mountains. Get better. Get help. Please." Her soft sobbing turned into a shrill weeping and she dropped her paper into her lap. "I'm sorry," she said, dabbing the tears away with her crumpled up tissue, "I can't read anymore. I just can't."

"Are you sure, Cindy?" Deborah said.

"Yes. I can't. I just can't."

"Okay, thank you, Cindy. I know how difficult that was. Monty? Did you hear what your mother just said?"

Monty nodded without looking up from his spot on the floor.

"So you know what's at stake here if you don't accept treatment?"

"Yeah, I get it. I'll be cut off. Fine. Now, are we done?"

"No, we are not done." Deborah glared at him for a few moments, clenching her jaw, and clasping her fists. Monty could tell he was starting to get to her. That phony smile had completely evaporated from her face. She took a deep breath then turned towards Robby and Susan sitting together on the edge of the bed. "Robby, Susan, would either of you like to say a few words?"

Robby popped up from the mattress, a Styrofoam spit cup in his left hand. "Yeah, I'd like to say a few words if you don't mind."

Oh great, thought Monty. Here we go again.

"Hey Monty. Hey." Robby started snapping his fingers. "Look at me man. Look at me god damnit."

"What?"

"You listen to me. You got one chance at this man. If you fuck this up, I ain't gonna be around to pick your ass up off the ground. You got me? I can't take this shit no more. It's too much and I just can't do it. I gotta worry about my recovery too, and I will be damned if I'm gonna let anything get in the way of that."

"That's right," Monty said. "It's all about you, isn't it Robby?"

"You're god damn right it is. I can't let nothing get in the way of my recovery, and right now, you're about as close to fucking that up as I've ever let anybody get in my entire life, and I just can't let that happen, not now, not after all I've been through with this shit. You're my best friend and I love you, but if you don't go to this place and get some treatment, you're on your own. And let me tell you, that's a scary fucking place to be; all alone with no one to turn to, nothing but that shame and guilt bouncing around in your head. Believe me man, I know. The time I was most scared in my life—it wasn't prison, fuck prison. Hell, prison saved my ass. You know when it was? It was when I was all alone with that fucking needle in my arm and that cold, steel barrel lodged down my throat."

"Yeah I know, Robby. I've heard your story before. Why don't you save it for someone who gives a shit? Save it for your fucking home group."

Robby threw down his spit cup and ripped across the carpet, getting right up in Monty's face. "You're my fucking home group! You are! This ain't a game, Monty. This is life and death. Don't you get that?"

"Yeah, I get it."

"So what? You just gonna kill yourself? Is that it?"

"Hey, you're finally catching on. Congratulations man. Maybe you're not as dumb as I thought."

"You think by killing yourself you're gonna bring back Victoria? Is that what you think?"

Monty's posture stiffened. The sound of her name was like a needle scraping the inside of his ear canal. "Leave her out of this. She's got nothing to do with this."

"That's bullshit. She's got everything to fucking do with this. What do you think she'd say about you trying to drink yourself to death? Huh?"

"I don't know."

"Yeah you do. You know exactly what she'd say. She'd tell you to quit being such a fucking pussy and get off your ass and do something with your life. That's what she'd fucking tell you, man."

"Fuck you, Robby."

"Fuck me? Fuck me? No. Fuck you. Fuck you Monty. You think she'd want you to just give up and throw your life away? Huh? And what about Tommy? You just gonna give up on him too?"

"Shut up Robby, I'm warning you."

"That kid loves you, man. You're the closest thing he's ever had to a real fucking father. Have you ever stopped to think how this would make him feel? No, you didn't think about that did you?" Robby paused then took a few steps backward and turned his attention towards the hotel door. "Well, why don't we ask him? Why don't we ask Tommy how it would make him feel?"

"What?"

"He's here. He's right outside in the hallway. Let's fucking ask him how it would make him feel."

Monty looked at the door then back at Robby, and for a second, he actually almost believed his lie. But then he quickly came to his senses. The kid was in New Mexico with his grandparents—there was no way in hell they'd bring him all the way out here. "You're full of shit," Monty said, slouching backwards, calling his bluff with a confident smile.

"Oh am I?" Robby smiled and reached into his pocket then pulled out his phone and flipped it open. "Care to make a wager on that?"

Monty looked at the phone. His heart began to flutter, his hands began to shake, and his eyes grew wide.

"Come on Monty, make a wager. How much you wanna bet he's not right outside that door?"

He knew right then that Robby was serious. He could tell by the sadistic look in his eyes.

"No wait," Monty said, reaching outward, like he was trying to pull Robby away from the door. "Don't do it. Please. I can't.

"Oh, yes you can, Monty. That kid just lost his mother and, now, you're gonna explain to him why he's about to lose his best god damn friend."

Robby looked at the display on his cell phone then turned toward Deborah and said, "They're here, Deborah. Is it okay if I bring 'em in?"

"Yes, Robby, go ahead. Bring them on in."

Monty shot up from his seat and pleaded with Deborah: "No please, I can't. I just can't."

"You have to."

"No, I can't."

"Yes, you can."

Robby walked to the door and removed the deadbolt, then grabbed the handle and opened the door. "Come on in ya'll," he said, as he held the door open. "We're right in here. Come on in."

It was Vicky's parents, Al and Martha. They walked in like they were in a funeral procession—heads down, hands folded, neither one of them uttering a single word. Tommy trailed in right after them, his little hand tugging at the back of his grandmother's black dress.

"Tommy," Robby said, getting down on one knee in the center of the room. "Can you come over here for a minute?"

Tommy looked around the room like a frightened rabbit then hid in terror behind his grandmother's leg.

"Please Tommy. It's just for a minute."

The kid looked to his grandmother for some kind of direction. His grandmother nodded and said, "it's okay honey. It'll be okay." Then, she placed her hand on the kid's shoulders and led him to Robby in the center of the room. Robby put his hands around the kid's tiny abdomen and leaned him back against the side of his knee. "I want you to take a good look,

Monty. Take a good look at this kid right here and tell him. Tell him that you're gonna die."

Monty stood frozen, completely paralyzed, unable to speak, unable to blink. It was eerie—the kid looked just like his mother, everything from his dark, curly hair to his chipmunk-like cheeks—same nose, same eyes, same olive skin complexion, the resemblance was so close that it made it hard to breathe.

"Tell him, Monty," Robby said.

"God damn you, Robby, don't do this to me."

"Tell him. Tell him you're gonna die."

Tommy pushed himself out from between Robby's knee caps then walked towards Monty on the other side of the room. When he got to him, the boy reached outward, and took Monty's hand and put it in his. "Monty," he said, looking up at him, his small body trembling like a puppy shivering in the snow. "Please don't die. I don't want you to die."

The words were like razors ripping through Monty's insides, tearing away the dead layer of his calloused heart. "I'm sorry, Tommy," he said, looking down at him, holding back the tears pounding against his eyes. "I'm so sorry. It's my fault. It's all my fault."

"Please don't die, Monty. Please don't leave me."

Monty could barely stand up straight. The room was spinning. He had to get out of here. He had to leave.

He released the boy's hand and moved towards the doorway, but Deborah got up and blocked his path. "Where are you going?" she said, her flabby arms raised outward, like a rodeo clown trying to coral a wild bull.

"I'm leaving," Monty said. "I'm not going to some fucking rehab. And there's nothing you can do that'll make me go."

"Oh yes there is," Deborah said, nodding her head slowly, meeting his eyes with a grave snarl. "I didn't want to have to play this card. I was hoping you'd agree to go on your own fruition. But, since you're obviously not going to cooperate, I have no other choice."

She reached into her bag and pulled out a manila file folder that had the seal of Colorado stamped on the front. "Do you know what this is?" she said, as she opened the folder, pulled out a form, and held it print side up. "This is what's called an Application for Emergency Commitment. Colorado is one of a few states that allow for a person to be involuntarily committed if they are both intoxicated and clearly dangerous to themselves and/or others. And I think last night, with your little escapade in the hospital, you've proven that you fit both criteria."

"You can't do this to me," Monty said, as he inched towards the doorway. "This isn't legal."

"I'm afraid it is. The application's been signed by myself, your parents, and the attending physician at the hospital. We've all recommended that you be committed to a detoxification program. Now, it's your choice—you can either go back to the hospital and spend your detox strapped to a bed by your wrists and ankles, *or* you can go up to Sanctuary, where I think you'll be a little bit more comfortable. I'll let you decide. Either way, you're going to get treatment even if we have to get you there by force."

Deborah nodded in Robby's direction.

"Now?" Robby said.

"Yes, you can call them."

Robby got up from the bed and moved towards the doorway, while punching the keypad on his cell phone. "Hello," he said, as he held up the receiver, "yeah, this is Robby. We're ready for you. It's room 1520."

Monty looked around the room in a state of panic. What the hell was happening? Who was he talking to?

As Robby flipped the phone closed, he removed the deadbolt then pulled open the door and propped it open. A few seconds later, a pair of uniformed policemen appeared in the doorway, their heavy black boots clunking against the hotel's pistachio green floor.

"Come on in," Robby said, as he ushered them forward, "we're right in here. Thanks for coming."

"What the hell's going on?" Monty said, as he backed away towards the windows. "What are they doing here? Are you're having me arrested?"

"No," Deborah said, "they're not here to arrest you. They're only here to observe and make sure no one gets hurt."

"That's bullshit," Monty said. "They're here to arrest me. They're here to put me in a straight jacket and take me to a fucking mental hospital."

"No, I assure you," Deborah said, "that's not what's going to happen. Not as long as you're willing to cooperate with us."

Monty glanced at his parents. They were both quiet, holding each other's hands, staring down at the floor. "Why are you doing this to me?" Monty screamed at them. "What are you hoping to accomplish? Don't you know this isn't going to change anything?"

"Now wait a minute," Deborah snapped, "it's not just their decision. It's all of ours. Everyone in this room wants to see you get better."

"Fuck you, you cunt. I don't even know you. Who are you? Why are you even here?"

"Hey," one of the officers said, as he lifted his gloved hand out towards Monty, "there's no need for that. We're only here to help you. But, if you start putting up a fight, we're going to have to detain you."

"It's okay," Deborah said, motioning to the officer. "He's not going to fight. He's going to do the right thing. Aren't you, Monty?"

Chapter 19

The Pod

The pod is what they called it. A small housing cluster consisting of two tiers of cells—ten on the top and ten on the bottom arranged in a perfect octahedron around a central, open dayroom. The dayroom was where Dave and his fellow inmates at the Boulder County Detention Center ate their meals, watched television, played checkers, and made phone calls. The dayroom was small, probably not much bigger than the faculty lounge at Dave's high school, with a couple of metal tables scattered unevenly around an old, tube television that was bolted to the top of a concrete pillar standing in the middle of the floor.

Dave sat by himself at one of these tables, his eyes transfixed on the telephone in the corner of the pod. He'd been staring at that phone all fucking morning, waiting for his turn to make a call. Unfortunately, it had been occupied by the same guy for the last two hours—a six-foot tall ape of a human with biceps twice the size of Dave's puny skull. His hands were as big and black as a gorilla's and his fingers looked like bruised bananas wrapped around the phone. Dave didn't dare go up there and stand next to that monster. One false move and the guy could swat him like a fly. Plus, if he got up now, he might lose his spot at the table. He was lucky the other inmates let him have it all to himself. He could tell already he wasn't very welcome. It seemed he was the only white guy in the pod. Everyone else was either Black or Mexican, with maybe a few Asians sprinkled in here and there like vegetable stir-fry. He could feel their eyes all pointed in his direction, like radioactive waves burning holes through his uncomfortable, blue, prison-issued shirt. They were sizing him up, looking for his vulnerabilities, waiting for the chance to pounce on his face.

No, he'd better not get up and just stay where he was seated. Only fifteen more minutes and it'd be visitation time. With any luck, Cheryl would be there waiting for him, standing at the very front of the line. He couldn't stand not knowing what happened to Larry. These assholes in here wouldn't tell him a god damn thing. The thought of the poor kid lying there while those bastards tased him was enough to make him want to gouge out his own eyes. What were those idiots thinking? How could they be so stupid? How could they not realize he was just a little boy?

Dave sighed and lifted his hands to his forehead and slicked back the sweat that was caught in his eyebrows. Why was it so hot in here? Didn't they have air conditioning? How could it be this hot when it was snowing outside? He was so damn dehydrated, he could barely even swallow. It was like he had no saliva, like he was all dried up inside. His head was pounding, his hands were shaking, and his throat felt like it was gonna collapse in on itself. What were the guards doing? Were they trying to make him miserable? Were they betting on how long it would take until someone died? "Fuck." He slammed his fists down against the table, so hard that it caused a few inmates at the table in front of him to turn around.

"The fuck's the matter with you?" one of them said, his dark, bug-like eyes scanning Dave up and down.

"Who me?"

"Yeah you. What's your problem?"

"Uh...nothing. I'm fine." Dave forced a smile then hunched forward, retreating into himself like a frightened hermit crab.

The inmates shook their heads then turned back towards the television, focusing on the program that was playing on the screen. It was hard to hear above all their hooting and howling, but it looked like the program they were watching was a talk show of sorts. The guy with the microphone, a familiar looking man, with a big nose and curly, unkempt sideburns, appeared to be conducting some sort of carnival-style group therapy session with the mothers of what looked like morbidly obese children. The mothers sat up on stage on rows of sofas next to their two-ton babies, while the man with the microphone took questions from the people in the crowd. The people in the audience were the real freaks of this circus sideshow, not the two-ton babies sitting on the couch. They had bad skin, bad hair, and bad hygiene with brown holes in their gums where their teeth used to be. Their eyes bulged outward from their sockets and their skin sagged like pudding from their cheeks.

After the Q&A session, the camera cut back to the row of fat babies, and one of the black guys in the pod turned to his buddies and yelled: "That ain't no kid, that be a mothafuckin' baby gorilla. Shit."

His buddy next to him said: "That ain't no fuckin' gorilla, that's yo momma muthafucka!"

"Fuck you nigga. Don't be talking about my momma. Yo momma so fat, when she steps on the scale, it says one at a time please."

The black dudes threw their heads back and started laughing; the fat rolls on their necks squishing together like a stack of Goodyear tires. The back of their bald heads looked like half-sucked milk duds, shiny with perspiration from the lights that hung overhead.

Oh great, Dave thought, again with the momma jokes? How many more of these could they possibly have?

"Shit. Yo momma so fat, her cereal bowl came with a lifeguard."

More giggles, more shouts, more hooting, more hollering.

"Man, fuck you. Yo momma so fat, when she ran away, they had to use all four sides of the milk carton."

"Oh yeah? Well yo momma so fat, when she goes to an all you can eat buffet, they gotta install speed bumps."

At this point, the milk duds were falling out of their chairs and holding onto their bellies trying to keep their stomachs from splitting open at the seams.

Dave just sat in the back and said absolutely nothing, trying to keep his eyes glued to the television screen. He couldn't understand how these guys could be so indifferent. Didn't it matter that they were stuck in prison? Maybe this was normal for them. Maybe it was a typical weekend. Maybe they actually enjoyed being in this place.

A few minutes later, the doors at the opposite end of the pod slung open and a pair of uniformed guards came walking out. They were dressed in all green with a pair of leather, workout gloves and set of white, plastic twisty-ties dangling from their black, utility belts.

"Alright," one of them said, as he approached the center of the dayroom. "Everybody listen up. It's visitation time. If I call your name, I need you to come here and stand at this black line."

The guard unfolded a white sheet of paper and called out the names that were written on the top: "Hernandez, Ramirez, Washington, Bell."

Oh thank god, Dave thought. It was Cheryl. Hopefully, she was gonna get him out of this fucking hellhole.

He stood up and shuffled quickly across the dayroom. As instructed, he placed the balls of his feet on the solid black line.

"Okay," the guard said, turning to his partner. "Let's get these guys down to visitation C."

"Ten-four."

The guards pulled off a couple of plastic twisty-ties then tightly secured them around each of the inmate's wrists. Once they got everyone tied off, one of the guards radioed to the control booth and said he had four prisoners that were ready to be walked down. A voice came back and said, "Ten-four. Copy. Go ahead, bring 'em on down."

The guard nodded then turned towards the line of inmates and said, "Follow me. Single file."

Dave was the last one in line. He followed the guy in front of him to a set of metal doors on the opposite side of the pod. Once the doors opened, they marched single file down a long, fluorescently lit hallway that was lined with windows and security guards working on the other side. The guards sat at long, angular desks, and stared at sets of video monitors that were stacked on top of one another in rows of perfectly lined cubes. They glanced up at the inmates as they walked past them, nodded their heads at the guards then returned to their cubes.

When they got to the end of the hall, the guards stopped at another set of large, metal doors then turned around to face the men. "Alright," the one in charge said. "Who hasn't done this before?"

Dave looked around and slowly lifted his hand. He wasn't surprised that his was the only hand in the air.

"It's simple," the guard said, looking in Dave's direction. "We're going to get you in there one at a time. When these doors open, you go in and stand in front of the black line. State your name into the camera and wait for the next set of doors to open. Once they do, go into the holding area and take the number that the guard's going to give you. Match that number with the number written on the top of the viewing stall. Then, go to that stall and look directly into the video monitor and pick up the phone that's mounted on the wall. You can see them and they can see you. Any questions?"

Dave shook his head.

"Alright," the guard said, "Hernandez, you're first...then Ramirez...then Washington...and, finally, Bell."

The men disappeared through the doors in five-minute increments, one after the other, like they were being ushered into an exclusive nightclub. Dave waited patiently staring at the back of the man's head in front of him, watching as the sweat beaded down his neck. Once it was his turn, the guard put his hand on Dave's shoulders and guided him to the front of the metal doors. There was a camera mounted on the wall just above the doorway with a little red light blinking beside the lens. The guard looked up into the camera and said, "Last one to go. Dave Bell. Open it up please."

Something unlocked and the doors opened slowly. Dave waited for the guard's permission then slowly shuffled through. But the room wasn't a room—it was a small holding area, like the bucking chute a bull stands in before it's released into the pen. Dave walked to the end of the chute and placed his feet squarely on the black marking, then looked up into the camera and stated his name.

He waited a few seconds, but nothing happened. A few minutes later, still, there was nothing. Exactly five minutes later, the next set of doors opened. Dave moved from the line and walked on through. There was a female guard on the other side, Hispanic or maybe Italian, with those familiar black gloves strapped to each hand. She looked up at Dave then down at her clipboard, checked something off and held out a small, laminated card, "Dave Bell," she said, "you're gonna be in stall number twelve today."

Dave took the card and flipped it over—the number twelve was written on the back. He looked back up at the guard for some kind of guidance. "Go on," she said. "Right through there. Your stall's the last one on the left."

Dave nodded and limped down the hallway into a room that was more dimly lit. It looked like the pod, only smaller, with rows of video booths wedged up against the walls. The booths looked like urinal stalls at the airport, only the partitions that separated them were concrete instead of plastic and had phones instead of flushers.

Dave looked down at his card then back up at the video booths. The numbers were painted in dark black blocks above each stall. He walked to the end and found his number; number twelve, the very last one. But there was nowhere to sit, just a blank video screen and a phone with a metal cord running out of the wall. He picked up the phone and held it to his ear. The video screen flashed blue and slowly came alive. He could see Cheryl. She was sitting on the opposite side of the video screen, a phone trembling in her hand. Her lips were moving but he couldn't hear what she was saying. Something was wrong. The audio was turned off.

He lifted his hand and tapped on the screen gently. "Cheryl?" he said. "Hello? Can you hear me?"

But there was nothing, just silence. A man's voice cut through the receiver: "Mrs. Bell," he said, "you have a bad connection. Please hang up the phone and try again."

Cheryl nodded her understanding. She hung up the phone and the screen went dead.

"Hello?" Dave said, tapping the screen more forcefully. "Hello? Can you hear me? Cheryl? Cheryl?" A few seconds later, the screen started flashing and Cheryl's image reappeared. "Cheryl? Cheryl?"

Her voice came on. He could finally hear her. "Hello?" she said. "Dave, can you hear me?"

"Yes, Cheryl, I can hear you. Can you hear me?"

"Yes."

Dave leaned in close. His forehead was nearly touching the monitor. "I can see you, Cheryl. Can you see me?"

She nodded. Her eyes were all red and puffy and she had blots of mascara running down her cheeks.

"Oh Cheryl, it's so good to hear your voice. Thank God, thank God you came."

"Of course I came, Dave. What was I supposed to do?"

"Oh Cheryl, I'm so sorry, I'm so fucking sorry."

"Oh Dave," she said, dabbing her tears with a crumpled tissue. "What have you done? What were you thinking?"

"Cheryl, listen to me. I don't know how much time we have. How's Larry? Is Larry okay?"

Cheryl nodded, the fat twitching underneath her chin. "Yes Dave. He's fine. Larry's fine."

"Oh thank God." Dave closed his eyes and leaned his head forward, letting out a sigh of intense relief. Thank God the kid was alright. Thank God nothing happened.

"How could you do this, Dave? What were you thinking? I told you specifically not to take him on that bus."

"I know Cheryl. I fucked up. I'm sorry."

"If you'd just listened to me and taken him to my sister's, none of this would've happened."

"I know."

"I wouldn't have had to—" She bit her tongue, abruptly stopping mid-sentence.

"What?" Dave said, peering into the monitor, trying to get a read on Cheryl's face. "You wouldn't have had to what?"

She turned away and shook her head in frustration, wiping the mascara that was running down from her eyes. She was hiding something. Dave could tell by the way her lips were twitching. They always did that when there was something she didn't want to say.

"Cheryl, what is it? If I would've dropped off Larry, you wouldn't have had to what?"

She lifted her head and looked back into the video monitor, her hair like spaghetti falling over her face. "I wouldn't have had to call the cops, Dave."

Dave's skin turned cold. His stomach began to tighten. He could actually feel the knife being plunged into his spine. "What...what are you saying? You did this? You called the police?"

"What was I supposed to do, Dave? You wouldn't pick up your phone, I couldn't find Larry. I didn't know if he was hurt or in trouble or lying somewhere dead on the side of the road."

Dave clenched his jaw and pressed his forehead against the video monitor trying to push back the rage that was boiling inside his blood. That's how the cops knew his name. That's why they pulled him over. Not because he was speeding or driving erratically, but because Cheryl called them and told them to. But was that even legal? Could they just pull him over? Didn't they need probable cause?

He shut his eyes and tightened his hand around the receiver, squeezing it until his knuckles turned bloodless white. He wanted to take the phone and smash it through the video screen and drive it right in between Cheryl's blubbering eyes. He wanted to slam it against her face until she turned bloody, until she screamed and cried for him to stop.

"Dave," she said, her voice slightly cracking in that same pathetic sounding cry. "Don't just stand there. Say something. Talk to me."

Dave opened his eyes, lifted his head slowly, and spoke with an almost inaudible growl: "How could you? How could you do this to me? Do you realize the shit you've gotten me in?"

"Don't you dare blame this on me. This wasn't my fault. I didn't cause this. You did, not me. You're the one who was out there driving around intoxicated. You're the one who was out there high on crack with our son."

"I was not high, Cheryl. I had everything under control. Besides, the only reason I was smoking was because my fucking knee was throbbing, which, by the way, we all know is your fault."

"Don't you dare try and use your leg as an excuse."

"Why not? I can't hold down a clutch if my fucking knee is throbbing. How do you expect me to watch Larry *and* drive a bus full of screaming high school girls? Larry wasn't even supposed to be with me in the first place and you know it. If you hadn't fucked up the schedule and picked him up like you were supposed to, none of this would've happened. I would've gotten to the game and everything would've been fine."

"Fine? Are you kidding me? You would not have been fine. What if you flipped that bus? What if you got into an accident? You could've killed those kids. You could've killed your own son. You're lucky I called the cops when I did before something worse happened out there. You could be sitting here facing a dozen manslaughter charges. But instead, because of me, because I happen to have a relationship with the judge, you're going to be getting out of here with nothing more than a slap on the wrist—a five thousand dollar fine, a suspended license, and three months probation at a rehabilitation facility of our choice."

"What? What are you talking about? What facility?"

Cheryl bent down away from the monitor but reappeared a few seconds later holding a manila file folder. "It's called Sanctuary," she said, as she opened the folder and fixed her reading glasses to the tip of her nose. "It's a dual diagnosis facility, up in the mountains, down I-70 up around Breckenridge. It's a top-notch facility with a staff of psychologists and counselors who can help people with both addiction and mental illness."

"You mean an insane asylum?"

"No, Dave, not an insane asylum. It's a clinic for people with addictions to alcohol and drugs."

Dave shook his head adamantly. "I don't care what it is. I'm not doing it. I'm not going to some fucking nut house."

"Well, you don't really have a choice, do you? You can either get help and go to this *rehab,* or…" Cheryl paused and looked down at the table, clenching her jaw like she was about to explode.

"Or what?"

She looked back up—her eyes were solemn, her expression unnervingly cold. "Or you're on your own. I'll leave you, Dave. I'll divorce you. I'll take the kids and leave you here to fend for yourself. And good luck finding a judge to take pity. Without me, you're just another criminal in the system…another crack head to be tossed out like the garbage you are. That judge in there will have no problem sending you up to Lincoln County with all the other low-life degenerates. All it takes is the flick of his pen and you'll be up there serving ten to twenty, living with a bunch of rapists and murderers."

"Bullshit. I know you, Cheryl. You wouldn't do that. You'd never let that happen."

"Oh no?"

"No. You're too proud, too damn conceited, too damn worried about what other people would think."

Cheryl cocked her head and leaned in towards the monitor and met Dave's eyes with a cold, glazed over stare. "Try me, Dave. Just try me."

Dave held her stare. This was bullshit. She had to be bluffing. There was no way in hell she'd just leave him here like this. "Well, what about the kids?" he said, straightening his posture. "Are you just gonna let them visit their dad in prison, behind a plate of bulletproof glass? I don't believe it. You wouldn't do that. You'd never let something like that happen."

Cheryl smiled and nodded slowly, as if she knew something that Dave didn't. "You know what? You're absolutely right. I wouldn't do that. I wouldn't bring those kids within a hundred miles of this place. Why do you think I didn't bring them here today? Huh? You think I'm going to let them see you like this, in prison, through a video screen?" Cheryl let out an insane sounding giggle then tossed her hair back away from her face. "No Dave. No way in hell I'm going to put them through something like that. They deserve better and you know it. They deserve a father who's not a lowlife crack head."

"Are you threatening me, Cheryl?"

"You're damn right I am. I swear to God Dave, if you don't go to this rehab and take this opportunity, you will never get to see those kids again. I promise you that. It's either the crack or your family. You can't have both. You have to choose."

Dave lowered his eyes away from the video monitor feeling as the jaws of fifteen years of marriage clamped down like a vice on his groin. Was she bluffing? Was she serious? Would she really leave him here to rot in this hellhole?

He exhaled deeply and looked over his shoulder, his eyes scanning the entrails of the visiting room. There were dozens of inmates dressed in blue polyester, standing like defiant, blue statues in their concrete viewing stalls. Some of them were shouting, others were crying, while some just stood hardened and rigid, saying nothing at all. Look at them—animals, every single one of them. Platinum capped teeth, huge, veiny forearms, and tattoos like hellacious graffiti scrawled all over their dark, sweaty skin. Christ, he couldn't stay here. He didn't belong here. He wasn't a criminal or some fucking junkie. He was a father, a coach, an Olympic athlete.

He lowered his head and sighed deeply while squeezing the bridge of his nose. Maybe Cheryl was bluffing and maybe she wasn't…there was really no way he could know for sure. But what he did know, was that he wouldn't last five more seconds in this facility, cooped up with all these gorillas, just waiting to get their paws around his throat. No. No fucking way. Any place had to be better than this shithole. Three months up in the mountains? Hell, that was nothing. Plus, it would give him enough time to hire his own lawyer. What Cheryl and those cops did had to be illegal. They couldn't just pull someone over without probable cause. He could fight this. He could prove his innocence. Then Cheryl would be the one in this fucking pod.

He smiled to himself and peered into the video screen then brought the phone against his ear. "Alright Cheryl, you win. I'll do it. I'll go to this rehab, but only because I have to get out of here. I can't stand one more minute in this fucking pod."

Chapter 20

Intake

It felt like they'd been on this road forever—a dangerously skinny, two-lane artery that switched back and forth along the edge of a flinty, snow-laced facade. Monty scooted forward and peered out the window, his forehead pressed against the icy glass. It was quite a drop—two hundred feet, maybe three hundred, to a jagged, icicle-spiked forest below. "You sure this is safe?" he said, as he scooted back from the window, trying to get as close he could towards the center of the van.

The driver snorted and glanced over at Monty, wearing what seemed to be a permanently amused grin. He reminded Monty of a billy goat. He was an older gentleman, African American, with a silky white beard, like coconut cotton candy, sprouting from the center of a strong, protruding jaw. "Oh yeah man, it's safe," the old man said then flipped on the wipers and adjusted the volume button on the radio.

"You sure?" Monty said, peering out over the edge of the summit, staring at the miles and miles of snow-covered Douglas firs. "It looks kind of dangerous."

"Aw nah man. It ain't no thing but a chicken wing." The old man laughed as he reached for his coffee, took a long slurp then set it back down. "I do this all the time, sometimes twice in one day. You just sit tight and try to get some sleep. We'll be up at the house before you know it."

Sleep? Yeah right. How was he supposed to sleep after what he'd just gone through? Just a few hours earlier, he was strapped to a hospital bed by his wrists and ankles, with an IV in his arm and a catheter in his dick. Then his own parents, his own flesh and blood, had the nerve to arrange an ambush and hire some interventionist who had him committed. How could they get away with this? It had to be illegal. There had to be a way out of this. There must be some kind of loophole.

He reached into his pocket, pulled out the form that Deborah had issued him, and began reading down the lines and lines of fine print:

"NOTICE TO PERSONS ADMITTED FOR INVOLUNTARY COMMITMENT: Pursuant to provisions of Section 27-81-111, C.R.S. You are hereby notified that you have been accepted for emergency treatment on the basis of the application as shown above. You are further advised that you may be held for a period no longer than five (5) days unless a petition for involuntary commitment has been filed with the court."

Ah-ha. There it was. He knew there had to be some kind of time limit. Five days? Hell, that was nothing. He could get through that, no problem.

He blew a sigh of relief as he sank back against the seat cushion, feeling as the anxiety released its grip around his throat. Thank God, that was a close one. He knew they couldn't legally hold him for as long as they wanted. After all, he wasn't a minor. He was an adult. He had rights.

He lifted the form and went to read on further, but his hands were shaking so bad that he could barely follow the rest of the paragraph. God damnit, the withdrawals were getting stronger. It felt like a cluster of hand grenades were going off in his head. His teeth were chattering, his hands were shaking, and it felt like his skin was crawling with an army of red fire ants.

He folded the form and shoved it back in his pocket then leaned slightly forward and peered out the windshield. The snow was coming down harder and harder, the white haze of flurries making it difficult to see the highway.

How much longer? How much farther? If he didn't get some meds soon he was going to have a seizure. He needed something to calm his muscles, to relax his breathing…Benzos, Valium, Ativan, anything.

He reached back behind him and pulled his hood up over his head. Folding his arms, he turned his body sideways then slunk back into his jacket like an eel retreating into its underwater cave.

Sleep? Yeah right. Maybe he was sleeping. Maybe this was all just one long, bad dream. Maybe any moment he'd wake up and be back in his apartment resting sweetly in Vicky's soft, warm arms. Maybe if he concentrated hard enough he could pull himself from this nightmare. Maybe if he closed his eyes, he could make it all go away—the shaking, the sweating, the headaches, the tremors…the bleakness, the mountains, the snow, the cold.

He closed his eyes and focused on his breathing, listening as the tires splashed against the soggy road. He could see her. He could see her smiling, her face illuminated by the rays of sun pouring in through the blinds. She was lying in bed right beside him, her soft, sweet breath blowing against his neck. Her left leg was draped across his stomach and her head was nuzzled tightly against his chest. "I love you," he whispered, as he stroked her stomach, making a small circle around her belly button.

"I love you too," she said, looking up at him, her lips pursed together like two rose petals pressed in between a book.

He closed his eyes then fell into her and swallowed her mouth with his lips. As he kissed her, he could feel her body rising and falling, her left leg coiling tightly around his hip. Then something went wrong. Her mouth felt freezing, as if it was filled with buckets of ice. He opened his eyes and tried to separate from her, but his tongue was sealed frozen to her teeth.

His eyeballs darted around in all directions as the cold traveled through him and down his throat. It felt like liquid nitrogen was running down his larynx, freezing his body from the inside out. He couldn't move...he couldn't breathe...she was sucking the air out of him. The vacuum from the cold was collapsing his lungs. She threw her bare arms and legs around his body and squeezed him so tight that he couldn't even scream. Almost immediately, their skin fused together, like a moist tongue to a flagpole on a freezing December day. Then, the ceiling and the walls started weeping and the sound of rushing water began to fill the room. The windows cracked, the glass shattered, and a surge of water broke onto the bed. But the water was warm— warmer than Vicky—and melted the seal between their skin. "Go," Vicky screamed, looking up in horror, as a layer of ice began to encase her skin. "Get out of here. Leave me. Save yourself. Go."

"No," Monty said, "I can't leave you. You're my only reason for living. You're the only one I have left."

"Don't say that, Monty. You have to get out of here. Don't worry about me. Save yourself."

"I can't."

"Yes, you can. I believe in you, Monty. Go now. Get up! Get up!"

Just then, Monty's eyes shot open as his head bounced against the window's glass. The bed was gone and Vicky's screams had vanished, replaced by the squeal of brass horns coming from the van's speakers.

"Come on, get up, Monty," the old man whispered, as he tugged and pulled on Monty's wrist. "Get up. We're here."

Monty groaned and peeled himself from the headrest then rubbed his eyelids and let out a deep yawn. He could see the house emerging through the clearing. It looked like something out of a Shakespearean play. It was three stories high, white and colonial, surrounded on all sides by an imposing wall of Ponderosa pines. The trees' branches were curved, long, and intrusive, embracing the house like a pair of giant, wooden hands. The north side of the house was completely covered in ivy, shrouding the white stone walls with a cloak of ice-laden, emerald vines. An impressive wooden porch painted as white as the snowflakes wrapped from one side to the other like a giant, albino anaconda all the way around the stone. Fat, Greek columns spiraled up towards the heavens supporting the weight of a curved balcony that sat on the top floor. It looked like the only way up was a brass, spiral staircase that commenced from the bottom and wound upwards towards the top.

The old man squeezed the brake as he pulled around the semi-circle driveway, stopping right in front of the grand, white porch. "Alright," he said as he cut the engine. "Here we are. Home sweet home."

Monty cracked the door open and carefully eased himself down from the van. His legs were still asleep from the long haul up the mountain and he barely had enough coordination to even stand. He stood idle for a moment while the blood returned to his muscles, the pins and needles poking into his skin.

He couldn't believe this place. Even the driveway was a thing of beauty. Not one stone was the same as the other. Some were rich, like dark chocolate, scattered in crazy jig-jag patterns, while others were smooth and round with a light shade of brown sugar fitting together in perfect symmetry. There was a massive granite fountain overrun with tangles of ivy, its impressive four tier stone basins casting shadows against the snowy ground.

The old man shut the trunk and came around with Monty's green gym bag. "Alright Mr. Monty, you ready to go?"

Monty nodded and moved forward slowly, following the old man up the creaky porch steps. His legs were so weak that he could barely keep his posture. He had to take a break about halfway up the porch.

"You alright?" the old man said, looking back at him.

Monty nodded then grabbed hold of the icy, iron railing and used both hands to slowly pull himself up the steps. When he finally got to the top, he pressed his back up against one of the spiral columns and put his hands on his knees to try and catch his breath.

"You sure you're alright?" the old man said.

"Yeah. I'm fine."

"Okay. Whatever you say." The driver dropped Monty's bag then turned his fist into a knocker and pounded it against the door so hard that it sounded like he was trying to break it in. "Hello? Is anybody home?"

They waited a few seconds, but there was no answer. So, the old man mashed the doorbell with the club of his thumb. But still, there was nothing—no answer—and so he tried the doorknob, but it was locked. "Well," he said, as he scratched his scraggly chin hair, "looks like we oughta head around back."

Just as they were about to leave, the door flung open, and a tall, lanky black man stood grinning in the doorway, his bald head reflecting the glow of the overhead porch lamp. He was somewhat academic looking with oval shaped glasses, neatly pressed khaki's, and a gray, wool sweater vest. "Well, hello there," he said, as he pushed the screen door open. "You must be the young man I've been hearing so much about—the chemical engineer from Denver. My name's Dexter, but you can call me Dex. Welcome to Sanctuary."

Monty looked down and inched forward. He noticed that the guy's hand was balled into a fist. Oh great. He probably wanted one of those ridiculous fist bump things. Whatever happened to just a normal handshake? He forced a smile then gave the man a slight knock of the fist. "Hi," he said, retreating backwards, trying to keep his back against the column's support. "Nice to meet you. I'm Monty…but you can call me Monty."

Dexter threw his head back and started laughing. His cackle was a booming, baritone crack. "I see you still got your sense of humor. That's good, that's good. You're gonna need it."

Monty tried to be a good sport and smile with him, but all he could muster was a faint snort.

"So listen," Dexter said, grinning like a court jester, looking Monty up and down. "I understand you're one of Robby's sponsees."

"Yeah. Why? Do you know him?"

"I sure do. He was *my* sponsor. In fact, everything I know about addiction, I learned from him."

Oh great, Monty thought, just what he needed—another disciple of Robby to make him feel right at home.

"He used to have this job, you know?"

"Really?"

"Yep. He was running this place back when I came through."

Of course, now it was all starting to come together. No wonder they made him come here. It was Robby's fucking alma mater.

"Let's see," Dexter said, musing up at the porch lights, "that was back in '95. Nearly, ten years ago. Wow." He shook his head and let out a long whistle. "I can't believe it. Time sure flies by fast, doesn't it?"

"I guess."

"Well,"—Dexter clapped his hands together—"what do you say we get you in here and out of the cold?"

Finally. He was about to have a convulsion. Any more chitchat and he was going to keel over right in the snow. "Sure," Monty said, then peeled himself from the column and carefully shuffled towards the front door.

"Alright. Come on in here and we'll get you processed."

With his hand on his shoulder, Dexter ushered Monty forward then turned toward the old man as he pulled open the screen door. "Thanks Cap. I got it from here. You got anymore tonight?"

"Yeah," the old man said. "I got one more after supper. Gotta pick him up from the courthouse."

"Back in Denver?"

"Yep."

"Dang Cap. You're in for a long haul tonight, aren't ya?"

"I sure am."

"Well, you be safe out there my friend and don't stop for any hitchhikers."

"No sir." Cap chuckled and turned to Monty, extending his wrinkled, raisin-like hand. "It was a pleasure meeting you, Mr. Monty. You take care of yourself now, you hear?"

Monty took the old man's hand and shook it, struggling to give it a firm enough squeeze.

"And do everything these guys tell you to. They know what they're talking about."

Yeah right. Monty had heard that one before.

"Thanks. I will," Monty said as he released the raisin then bent down and scooped up his gym bag from the porch.

"Alright," Dexter shouted. "Let's do this thing. You ready?"

Monty nodded and took a deep breath inward then followed Dexter inside the grand, old house. He tried to move in small, calculated movements, afraid that if he moved to abruptly his knees might bow inward like a flamingo.

"Right this way," Dexter said, as he pushed a set of French doors open and flipped on a light switch that was mounted on the inner wall.

Monty readjusted the strap of his bag higher against his shoulder then followed Dexter into a modestly sized, windowless room. The room was carpeted and must've just been vacuumed, because he could still see the long striations in the fibers underneath his feet. There was a large, rectangular desk sitting in between two bookcases and a couple of armchairs and couches strewn along the sidewalls.

Dexter moved around behind the desk and collapsed backward into a swivel style, leather office chair. "Have a seat," he said, motioning to a large green armchair that was sitting a few inches from his desk.

Monty let his bag fall off his shoulder then carefully eased himself into the chair. He took another deep breath and leaned forward, squeezing his elbows with both hands.

"You okay?" Dexter said, as he began rifling through the bottom drawers of his desk.

Monty shook his head and shut his eyelids, swallowing as often as he could to try and suppress the bile.

"Don't worry. This won't take long. We'll get you all set up in detox and have you feeling better in no time at all. But first, we're gonna need a picture."

Monty lifted his head. "A picture? What for?"

"Don't worry. We take everybody's picture. We like to do a before and after kind of a thing. Ah-ha! Found it." Dexter pulled out a bright, red digital camera and proudly held it up as if he'd just caught a fish. "Now we're in business," he said, as he hit the power button and brought the camera up to his face. "Okay Monty, would you mind looking here for a minute?"

Monty leveled his eyes and stared blankly into the camera, but he was shaking so bad that he could barely hold himself still.

"Okay, I'm gonna need you to try and stop moving. Can you do that for me?"

Monty wrapped his hands around his elbows and squeezed like he was giving himself a tight hug. He tried as hard as he could to stop the trembling, but the more he tried, the more he shook.

"Come on, Monty, I need you to try and hold still."

God damnit—what the hell was this guy's problem? Didn't he know anything about alcohol withdrawal? He couldn't hold still. He could barely even swallow. Everything inside of him was about to explode.

"Okay Monty, just give me a big smile and say...*Recovery!*"

The flash went off and Monty winced forward, clenching his teeth as tight as he could.

Dexter lowered the camera and glared at the picture with what looked to be a sick, perverted smile. "Oh, this is a good one. You look like you've been run over by a garbage truck."

What the hell was wrong with this guy? Was he actually enjoying seeing him in pain? What kind of sadistic counselor was

Monty dealing with? Could someone in his position be this deranged?

"This one's gonna have to go in my scrapbook."

"Can I see it?" Monty said, leaning forward, trying to sneak a peek over the large oak desk.

Dexter quickly pulled the camera away and nestled it tightly into his lap. "Nope, sorry. Not until your time here with us is up. Don't worry, we'll give you a copy when you get ready to leave. That way you'll never forget just how messed up you were when you first showed up." Dexter studied the picture for a few seconds longer then shut off the camera and set it aside. "Okay," he said, as he grabbed a pad of paper and fountain pen from a fancy gold plated holder that had his name etched across the top, "enough messing around. Let's get down to business."

Monty took a deep breath and swallowed, staring at the carpet fibers underneath his feet.

"I understand that alcohol is your drug of choice. Is that correct?"

"Yes."

"Do you remember how old you were when you had your first drink?"

"No, not really."

"Just ballpark it. What were you...twelve, fourteen, sixteen?"

"Yeah. Sure."

"Which? Sixteen?"

"Yeah."

Dexter mumbled the number to himself as he marked it down in his note pad. "Okay, now—how much would you say you drank per day, on average?"

"When?"

"When what?"

"Well, I drank different amounts at different points in my life. When specifically would you like to know how much I drank?"

"Oh, uh, right before you got here would be fine."

Monty dropped his head and leaned forward, rubbing his forehead with both hands. "I'd say about…a handle a day."

"Of liquor?"

No, prune juice. Yes, of course, liquor. What the hell else?

"Yes. Liquor."

"But a handle per day? That's what, like a half a gallon, right?"

"Yeah. That sounds about right."

"You sure? That's quite a bit."

"Yes, I'm sure. Why? You don't believe me?"

"No, no, I do, I do, it's just…"

"What?"

"Well, a half a gallon is quite a lot. I mean, I'm not sure if anyone could survive that much."

"Well, I'm not just anyone. I'm an alcoholic."

"So, you admit it?"

"What?"

"That you're an alcoholic."

"Of course. Why else would I be in here?"

Dexter laughed and cocked his head sideways then set his fountain pen down on the desk. "That's great, Monty. That's just fantastic. Do you know how much easier that makes my job?"

"I'm glad I could be of service."

Dexter shook his head and reclined backward. He looked like he was enjoying himself at a comedy club. "Well Monty, you should have no problem here. I mean, you already admit you're an alcoholic. Now, all we gotta do is get you to stop drinking."

"A little easier said than done, don't you think?"

"Have you ever tried?"

"Of course."

"What was the longest stretch you've ever stayed sober?"

"A year."

"Really?"

"Yep."

"Interesting. Very interesting." He marked it down in his note pad. "And when was that?"

"This past year."

"Really? Well, what happened?"

"I relapsed."

"Well, yeah, but why?"

"I just did."

"No reason?"

"Nope."

"Aw come on, there's gotta be a reason. How does someone with a whole year under their belt suddenly start drinking again?"

"I don't really want to talk about it."

"Come on, don't be like that, Monty. I'm here to help you. How do you expect me to help you if you don't tell me what's going on?"

"I don't want your help."

"Well, what do you want?"

"I don't know."

"Do you wanna stay sober?"

"I don't know."

"Then why are you here?"

"I don't know."

"Do you know what will happen to you if you start drinking again?"

"I have an idea."

"And what's that?"

"I'll probably die."

"No, not probably. You *will* die. You will most certainly die."

"Okay, fine. I'll die."

"Is that what you want?"

"I don't know."

"What do you mean you don't know?"

"I mean I don't know!"

Dexter shook his head and reclined backwards, folding his arms over his chest. He sat there, unblinking, for what felt like an eternity, glaring at Monty like he was trying to see inside his head. Then he cleared his throat, took off his glasses, and began cleaning them with the tail of his shirt. "You know what I think, Monty?"

"No, but I have a feeling you're going to tell me."

"I don't think you want to die at all. I think this whole thing is just an elaborate cry for help."

Monty would've laughed in his face if he wasn't afraid he might vomit. A cry for help? Was that really the best he could do?

"You're just scared, Monty, like everyone else that comes through those doors—scared by the power of your own addiction—scared that if you don't have your alcohol you won't be able to cope with life on life's terms."

Oh great, clichés already? Couldn't he have at least waited 'til tomorrow to give him the "life on life's terms" sermon?

"Have you heard that before, Monty? Life on life's terms?"

No, never. Only from my sponsor a million fucking times.

"Yes, I've heard it."

"Then you know what I'm talking about."

"Yes."

"You see Monty, you don't really wanna die. If you did, then why not just put a gun in your mouth and pull the trigger? It'd be quicker and a hell of a lot easier than trying to drink yourself to death."

"I've considered that."

"I don't doubt you have. But here's the thing,"—Dexter leaned forward, fixing his glasses back on his face—"I don't think you wanna die. I think you wanna live. But your problem is, you haven't figured out how to deal with life on life's terms."

Why did he have to keep saying that?

"You'd rather give up on life and go hide inside a bottle than have to deal with life's little unpleasant inconveniences."

What? Monty lifted his head. Did he really just say that? Who in the hell did this guy think he was? Had he ever lost anything before? Had he ever lost a loved one? Had he ever had to watch his fiancé drown in a fucking car? If anyone deserved to drink, it was Monty. He earned the right to be a miserable drunk. He lost everything that night—his heart, his love, his friend, his soul mate…the one thing in his life that made him who he was. What had this guy lost? Anything? What made him think he had a right to judge? What did he know about pain? What did he know about suffering? As far as Monty could tell, this guy was a fucking joke—probably some washed-up, born-again, recovering crack head who thought that just because he found God and got clean and sober then everyone else should too. Well, fuck him. Fuck his superiority. Fuck his invasiveness. And fuck his questions.

"Well," Monty said, trying as best he could to remain collected, taking deep breaths in and out through his nose, "you're entitled to your own opinion."

"That I am," Dexter said, smirking and nodding, scribbling something down into his pad. "That…I…am."

Monty couldn't do this. He couldn't last much longer. Anymore questions and he was going to hurl. He was cold but hot, sweaty but dehydrated…it felt like his internal organs were coming up out of his throat. How much longer was this guy going to continue? How many more questions could he possibly ask?

"Alright," Dexter said, looking up from his notepad, "let's switch gears here for a moment. I understand this isn't your first time through treatment."

"That's right."

"And where were you before you came here?"

"I don't know."

"You don't know?"

"I can't remember the name right now."

"You can't remember? Are you sure? It's important that we get it into the file."

"Look,"—Monty stared up at him. His face was sweating, his hands were shaking, and his teeth were chattering so hard it felt like they were about to shatter into a million pieces on the floor—"how much longer is this going to take? I really need some medication. I don't feel well at all."

"Well,"—Dexter rolled back his sleeve and checked his wristwatch—"we still have a ways to go."

A ways to go? Jesus, he needed some fucking medicine. What was it about withdrawal that these people didn't understand?

"But, I suppose we could finish up some other time, if that works for you?"

"Please."

"Okay. Let me see if I can get the RA up here."

Thank God. Finally.

Dexter picked up the phone and punched in a couple of numbers, then swiveled away from Monty holding the receiver between his shoulder and his ear. "Yeah, hi, this is Dex. Is Nicholas down there? He is? Can you send him up please? I have a patient ready for check-in. Yes, tell him we're in the front room foyer. Thank you."

Dexter put the phone back into its cradle then set his pen and pad of paper back into the drawer. "Okay, we'll finish the intake when you're feeling a little better. I think I'm probably gonna be your primary counselor, so we'll be seeing a lot more of each other. For now, I want you to think about what I said about life on life's terms, and when you feel up to it, I want you to read through the first couple chapters in the Big Book. Do you have a copy?"

"No."

Dexter got up from his chair and walked over to one of the cherry wood bookcases that were set up on either side of his desk. He pulled down a book from the very top shelf then took it back with him over to Monty's chair. The cover was dark blue and made of soft vinyl with the words, *Alcoholics Anonymous* in gold lettering imprinted on the front.

"You ever read it?" Dexter said, as he held it outward.

"Kind of."

"What's kind of?"

"I've browsed through it once or twice."

"Well, it's not enough just to browse through it. You have to own this thing. Digest it. Go through it cover to cover. You know?"

"I know."

"Start with the first chapter, *The Doctor's Opinion*, and try to find the similarities between you and Dr. Bob. We can talk about it tomorrow morning when you're feeling better. Deal?"

"Sure."

"Excellent. I'll be looking forward to it."

I won't.

Monty took the book, thanked him, and stuffed it in the side pocket of his gym bag.

Just then there was a loud thud against the door like a reindeer butting its antlers against the fender of a car. Monty turned and looked. There was a kid, standing in the middle of doorway, wearing big, baggy jeans and a white t-shirt that was three sizes too big. "What's up, Dex?" the kid said, out of breath and panting, stains like mustard caked in both armpits.

"Oh hey Nick. How's it going?"

"Oh pretty good, pretty good. You know me...I can't complain." The kid looked over at Monty and shot him a bright, blinding smile. "What's up dawg?"

Monty didn't respond. He was too entranced by the kid's metallic set of incisors. They looked like the front grill of a Roll's Royce convertible—every single tooth had been capped with platinum and he had another five pounds of it dangling around his neck. He looked like a caricature of one of those thugs from an MTV rap video, only this kid was Caucasian, very Caucasian, and his jeans were so baggy he had to hold them up by the crotch.

"Monty," Dexter said, placing one arm over the kid's scrawny shoulder, "this is Nick. He's the RA for the men's side of things. He's gonna be checking you in this evening."

Monty nodded his understanding, trying not to stare, which was almost impossible.

"Be careful with this one, Nick. He's a sly one—chemical engineer all the way from Denver."

"No shit? You a chemical engineer, dawg?"

Monty nodded.

Nick's eyes lit up like a Roman candle. He covered his mouth and let out an ecstatic cry. "Oh shit. So, do you know how to make meth and shit?"

Monty couldn't help but laugh at the kid's impulsiveness. "I don't know," he said. "I never really tried."

"Fuck dude. I bet you could whip up a wicked batch of that shit."

"Hey come on," Dexter interjected. "Don't forget where you are now."

"Oh yeah, yeah, my bad, my bad. I guess I get carried away sometimes. It's that disease, you know? It's a fucking sickness— a sickness in my fucking head." The kid started slapping his head like he was trying to knock water out of his eardrum. "You know what I'm saying dawg? It's a fucking illness."

"Yeah, I can see that," Monty said, scooting backwards, trying to get as far as he could away from the kid.

"Pretty fucked up, isn't it?"

"It sure is."

"Alright," Dexter said, checking his wristwatch. "I need to head on down to group. You take good care of my patient now, Nick. No screwing around. I need him over at detox just as soon as you're finished checking him in."

Nick stood on his tiptoes and gave Dexter a kind of mock salute. "Aye, Aye captain. You can count on me."

Dexter nodded somewhat suspiciously, as if he didn't trust a word that the kid just said. "Hey Monty, you hang in there, alright? And think about what I said. Next time we see each other, we're gonna dive into your recovery, and you're gonna have to be open with me, otherwise this thing's not gonna work. Got it?"

Monty nodded just to get rid of him. In reality, he had no intention of telling this guy a damn thing. He just wanted to do

his five days detox and get the fuck out of here, then he could go
back to his apartment and complete the plan.

"Alright," Dexter said, "I'll see you later. Have a good night
and try and get some sleep."

Yeah right.

Nick waited until Dexter was out of the office then turned
to Monty and clapped his hands. "Alright, dawg. Let's get you
checked in. Where's your shit?" He motioned to Monty's green
gym bag on the floor. "Is that it?"

"Yeah."

"Alright then. Bring it on up here big boy." He slapped the
top of Dexter's desk. "I need to check your bag, make sure
you're not trying to sneak any paraphernalia up in here."

Monty gripped both sides of the armchair and slowly pushed
himself up. Crouching to the floor, he grabbed his green gym
bag, lifted it by the shoulder strap, and set it on the desk. As he
returned to his chair, he could feel his heart rate beginning to
quicken as cold beads of sweat ran down from his head. Damn,
he felt sick. He wasn't going to last much longer. The simple act
of lifting a gym bag was enough to make him out of breath.

He bent his knees and sank back into the armchair, watching
as Nick furiously opened and closed the bottom desk drawers.
After a few minutes, he found what he needed—a black
permanent marker and a box of Ziploc bags. He unscrewed the
cap and brought the tip of the marker underneath his nostrils
then took a deep whiff and arched his eyebrows. "I'm just
kidding," he said then doubled over, grinning, with that metal
toaster shoved inside his mouth.

Jesus, this guy was messed up. There were definitely a
couple screws missing. Wonder what did it to him? Was he
mentally challenged? Could it have been all the drugs? Or maybe
he was always like this. Maybe he was that kid in kindergarten,
the one who ate all the other kids' crayons. Then again...maybe
once upon a time he was the most popular kid in high school—

the quarterback, the prom king, the president of the student council. Then, one day, he started self-medicating and look at what happened—he became this twisted, perverted pile of platinum deteriorating right before Monty's eyes.

As Nick collected himself, he cocked his head sideways and stuck out his tongue like he was doing an impersonation of Michael Jordan. Then he took the magic marker and began printing Monty's name, spelled *MONTEY,* in all capital letters on the side of the bag. He paused mid-stroke and looked up at Monty and asked him what his last name was. Monty told him: "Miller." Nick nodded and mouthed the word slowly as he printed the name onto the side of the bag.

Once he finished, he leveled his head and studied his penmanship then blew on the ink so it would dry. "Okay," he said, as he walked over to a metal file cabinet, opened the top drawer, and pulled out a box of blue latex gloves. "Time for inspection."

Oh great, again with the latex?

Nick snapped on the gloves, one after the other, then began rubbing his fingers together, making a terrible popping sound. He pulled up his jeans and straightened his posture then began circling the green gym bag like a shark stalking its prey.

Oh great, now what? What was he doing? Why was he just walking around the bag in aimless circles?

Suddenly, Nick stopped and pointed to the zipper, like a detective on a crime scene investigation show. "Wanna go ahead and unzip that for me?"

Monty sighed and stood up from the armchair then, with his hands trembling, he carefully unzipped the bag.

"Okay. Start taking everything out and place it right here for me."

"Everything?"

"Everything."

Monty started digging out his belongings, laying them down on top of the desk. First, came the undershirts and his plaid, cotton boxers sitting on the pile near the very top…then came the jeans and long-sleeve sweatshirts underneath layers and layers of plain white socks. He began to wonder where all these clothes came from. Did his dad pack it? He must have, because he sure as hell didn't remember packing any of it. When he got to the bottom, he found his black leather shaving kit and set it with his clothes on top of the desk.

"Whoa," Nick said, stepping forward, his eyes fixed on the shaving kit. "What do we have here?" He picked up the kit and pulled open the zipper then dumped the contents out onto the desk. "Uh-oh. Jackpot." He picked up a bottle of cologne and read off the label: "Chanel Sport. Very nice. Too bad you can't have it. Contains alcohol. See?" He pointed to the small print at the bottom of the label. Sure enough, it said fourteen percent alcohol by volume.

So what? What did he think he was going to do, drink it? He'd have to be a lunatic to try and drink that stuff.

"I know what you're thinking," Nick said, as if he could read him. "You'd have to be crazy to drink this shit. But, I've been here a long time, and believe me, people do some pretty fucked up shit in here. You know those hand sanitizers? The ones they got in the restrooms at the airport?"

Monty nodded. He happened to know exactly what the kid was talking about. He hated those things. They made his hands feel gross.

"Well, we used to have those in the cafeteria, so people could wash their hands before lunch and dinner and shit. Well, some crazy-ass alcoholic figured out that there was like fifteen percent alcohol in there. So, you know what he does? He gets up one night, sneaks down to the cafeteria, and busts all the containers wide fucking open. Then, he takes that shit upstairs to his room, shuts the door, and sucks it down like it was Coca-Cola."

"You're kidding me."

"Nah man, I wish I was. You know what happened to that poor motherfucker?"

"What?"

"Well, alcohol ain't the only thing they put in that shit. Also has a whole bunch of chemicals, but you probably know all about that, being a smart chemical engineer and all." Nick grinned and poked Monty in the shoulder to which Monty just lowered his eyes and looked away. "Anyway, all them extra chemicals made him sick as a dog. Dude looked green when they brought him down in that gurney, like the fucking jolly green giant. Only this dude was pretty far from jolly. It looked like his head was about to pop off like a fucking piñata. They had to rush him to the ER down in Frisco and pump his stomach like they was pumping a well."

Monty put his hand over his stomach. The thought of getting pumped full of charcoal made him feel like he was going to hurl.

"Since that happened, we had to get rid of all them sanitizers and now we check everything. So, stuff like mouthwash, cologne, cough syrup—you can't take any of that shit up in here with you."

Nick continued to sift through the contents of the shaving kit, using his black felt pen like he was some kind of forensics expert. When he came to a set of shaving razors, he looked up at Monty as if he was the dumbest person in the world. "Razor blades? You kidding me? You definitely can't have these."

"Don't blame me," Monty said, defensively. "I didn't pack any of this. My dad did. I have no idea what's in there."

"Oh, yeah right, I've heard that one before. You think I was born yesterday? I hope I don't need to tell you why you can't have razors in here."

This kid was really starting to get on Monty's last nerve. All he wanted to do was get some sleep and some god damn medication. Didn't they understand what he was going through? He was sick. He needed medication—something, anything to take away the withdrawals.

"Now, don't worry, man. You can still shave. You'll just have to check these razors out when you're ready. They'll be right here in this safe along with all your other shit." He pointed to a metallic safe on the floor behind the desk. "When you're ready, just come down and someone will check 'em out for you." His eyes moved up and down Monty's torso then stopped abruptly at his feet. "I'm gonna need those shoe laces too my friend."

"My shoe laces?"

"Yep. Can't have 'em in detox, or your belt for that matter. I'll need 'em both."

"What for?"

"They don't want you trying to hang yourself in here. Nurses can't keep an eye on you crazy motherfuckers twenty-four seven."

Monty unbuckled his belt and slung it out from around his waistband.

"Come on, chop-chop, pick it up. Shoe laces too."

He squatted down to the carpet then started pulling the laces from his shoes.

"Don't worry, dawg. You can have your laces and belt after you get outta detox. Oh by the way, what's your drug of choice?"

"What?"

"Your drug of choice? What is it?"

"Alcohol."

"Alcoholic, huh? That figures."

"What's that supposed to mean?"

The kid shrugged. "Nothing. You just look like an alcoholic…talk like one too. Shit, you even dress like one…Mr. Chemical Engineer." The kid snickered as he picked up the belt and laces and stuffed them into the Ziploc bag. "Shit, we don't get too many of you guys in here."

"Well, what's your drug of choice?"

The kid looked at Monty like he was offended. "What? You can't tell?" He stuck his palms out and started twirling as if he was a model at a fashion show. "Isn't it obvious?"

Monty shrugged.

"I'm a meth head, dawg. Smoked it, snorted it, injected it...you see these things?" He opened his mouth so Monty could see his teeth. "Had to get these bitches capped. My real teeth rotted out. That's what smoking that shit does to you, man. Makes your damn teeth rot out. You're lucky you're just an alcoholic. All that other shit just fucks you up."

Yeah right. Monty was real lucky. He was trapped in a rehab in the middle of the god damn mountains.

"Alright, let's take some stock here." The kid went to the drawer and pulled out a clipboard then started checking the items off in the bag. "Okay, so we got some shoe laces...Check...one belt...Check...one bottle of Chanel." He paused and looked up at Monty. "Very nice, by the way." He winked and started giggling. "And one, two, three, four razor blades...Check. Oh, you got a cell phone?" Monty didn't say anything, just shrugged his shoulders. Nick laughed and skipped the box. "No sweat man. You don't gotta tell me. Just don't let them catch you with it. They'll take it away and give me a bunch of shit for not snatching it off you. Okay, now last thing—I'm gonna need your wallet."

"My wallet?"

"Yeah man. We can't have you ordering a bunch of pizzas in here."

Monty sighed and patted his back pocket, but his wallet wasn't there, so he tried his jacket pockets, but it wasn't there either, so he tried his green gym bag, and found it buried in the very bottom of the side pocket. Thank god, at least he still had it. At least his dad didn't try and take it from him. He pulled it out and unfolded it. There was no cash inside, but at least he still had his health savings debit card. "Here you go," he said, as he handed it over.

"Thanks." The kid snatched it and stuffed it inside the Ziploc bag. "Alright, that about does it. I just need you to sign right here." He pointed to a dotted line at the bottom of the checklist. "It just says I searched your shit and pulled out all the items checked off here in these boxes."

Monty picked up the pen and tried to sign, but his hands were shaking so bad he could barely hold his fingers around the grip.

"You can just put an X if you want."

Monty drew an X, but it looked more like a capital Y.

"Okay. Good. You can go ahead and toss your other stuff back in the bag."

The kid folded up the checklist and placed it in the Ziploc bag, then sealed it, walked over to the safe and squatted down. Turning his back so Monty couldn't see him, he punched in some numbers on the digital keypad. He opened the safe and tossed in the plastic baggy then shut the door and stood back up. "Okay, so all your stuff will be right here when you get out. Remember, once you get out of detox you can come in here and grab your belt and shoelaces. Don't want you running around here with your britches falling off." He winked at Monty, holding his jeans up by the crotch. "Alright you good?"

Monty nodded.

"Got everything?"

Monty nodded again.

"Alright let's get you some medicine and under them covers."

"You read my mind."

Chapter 21

The Trailer

Monty followed Nick back through the main foyer and out into the bitter Colorado evening cold. The snow was coming down in fluffy, white flurries and the wind, like a freight train, whistled through the trees.

"Shit man," Nick said, as he zipped up his hoody, "it's colder than a motherfucker out here. Weatherman says we're supposed to get a couple feet of this shit by morning. Can you believe that?"

Monty nodded as he clutched the porch railing and carefully descended the icy, wooden steps.

"Careful dawg, that shit's icy. Don't want you breaking your neck before you get detox'd."

"Where are we going?"

"There's a trailer out back. It's the detox slash hospital. That's where you'll stay for the next couple of days, until you get that liquor outta your system. You'll like it over there. It's nice and quiet and you can pretty much do whatever the fuck you want. There's no meetings, no groups, no prayers, none of that bullshit. You can sleep in as long as you want, eat whenever, shower whenever, plus man, who knows, maybe there'll be a cute little girl in there for you to play with. They don't keep the men and women separated like they do in the main house. If you're quiet, you can sneak up in her bed and give her a little something, something. She'll be so out of it from them detox pills she won't know what hit her. You know what I'm saying?" The kid clenched both fists and started thrusting his pelvis forward. "Pow! Pow! Pow!"

Monty shook his head. Didn't this kid have any decency? Or was he so far gone that he just didn't care? He sighed and dug his hands into his pockets, then carefully followed the kid around the side of the house. The snow was deep, probably about eight inches—like fiberglass insulation, it seemed to sag as he walked.

"Come on," Nick said, looking back at Monty, his hand motioning to a rectangular structure up ahead in the dark. "There it is."

The kid wasn't joking when he said it was a trailer. That's exactly what it was—an old, dilapidated doublewide. It wasn't something he'd expect to see up here in Colorado—maybe where he grew up in white trash north Florida, but not up here, not in the mountains. The roof was coming off, the paint was chipping, and the snow was piled so high around it that it looked like it was sagging into a sinkhole.

"Come on," Nick said, waving Monty onward, jogging the last couple yards up to the trailer's front steps. "It's cold as shit out here."

Monty readjusted the gym bag higher around his shoulder then cautiously ascended the set of short, narrow steps.

The inside of the trailer was ratty and smelled like mildew. It resembled the reception area at a dentist's office. There was a brown suede couch parked against the windows and a half dozen folding chairs sitting directly across from it. In between the couch and the chairs, sat a dusty, brown coffee table, its legs bowed inward like a four-legged bug. The walls were white, the carpet was pistachio, and there was a sliding glass window set up in front. Beneath the window was a sign-in sheet with a pen attached by a silver chain to the counter and a sign that read, *Visitors Please Sign In Before Entering.*

Nick closed the door and stepped into the trailer then cupped his hands around his mouth and yelled, "Yo Mrs. Jill! You in here?"

Something moved around behind the window. The glass door slid open and a woman's head popped out from behind a computer monitor. Her face was chubby and she had a bright red, beehive hair-doo with a pair of thick, square glasses dangling from a silver chain around her plump neck. "Is that you, Nicholas?"

"Hey Jilly bean. How's my favorite nurse?"

"Oh just peachy. You got another one for me?"

"Yes ma'am." Nick put his hand on Monty's shoulder and inched him forward up to the window. "This one's called Monty. He's a chemical engineer. Came all the way from Denver."

"Wow. City boy, huh?"

Monty picked up his gym bag's strap and slid it with him as he walked up to the window.

"Oh my goodness," Jill said. "What on earth happened to your chin?"

Monty dropped the strap and lifted his fingers, touching them to the gash on his chin. Oh shit. The cut, it was bleeding. The damn thing must've opened up again.

"What happened, sweetie?"

"I fell."

"He's an alcoholic," Nick chimed in. "They tend to fall down a lot, you know."

"Yes, yes, they most certainly do." Jill wagged her head from side to side like a doting grandmother then turned to Nick and said, "Well, thanks for dropping him off. I'll take it from here. You got anymore coming in tonight?"

"Not that I know of."

"Is the snow still coming down out there?"

"Yes ma'am. Been coming down all afternoon."

"Well, you be careful out there sweetie."

"Will do." Nick turned toward Monty and patted him on the shoulder. "Later, dawg. I'll see you when you get outta here. Remember what I told you." He leaned forward, his lips like a snake hissing beside Monty's ear. "This might be the best chance you got to get some pussy, so make it count. There's a cute little pill head up in here. Girl by the name of Jenny. I dropped her off a few days ago. You'll know who I'm talking about when you see her. Got an ass like a watermelon"—The kid brought his hands up like he was holding a watermelon then opened his mouth and took an imaginary bite—"*Juicy!* You know what I'm saying, dawg?" The kid rolled his head back and started laughing hysterically like a jack in the box that had been wound up too tight. Then he opened the trailer door and winked at Monty, pulled up his baggy jeans and disappeared off into the night.

"Well, Mr. Monty," Jill said, pulling on her glasses, "from the looks of it, I'd say you're in dire need of some meds. Let's see if we can't get you feeling better." Jill disappeared from behind the window then reappeared seconds later through a set of saloon-style swinging doors. "Now, the doctor won't be here until later tonight, but I'm going to go ahead and start you on some benzodiazepine. It should help slow down the withdrawals."

About damn time. That was all he wanted, ever since he left the hospital more than eight hours ago.

Jill handed him a small plastic cup about the size of a shot glass with three different colored pills crammed inside. "One's the benzo and the other two are vitamins. You can get some water from the fountain over there."

Monty turned his head to see where she was pointing. There was a freestanding water fountain next to the brown, suede couch. He lifted the cup and dumped the pills into his mouth then walked behind the couch and stuck his head under the fountain. The water was freezing. It sent a jolt of pain through his teeth to his gums. But, he swallowed the pills and walked back to the counter, wiping the water from the corners of his mouth.

"Come on," Jill said, propping the door open. "Let's get your blood pressure."

Monty nodded and picked up his green gym bag then followed Jill through the saloon style swinging doors. They took an immediate left and walked down the hallway, entering what looked to be an examination room. The walls were cracked and the carpet was shoddy, and there was an archaic looking hospital bed parked in the center of the room.

Jill plopped down in a chair next to a four-wheeled, plastic pushcart that was loaded with stethoscopes, needles, tubes, and green bags that said *Bio-waste*. "You wanna go ahead and sit down for me?"

Monty nodded and dropped his gym bag then made his way over to the hospital bed. The bed was covered with a thin layer of paper that crinkled underneath his legs as he lowered himself down.

"Can you take your jacket off for me, sweetie? I need to get your blood pressure."

Monty pulled off his jacket and draped it across his legs. He watched intently as Jill fastened a Velcro strap around his bicep then pressed a green button on a computerized machine. The machine began to make a grinding noise, as if it was angry, the strap winding tighter and tighter around his arm. Then it stopped for a few seconds, exhaled, and slowly reduced the tension. Jill mumbled to herself as she jotted down some numbers onto a clipboard that she held in her lap. "One-sixty over one-twenty. It's a little high. The benzo should help bring it down. We'll check it every six hours or so." She set down her pen and clipboard then dug through a plastic box on the second shelf of the cart. "Alright sweetie...now, we just need to get some blood." She pulled out a needle and some rubber tubing that she unwound and set in her lap. "Let's take it from the other arm, okay?"

Monty nodded and shifted his body sideways so that his left arm was closest to Jill. Jill grabbed his wrist and pulled it over gently such that his forearm was resting flat across her thigh. She fastened the rubber cord around his forearm then knotted it tightly at the end. She took two fingers and slapped them against his forearm looking for the green vein hiding underneath his skin. When she found it, she took some isopropyl alcohol and dabbed it with a cotton ball onto his skin. The stench was strong and caused Monty to recoil. He breathed through his mouth instead of through his nose.

"You alright sweetie?"

"Yeah."

Jill positioned the syringe over his forearm then asked "You ready?" Monty nodded and turned away. The stick of the needle was no worse than a bee sting—it was in and out, then gone. Jill placed a cotton ball over the puncture and fastened it down with a piece of blue medical tape. "There," she said as she fastened down the corners. "Can you hold that there for me?"

Monty put his fingers over the tape. Jill unfastened the small serum of blood from the end of the syringe and laid it in a little spice drawer inside the cart. She tore off another piece of tape and crisscrossed it on top of the other, making a blue X over the cotton ball.

"That about does it," she said, patting his knee. "You hungry?"

Monty grimaced. The thought of eating right now made him feel sick. "No thanks. Maybe later."

"How about some ginger ale?"

That actually sounded good. Plus, it was something he could keep down. He nodded. "Okay."

"Alright, let's get you tucked in first then I'll bring you some ginger ale."

"Where's the bathroom?"

"Oh, it's down the hall and to the left. You go and I'll get your ginger ale, okay?"

"Alright."

When Monty got inside the bathroom, he flipped on the light switch then pushed in the small silver lock on the knob. He was a little nervous. This would be his first piss since he pulled out the catheter and he didn't really know what to expect. Hopefully, everything would come out normal. Hopefully, there was no permanent damage to his dick. He unbuttoned his jeans and reached inside his boxers, but was surprised when he didn't feel his hand against his flesh. It was completely numb—there was no feeling, and the foreskin was all shriveled up like a stack of dimes. The blood had dried around the soft part of his pelvis creating a crusty adhesion between the hair and the foreskin. He took a deep breath and bent his head forward and, one by one, surgically peeled away the hairs from the skin. Once it was free, he grabbed it by the tip, pulled it out of his boxers, and aimed it down into the porcelain bowl. He could feel the pressure rising in his belly—it wasn't gushing to come out, but he knew it was there. Maybe some water would help him get going. He reached over and turned on the faucet then closed his eyes and listened to it flow. He could feel something sharp creeping upwards, like a golf ball being sucked through a garden hose. Then, it came, jagged and relentless, like razors wrapped in barbed wire and doused with gasoline. His eyes bugged out, his mouth dropped open, his legs and arms wobbled and tears ran down his cheeks.

It was so painful that he had to steady himself with one hand against the counter, afraid that he was going to black-out and collapse. He gritted his teeth and let out a soft, pain-filled whimper, as the razors cut into him at a slow and painful crawl. He had to stop; it was too much anguish. So, he sucked it back and squeezed his urethra shut. But a remnant drop of blood clung to the tip of his penis like a red-colored spider trying not to get flushed. He flicked his middle finger against the foreskin and the spider fell off and into the bowl. The blood was so dark it almost looked like oil, spiraling downward into the pale yellow bowl. Monty inhaled and exhaled deeply, burying his face into his arms. The razors retracted up into his belly, like the teeth of a great white into its gums.

"Okay, okay," he whispered to himself, one hand on the counter, the other around his nuts. He knew what he had to do. He had to get a good stream going. Get it all out in one good push. The slower he went the more painful it would be for him, but he couldn't do it standing, his legs were too weak. So, he pulled down his jeans and eased onto the porcelain. The seat was so chilly it sent goose bumps up his thighs. He leaned over and twisted the other knob of the faucet. The water gushed out and splashed into the sink. A bank of steam rose up from the water and floated around the lights above the mirror. He reached between his legs and grabbed his penis, directing the tip down into the bowl. Then, he shut his eyes and took a deep breath inward and pushed and pushed as hard as he could. The razors came shredding back up to the surface—the great white was back and ready for its meal. Monty covered his mouth and let out a muffled whimper as the first couple drops dribbled into the bowl. He grabbed hold of the counter and pushed harder and harder, squeezing his fists and gnashing his teeth. The drops became more frequent and evolved into a dribble then eventually developed into a full-fledged stream. The pain subsided and the razors became blunted, like the blade of a knife dulled with a metal file. He looked between his legs. The viscous, brown oil was now a mixture of reddish-yellow, flowing into the toilet in a nice, smooth line. But, as the stream began to weaken, the razors regained their sharpness and the last couple drops felt like they were eating away at his urethra walls. He shook vigorously trying to eject them, but they clung to his tip like they didn't want to go. In one swift motion, he flicked his penis and the last couple drops fell off and splashed into the water. A feeling of relief began to ripple through him as he watched the razors disappear into the bowl. He leaned forward and hit the flusher, and just then, there was a light knock at the door.

"Monty sweetie? Are you alright in there?"

It was the nurse. What did she want from him? Why couldn't she just leave him alone? He grabbed his jeans and pulled them up quickly then zipped his zipper and buttoned his button.

"Monty, are you okay?"

"Yes, I'm fine."

With both hands on the counter, he leaned over the faucet and studied his reflection in the mirror. He looked awful. His face was flushed, his eyes were swollen, and the gash on his chin was crusted over with mucus and blood. He let out a soft whimper as he stuck his hands under the faucet then threw some hot water up on his face. The knocking continued in a gut wrenching intonation, like an angry punk band who didn't know how to play their instruments.

"Monty? You okay sweetie?"

"Yes. I said, I'm fine. Jesus." He dried off his face with a hand towel then took a deep breath and opened the door.

Jill was standing there in the hallway, a look of concern on her freckled face. "You okay?"

Monty shook his head. He couldn't hide it. He sniveled into his shirt and wiped away the snot.

"What's the matter, sweetie?"

"Something's wrong. I'm pissing blood."

"*What? When?*"

"Just now."

"What happened?"

"At the hospital. I pulled out my catheter."

"The hospital? What hospital?"

"In Denver."

"Oh my God, you poor thing. What did it look like?"

"It was sort of reddish-brown."

"Any chunks?"

"I don't know. Maybe."

"Oh, Monty. Was the balloon deflated when you pulled it out?"

"I don't think so."

"Oh Monty. You poor thing. You probably scraped it."

"What should I do?"

"Well, it'll probably bleed a couple more times. You're just going to have to keep going until it clears up. I'm sorry, sweetie. Here, drink this." She handed Monty a small, paper cup filled with crushed ice and ginger ale. He took it and lifted it to his lips and let the liquid slowly trickle into his mouth. He swished it around for a few seconds then closed his eyes and gulped it down. It was cold and wet, sweet and frosty—the perfect remedy for his dry, chapped lips.

"You want some more?" Jill said.

Monty nodded. It was the best thing he'd tasted in a long, long time.

"Okay sweetie, I'll get you some more, but first, let's get you in bed."

Monty followed Jill down the short, dark hallway as the wind outside gusted against the flimsy, metal trailer walls. An exit sign glowed red above the back door staircase, splashing red against the silver of an oval bedroom doorknob. Jill stopped in front of the door then carefully pushed it open. She put her hand on Monty and quietly ushered him inside. There were three beds—two of them looked occupied, just lumps of blankets rising and falling with the cadence of short breaths.

"Quiet," Jill said. "Don't wanna wake the others." Monty nodded and followed her to the vacant bed. He crawled in, one leg after the other, then grabbed the covers and pulled them up to his neck. The mattress was hard and flat and way too short for him. His feet dangled by more than a foot off the edge. The sheets were cold and coarse like sandpaper, but he didn't care. He'd been through so much hell today, it felt good just to be able to lie there, stretch out his muscles and finally relax.

"I'll be back with your ginger ale," Jill said as she crept across the bedroom then disappeared into the hall.

As she closed the door, the room fell silent except for the scraping of a tree branch against the window directly above his head. He shifted his body underneath the blankets then stole a quick glance at the other beds. One of the lumps was beginning to shudder, making a soft moan like someone having a bowel movement. He quickly turned away and tried to focus on his own breathing, curling his knees up against his chest. His toes began to thaw and his heart rate grew steady. Finally. It seemed the Benzo's were kicking in.

As he listened to the wind, his mind drifted to Victoria, her curly, black hair, her warm brown skin. He could feel her there, lying next to him, her soft breasts pressed tightly against his chest. He draped his arm around her body and nuzzled his nose against her neck. "Goodnight," he whispered into his pillow. "I love you, Vicky."

Vicky didn't whisper back.

Chapter 22

No Fraternizing

The next thirty-six hours were an endless stream of ginger ale and Benzo's, nightmares and hallucinations, puking and pissing, sweating and shivering. Most of the time, Monty couldn't tell if he was awake or dreaming—the nightmares and reality seemed to fold in on top of themselves. Was the wind outside really slamming against the walls of the trailer or was it all just part of an ongoing dream? Was he really here in bed, inside this trailer, sweat slicking the backs of his arms and legs? Why couldn't he think clearly? Why was everything all muddled? And why did it feel like he was paralyzed from the neck down? It was like his brain wasn't connected to the rest of his body—like it was on the floor spinning in circles, like a dog chasing its tail around and around. He had no control over the tremors running up and down his muscles or the sweat pouring from his back and sliming the thin, rough hospital sheets. He couldn't stop the images that materialized before him—the figments of an imagination sick from the fever boiling inside his brain—images of Vicky holding a knife to her son's jugular, threatening to slice it open if he didn't read the twelve steps of AA...the counselor from last night, Dexter, standing naked behind her, his partially erect penis grinding against the cleft of her ass. "Read them,"

Dexter said, wiping the lens of his glasses. "Say them with conviction, with passion, with pride. This is your life we're talking about here, not some game of Monopoly. Without these steps you'll never survive."

"Do it," Vicky pleaded. "Do it for me, Monty. Do it for Tommy. Save us. Don't let us die."

Monty's eyes shot open. He ripped off the covers then swung his legs out over the edge of the bed. He couldn't do this. He couldn't lie here any longer, conjuring up these perverted images, allowing them to run wild inside his imagination. He had to get up. He had to get out of here, out of this room, out of this trailer.

He planted his feet into the carpet then slowly straightened his legs. Looking around the room, he noticed the other beds were empty—nothing but indentations where people once slept. Where was everyone? And what time was it? How long had he been asleep?

He crept across the bedroom towards the windows, parted the curtains, and wiped away the fog. It was light out, but not light enough to be lunch time, and certainly not dark enough to be time for dinner. The sun was out but shrouded by a canopy of snow-laced treetops, which bent and swayed with the gusting of the wind. Across the yard, he could see the main house's back porch area where people sat like stumps on benches, clinging to their cigarettes like dead leaves clinging to the trees. How did he end up here? How could he be so stupid? How could he allow this to happen again? He should just leave now before anyone noticed, before everyone out there knew him by his face and name. He could sneak out the back door and trudge through the forest, find that ravine and throw himself off the edge. It would be so simple, so quick and so painless—a moment of freefall followed by a sudden, bone-shattering blow. But what if he didn't die on impact? What if he survived the fall? Would he freeze to death alone in the forest, his blood spilling out into the snow? How long would that take—an hour, maybe two hours?

What if someone found him and took him to the ER? What if he ended up a vegetable, brain dead and paralyzed, sucking oatmeal through a plastic tube? Would his parents cut the cord? No, of course they wouldn't. They were too damn weak to ever let him go. They'd keep him on that life support, hoping for a miracle even when the doctors said he'd have no chance in hell. And he'd just have to lie there and take it while his mother bawled all over him, unable to speak, unable to move. He should've just done it back when he had the chance in Denver, back when he still had a little bit of control. Now, he had none. He was trapped up here in these god damn mountains surrounded by miles and miles of nothing but snow. Even if he did sneak away, how was he going to get back inside his apartment? How was he going to get money to pay for a ride home? His wallet was locked away in that safe in Dexter's office, along with his health savings card and all his keys.

He sighed as he released the curtains then tiptoed across the carpet and sat on the bed. After pulling on his shoes, he reached into his gym bag and pulled out his gloves and his black, wool hat. He put them all on then grabbed his snowboard jacket, opened the door and wandered out into the hall.

As he approached the nurse's station, he heard the sound of country music playing through a set of static-filled speakers. Jill, the nurse, was behind her desk staring at the computer, playing with a strand of red, curly hair. She looked up at Monty as he walked through the saloon-swinging doorway, and gave him a bright, red lipstick-smeared smile. "Well, look who's up," she said, a little too cheery, especially for someone who was stuck in this trailer too. "And how are we feeling this morning? Did you sleep okay?"

"Not really."

"Aw what's wrong, sweetie? You still got the shakes?"

Monty nodded.

"Well, let's see what we can do about that." Jill sifted through a stack of manila file folders and propped one open on the top of the desk. "Let's see, it says you're due for another dose at"—she looked up at the clock ticking above the freestanding water fountain—"right now, actually." She stood up and disappeared from the glass window then came out through the saloon doors carrying a small, plastic cup. "Here you go, sweetie. This should help."

Monty took the cup and dumped the pills into his mouth then walked over to the fountain and got a mouthful of water. He threw his head back and swallowed the pills.

"You hungry sweetie?"

"No."

"You sure? I think they stopped serving breakfast, but you could probably get a bowl of cereal. You should really try and eat something. It might make you feel better. Help to even out that blood pressure."

"No thanks."

"Alright, well, is there anything else I can get you?"

"I guess not."

"Why don't you go back to bed and try and get some more sleep?"

"I can't sleep anymore."

"Well, if you're interested, I think Dexter's giving a lecture this morning. You're more than welcome to attend. It might be nice for you to get out and get some fresh air, meet some of the other patients."

"Okay."

"Oh good. You know how to get over there, right? Just walk straight out this door and go around through the back way. No need to go in through the front of the house. You can just go right in through the back gate and over by the dining hall. I'm sure they'll all be out there smoking and drinking coffee. You can't miss 'em."

Monty walked out the trailer door and trudged his way over, wading through the snow around to the house's back gate. Jill was right. They were still all outside bundled up in their winter jackets, smoking and chatting, braving the early morning chill.

Monty kept his head down and slogged right past them, trying to ignore their curious stares. He was sick and cold, shaky and nauseous and wasn't really in the mood for an exchange of pleasantries. When he got by them, he slid open the door to what must have been the main meeting area, judging by the way the chairs were set up in a semi-circle in the middle of the room. The chairs were empty except for a few people, scribbling in spiral bound notebooks that were unfolded in their laps. Most of the people were up standing around an industrial sized percolator anxiously waiting for the brewing light to turn red.

Monty did his best not to make any eye contact and shuffled his way through the cluster of folding chairs. He picked the chair with the fewest people around it then bent his legs and carefully sat down. With his elbows on his knees, he bent slightly forward and took deep breaths in and out. Maybe this was a mistake. Maybe he should have just stayed in the trailer. But what was he supposed to do? He couldn't sleep. Maybe if he just sat here quietly no one would bother him. Maybe he could just blend in with the rest of the group.

A few minutes passed and the glass door slid open and the patients began to meander in from the outside porch. They smelled like smoke and sounded like hyenas, laughing and chatting, their cheeks bright red from the morning cold. Monty made the mistake of looking towards the doorway when his eyes accidentally locked with a short, grungy looking man's. He had a reddish-brown beard and was walking kind of funny, balancing two cups of coffee, trying not to spill any on his hands.

Oh no, Monty thought, looking away quickly…please don't come over here…please don't sit next to me.

The man limped his way down the line of perfectly good empty folding chairs just so he could stop at the one right next to Monty's. "Is anyone sitting here?" the man said, gnashing his teeth together, like he was chewing on a piece of bubble gum that wasn't really there.

"No," Monty said, scooting his chair over, trying to make as much space he could between him and the other chair. "It's all yours."

"Thanks." The guy crouched down and set his two cups of coffee on the carpet, then took off his jacket and draped it across the back of the chair. With one hand on the seat and the other on his knee, he carefully eased himself down into the chair. "I'm Dave," he said, as he snatched one of the cups from off of the floor.

Monty said nothing and just nodded, slowly breathing in and out through his nose.

"You got a name, kid?"

"Yeah."

"Well, what is it?"

"Monty."

"Monty?"

"Yeah."

"Cool name."

"Thanks."

The guy blew into his cup then took a long slurp of coffee, making a repulsive gurgling sound with his throat. "So, when'd you get here, Monty?"

Oh for Christ's sake. Why? Why did people always do this? Was there a sign on his back that said I'm lonely, please come and talk to me?

"I got here uh...two days ago, I think."

"No shit? Me too. Where'd they put you?"

"What?"

"What floor did they put you on?"

"Oh, I uh...I'm not in the house. I'm in the trailer."

"What trailer?"

"It's around back."

"What's it for?"

Monty sighed and leaned forward. Couldn't this guy tell he didn't feel like talking right now? "I don't know. I guess it's supposed to be some sort of makeshift hospital. It's where they put the people coming off of stuff."

"Oh yeah? You coming off something?"

"Alcohol."

"Alcohol? What? That's it?"

"Yep."

"Shit man, that's nothing. I'm coming off crack and they didn't put me in no detox."

Oh great, Monty thought, another crack head. He should've known by the way the guy was chomping on his fingernails. "Yeah, well, crack's a stimulant."

"Yeah. No shit. So what?"

"So, it doesn't have any of the physical withdrawal that sedatives have."

"You sure about that?"

"Positive."

"Well then how come I feel like I'm about to die?"

"It's psychological. You might feel like you're about to die, but you won't—at least not from cocaine withdrawal."

"You sure?"

"Yep."

"Well then what about heroine?"

"Heroine's a different story. It's a sedative, like alcohol. Depending on how much you've been taking, if you suddenly stop without the proper detox, you could end up going into convulsions and dying from a seizure."

"How the hell do you know all this man? You a doctor or something?"

Monty laughed. "No. I almost finished my PhD, before…well, before all this."

"No shit? So you're a scientist?"

"Not really."

"What's your major?"

"Chemical engineering."

"Chemical engineering?"

"Yep."

"God damn kid, are you sure you're supposed to be here? I don't even know what a chemical engineer does, but the last place I thought I'd meet one is in a fucking drug rehab."

"Yeah, well, I didn't exactly elect to be here."

"Oh yeah? What happened? You get court ordered?"

"Sort of."

"No shit?" Dave's eyes lit up like two atom bombs in the desert. "Me too!"

"Oh yeah?"

"Hell yeah. You think I wanna be here? Fuck no. This place is for loonies." Dave looked back over his shoulder to make sure no one was listening then covered one side of his mouth like he had a secret to tell. "You see that guy over there, the one with the leather jacket and mustache...looks kinda like Geraldo Rivera?"

Monty looked over his shoulder and saw who he was talking about. The guy did look a little like Geraldo Rivera, bushy mustache and all. "Yeah, I see him."

"That motherfucker told me that he was blessed to be in here—that this was some kinda fucking vacation for him. Can you believe that shit? A fucking vacation?" Dave shook his head and took another slurp of coffee. "I'm glad I sat next to you. You actually seem somewhat normal. Some of these other people in here are just plain nuts."

"Yeah, well, I guess some are sicker than others."

"Ain't that the truth." Dave laughed and reclined backwards, scratching the splotches of reddish brown hair on his neck. "So, what kind of drugs they giving you over there?"

"Where?"

"In the trailer."

"Oh uh...just benzos."

"The fuck's that?"

"It's a depressant...supposed to keep people from going into seizure, but I've heard doctors prescribe it for insomnia as well."

"Oh yeah? Makes you tired?"

"Yeah. It makes me groggy."

"That sucks."

"It's better than the alternative. I'd rather sleep than have to go through alcohol withdrawal."

"I hear that. I didn't sleep a fucking wink last night. They stuck me with some dude who has chronic sleep apnea. He had on one of those fucked-up looking prescription sleeping masks. Looked like Darth Vader or some shit, like he had a fucking vacuum cleaner attached to his face."

"What's it for?"

"He said it was supposed to muffle his snoring."

"Did it work?"

"Hell no. The dude still snored all fucking nightlong. The god damn walls were shaking so bad I thought a tornado was ripping through the house. Shit, talk about feeling groggy. I feel like fucking shit right now. I didn't even get a good five minutes."

Monty smiled and motioned to the line of cups underneath Dave's chair. "Well, I see you got your coffee. That should help wake you up."

"Nah, this shit's watered down or something. I've had three cups and I still feel like a fucking zombie."

"Yeah, I think they do water it down. Probably afraid that if they give us real coffee we might start tearing the place apart."

"That's bullshit."

"It was like that at the last rehab I was in. The stuff tasted more like dishwater than actual coffee."

"You were in rehab before this?"

"Yeah, unfortunately."

"What happened? You couldn't stay sober?"

"No, I guess not."

"That sucks man. I'm glad I don't have that problem. Shit, I can quit whenever the fuck I want."

Monty looked up at Dave, surprised he just said that. Was he serious? Or was he just joking around? He waited for him to break into laughter, but he didn't—his face was as serious as a man choking on an atomic fireball. "Wait a minute," Monty said, turning in his seat towards him, "if you can quit whenever you want, then how'd you end up here?"

Dave sniggered as if that was an unmerited question, as if Monty was an idiot for even having asked. "Well," he said, as he reached for his coffee then blew across the surface and took a small sip, "it's a long fucking story, kid." He took another sip and winked at Monty when something caught his attention on the other side of the room. "Uh-oh. Watch out. It looks like they're about to get this show on the road."

Monty turned to see where Dave was nodding. Sure enough, there was Dexter, bouncing down the kitchen steps. He was dressed to the nines with a tie, lapels, and a double-breasted jacket, shiny, black shoes and an elaborate, gold watch. He had a big grin on his face and was singing and dancing. He looked like a preacher about to give a sermon at a Pentecostal church. "Good mornin' everybody," he said, as he glided across the meeting room and bumped fists with the people sitting in the front row.

"*Good morning, Dexter,*" the room replied somewhat unenthusiastically, like they'd seen this act a couple times before.

Dexter frowned and grabbed a chair from against the back wall and propped it open in the center of the room. "That was a little uninspiring. Let's try that again, shall we?" He cupped his hands around his mouth and shouted as loud as he could: "GOOD MORNING EVERYBODY!"

"GOOD MORNING DEXTER!"

The reply was so loud it nearly knocked Monty right out of his chair.

"Now, that's more like it," Dexter said, nodding with conviction and pumping his fist in the air. "That's what I like to hear. Yeah." He whipped his chair around and sat in it backwards, resting his pointy elbows on the top of the metal back. He smiled and nodded as he pointed his finger, counting the patients off around the room. "I see a lot of new faces out there this morning. That's wonderful, just wonderful." He got to the end of the row and paused at Monty then gave him a smile and a wink. "I'm so glad you all could make it. For those of you who don't know me, my name is Dexter and I am a grateful, recovering heroine addict."

"*Hi Dexter*," the room chimed.

"Hi everybody." Dexter laughed and threw his bald head backward, arching like a bow and arrow in his seat. "Before we begin today's group, I want to ask you all a question. How many of you, by show of hands, got down on your knees and prayed this morning?"

About half the hands in the room went up.

"You," Dexter said as he stood up and pointed to a kid who didn't have his hand raised. "What's your name?"

Monty leaned forward to get a better look. It was a Hispanic kid, with wild tattoos scrawled across his neck and forearms, and a black wool beanie pulled over the top of his head.

"Me?" the kid said, indignantly, his finger pressed against his chest.

"Yes, you. What's your name?"

"Miguel."

"Miguel, let me ask you something." Dexter paused and looked down at the carpet, folding his hands behind his back. "Do you believe in God?"

The Hispanic kid scoffed and slouched backward, like a kid getting reprimanded in Sunday school. "Yeah, I believe in him."

"But you chose not to pray to him this morning? Why?"

"Man, I pray. I just don't pray how ya'll want me to pray."

"And why not?"

"I don't get down on my knees for nobody. I ain't no fucking punta, man."

Sniggers eked out from around the circle.

Dexter quickly put up his hand to shush them. "Miguel, let me ask you this. Do you want to get sober?"

"Yeah, I'm here, ain't I?"

"Yes, you most certainly are. But I'll tell you this, Miguel...I guarantee you—*guarantee you*—that you will not get sober unless you get down on your knees and submit to God. And that goes for all of you. If you want to get sober and stay sober, you must get down on your knees every morning and submit to God."

"But what if you don't believe in God?" a voice blurted from somewhere in the back.

Dexter's eyes went wide and his neck craned forward. He looked like a perturbed owl peering out into the center of the room. "Who…who said that?"

Monty turned his body and leaned forward, trying to get a better view so he could see who it was. A small, unsure hand slowly surfaced from beneath the sea of people's faces. The hand was a girl's, petite with black nail polish and silver rings on all the fingers except for her thumb and her pinky. "Uh…I did," the girl said with shy hesitation as if she wished she could take it back.

Dexter's face relaxed and his eyes softened—he went from a perturbed owl to an amused raccoon. "Ah, young, Jenny," he said. "You bring up an excellent question."

"I do?"

"Absolutely, you do. And you already know the answer. You just don't realize it yet."

"I do?"

"Of course you do. It's in your literature. Who has their Big Book? Anyone?"

"I do," Jenny said, as she bent underneath her folding chair then pulled out her Big Book and waved it in the air.

"Ah excellent," Dexter said. "How 'bout flipping to page fifty nine and reading what it says on the top?"

"Okay." Jenny brought the book down and cracked it open, then cleared her throat and began: "Step one—"

"On second thought," Dexter interrupted, "why don't you come up here and read? That way we can all hear you."

"Up there?"

"Yeah, come on. You got your first step coming up. This'll be good practice for you."

"Um…ok."

"That's the spirit. Come on up here, girl. Front and center."

The girl stood up and made her way out of the folding chair horseshoe, clutching her book against her chest. She was young, probably a little younger than Monty, wearing dark rings of purple eye shadow and a dark brown ponytail that seemed to bounce as she walked. Her hips seemed to wag like the tail of a puppy, her butt perfectly curved against a pair of skinny blue jeans. As she planted her feet a few steps behind Dexter, she smiled anxiously at the patients around the room. Monty could tell she was nervous. She was blushing and rocking back and forth on her tiptoes, her hands tightly clutching the book pressed against her lap.

"Alright, Ms. Jenny," Dexter said, as he put his long arm around her and guided her forward to the center of the stage. "I want you to read steps one through three for us, okay?"

Jenny nodded and cracked the book open, her eyes focused intently on the words on the page. "Step one," she said softly, her voice no louder than the chirp of a cricket.

"Louder," Dexter interjected. "Like you mean it."

She smiled and Monty smiled with her. He felt himself pulling for her, but didn't know why.

She took a deep breath and pulled back her shoulders—her shirt came up just enough so that Monty could see some belly skin. "Step one," she said with a little more volume, "we admitted we were powerless over alcohol, that our lives had become unmanageable."

"Good," Dexter said, pacing behind her. "Go on. Step two?"

"Step two. We came to believe that a power greater than ourselves could restore us to sanity."

"Okay, and the last one?"

"Step three. We made a decision to turn our will and our lives over to the care of God as we understood him."

Jenny looked up, beaming with confidence as if she was the Valedictorian giving her class's graduation speech.

"Good," Dexter said, beaming with her. "Thank you, Jenny. Thank you very, very much. You may go sit down now."

Jenny smiled and did a little curtsy then returned to her seat in the back of the room. As she walked back to her chair, Monty's eyes followed her, watching as her ponytail bobbed up and down. She must have felt his gaze, because she looked right at him and gave him a cute, endearing smile. Monty smiled back then quickly looked away from her, turning his eyes back towards the front of the room.

Dexter now had his jacket off—laid across the back of his folding chair—and was rolling his sleeves up to his elbows. "Did you all hear that?" he said, nodding emphatically, his eyes the size of two white golf balls. "Step three says, we made a decision to turn our will and our lives over to the care of God as *we understood him*. What does that mean? Does it mean you have to be a Christian to stay sober? No. Does it mean you have to be a Muslim to stay sober? No. It says God, as *we understood him*. That means whatever higher power you choose to believe in—something or some force beyond the realm of human understanding—a supreme creator, an infallible entity. It doesn't have to be a Christian God or a Muslim God or a Hindu God. God can be anything you want him to be. Okay?"

Dexter paused for a moment and reached into his front pocket then pulled out a white hanky and used it to wipe his sweaty brow. "Okay," he said, as he stuffed the hanky back in his pocket, "before we go any further I'd like to go over some of the ground rules."

A couple groans eked out from around the horseshoe.

"I know, I know," Dexter said. "You are all sick and tired of hearing me harp on this stuff, but I need to go over it for the benefit of the new folks." He glanced in Monty and Dave's direction. "It's pretty simple really. It's all about respect. Respect for the staff, respect for each other, and respect for this disease." He pulled a magic marker from his pocket and walked over to a white board parked against the back window. He wheeled it forward to the center of the horseshoe then flipped it over and wrote *RESPECT* in all caps. He underlined it then wrote *STAFF* directly beneath it and then *ONE ANOTHER* directly beneath *STAFF*.

He turned back around and glared at the patients while screwing the cap back on the marker. "Respect," he said, pointing to the whiteboard. "Respect for the staff. We have a lot of qualified counselors here who are trained to conduct your group therapy sessions in a well-organized and controlled manner. Please remember, that they are the professionals, and you"—he pointed his finger in a stabbing motion toward Dave and Monty—"are the patients. That means if your counselor tells you to do something, I don't want you to argue. Just do it. I don't care how smart you think you are. You are not a psychiatrist and you are not qualified to play doctor. Everyone will get a chance to share their feelings, but only one person should be talking at a time, and whoever that person may be, I want you to give them your full, undivided attention. That means if someone else is talking during group, you shouldn't be. Okay? That's respect for one another."

He put a check mark next to *STAFF* and *ONE ANOTHER* then wrote *DISEASE* right beneath *ONE ANOTHER*.

"Now, respect for the disease. What does that mean? Well, right now, every single one of you is going through chemical withdrawal. Your brain is confused and your body is in a state of complete and utter panic. This is the first time in a long time that you've been without drugs and alcohol, and your body is still trying to figure it all out. You've spent the last several years of your life suppressing your emotions and dulling down your true feelings with massive amounts of booze, drugs, and pills, and whatever else you could get your grubby, little addict hands on. But now that those poisons are leaving your body, those emotions, those raw, uninhibited feelings are bubbling back up to the surface. And believe me when I tell you that once those emotions begin to resurface, they will erupt, and they will be razor sharp. I've been doing this a long, long time, and I can tell you that the very first emotion that comes bubbling up to your brain with the force of that raging Colorado river out there, is gonna be your sex drive. Hell, some of you are probably already feeling it. You've been without those poisons for a couple weeks now, you're starting to feel a little better, you've gotten your appetite back, a little spring in your step, and you're starting to feel that tingle in your loins."

The room filled with a couple of giggles.

"See, you all know what I'm talking about. You're starting to notice your fellow patients and their perky breasts and their cute little behinds."

Even more giggles.

"Am I right? Then, before you know it, this gal or guy you've been noticing is pouring out their guts in group therapy, going on and on about their innermost, personal feelings and you think to yourself, *oh my god, I'm in love.*"

More chuckles…more giggles.

"But please, believe me when I tell you, that it is most certainly not love. It is your disease. It is your disease tricking you. It wants you to take attention away from your recovery. It wants you to think you've found your true love here in rehab and are ready to go away, get married, quit the program, and start having babies. But that's not true. That's not reality. You cannot have a normal relationship until you first learn how to live without drugs and alcohol. And you cannot love somebody else until you first learn how to love yourself."

Dexter paused and looked directly at Monty, as if what he'd just said was supposed to have some kind of special meaning. But it wasn't new, it wasn't special—it was the same bullshit he'd been hearing the past year from Robby…how he and Vicky shouldn't have been together…how they were too young, too early in their own recoveries…how they needed to wait at least a year before they started seeing each other, otherwise they might relapse and leave the program. But, was Robby right? Did any of that happen? Hell no. Nothing could take away what he felt for Vicky—no drugs, no alcohol, no sponsors, nothing. Their love was stronger than this so-called *disease*. And if it hadn't been for the accident, they'd still be together, engaged, in love, clean and sober. If he would've just pulled over and spent the night in Boulder, none of this would've happened—she'd still be here.

Monty sighed and took a deep breath inward while rubbing his forehead with the tips of his fingers. When he looked back up, he noticed that Dexter had switched from evangelical preacher to traveling salesman and was talking about how wonderful a rehab this was to be in. "Now, this facility," he said, pacing in front of the horseshoe, "is the only one of its kind in the entire nation. In other places, they keep the men and women completely segregated. But, I and the other counselors here believe that severely limits what you are able to learn in here. We believe it is tremendously valuable to learn from one another, including members of the opposite sex. We believe that quantum leaps can be made in recovery by listening to one another, and I would never, ever, ever, wanna take that away from any of you. But, for your safety and the safety of your fellow patients, there shall be no touching, flirting, petting, hugging, kissing, or anything even remotely close to it. If one of your fellow patients is going through some trauma, please do not be a shoulder for them to cry on. Give them a tissue and let your counselor know that someone is having a problem. Let the counselors handle it. They are the professionals. That goes back to respect for the staff."

He pointed back up to the word *STAFF*.

"You are here to learn about your disease and work on your own personal recovery. You are not here to work on each other's recovery. Each and every one of you is sick. Some are sicker than others, but we've all got to work on our own personal recovery. And under no circumstance, should the men be on the women's floor and the women on the men's floor. In fact, no one should be upstairs during the day at all, unless you have first gotten your counselor's permission. If you are caught upstairs, where you aren't supposed to be, without your counselor's approval, you will be asked to leave Sanctuary. No refund. You will be kicked out of here faster than you can zip up your jeans and put your thingy back where it belongs. Then you can explain to your family why you wasted their money and abused their trust just so you could satisfy a little tingling in your loins. Are there any questions about this?"

He paused and waited for any questions, but no one's hand went up.

"No questions?" he said. "Going once...twice...okay, gone. Thank you for your time everybody and I will see you back here after lunch for your break-out groups." Dexter smiled and pulled on his double-breasted jacket then trotted up the steps and disappeared into the kitchen. The patients all stood up and pulled on their winter coats and beanies then wandered out the door onto the back porch.

Dave let out a groan then leaned forward and stacked up his empty cups of coffee. "Well kid," he said, as he pulled his right leg out in front of him, "I guess we're outta luck. It sounds like we're not gonna get to do too much fooling around in here. That sucks. There sure are a lot of good-looking girls in here. Did you see that one up there who was reading? What was her name, Jenny?" He drew out a long whistle. "She was pretty cute, wasn't she?"

"I guess."

"Hell yeah she was. Better be careful though. I bet most of these girls in here are nut jobs." Dave smirked and reached into his jacket pocket then pulled out his lighter and a pack of cigarettes. "Come on," he said to Monty, "let's go get a smoke."

"I don't smoke."

"You're shittin' me. You don't smoke?"

"Nope."

"Shit, you're probably the only one in here who doesn't."

"Yeah, I know. I usually am."

"Well, good for you." Dave patted him on the shoulder. "Shit's bad for you. Come on outside with me anyway. I don't wanna be alone with these fucking whackos."

"What the hell." Monty pushed himself up and struggled into his black jacket then followed Dave across the meeting hall and out onto the back porch. The sun was out and the snow was melting, turning the yard into a giant, vanilla Slurpee.

"Hey, look at that," Dave said, pointing across the yard. "It looks like it's actually starting to warm up for a change."

"Yeah, finally. I can't stand this cold."

"Ah, it's not that bad once you get used to it. So, where you wanna sit?"

Monty shrugged. "I don't care."

"How 'bout up there?"

Monty looked to where Dave was pointing. There was a small, white veranda looking out over the backyard picnic tables. "You think we're allowed to go up there?"

"I don't see why not. Come on, let's check it out."

"Okay."

They walked through the backyard and ascended the spiral staircase. The steps were icy and a bit narrow. Monty had to concentrate. He was still a little woozy from all those Benzos.

When he got to the top, he went to the railing and looked out over the stretch of snow-covered forest. There was nothing but miles and miles of evergreens in every direction—it looked like something out of a Robert Frost poem. No towns, no cars, no bars, no traffic…no drugs, no dealers, no liquor stores, no nothing. He took a deep breath and placed his hands on the railing then closed his eyes and soaked in the warm sun. "It's nice up here."

"Yeah, it sure beats being down there with all those nut jobs."

Monty opened his eyes then turned away from the railing. Dave was sitting at a glass table underneath the house's overhang. "You wanna sit down?" he said, as he lit his cigarette then took a drag and let the smoke curl away from his lips.

"Sure."

Monty pulled up a chair and sat down next to him. The seat was wet from the snow melting and dripping off the overhang.

"Careful," Dave said. "It's a little wet."

"Yeah, I noticed."

Dave took another drag and expelled it upward then looked over at Monty as if he wanted to say something. "So," he said, contemplating the end of his cigarette, "you still wanna hear my story?"

"Sure. But, only if you want to tell me."

"I do, but you gotta promise not to tell any of these other whack jobs in here. I don't want any of 'em knowing my business."

"Okay, I promise…but I have a feeling they're going to find out sooner or later. I've been in these kind of places before and by the end of the first week everybody usually knows everybody else's business."

"Well then fuck it. I guess it doesn't really matter then, does it?" Dave sat up and readjusted his posture as if he was about to launch into a serious dissertation. "The reason I'm in here isn't because I'm an addict."

"No?"

"Nope. It's because my bitch of a wife called the fucking cops on me."

"Really?"

"Yep."

"What were you doing?"

"What do you mean?"

"Why'd she call the cops on you? What were you doing?"

"Oh." Dave snorted and leaned forward. Monty could see the annoyance bubbling on his face.

"You don't have to tell me if you don't want to."

"No, no, I'll tell you. You seem cool." He took another drag and put out his cigarette then loosened his collar as if he was a criminal on the stand being cross-examined. "Alright, here it goes."

He took a deep breath then launched into a story about how he got pulled over while driving a school bus up to Estes Park. It seemed his wife called the cops on him and got him arrested for kidnapping his son, Larry, and taking him on the bus. The story was kind of convoluted and didn't make a whole lot of sense to

Monty. Why would his wife call the cops on him? And why would they arrest him? What was he doing? Was he being reckless? Was he driving too fast?

"Wait a minute," Monty said, interrupting him, "I'm a little confused. Why did the cops arrest you? Were you driving too fast?"

"What? No, I told you. It's because my wife called them."

"Yeah, I understand that, but what grounds did they have for arresting you? I mean, they can't just throw you in prison for no reason."

"Oh, well they found my stash."

"Stash of what?"

"Crack."

Ah-ha. There it was. That explained it. Finally, the story was starting to make some sense. "Okay, now I see," Monty said. "So, you were smoking crack and driving a school bus?"

"Well, not at the same time. I mean, I pulled over at a gas station. I'm not an idiot."

"Right, right." Monty tried his best to conceal his laughter, but the mental image was horrifically hilarious—this guy high off of crack behind the wheel of a school bus barreling down the mountains with the cops chasing after him. It sounded less like reality and more like television, like something he'd seen in a Bill Murray movie.

Monty sat up and put on his best poker face, squeezing the ends of the armrests. "So, your wife called the cops on you?"

"Yeah."

"Was she on the bus too?"

"What? No man. She was at court all day."

"Well then how did she know where you were?"

"She always knows where I am. She's a fucking lawyer."

"Oh, okay, that explains it." Monty rolled his eyes. He couldn't believe this guy was serious. What was he talking about? Was he crazy? "Okay," Monty said. "So, your wife's a lawyer."

"Yeah."

"And she called the cops on you."

"Right."

"Because you kidnapped your son, Larry?"

"Yes—I mean, no. I didn't kidnap him. He's my son too for Christ's sake. I didn't have time to take him all the way to Broomfield so I just took him with me up to the volleyball match. What's so bad about that?"

"Nothing, except…"

"Except what?"

Monty paused and considered his next words carefully. He didn't want to get this guy too riled up. In addition to being mentally ill, he could also quite possibly be homicidal. "Well, you *were* driving around under the influence, right?"

"Yeah, so?"

"So, don't you think that's a little irresponsible?"

"Don't tell me you've never driven around a little fucked up."

"No I have, but—"

"But what? What's the difference?"

"Well, I guess there is no difference, but I mean, if I got pulled over, I'd definitely know I deserved it."

"Well, there's the difference right there—I didn't deserve it. The cops pulled me over for no fucking reason. I wasn't doing anything wrong. I wasn't speeding."

"But you were smoking crack."

"Yeah, but how would they know that?"

"Well, your wife told them, right?"

"Yes. Exactly. That's what I've been trying to tell you. The bitch turned me in. She betrayed me."

"Well, maybe she was just worried about you. Maybe she thought you'd get into an accident."

"No, Cheryl doesn't care about anyone but herself. Why do you think she put me in here?"

"Uh…because you need help?"

"Fuck no. The only reason she put me in here was so she could divorce me. I won't give her another kid, so she's trying to get rid of me. She's fucking evil, man, I'm telling you. Hell, I wouldn't be surprised if she's cheating on me right now with one of her little, fucking lawyer buddies."

Monty just shook his head. He didn't know what else he could say to him. The guy was obviously too far in denial to listen to any reason. But, what did he care? It wasn't his responsibility to try and play counselor. Why not just let the guy have his crazy delusion? He seemed harmless, albeit a bit deluded. At least he was in here and not out on the highway. It was only a matter of time before the crazy bastard killed someone.

Just then, Monty heard someone shouting at them from the backyard patio. He got up from his chair and peered out over the railing. It was Dexter. He was in the yard, calling up to them, yelling something about coming down for lunch.

Monty walked back across the veranda, turning to Dave before he started down the spiral staircase. "I think they're starting to serve lunch. You want to go down there?"

Dave nodded and finished his cigarette then stomped it out on the balcony. "Hell yeah, let's go. I'm fucking starving."

The meeting hall had been transformed into a banquet style cafeteria. The horseshoe of chairs was gone, replaced by two columns of white, fiberglass top folding tables. The women were on one side and the men were on the other, and there was a constant carousel of patients going up and down the steps to the kitchen. They carried plastic plates that were loaded with fried chicken and what looked like mashed potatoes swimming in an ocean of gravy.

Dave stepped forward and got behind the last person in line. He clapped his hands together and turned to Monty with a big smile. "Smells good, doesn't it? I'm starving."

The fried grease and hot gravy was overwhelming, like a wall of nausea slamming right into Monty's nose. As he got closer to the kitchen, his stomach started turning like an eggbeater churning a bowl of rancid butter. He couldn't do this. He couldn't eat here with all these people. He stepped out of the line and turned back towards the porch.

"Hey, man where you going?" Dave said.

"I gotta get out of here."

"Why? What's wrong?"

"I don't feel well."

"Well, here, let me help you." Dave got out of line and grabbed Monty's bicep then helped him forward towards the door.

"No, it's alright," Monty said. "I think I got it. I'm probably just going to go back to the trailer and lie down."

"You sure?"

"Yeah."

"I don't mind going over there with you. Don't want you passing out and freezing in the snow."

"No, it's okay. I'll be alright. I think there's just too much commotion in here right now."

"Alright man, well I hope you feel better."

"I will. I just need to lie down."

"You think you're gonna be at the next meeting?"

"I don't know. Maybe."

"Well, I'll save a seat for you just in case."

"Okay."

"Hey, it was nice meeting you, Monty."

"Yeah, you too."

Monty took a couple deep breaths then turned and staggered out onto the backyard patio with his hand over his stomach and his eyes on the ground. The yard was wet and the air was quiet, only the sound of snowmelt dripping from trees. As he walked back towards the trailer, he turned his chin up towards the sunlight and let the warmth caress his tired face. Christ—how in God's name was he going to do this? How was he going to last another four days? He couldn't even stand the smell of fried chicken. Just the thought of eating something made him feel like worms were burrowing into his intestines.

Well, at least he made a friend, at least he met Dave. He usually didn't make friends in these kinds of places. In fact, he usually didn't make any friends at all. He just sort of kept his head down and his mouth quiet and buried his nose in some book that he never even read. But this time was different. He felt a little more comfortable. It was nice to get out of his own head and listen to someone else for a change, especially someone so new in their addiction, someone so fresh, so naïve like Dave. The guy was pretty amusing, although a bit misguided. He had some serious issues with denial and pride. It was almost like he was impervious to self-reflection, like he lacked that basic human function that allowed him to see his own faults. But maybe that was the way to go, with no culpability, never accepting responsibility, never taking any blame. If ignorance was bliss then that guy must be ecstatic. He could just float through life without ever having to feel any real pain. Because *real* pain wasn't external…it was internal. It was having to look at yourself in the mirror every fucking day. If Monty had a choice, he'd take what Dave had, bottle it, and drink it, because anything was better than living in this hell.

He sighed and pulled the trailer door open then walked down the hallway and collapsed onto his bed. He didn't even bother kicking off his shoes or pulling off his jacket—he just closed his eyes and pulled the covers over his head.

Chapter 23

A Moment of Clarity

Dave is driving his Volkswagen along the top of a frozen reservoir, one hand on the steering wheel, the other around his crack pipe. Larry is in the passenger seat laughing and dancing, singing along to a song that plays out over the car's speakers. The song sounds familiar, but Dave can't quite place it. Everything is all muddled—the song, the car, the reservoir, even Larry. Where the hell are they? What are they doing? And why in God's name are they driving across a frozen-over reservoir? What if the ice breaks? What if they fall into the water? How will they get out? Larry can't swim, can he?

Dave tries to get off the ice and back onto the highway, but every time he turns the steering wheel, Larry yanks them right back onto the ice.

"Stop it, Larry. What the hell are you doing?"

"We have to stay on the ice, daddy."

"Why?"

"Because the song's not over."

"Fuck the song." Dave hits the eject button, but the song keeps playing. God damnit. What the hell's wrong with this thing? Why isn't it ejecting?

Just then, he hears something like trees toppling over. When he looks in his rearview mirror, he sees that it's not trees—it's the ice, it's breaking. Shit. Now what is he supposed to do?

He tries to turn the steering wheel, but the wheel just oozes between his fingers, all wet and gummy, as if it's made of putty. What the fuck? He goes to slam down the brakes, but something isn't connecting. It's like there's nothing there, like something is missing. When he looks down in his lap, he notices that his legs have been severed and all that's left are two stumps, all bloody and mangled. Jesus Christ—what the hell's happening? Where are his legs? Did somebody take them?

"Oh daddy," Larry says, with an air of flirtation, "are you looking for these, you silly wittle wabbit?"

Dave looks at Larry. The kid is giggling. He has his legs and is banging them against the dashboard like a pair of drumsticks.

"Larry," Dave says, "what the fuck are you doing? Those are my legs. Give 'em back to me." Dave reaches across the seat, but the kid pulls them back from him. "Nope, sorry daddy. They're my legs, now. I found 'em."

"God damnit Larry, give 'em back to me. I need them."

"Nope, not until you admit you're an addict."

"What? I'm not an addict."

"Then what are you?"

"I'm a runner."

"Not anymore, you're not."

The kid giggles, then rolls down the window and dangles his legs out of the Volkswagen.

"No Larry, wait, what are you doing?"

"I'm going to save you, daddy."

"No, please, don't, I beg you."

The kid takes the legs and tosses them out the window, but Dave leaps across the seat and goes out after them. "No daddy, don't!"

As he dashes out the window, he's able to grab a hold of the ankles, but the skin is so slick with blood that he can't hold onto them. They slip from his hands and splash into the reservoir like a pair of Fun-noodles falling into a swimming pool. "No!"

Dave screams and jumps through the window, his legless body hurtling towards the dark, cold reservoir. Like being run over by an ice truck, his body hits the water, belly first, knocking the air right out of him. He flails around for a while like a flipper-less sea cow, trying to turn himself over so his head won't be submerged in the water. When he finally gets right side up, he looks underneath him and spots his legs sinking towards the bottom. He takes a deep breath and tries to go in after them, but he can't stay submerged and floats back up to the surface. "No! No!" He screams and hollers for someone to help him, but no one comes. He's all alone, bobbing up and down in the water, the blood from his legs slowly draining out into the reservoir.

When Dave woke up, he was wet with perspiration—a slimy, film of sweat covered the back of his legs and the middle of his forehead. As he lifted his head, he looked down the line of his body then pulled off the sheets to make sure his legs were still connected. They were. Thank God. It was just a nightmare. What the hell was that all about? That was fucking awful.

As he rubbed the sleep from his eyes, he heard something stirring beside him. He looked across the room and saw that it was just his roommate, Frank, gurgling in his sleeping mask. Bubbles of drool were foaming out over the corners of the mask's plastic, like a dishwasher that had been filled with liquid soap instead of dishwashing detergent. Jesus—how could he sleep in that thing? Didn't it suffocate him? The thing didn't even work right. He could still hear the fat bastard snoring.

After popping his neck a few times, he pushed himself up from the mattress then knelt beside the dresser and grabbed his shaving kit and a fresh pair of clothes from his Catholic High Crusaders duffle bag. With his shaving kit tucked under his arm, and a red flannel shirt, jeans and underwear thrown over his left shoulder, he walked out into the hallway and got into line for the bathroom. There were two people in front of him and one still in the shower. How could there be only one bathroom for an entire floor of eight male patients? It didn't make any sense. It was idiotic. He couldn't wait to get out of this shit hole. It was almost worst than prison—well, almost.

About half an hour later, Dave finally got to take his turn in the shower, only there was no hot water left. The bastards had used it all. Motherfuckers. It was so cold he could only stand it in three-second increments, and by the time he was done, his dick had shriveled up to the size of a nipple. God damnit, this was awful. He couldn't go through this again. Tomorrow morning, he was gonna wake up early and be the first one out here.

As he stepped out of the shower, he grabbed a towel then dried his hair first followed by his legs, arms, and butt crack. After throwing on his shirt, he pulled on his underwear then slipped into his jeans and rolled on some deodorant. Just as he was about to leave, he saw that someone had left their toothbrush. It was sitting on the sink right next to a bar of soap and some uncapped toothpaste. Hmm. It probably belonged to one of the assholes who took up all the hot water, the same asshole who didn't even bother to flush and left a bunch of piss in the toilet. Dave thought about it for a moment. Should he do it? Yeah. The bastards deserved it for making him freeze his ass off.

First, he took the toothpaste and squeezed as much as he could into the piss-filled toilet then grabbed the toothbrush and dunked it into the bowl, scrubbing the bristles against the shit-stained porcelain. Next up was the soap bar. He took a bite out of it and spit half of it into the toilet, then hit the flusher and put everything right back where he'd found it—the empty tooth paste tube, the feces-scrubbed toothbrush, and the half-eaten bar of soap that had his teeth marks in it. There. Enjoy that, you bastards. Last time you fuck with me, you inconsiderate assholes.

He smiled in victory as he gathered up his dirty laundry then swung open the door and limped back to his bedroom. After tossing his dirty clothes on the floor, he put on his green and gold Catholic High Crusaders jacket, then pulled on his black and yellow bumble-bee running shoes and headed down for breakfast.

When he got downstairs, the smell of bacon grease began to waft under his nostrils, causing his mouth to salivate and his stomach to grumble. Damn, he was hungry. It had been a long time since dinner. Why they served it at five o'clock, he still couldn't understand it.

He got behind the last person in line at the entrance to the kitchen and inched forward slowly while eyeing the glorious spread of food set up on the table. There were scrambled eggs, bacon, sausage, and blueberry pancakes. Dave loaded up his plate with a little bit of everything then reached into the cooler and grabbed a can of orange juice. He found a seat by himself on the men's side of the dining hall.

He didn't waste any time and dove right into the sausage, cramming it into his mouth almost as fast as he could swallow. When he was finished with the sausage, he went for the bacon, then the eggs, and then the pancakes, which he smothered with hot butter and drenched in maple syrup. It was all so good. Every single bite was delicious. He couldn't remember the last time he ate a breakfast like this. It was probably back when he was still running races.

Once he finished with his plate, he went back up and grabbed another, but this time instead of eggs and pancakes, he got twice the serving of bacon and sausage. It looked like a whole dead pig was on his plate, all cut up and processed, the steam from the grease rising up like the pig's deceased spirit. As he sat back down, he bent over the plate and took a deep breath inward, letting the hot grease fill up his lungs and nostrils. Then, he arranged his can of orange juice directly in front of him, grabbed his plastic fork and knife and went to work again savoring every single morsel.

Once he was finished, he took his plate, cup, and napkins and threw them all in the trash. Then he got a fresh cup of coffee and took it with him outside to the back porch patio. There was a small group of patients out there huddled together. They were under the red glow of two umbrella-shaped space heaters playing a game of Monopoly that was set up on one of the green picnic tables.

Dave tried not to look at them as he grabbed a metal folding chair and propped it open beside the payphones. Unfortunately, one of the patients got up, walked over, and asked if he wanted to play Monopoly. He told them no, because he didn't really like board games. Of course, what he really meant was that he didn't like any of them. He still couldn't understand why these people would elect to be here and why they seemed so damn happy about it. His roommate even said this was a vacation for him. A vacation? Really? Was he serious? This place was a shit hole. If he wasn't court ordered, he'd be fucking out of here.

After two cigarettes and two cups of coffee, Dave decided to go for a walk around the backyard's perimeter. He took his cigarettes and lighter and stuffed them into his jacket pockets and was about to get up when Dexter, the black counselor from yesterday, poked his head through the sliding glass doors and said, "Come on peeps. It's time for morning group. Let's get this thing started."

The patients all groaned as they began packing up the Monopoly pieces then stuffed the game board into the box and shuffled by Dave back into the cafeteria. Oh great, Dave thought, guess he had to go in there with them. Another group? Christ—how many more of these things did he have to go through?

After tossing his two coffee Styrofoam cups into the trash can, Dave followed the procession of patients back inside the cafeteria. But the cafeteria tables were gone—stacked up by the windows—and all the chairs had been put away except for a dozen or so sitting in a circle in the middle of the meeting room.

Before he sat down, Dave grabbed two more cups of coffee and loaded them each up with two packets of Sweet'n Low and two miniature cartons of half and half Mini Moo's. He picked a spot on the outer edge of the circle and grabbed a chair for himself and one for his bad leg. After setting his cups on the carpet, he positioned the extra chair directly in front of him then propped his bad leg up on the seat and folded his hands behind his head. There. Now, he was set. Now, he was ready. He was ready for whatever bullshit group therapy he had to listen to today.

A couple minutes later, Dexter appeared at the top of the kitchen staircase with a pen in his mouth and clipboard tucked under his armpit. "Good morning everybody," he said, as he trotted down the staircase, clapping his hands together like a seal at Sea World.

"*Good morning Dexter,*" the group chimed like a cult following, entranced by their leader's demonic swagger.

Dexter smiled and grabbed a chair from the stack against the back windows and plopped it open right in the center of the circle. "How's everybody doing today?"

"*Good.*"

"Looks like we got some fresh faces today. That's great." He started pumping his fist and chanting like a frat guy at a toga party. "Fresh fish! Fresh fish! Fresh fish!" He was all teeth and bright, white eyeballs, his head black and glossy like a freshly waxed bowling ball. "Alright peeps," he said, then dropped his clipboard and slid it with his heel underneath his chair. "It's nearly nine o'clock, so let's go ahead and get started. For those of you who don't know me, my name is Dexter and I am a grateful, recovering heroin addict."

"*Hi Dexter.*"

"Hi everybody. This is my group. The nine o'clock group therapy group, for lack of a better name."

Dexter smiled and nodded in Dave's direction. What the hell was he smiling at? What was he, gay or something?

"Since we have some new faces with us today, I want to go over the ground rules real quick."

Grumbles rippled from around the circle. Dexter frowned and leaned forward, pointy elbows on top of pointy kneecaps. "Alright, pipe down. If you already know the rules then you don't gotta listen. This is for the new folks, alright?"

The grumbles turned to nods then to sounds of approval. Dexter waited for the room to settle then cleared his throat. "Alright, rule number one: *No Cross Talk.* What does that mean? That means if someone else in the circle is speaking, you shouldn't be. Everyone in this room will have a chance to share, and when it's your turn to do so, I do not want you to direct it towards anyone else in the group but yourself. You are here to work on your own recovery and not somebody else's, okay?"

Yeah right, recovery? What a bunch of horseshit. What was he supposed to be recovering from? What was he, sick or something?

"Rule number two: *Surrender.* If the topic of conversation is making you uneasy and you just can't bear to hear anymore, you are permitted to leave the group. Touch your knee to the floor, like this"—Dexter got down on one knee and stuck his right hand up in the air—"and say, I surrender. This lets me know that you are surrendering and leaving the group. Now, if you do this, you must go sit in the front foyer and notify the other counselors that you have left the group. Under no circumstances are you permitted to go outside and have a smoke while group is going on. Understood?"

Damn, in that case, he may as well get down on one knee right now and just get it over with. He'd rather sit up in the foyer than have to listen to this bullshit.

"Alright, last one. Rule number three: *The Foot Rule.* Your feet must be touching the floor at all times while you're in here. I want you listening and paying close attention to what's going on and not slouching backwards in your chair with your feet propped up." Dexter lowered his glasses and looked around the circle. He stopped and stared at Dave. Oh great, just when he was starting to get comfortable. "That means you sir. One foot on the ground please."

"Me?" Dave said, trying to sound innocent, seeing if he could work the pity card on him.

"Yes, you. I need both feet on the floor, please."

"But I have a medical condition," Dave said, pursing his lips together. "I have to keep this leg elevated or I'll lose blood flow and I won't be able to stand for like an hour. See, look, look." Dave rolled up his pant leg, revealing the long red scar that began at his thigh and ended at his ankle.

The patients around the circle all gasped and starting making gagging noises. One of 'em even got down on one knee and tried to surrender.

"Alright, alright, everybody just calm down," Dexter said. "There's no need to flip out. It's just a leg." Dexter turned to Dave and scowled, shielding his eyes as if he was blocking out the sunlight. "Alright, you can keep it propped up. But I want the other foot to remain on the floor. Deal?"

"Deal." Dave smiled to himself as he rolled down his pant leg. Yes, another victory. He was actually starting to enjoy himself.

"Alright good. Is everybody else good?"

"*Yes Dexter.*"

"Alright then. Let's go ahead and get started."

Dexter clapped his hands and turned towards one of the patients—a good-looking woman, probably in her late forties, with long, sexy legs and a big ol' set of D size titties. "Angie, sweetie? Are you ready?"

The woman smiled shyly and reached behind her then pulled out a poster board and made her way to the center of the circle.

Dave was absolutely mesmerized. He couldn't take his eyes off of her. The woman was a ten—no, scratch that, an eleven, maybe a little old, but in a mature Kim Basinger kind of way. She had a long, graceful neck and a pair of full, luscious lips as red as the skin of a Red Delicious apple, with a wild mane of dirty blond hair that seemed to roll in waves over her skin tight, white sweater. The only flaw he could see were the little red dots speckled across her forehead, but, that was okay—she was probably just having a bad pimple break-out or something.

As the woman pulled her hair back, Dave craned his head forward and suddenly realized that he'd seen this woman somewhere before. But, it wasn't just her face—even her physique looked somewhat familiar. Those long, sexy legs, those broad, swimmer-like shoulders—he'd seen them somewhere, but where? Where had he seen them? Was she one of Cheryl's friends? No, Cheryl wouldn't know anyone in here. What about a teacher from the high school? No, of course not. They wouldn't hire anyone who was this sexy. Then where? Where had he seen her?

Dexter popped up from his chair and took the poster board from the woman then set it up on the seat cushion and dragged the chair more towards the center. "Okay," he said with one eye closed and his hands raised outward, like he was a director appraising the next shot of a movie, "why don't we all move our chairs this way so we can see Angie's poster?"

Everyone got up and shifted in closer, making a kind of distorted horseshoe in front of Angie and her poster. "Alright, can everybody see now?"

"*Yes, Dexter.*"

"Alright good." Dexter got another chair from the stack against the back windows and sat down in it at the head of the horseshoe. "Okay, so today, we're gonna do Angie's first step. The first step is probably—no wait, scratch that"—Dexter slapped his lips as if he'd said something inappropriate—"The first step is without a doubt the most important step that you all will take in here. It is an affirmation of the powerlessness that each of you have over your disease. Everyone in here will have the opportunity to put a life collage together, like the one Angie has so marvelously constructed, and present it to your fellow addicts and alcoholics. As you can see, your life collage is a quick summary of the events of your life in visual representation. Each of you will get a poster board, just like this one, and use the hundreds of magazines and newspapers we have over there on the counter to cut out pictures or words or phrases that describe your life up to this point in time. You can arrange it any way you like. Some people, the type A personalities, like to arrange theirs in linear form. Others, the type B personalities, like me, usually just scatter them all over the place in no particular order. It is completely up to you how you want to present it. The key to making a successful life collage is to pick out things that show the powerlessness you have over your addiction. For instance, I once had a guy who found a picture of a Ford truck that was all bent up and twisted. He explained that not only could he not stop drinking, but he also couldn't stop from driving around drunk. He admitted his powerlessness and said that if he didn't stop drinking, he'd end up like the guy in that truck. So, that's what we're after here people, an affirmation of your powerlessness. I'm sure every single person in here can give a specific example that shows exactly what that is."

Dave's mind flashed back to images of his blue Volkswagen, the right fender smashed in and the side mirror knocked off. He never did figure out what in the hell had happened. Maybe he hit a deer. Those fuckers were all over the place in Boulder. But would a deer explain that red shit smeared all across the side panels? Yeah, it was probably just dried up deer blood. Stupid animals. They oughta make 'em extinct or something.

"Okay, Angie," Dexter said, as he picked up his clipboard and pulled the cap off his ballpoint. "Are you ready?"

Angie nodded and smiled timidly, revealing a pair of shiny, metallic braces. Damn, strike two, Dave thought. What else was she hiding? Oh well, at least her body was still pretty damn flawless. Her tits were definitely D's, maybe even double D's, if he wasn't mistaken.

"Whenever you're ready," Dexter said.

Angie took a deep breath then pulled her long, blond hair back behind her. "Hi everyone," she said, a bit shaky, lifting her hand in a shy, little wave. "My name's Angie."

"Hi Angie."

"Um, hi." She cleared her throat and turned toward the poster, pointing to a picture of the U.S. map, right around southern Wyoming. "So, I grew up in a little town called Rock Springs, Wyoming." There was a green thumbtack stuck to the southwest quadrant of Wyoming, just north of the border between Colorado and Utah. "This is my mom, Laurie and my childhood dog, Ralphie." Her hand moved down to a couple photographs that were all chewed up, like they'd been pulled out of a fire. "I was an only child. My dad died when I was real little. His name was Doug."

She pointed to an old, grainy black and white photo of a man posing in front of a Chevy Camaro. He looked Greek, maybe Italian, kind of handsome, like Robert Deniro, with dark, wavy hair and a little mole on his right cheek.

"He was an alcoholic and a schizophrenic and he shot himself in the head when I was only three." Below the photo was a cutout of a cartoon revolver that had hand-drawn smoke curling up from the barrel. "My mom's also an alcoholic—a *recovering* alcoholic—and she's been sober for like five years now." Beside the revolver were some crude, hand drawn pictures of bottles of booze with skull and cross bones emblazoned on the front label. Dave had to strain his eyes and scoot his chair forward so he could read the penciled-in lettering underneath. It read *Poison*.

"Let's see," Angie said, glancing back at her poster, nervously wringing the tips of her fingers.

"Um…I was a pretty bad student. I was always getting into trouble at school, breaking the rules, skipping class, and smoking weed out by the jungle gym." She laughed nervously, her eyes cast down towards the floor. "My mom sent me to a shrink when I was in the eighth grade. I guess I was fourteen at the time, or around there. The doctor told my mom that I had attention deficit disorder and that I needed medication to calm me down. So, he prescribed me a bunch of Ritalin, and when that didn't work he prescribed me Xanax, and when that didn't work, Dexedrine. I started taking a whole bunch at a time, and even started stealing my mom's pain pills from her medicine cabinet. My mom was still drinking a lot then, and so I'd steal her liquor and take a bunch of her pain pills up to school and sell them and use the money to buy weed. I started getting really, really messed up when I was…I guess a sophomore in high school. Sometimes I'd just start crying in the middle of class for no particular reason and the teacher would make me go down to the principal's office and all the kids would laugh at me and call me names, like crazy Angie, or loopy Angie, or just basket case. Then, one day I got caught smoking weed with some friends—" She paused and looked up, a sad smirk on her face—"well, I mean, I don't know if you could call them friends. They only hung out with me because I could get them high. Anyway, we were in the park smoking weed and some patrol cars drove by. My friends took off running, but I just sat there and finished my joint, then swallowed a whole bunch of pills and washed it down with some vodka. At that point, I didn't really give a damn. So, the cops picked me up and I had to spend a couple of nights in the juvenile detention center while my mom was passed out drunk at the house. It took her five days just to sober up so she could come get me. I remember the ride home. It was cold and rainy and she didn't say a single word to me. She just went back inside and polished off a box of wine. The next week, I was on my way to an all girls reform school at some place in northern Wyoming." Angie paused and took a deep breath inward, tears beginning to form at the base of her eyes.

"That was the worst," she said, wiping her eyelids, "being trapped in that hell hole. The teachers there were so messed up. They would beat us with leather belts and lock us in our rooms. We hardly ever got to go outside. We lived in these cramped little spaces, like ten girls to one bathroom. It was awful. I've tried to block out most of the memories, but there was one that I could never forget. There was this teacher named James. He was the only guy in that place. The rest were nuns. He was like thirty, maybe thirty-five, and he taught our history and geography classes. He was really smart and funny and even kind of cute, but he would always single me out and yell at me in front of everyone in class. I never knew why, until one day after class, he sat me down in front of him and told me that the only reason he was making an example out of me was because he liked me and wanted to see me succeed in life." She paused for a moment and looked down at the carpet, twisting her finger like she was trying to pull off a ring.

"It's okay," Dexter said. "You can do it. Go on, Angie. Tell us what happened."

She lifted her head and looked up at the horseshoe. Tears streamed down her face and dripped to the carpet.

"Come on, Angie," Dexter said. "Tell us what happened. Don't be afraid."

What an asshole, Dave thought. Why was he pushing her? It was obvious she didn't want to tell the god damn story.

"Well," Angie said, wiping her eyelids, pushing her hair back away from her face, "he started getting really close to me. He put one hand on my shoulder and slid the other in between my knees. Then, he started undoing my blouse and breathing on my cheek. I was frozen. I couldn't move. I couldn't do anything. He got up for a minute and shut the classroom door. Then, he came back and forced me down on top of his desk. He put all his weight on top of me, pulled off my underwear, and unzipped his pants. It hurt so much. I just shut my eyes and cried and prayed for it to be over. Once it was over, I ran back to my room, and cried into my pillow until I fell asleep. I didn't go to class, I didn't go to the cafeteria, I just stayed in my room and cried and cried and cried. No one knew what was wrong with me. They all just thought I was crazy. The nuns tried to make me come out but I didn't want to, so they dragged me out of there and locked me in confinement. I tried to tell them what happened but no one believed me. They all said I was making it up to try and get attention. They all said I was evil and crazy. I guess I don't blame them. I mean, why would anyone believe me? I was a bad kid, a rotten apple."

No, Dave thought. She wasn't a rotten apple. She just got fucked over by people she was supposed to be able to trust. Poor woman. Why was Dexter making her do this? It was obvious she didn't want to be up there telling this story. As if it wasn't bad enough being locked up in this hellhole—you also had to feel like shit in front of a room full of people you didn't even know? What was the point? To make you feel lousy? Dave didn't get it. It seemed counterintuitive. Why would you want to be powerless over something you could otherwise control?

Dexter got up and grabbed a box of tissues and handed them to Angie as he studied his clipboard. "Take your time, Angie," he said, as he returned to his folding chair and crossed his legs like the big shot counselor he probably thought he was.

Angie nodded and took out a tissue. She blew her nose then set the box behind her on the floor. "I was there at St. Catherine's Reform School for a whole year. They finally sent me home when my mom decided she didn't want to pay the tuition anymore. So, I went back to my old high school and started my senior year. And that's when I met Bill." All of a sudden, Angie's demeanor completely shifted. Her face lit up like one of those Oriental ball lamps.

"Bill was the most gorgeous man I'd ever laid eyes on. Starting quarterback and president of the student council, he wasn't only a real man's man, but he was intelligent too. And he had the hots for me, big time. I could tell by the way he was always smiling at me in P.E. But, being the bad girl I was, all of his buddies said he should stay away from me. Thank God he didn't listen to them and asked me out on a date. I'll never forget it. We went and saw *Footloose* at the Star Stadium theatre. Bill was a big fan of Kevin Bacon back then. After the movie, he took me to the top of Lookout Mountain and made love to me until the sun came up. It was like something out of a dream. Almost overnight, I went from crazy Angie to Cinderella...from the Hunchback of Notre Dame to the Belle of the Ball. Bill was my Prince Charming...my knight in shining armor. With him, I didn't feel the need to get high or wasted. For the first time in my life, I was just fine with who I was."

Angie closed her eyes as if she was trying to savor the memory. When she opened them back up, she seemed peaceful and pleasant, like someone who had just devoured a bar of Godiva dark chocolate.

"We fell deeply in love right after Homecoming and by the time graduation rolled around, I was pregnant with my first son, Jonathon." She returned to her poster and pointed to a clipping of the Gerber baby that she'd obviously gotten from a magazine advertisement. "After the wedding, Bill got a job at his uncle's construction company in Boulder, so we packed up everything and moved out to Colorado."

She lived in Boulder? Well hell, he probably did know her. Maybe he'd met her ex-husband. Maybe he'd worked with him before.

"We bought a little house in Broomfield—we couldn't afford a house in Boulder—and Bill went to work while I stayed at home with little Jonathon. Everything was going pretty good. We had two more babies, Joshua and Sarah." She pointed to two more pictures of cutout babies—one was from a Charmin toilet paper advertisement and the other was from an ad for the Kid's Gap outlet. "I have a real picture to show you. It's in my day bag. I didn't want to glue it to the poster, 'cause I was afraid I might tear it when I tried to get it off." She shuffled back to her chair and knelt beside a red leather handbag then carefully pulled out a photo and took it back with her up to the front of the circle. "They're such beautiful children," she said, as she proudly held up the photo, "especially my youngest, Sarah. She's such a smart young lady and a great athlete too."

Dave strained his eyes and leaned as far as he could forward, narrowing in on the girl who was sandwiched between her two older brothers. She had straight, blonde hair, just like her mother's, with a long, swan-like neck and skin as milky and smooth as freshly churned butter. The white dress she wore was sleeveless, such that you could see her shoulders, which were almost as defined as either of her brothers'. Suddenly, it hit Dave, like someone had just slapped him in the forehead. Wait a minute, he knew this girl. It was Sarah, Sarah Mallard—the captain of his volleyball team, his best middle blocker. That's how he knew this woman. That's why she looked so familiar. She was Sarah's mother—same blond hair, same muscular shoulders, same sexy, long legs, and same juicy, double D melons. Holy shit. He couldn't believe it. What were the odds of running into Sarah's mother? And in a rehab of all places? Maybe it was a sign, like a message or something. Maybe the universe was trying to tell him something.

He sniggered to himself as he sank back against his folding chair. Yeah right. What was the message? That he was stuck in rehab with his middle blocker's mother? So what? What good did that do him? How was that gonna help him get out of here? He was still trapped in this shit hole.

As he watched Angie carefully place the photo back in her handbag, something hit him—something roused his senses like being doused with a bucket of freezing cold ice water. If only for a moment, it was as if he had perfect clarity, as if everything in front of him was aligning in perfect harmony. He thought back to what his lawyer, Weinstein, had said—that the cops couldn't just arrest him without probable cause—that they had to witness him doing something suspicious first in order to have reasonable suspicion to pull him over. Meaning, he had to be swerving, or speeding, or driving erratically, but since he wasn't doing any of those things, they could prove the cops didn't have reasonable suspicion and the case could be dismissed and he could get the fuck out of here. All he had to do was prove that he wasn't speeding or swerving, and who better to prove that than this girl Sarah? She was there. She saw what happened. She saw them choke him with the billy club. She saw them shoot Larry with a fucking Taser. Holy shit. This was it. This was the break he'd been waiting for. All he had to do was get Angie to get Sarah to testify for him.

Dave could barely sit still for the rest of the meeting. He was so antsy that chomping on his fingernails was the only way he could keep from digging out his own eyeballs. He couldn't even listen to the rest of Angie's story, because he was too busy congratulating himself on what a genius he was. She said something about a divorce, a settlement, and a guy named Rick with a dingy trailer. He didn't really pay close attention. He was too busy plotting out what he was gonna say to her. He knew he couldn't just run up to this woman and spring the idea on her. She seemed like the kind of gal who might scare away pretty easily. He had to take it slow, nice and easy, use his powers of seduction, finesse her a little.

First, he'd introduce himself and tell her what a great job she did with her First Step story, tell her it inspired him and made him feel uplifted. Then, he'd tell her who he was and establish the connection, tell her he was Sarah's volleyball coach and talk about what an outstanding player Sarah was. That oughta give her some kind of reassurance. What mother wouldn't like hearing wonderful things about their daughter?

Once the meeting was over, the patients got up and went out for a smoke break on the back porch patio, except for Dave who hung back a bit and waited for the right opportunity to talk to Angie. Unfortunately, Dexter and a few other patients had her surrounded. They were congratulating her on what a great job she did and basically kissing up to her.

Come on people, Dave thought. Get the fuck out of here. Couldn't they see he needed to talk to this woman? She was his only ticket out of here.

After a few minutes, Dave finally gave up and retreated to the kitchen for a fresh cup of coffee. He poured in his standard two packets of Sweet 'n Low and two cartons of half & half Mini-Moos. He stirred it up, tossed back a gulp, then limped down the steps into the meeting hall, and wouldn't you know it?

Angie was gone. The bitch had vanished. Fuck. He was only gone for a minute. Where the hell did she go? Who was she, Houdini or something?

He cursed to himself as he limped across the meeting hall then slid open the sliding glass doors and stepped out onto the backyard patio. Most of patients had re-assembled back behind their stacks of multi-colored, paper money. They were all huddled together with wool blankets pulled up around their shoulders like prisoners in a concentration camp waiting for the guards to come gas them.

He took a quick look at the table, but didn't see Angie, and so he squinted his eyes and began to scan the backyard's perimeter. Ah-ha—there she was, out by the garden, sitting on a concrete bench, having a cigarette. And she was alone, thank God. This was his opportunity. There was no one around. It was now or never.

He spit on his hand then parted his hair down the middle, took a deep breath and made his way out across the winter wonderland. The snow was about three inches deep, all soft and squishy. It seemed to squirm out from underneath his feet like a tangle of garden snakes. Great, now his favorite running shoes were gonna get ruined. How could Cheryl not think to pack any boots for him? What was she, fucking stupid?

As he approached the bench, Angie's face came clearer into focus. She was sipping on coffee and sucking down a cigarette. "Hey," Dave said, smiling down at her, his eyes bouncing between her face and the perfect little triangle that formed between her legs where the crotch met the pelvis. "What are you doing out here? Aren't you freezing?"

Angie looked up, surprised and uncertain. She laughed anxiously then nodded her head. "Yeah, a little, but I don't mind it. I grew up in the mountains, so I'm kind of used to it."

"Yeah, me too."

Dave smiled and the woman smiled with him, revealing those two rows of shiny braces. Somehow, the braces made her look twenty years younger, like she was just a girl in high school waiting for her boyfriend. "I'm Dave, by the way," he said, as he extended his hand outward.

Angie smiled and fumbled with her cigarette, switching it to her left hand so she could offer her right. "Nice to meet you, Dave. I'm Angie." Dave held her hand for a few seconds longer than what was probably acceptable. But he didn't care. Her touch felt good to him.

"Nice to meet you, Angie," he said. "You mind if I sit down?"

"No, go ahead." Angie scooted down the bench and made room for Dave and his two cups of coffee. Lucky for him, she'd warmed the spot for him. For a split second, he thought how great it would be to be this bench for just one minute and feel the warmth of this woman's ass on top of his lips and across his forehead.

He shook off the fantasy as he pulled out his cigarette, flipped it in between his lips then lit the end. "So," he said, trying to think of something clever, something that would get this conversation rolling along nicely, "how long have you been here?"

"Oh…about a week."

"Really? That's it?"

"Yeah. Why so surprised?"

"Well, you just looked like such a pro up there."

"Thanks." She smiled then took a quick puff of her cigarette. The smoke drifted off into the vanilla-colored sky. "It was an interesting experience. Kind of weird telling that stuff to a room full of strangers. Could you tell I was nervous?"

"No, not at all. You did a good job. Very natural."

"Thanks. I appreciate that."

She smiled and returned to her cigarette, lifted it to her lips and took another deep drag. "So what about you?" she said, as she flicked away the ashes, which drifted like charred leaves to the rich, creamy ground. "How long have you been here?"

"Oh, about three days."

"Really? So, you're pretty new here?"

"Yep."

"What's the one that did it?"

"Excuse me?" Dave said.

"Your drug of choice."

Dave laughed and looked at the end of his cigarette. "Why the hell does everyone keep asking me that?"

"Oh, I'm sorry. They all asked me the same thing when I first got here. I think it's how people introduce themselves around here."

Dave nodded and took another sip of coffee. Stupid way to introduce yourself, he thought.

As he looked down at the bench, he noticed that Angie's hands were shaking, and she had little red lesions, like the ones on her forehead, covering the backs of her knuckles. "You alright?" he asked.

"Yeah. Why?"

"Your hands—they're shaking. Are you cold?"

"No, I'm fine."

Yeah right. Dave knew she was lying. He could tell by the way she quickly pulled her hands away and wedged them underneath her thighs. "You sure you're alright?" he said, as sincere as possible, trying to sound like he actually gave a damn.

"Well," she said, as she tilted her chin upright and pushed her bangs back away from her eyes, "according to Dexter, I'm an addict...but here's the thing." She whipped her head around abruptly, wielding her cigarette like she was waving a gun. "I never had any problems until I started taking that Dexedrine crap."

"Dexe-what?" Dave said, leaning away from her so the cigarette didn't accidentally wind up in his eyeball.

"Oh, it's this stupid stuff my doctor put me on. He said it was supposed to help with my ADHD, but all it did was screw with my head and make me bloated."

"So, is that what you're here for? Dexedrine?"

"No, not really. I guess I'm what you'd call a meth head."

"Really?"

"Yeah."

"Well, that's surprising."

"Why do you say that?"

"Well, I never would've pegged you for a meth head."

"No?"

"Hell no. A pretty lady like yourself? Shit. Alcoholic, maybe, but definitely not a meth head."

Angie smiled and sniffled. Her face turned a shade of red that helped to camouflage her pimples. "Thanks, I think."

"Don't mention it."

"Well, what about you?"

"What about me?"

"Are you an alcoholic?"

Dave laughed then shook his head. "Who me? Hell no."

"Then what?"

Yes. Here it was. This was his opportunity to tell her what a bitch Cheryl was. "Well," he said then took a quick puff of his cigarette and turned to Angie with a sly, sarcastic smile, "if you must know, Angie, I'm here because my lying, cheating, two-faced bitch of a wife turned me into the cops."

Angie gasped, covering her mouth. "You're kidding me?"

"Nope."

"What happened?"

Dave paused for a moment to add dramatic tension then lowered his eyes and took a long, labored breath inward. "It's a long story," he said, as pathetically as possible, hoping that Angie would take pity on him. "All I can say is she's trying to get rid of me, probably so she can get custody of the kids and run off with her little lawyer boyfriend."

Angie gasped again, only this time louder. Everything seemed to be working. He was reeling her in. "Wait—she's cheating on you too?"

"Yep. I mean, at least I think she's cheating. I can't really think of any other reason why she'd be doing this to me." Dave clenched his fist and looked down at his knuckles, staring at the little wrinkled, red grooves imprinted in the skin. He tried to force some tears, but couldn't get them going, so he just dropped his head and let out another *woe is me* kind of sigh. "She's probably with the son of a bitch right now, filling out the divorce papers, just laughing it up, and humping away in my bed."

"Oh, you poor thing." Angie scooted close to him and put her hand on his kneecap, stroking it like she was stroking a cat.

Yes, it was working. Everything was moving along nicely. He was gaining her confidence. He was establishing a relationship.

"I'm so sorry," Angie said, moving her hand across his knuckles, the soft touch of her fingers sending goose bumps up and down his vertebrae. "That's just awful. I can't believe your wife would do that to you."

"Well, she's the devil. Satan dressed in a pants suit and stilettos."

Angie nodded like she understood him, like this was a story she knew all too well. "It sounds like you and I have a lot in common. My husband—well, ex-husband. He was the same way. I swear all that man ever cared about was what other people thought of him. He didn't give a shit about me. I was nothing to him, nobody, just a lousy trophy to wear around his arm." As Angie turned away, her lips started to quiver and her hands started shaking so bad it looked like she had Parkinson's. "That bastard. I can't believe he did this to me. It's all his fault, you know? None of this would've happened if he could've just kept his dick in his pants. We'd still be together. We'd still be happy and I'd still get to be a mother to my children."

Dave scooted down the bench a little closer and placed his hand gently on her left shoulder. "Well, if it's any consolation," he said in a delicate whisper, "I think your husband's crazy. I think you're absolutely gorgeous."

Angie smiled, revealing those cute braces, which sparkled like a row of quarters sitting on the tracks of a train trestle. "Thank you," she said, rubbing his knuckles. "You're sweet for saying that."

They held each other's stare for a little longer. Dave could feel the blood beginning to rush to his penis. He had to move his hand over his crotch to keep his dick from pressing up against the zipper. He crossed his left leg over his right then started counting back from twenty. By the time he got to three, the erection had deflated enough that he could uncross his legs and place his hand next to hers on the bench. Alright, this was it. This was his opportunity...time to tell her about Sarah...time to lay it all out there. "Well, you're probably not gonna believe this," he said, as he adjusted his posture, then cleared his throat and took a deep breath inward, "but I actually know your daughter."

Angie's head snapped around so abruptly that it almost knocked Dave right off of the bench. "What? Sarah? You know Sarah?"

"Yep."

"How? How do you know Sarah?"

"Well, it's the darndest thing, Angie. It just so turns out that I'm her volleyball coach."

Angie looked like she had just been zapped with a cow prod. Her eyes bugged out like a cartoon character and her mouth was dropped open so wide that a bird probably could've flown inside. "You're kidding me?"

"No, I'm not. I work at Boulder Catholic high school. I coach track in the spring and girls' volleyball in the winter. I'm her coach, coach Bell, coach Dave Bell."

Angie just stared at him with her mouth wide open, her head wagging back and forth in complete astonishment. "I don't believe this," she said, throwing her hands upward. "You know Sarah? You know my Sarah?"

"Yeah, she's one of my best middle blockers. Hell, she's probably got the best serve of anyone on the whole damn team."

"I don't believe this. This is crazy. This is absolutely insane."

"I know, I know. I tell you, I nearly fell outta my chair when you brought out that picture of her. I was like, wait a minute, I know that girl. She's on my volleyball team. Her name's Sarah. Small world, isn't it?"

"It sure is. My goodness. I mean, what are the chances? And in a rehab of all places—it must be some kind of good omen."

"I was thinking the exact same thing."

Dave snickered to himself as he picked up his cup of coffee then took a long slurp and set it back down. Okay, phase one was complete—the introduction. Now, all he had to do was introduce the plan. But, he had to be careful. He didn't want to just rush into it. Angie was liable to flip out once he told her about the bus incident.

He took a deep breath and turned slowly towards her. The woman was biting her nails and spitting them out into the snow. "So," he said, as casually as possible, "when was the last time you talked with Sarah?"

"Hmm." Angie rolled her eyes up towards the tree line then began mumbling to herself as she counted off on her fingers. "I'd say it's been about...eight weeks."

Eight weeks? Perfect. That meant she hadn't yet heard about what happened, unless of course she saw it in the papers, but then wouldn't she have said something already? Yeah, of course she would've.

"Really? That long?" Dave said then exhaled deeply feeling as the anxiety began to fall away from him.

"Yeah. Unfortunately, my ex-husband, Bill, won't let her talk to me. That asshole's probably got her phone locked away in his study."

Dave took another deep breath and let it out slowly. This was awesome. It was working out better than he could've possibly imagined. If Angie hadn't yet heard about what happened then he could tell her his side of the story. He could tell her what really happened on that bus, how the cops pulled him over without reasonable suspicion. But, he ought to wait a little bit first and let everything settle. He didn't want to give Angie the impression that he was just using her for her daughter. Besides, he still needed some time to get in touch with his lawyer. He had to find out if this kind of thing was even possible. Could someone like Sarah be called as a witness? Would her testimony even help? And when was the court date? He didn't even know yet. He was still in the early planning stages. He had to find out all of this shit first then he could get Angie to call up Sarah.

After he stamped out his cigarette, Dave tossed it in his coffee. The butt hissed like a snake as it drowned in the last little bit of sludge at the bottom.

"Where are you going?" Angie said, looking up at him.

"Oh I uh…I gotta go take care of some business. But I'll see you later."

"Oh, okay. Well, it was nice talking to you, Dave."

"Yeah, you too. And don't worry, we'll talk again later."

"Great. I'll be looking forward to it. I wanna hear all about my daughter and how great she's doing at her volleyball." Angie smiled and winked at Dave somewhat seductively. What the hell? If he didn't know any better, he'd say she was flirting with him. Holy shit. This was great. If she was this fucking horny then she'd be putty in his fucking fingers.

Dave smiled back at her with his own version of seduction—a slight roll of the shoulders to get his pecks protruding outward. He let her soak it in for a few seconds then did an about face and headed off towards the porch patio, making sure to flex his butt cheeks as he walked so that the fat wouldn't jiggle.

When he got to the patio, he went right for the payphones, trying not to acknowledge the patients who were still gathered around their silly, little Monopoly game. He didn't have time for small talk or pleasantries. He had to get a hold of Weinstein. He was on a fucking mission.

As he lifted the phone from its cradle, he fished out his lawyer's information. With the receiver wedged between his ear and his right shoulder, he flattened the lawyer's number out against the top of the payphone. He'd gotten the number from the yellow pages of the Boulder County phone book, underneath Attorneys at Law, subsection DUI Charges. The toll-free phone number was listed at the bottom in patriotic red, white, and blue ink right beneath his lawyer's name, Barry Weinstein, who was dressed up in a Benjamin Franklin outfit. Supposedly, this Weinstein character was one of the best DUI case lawyers in all of Colorado. In fact, Dave even remembered seeing his commercials on the local television station in Boulder. They called him "The Patriot" on account of his "unrelenting allegiance to the common American." There was no case he wouldn't take—big, small, even un-defendable. All he required was a credit check and a down payment. The guy wasn't cheap, but he seemed to be worth it. Hell, he'd better be. For five thousand big ones, the guy had better be a fucking miracle worker.

As Dave punched in the numbers, he switched the phone to his left ear. This call was way too important to trust with his weaker ear.

The phone began to ring…once, twice, three times, four…then the receptionist picked up: "Hello, Weinstein and Company, Attorneys at Law?"

"Yes, hello, my name is Dave Bell. I'm one of Mr. Weinstein's clients."

"Yes, hello, Mr. Bell. What can I assist you with today?"

"Yeah, well, I'd like to talk to Mr. Weinstein if I could. I have some new information for my case that I think would be very valuable."

"Oh, I'm sorry, but Mr. Weinstein is in court all morning. Can I have him call you back?"

Shit. Dave was afraid this might happen. The guy was hardly ever available. But that was a good sign, right? That meant he was good enough to be busy.

"Well, when will he be back?" Dave said, looking out across the lawn at Angie who was still sitting on the bench finishing her cigarette. "This is very important. Time is of the essence."

"Hmm...let's see." Dave could hear the sound of shuffling papers and a keyboard tapping somewhere in the background. "It looks like his last case is at ten-thirty, which means he should be back at the office after lunch, around twelve-thirty."

"Twelve-thirty?"

"Yes sir. Would you like to leave a number?"

"Yeah, but unfortunately I'm on a payphone."

"That's okay. What's the number?"

"Hold on, let me see." Dave leaned forward and found the number. It was written on a piece of tape just above the phone's keypad. "Okay, here it is." He moved his finger across the tape as he read off the number. When the receptionist finished taking it down she said, "okay, got it."

"Alright, so twelve-thirty?" Dave said, one more time for confirmation.

"Yes sir. I'll have him call you as soon as he gets in the office."

"Okay, thank you."

Dave hung up the phone and checked his Casio. It was nine-thirty now, which gave him another...one, two, three hours. Damn—why was this guy always in court? He needed to talk to him. This was a huge break. He finally found a way out of this shithole.

Chapter 24

The Patriot

Three hours later, the payphone began ringing. Dave was sitting in the same metal folding chair with a pile of cigarette butts beneath him. "Yeah?" he said, as he yanked down the receiver and stomped his cigarette out onto the pavement.

The voice on the other end was old and scratchy and had that whiny, Woody Allen New Yorker accent. "Uh yes hello...I'm calling for uh...Mr. David Bell?"

"Is this Weinstein?" Dave said, as he straightened his posture and switched the receiver to his other ear, the good one.

"Yes it is. Is this David?"

"It most certainly is. Where the hell you been, Weinstein? I've been waiting out here in the cold for like...four frigging hours."

"Oh you know how it is, David...busy, busy. Nothing but drafty court rooms and old, curmudgeonly judges." Weinstein began laughing into the receiver. It was a shrill kind of cackle, like that of a drunken hyena.

"Yeah, yeah, yeah," Dave said, waving his hand dismissively. "Listen, I got some great news for you. I think I may have just broken this case wide open."

"Really?"

"Yep. I just met this chick in here, a gal by the name of Angie Mallard. It just so happens that she is the mother of one of my best middle blockers, Sarah Mallard." Dave waited to see if Weinstein could put two and two together, but the guy didn't say anything. He just yawned and let out a lazy sort of grumble. "Can you see where I'm going with this, Weinstein?" Dave said, as he pulled out another cigarette, tossed it in between his lips, and sparked up his lighter.

"No, not really, David. I'm sorry, but you're going to have to elaborate."

Dave pulled the phone back and looked at it like it was growing fungus. What the hell was with this guy? Was he tired? Thought he was supposed to be "The Patriot," not some tired, old geezer.

"Sarah was there," he said, as he lit the cigarette then took a quick puff and spewed the smoke outward. "She was there when the cops pulled me over. She saw what happened. She can testify for me in the courtroom."

"Uh...I'm not sure I follow you, David. Testify to what exactly?"

"That I wasn't speeding or driving erratically. That the cops pulled me over without reasonable suspicion."

Finally, Weinstein let out a groan of understanding. "Oh, okay, I see where you're going with this, David."

"You get it now?"

"Yes, I get it."

"You think it might work?"

"Uh, well"—Weinstein's voice went up an octave—"I'm not so sure about that. It's seems a little...iffy."

"Iffy? What the hell do you mean iffy? It's brilliant. It's the best idea I've ever had. It's fucking genius."

"Well, let's not get ahead of ourselves now, David. It's certainly not something we should be betting the farm on. At least not just yet."

"Well, why not? You said that if we could prove the cops didn't have reasonable suspicion to pull me over, then the case could be dismissed and I could get the fuck out of here."

"Yes, but that was before I received the full police report from the Boulder County Sheriff's office."

"So what? What does that change?"

"Well, you didn't tell me they found you in possession of narcotics."

"I didn't think that was really important."

"Not important? David, are you kidding me? The arresting officer said he found eight grams of crack cocaine in your jacket pockets."

"So?"

"So how am I supposed to get a judge to even look at this case seriously? I mean, considering the amounts we're talking about here, you're lucky you didn't get an intent to distribute."

Dave tightened his hand around the receiver. He felt like driving the thing right against the fucking keypad. An intent to distribute? What the hell was this guy saying? Just three days ago, Weinstein said the case would be a slam-dunk, no problem. Now, all of a sudden, he was starting to get iffy? Where was all this coming from? What was this Jew trying to do...swindle him?

"Now just wait a minute," Dave said, as he tried to suppress his anger by pretending the phone was Weinstein's neck and squeezing it tighter and tighter. "You said I had a good chance at getting out of here."

"Yes, but—"

"You said all we had to do was prove that I wasn't driving erratically."

"I know but—"

"But nothing. Now look Weinstein, I'm not paying you so you can just sit on your ass and tell me what's not possible. I'm paying you so you can do your job and get me the fuck out of here. Now, I've done my part—I got you a fucking witness. I got you someone who was at the scene and can testify that the cops were acting inappropriately. Now, you do your job and get this girl inside of a courtroom and I'll make sure she does the rest. You got it?"

For a moment, there was a long, uncomfortable silence. Weinstein didn't say anything, but Dave knew he was there, because he could still hear the old bastard breathing. "Hello?" Dave said. "Earth to Weinstein. Did you hear me?"

"Yes," Weinstein finally grumbled, "I heard you,"

"Well, do you got it?"

"Yes, David, I got it."

"So, we're good to go then? We're not gonna have any problems?"

Weinstein let out another deep sigh, like a tire being deflated. "No, David, no problems."

"Good, so, I'll have this girl call you. Once again, her name is Sarah. She's a minor, but I'm gonna get her mother's permission, so that shouldn't be a problem."

"Okay, David, that's fine. You can have her call me, but I don't want you to get your hopes up. There's a very good chance her testimony may not be enough to convince a judge to release you."

"You just do your job and get us a court date. I'll do the rest. You can count on that."

"Alright, listen, you hang in there, David. And try to get some rest. Maybe even listen to what those therapists are telling you. Who knows? They might surprise you. You might find out something about yourself that you didn't know before all of this happened."

Dave couldn't help but chuckle. Yeah right. He wasn't gonna have time for any of this therapy bullshit. Especially, not now—he had a case to assemble.

Chapter 25

The Witness

Dave didn't see Angie again until after dinner. She was outside at the picnic tables sucking down a post-meal cigarette. She had changed her clothes. She had on a white wool beanie pulled down over the pimples on her forehead with matching white jeans and a bright red and white candy-cane striped ski jacket.

Dave took a moment to regain his composure. After spitting on his hand and patting his hair down, he tucked in his shirt then did a quick breath check. It wasn't too bad, a little garlic-flavored. He probably shouldn't have had all that garlic toast. Oh well, he couldn't brush his teeth now. He didn't want to risk losing Angie. He'd waited all day for her.

He limped across the patio and picked a seat next to Angie underneath the warm glow of one of the umbrella-shaped space heaters.

"Hey," he said, as he pulled out a cigarette, lit the end, and set down his lighter.

"Hey yourself," she said, smiling up at him. "How you doing?"

"Pretty good. How 'bout you? "

"Okay, I guess."

"Where were you this afternoon? I was looking all over for you."

"I had a meeting with my counselor."

"Oh yeah? How'd that go?"

"Horrible. I hate her. She makes me so uncomfortable."

"Yeah, I can understand that. The people in charge here are assholes. It seems like they wanna get up in everyone's business."

Angie sniffled. "Ain't that the truth."

The next few seconds were filled with nothing but silence. Dave wanted to broach the subject, but didn't want it to be too obvious. "So…" he said, looking at the end of his cigarette, "I talked to my lawyer today."

"Oh yeah? How'd it go?"

"Good. I think I may have even found a way out of here."

"Really?"

"Yeah. Actually, it's kind of funny, your daughter's name came up."

"What? Sarah?"

"Yeah."

"What for?"

"Well, my lawyer, Barry Weinstein, thinks she can help me."

"How?"

"Well, remember how I told you my wife called the cops on me?"

"Yeah."

"Well,"—Dave puckered his lips like he'd just bit into something sour. The words were on his tongue but he was almost afraid to say them—"your daughter was there when the cops pulled us over."

"What!" Angie shot up from the table and seized Dave's forearm. Her nails were so sharp he could feel them digging through the sleeve of his jacket. "What in God's name are you talking about?"

Dave tried to wrench his forearm away from her, but her grip was too strong. Jesus—what was she, a fucking weightlifter or something?

"What are you talking about, Dave? What happened? What do you mean the police were there? Tell me right now, god damnit."

"Alright, alright, Jesus, calm down, I'll tell you."

"Right now."

"Alright, alright. Fuck me." Dave cleared his throat and looked up at Angie. She looked liked a possessed woman in a need of an exorcism. "We had a match three weeks ago on Monday. It was all the way up in Estes Park."

"I know, I know, I was supposed to be there. But I couldn't make it. Why? Did something happen? What happened?"

"Well, that's when the cops pulled us over—on our way up to Estes. I was driving the bus like I always do…you know, not speeding or driving erratically…just trying to get the girls to their game on time so they could win the state championship."

"You weren't drinking were you?"

"What? No, of course I wasn't drinking."

"You promise?"

"Yes. I promise." That was actually the truth. He wasn't drinking, at least not while he was driving. He did stop to smoke for a little bit, but that was only for the leg pain.

"Well, then what happened?" she said, still holding onto his jacket, her fingers digging deeper and deeper into his forearm.

"Well, next thing I know, I look up in the rearview mirror and the cops are flashing their lights and riding my ass probably no more than two feet behind me. So, I pull the bus over, get out, and that's when the bastards grab me by the collar and slam me face down on top of the patrol car. I didn't even do anything wrong. They start patting me down in front of all the girls, like, like I was some kind of criminal. One of 'em even takes out his billy club and wedges it in underneath my chin. He was holding me in some kind of cop chokehold. He had me so tight I couldn't even get my feet on the snow. Next thing I know, the walls start closing in, I can't breathe, and everything's going dark. Of course, my mentally challenged son, Larry, is watching all of this from the front seat of the school bus. He gets scared and runs out to protect me, and that's when the bastards shoot him with a fucking Taser gun!"

"Your son?"

"Yeah. Larry."

"They shot him?"

"Yeah."

"They shot your son?"

"Yeah. He was only trying to protect me and they shot him. The fucking bastards shot my Larry."

"Oh my God." Angie gasped. She seemed to be going along with it. For now, he figured it'd be best if he left the whole crack thing out. There was no need to get her even more excited. She already looked like she was about to have a fucking coronary.

"Well, what about the girls," she said, tugging again at his jacket, her eyes as bright as those supernovas he'd lectured about in his Earth Science class. "Are they okay? Did they get hurt?"

"No, no, they're fine," Dave said, waving his hand reassuringly. "All the girls are just fine. The parents came, picked 'em up, and took 'em all back to Boulder. Hell, if anything, it probably gave 'em a good story to gossip to their little girlfriends about."

Angie let out a deep sigh. She seemed to be relaxing. She eased back down on the picnic table and released the death grip around Dave's forearm. "So everyone's fine? No one's hurt. Sarah, the girls, they're all back in Boulder, right?"

"Yes, yes, they're fine, I promise. I would never let anything happen to those girls. I love them like they're my own daughters."

Angie closed her eyes and smiled. That seemed to appease her. She let out another deep sigh then pushed her bangs back from her forehead. "Oh my God, you had me scared for a minute. I thought I was gonna have a panic attack or something."

"Yeah me too."

"Well, thank goodness everyone's okay."

"Well, almost everyone."

"What do you mean?"

"You forgot about me. I'm the real victim of this whole scenario. You know I had to spend three weeks in a fucking prison?"

"Really?"

"Yeah. And it's all because of my wife. She did this to me. She called the police. She had me arrested. She put everyone's life on that bus in danger…including your daughter's. I mean, if you think about it, your daughter's pretty damn lucky I'm such a good driver. The way those cops flew up on me like that"— Dave let out a whistle—"shit, almost anyone else would've freaked out and overcorrected. But not me. I'm as cool as a cucumber." Dave stuck out his hand and laid it flat in front of him. "You see that? Steady as a fucking mountain."

Angie shook her head and looked away from him, squeezing her fists and gnashing her teeth together. Dave could actually hear the grinding sound from where he was sitting—it sounded like a bone saw cutting through a fresh cadaver.

"You're right," she said. "I can't believe what those cops did to you wasn't illegal. I mean, what if they caused an accident? What if they made you panic? Sarah could've gotten hurt. She could've ended up in the hospital."

"I know, I know."

"How could they do that? How could they be so reckless? Cops can't just pull someone over because they feel like it, can they?"

Finally, Dave thought. This was what he'd been waiting for. Everything was falling into place, just as he'd planned it. "Actually, no, they can't." He reached into his pocket, pulled out his lawyer's information, and slapped it on the picnic table. "I found this lawyer in the phone book. His name is Barry Weinstein. Supposedly, he's one of the best DUI case lawyers in all of Colorado."

"Oh wait, I know him," Angie said, looking down at the advertisement, her eyes mesmerized by the picture of Weinstein dressed up as Benjamin Franklin. "I remember seeing his commercials on television. He's 'The Patriot' right?"

"Yep. You got it. Now, he told me that the cops can't just pull you over without what's called reasonable suspicion, meaning they have to witness you doing something suspicious before they can pull you over. And he says that since I wasn't speeding or swerving or driving erratically, we can prove the cops didn't have reasonable suspicion and the case can be dismissed and I can get the hell out of here."

"Really?"

"Yeah, all I gotta do is prove to the judge that I wasn't driving erratically, which shouldn't be too tough. I mean, after all, I got a whole bus full of witnesses, right?"

"Yeah, I guess so."

Angie studied the advertisement for a few more seconds. Was she gonna take the bait? Was she gonna go for it?

"Oh wait a minute," she said, her eyes growing bigger. "So, that's what you meant when you said Sarah could help you?"

Dave closed his eyes and nodded slowly with satisfaction. "Yep. That's it. Now, do you get it?"

"Yes, I get it. So, you just need Sarah to tell them that you weren't speeding?"

"That's it. Weinstein says Sarah's the best chance I have at getting my sentence commuted. He says her testimony could even clear my record."

"Really?"

"Yep. All we gotta do is get her to call up Weinstein and he'll do the rest. Easy cheesy."

Angie studied the advertisement for a few seconds longer.

"So, what do you think?" Dave said, holding his breath in anticipation. "You think you can help? You think you can call up Sarah?"

"I don't know," she said. "I'm a little bit worried."

"About what?"

"Well, we haven't spoken in so long. What if she doesn't wanna talk to me?"

"What do you mean? Of course, she'd wanna talk to you. You're her mother. She's probably worried sick about you."

"I know but, I've just let her down so many times. I mean, I haven't been there for her. And now look at me. Look at where I am. I'm stuck in this awful rehab."

"Well this is your chance to make things better. This is your chance to reconnect with your daughter. You said it yourself…good omen, remember? There has to be a reason we both ended up here. And I think this is it. I think we found it. I can't do this alone, Angie. I need you to help me."

Angie looked up at him with big blue hope-filled eyeballs. "You need me?" she said.

"Yes. I need you."

"Okay."

"Okay, what?"

"Okay, I'll do it."

"Yes, yes! Oh thank you, thank you! You don't know how much this means to me, Angie. You're a lifesaver." Dave leaned in and threw his arms around her then gave her a big smooch on the cheek, causing her to shy away like a little schoolgirl. "So, do you have her number?" he said, eyeing the payphone to see if anyone was on it, which no one was at the moment.

"Yeah, I do. I have it memorized."

"Great. Can we call her?"

"Now?"

"Yeah."

"Okay."

Dave took Angie's hand and shot up from the table. He went right for the payphone with Angie in tow behind him.

"You got a quarter?" he said, as he began patting his pockets.

"No, I don't think so."

"Shit." Dave slammed his fist against the top of the payphone. "Wait, hold on a minute." He limped across the patio to the far side picnic tables where a group of patients were playing another game of Monopoly. "Does anyone have a quarter?" he said, as nicely as possible, hoping to God someone would have the decency to help them.

The table just looked at him like he was crazy then shook their heads and went back to their stupid board game. "Please," Dave said, walking towards them, his hands out in front of him like a beggar, "we need a quarter. It's an emergency."

Some muscle-bound, bald guy looked up at him and started laughing. He looked like Mr. Clean, with tattoos on his neck and earrings in each earlobe.

"What's so funny?" Dave said, narrowing his eyes at him, his fists clenched, his heart pounding.

"You can't use the phones right now."

"Why not?"

"It's too late."

"But it's an emergency."

"It's the rules."

"Fuck the rules."

"What?"

"I said fuck the rules."

Mr. Clean took a deep breath and stood up slowly, folding his arms across his fat wrestler's belly. He was about to walk over to Dave when his buddy grabbed him and said, "don't worry about it, Wayne. It's not worth it."

"Yeah, Wayne," Dave mocked. "It's not worth it. Keep playing your little board game over there and mind your own fucking business."

Angie grabbed the back of Dave's jacket. "It's alright," she said, tugging him over. "Never mind them. I found one. I found a quarter."

Dave waited for Mr. Clean to sit back down at the table then turned away and watched as Angie punched in the keys on the keypad. His heart was beating like a hammer, knocking the blood against the walls of his corroded arteries. He couldn't believe this was actually happening. His plan was coming together perfectly.

"Hello? Sarah?"

Dave's heart skipped a beat and his stomach fluttered. Goose bumps like spiders scurried up and down his forearms.

"Hey sweetie, it's mommy. I need you to call me back as soon as possible—"

Fuck. It was just her voice mail. Where the hell was this girl? Why wasn't she answering?

"It is very important that we speak. I am still up here at this place in the mountains and I just met your volleyball coach, Coach Dave. He's here too and he needs your help. He says you were on the school bus the night he got pulled over. He says you can testify and tell the police what really happened. He wasn't doing anything wrong. He was just driving. His wife set him up. She had him arrested. Please call me back as soon as possible. We really, really need your help. You are Dave's only chance. The number here is"—Angie read the number listed above the keypad then said, "Please call as soon as you can, sweetie. I'll try you again in a few hours. And don't worry. Everything's gonna be okay. I love you. Hugs and kisses, hopes and wishes, may all our dreams come to fruition. I love you honey. I love you so very much."

As Angie hung up the phone, her eyes began to moisten. She turned toward Dave with a look of pain-filled hopefulness.

"Where is she?" Dave said. "Why isn't she answering?"

"It's that son of a bitch, Bill. He's not letting her answer. I just know it."

"Well, what are we gonna do? I need to talk to her. She's my only way out of here."

"I know, Dave, I know. Don't worry. We'll get a hold of her."

"How?"

"She'll call back, won't she?"

"I don't know, you tell me. You're her mother."

Angie brought her hands to her eyes. She tried to wipe away the tears, but more kept coming. What the hell was wrong with her? Why was she crying? It wasn't that emotional, was it? It was just a damn voice mail.

"It's alright," Dave said, trying to soothe her, cautiously placing one hand on her shoulder. "There's no need to cry. You're right, I'm sure she'll call back. You're her mother. She loves you very much. Heck, she told me so."

"Really?" Angie looked up at him. Her lips were trembling, her eyes were all puffy, and her mascara was running. "She told you she loves me?"

"Well, yeah." Dave's voiced cracked. He was lying. Sarah never talked about her mom, and if she did, he wasn't really listening. "She talks about you all the time," he said, looking away from her, unable to look directly into those big, hope-filled pupils. "About how wonderful you are as a mother...how she misses her time with you and wishes you were happy."

"She said all that?"

"Of course. I wouldn't lie about something like that."

"Oh thank you, Dave. Thank you for telling me that. It means so much to me."

Angie smiled and buried her head against Dave's shoulder. Dave allowed it and took a step closer, wrapping his arms around her body. "It's alright," he said, as he kissed her forehead then began rubbing her back in small circles. "Everything's gonna be okay. We'll get through this. Sarah will call back and everything will go back to normal. I'll get out of here and clear my record and you'll get to see your daughter again once you get out of here."

"You mean that, Dave?"

"Absolutely."

"I'll get to see Sarah again?"

"Of course you will."

"Oh thank you so much, Dave. This is unbelievable. I don't know why your wife would cheat on you. You seem like such a selfless individual."

Yeah, Dave thought. She was right. He was selfless. Why couldn't Cheryl see that? This woman obviously got it. He wasn't just using this woman...he was helping her. He was reconnecting a mother with her daughter. If that wasn't selfless, then he didn't know the definition. He was basically a martyr, a regular Mother Theresa.

He wrapped his arms tighter around Angie, feeling those double D's pressed up against him. She felt so good, so warm, so soft, and so beautiful. It had been a long time since he held a woman like this, so sexy and so curvy. He kissed her again, this time more deeply, then released her and moved a loose strand of hair back from her forehead. "Don't worry, Angie," he said. "We'll get through this. You, me, Sarah, and Larry...one day we'll all be a happy family."

Chapter 26

The Sexy Trailer

Day five. Finally, Monty was getting out of here. About time, too. He was sick of this facility—sick of detox, sick of this trailer, sick of Benzos, and sick of hearing Dexter's sappy lectures. He couldn't wait to get back home, back to his apartment, back to his booze, and back to his mission. He could almost feel the scotch already, warming the inside of his stomach, numbing the pain, dissolving the memories, and spinning its warm, nurturing cocoon around him. All he had to do now was go to the main house and check out his wallet. That health savings card in there was his only ticket to pure, alcohol-infused oblivion. He just hoped to God Dexter wouldn't give him any problems. He knew the guy was going to try and get him to stay, but legally he couldn't make him, right? Five days detox—that's all he owed them. It was spelled out in plain ink on the commitment forms right here in his pocket.

He took a deep breath then pushed himself up from the mattress, grabbed his black jacket and slipped into his shoes. Before opening the door, he flipped off the light switch then zipped up his jacket and walked out into the hall.

When he got to the nurse's station, he realized the place was empty and Jill, the nurse, was nowhere to be found. He checked the clock above the water fountain. It was almost ten-thirty, which meant she was probably over at the main house doling out the daily morning medication. Narrowing his eyes, he proceeded towards the exit, but just as he got to the door, he heard the sound of whispers coming from somewhere in the back room. He stopped, cocked his head, and pivoted towards the reception counter and saw the faint outline of two figures bobbing up and down behind the glass window.

He pushed down his anxiety and crept slowly towards the counter, the hairs on his neck standing on end like the bristles of a scrub brush. "Hello?" he said, as he got closer to the window, his heart like a machine gun rattling off shells against his sternum. "Is someone there?"

The shadows froze in straight, erect postures, like inmates getting caught by the spotlight of a prison tower.

"Hello?"

When he got to the window, he placed his hands on the counter, then took a deep breath and stood on his tiptoes. "Hello? Is someone there?"

The shadows disappeared, but the glass window flung open and Dave appeared on the other side grinning like a mischievous teenager. "Monty?"

"Dave?"

"I thought that was you, kid. God damn, you scared the hell out of us. We thought you were the nurse."

"Dave, what the—what are you doing over here?"

"Who is it, Dave?" a woman whispered from behind the counter, her head concealed by Dave's scarred appendage.

"It's okay Angie, it's just Monty."

"Who?"

"Monty. He's my friend. It's alright, he's cool. He's stuck here just like we are."

Monty peeked over the counter. Suddenly, a tall, blond woman shot up like a rocket upon ignition. She was out of breath, wide-eyed and grinning, struggling to pull her jeans up over her skimpy, black lace panties. "Hi," she said, wheezing exasperatedly, like she'd just got done with an aerobics class at Bally's. "Your name's Monty?"

Monty nodded and took a step backward, scowling at the little red lesions speckled across her forehead.

"My name's Angie, how do you do?"

Monty glanced at Dave then back at Angie. He couldn't believe it. In the detox trailer? "Jesus Dave," he said, holding his stomach, the thought of the two screwing making him feel a bit nauseous, "don't you have any self control?"

Dave pursed his lips together and started to snigger. He looked like a kid who just got caught smoking in the boy's room. "Aw come on now, Monty, we're not hurting anybody. I mean, just 'cause we're in rehab doesn't mean we can't have a little fun, right?"

"Uh, yeah, actually, it does. That's the whole point of rehab. Not to have fun."

Dave reared his head back and started laughing. "Come on, kid. Don't tell me you wouldn't do the same thing. I mean, look at this woman." He wrapped his arm around Angie's shoulder and pulled her face in close to his lips. "Have you ever seen a more beautiful specimen in all your life?"

Angie slapped him playfully and pushed him off of her. "Stop it, Dave. You're embarrassing me."

"Well it's true. You're beautiful. You're the most beautiful woman I've ever seen."

"You really mean that?"

"Of course, I do baby. Why else would I say it?" Dave leaned in and kissed her forehead, then licked his thumb and wiped the mascara that was running down her cheek. "Now, come on, let's get out of here before that nurse comes back."

Angie smiled and locked her arms tightly around Dave's waist, and using one another for balance, they staggered like a pair of drunks through the swinging saloon doors.

"What time you got, Monty?" Dave said, as he limped by him, stopping to pull open the front trailer door. "You think we got time for a smoke?"

"I don't know, I guess."

Once they got outside, Angie squealed and took off running down the trailer steps into the snow.

"What's she doing?" Monty said, watching her running as if she was a mental patient who'd just been let out of the institution.

"Fuck if I know." Dave cupped his hands around his mouth and shouted. His voice was like a dynamite stick detonating in the snow. "Yo Angie! What are you doing?"

Angie spun around and looked back at the trailer, throwing her hands up above her head. "I'm gonna go see if Sarah called."

"What?"

"I said, I'm gonna go see if Sarah called!"

"Oh, alright, well, me and Monty are gonna hang back a bit and have a smoke, but we'll see you over there for group, okay?"

"Okay! I love you, Dave!"

"I love you too, Angie."

Angie smiled and pulled her red hood up over her head, skipping off towards the house like Little Red Riding Hood.

Dave laughed and turned to Monty, knocking a pack of red Marlboros against the side of his wrist. "You want one?" he asked, as he pulled one out of the package and stabbed it in between his lips.

"No thanks. I don't smoke."

"Oh shit. That's right. I forgot."

Monty watched as Dave pulled out his lighter, rolled the flint, and sparked up the flame. Something wasn't right with him. He looked like a junkie, like he'd just smoked an eight ball or done a line of coke. His eyes were black and round like pieces of polished charcoal, and he had drops of saliva glistening the cleft of his chin. "Are you alright, Dave?" Monty said.

"Fuck yeah dude. I've never felt better in my entire life. You were right. They got a bunch of good shit back there. I felt like a fat kid in a candy store."

"You're pretty messed up, aren't you Dave?"

Dave smiled and reached into his pocket and pulled out a bottle of pills. "Fuck yeah dude. I'm fucking trashed. Check this shit out."

He handed the bottle over. Monty took it and read the label taped to the side: *Suboxone*. He'd heard of it before. It was similar to methadone, used for treating opiate withdrawal.

"Go ahead and take some if you want, man. I've got plenty."

"No thanks."

"You sure? You look like you could use it. You're startin' to shake and shit."

"I'm fine."

"Alright, man. More for me."

Monty shook his head in disgust and handed back the bottle, looking around the yard to make sure no one was coming in or out of the house. He didn't want to get caught with this guy. The counselors would probably think he had something to do with it. They'd probably think he helped him steal it. What if he got kicked out of here? Where would they send him? What if they made him do his five days over as some kind of punishment?

"Are you an idiot?" Monty said, turning back to face him, clenching his fists to try and suppress the rage.

"What?" Dave said, looking innocent, like this was no big deal, like this was just another day in rehab.

"I thought you said you were court ordered."

"Yeah. So?"

"So what if you got caught? What do you think would happen?"

Dave's eyes lit up like a Fourth of July sparkler. He turned toward Monty with a big, tobacco-stained smile. "Oh shit, man, I forgot to tell you. It doesn't matter anymore."

"What doesn't?"

"My parole—I don't have to worry about it anymore. Remember when I was telling you about how I got pulled over?"

"Yeah."

"Well, it just so happens that that chick Angie's got this daughter named Sarah who just so happens to be the captain of my volleyball team."

"So?"

"*Sooooo*, once we get a hold of her—if we can ever get her to answer her fucking cell phone—we're gonna get her to go to the courthouse and testify and get me the fuck out of here free of charge."

Monty scowled. What the hell was he blathering about? He wasn't making any sense. So what if he knew that woman's daughter? "I'm not sure I follow you, Dave."

Dave sighed and dropped his shoulders, looking at Monty as though he was the dumbest person in the entire world. "Sarah was there when those bastards pulled me over."

"Okay."

"She saw the whole god damn thing."

"I still don't get it."

"She can tell the courts what really happened. She can get me out of here. She can get me free."

"Testify to what?"

"Jesus Monty, weren't you listening to my story earlier?"

"Well, yeah, but—"

"Those cops had no right to pull me over. And they sure as hell had no right to shoot my son with a fucking Taser gun."

"But I thought you said you were smoking."

"That's irrelevant."

"Irrelevant? What do you mean irrelevant? You were smoking crack and driving a school bus. The cops were well within their right to pull you over. In fact, you're probably lucky they pulled you over when they did. You could've driven that bus right off the highway. You could've killed all those kids."

Dave laughed. "Listen to you, man. You sound just like my wife, Cheryl. I swear, if I didn't know any better I'd say you two were related." Dave bent forward and closed one nostril then blew the contents of the other out into the snow. "Aw fuck, that hurt." He threw his head back and sniffled up the mucus while squeezing the bridge of his nose. He bent forward again then did the other nostril. It looked like alien earthworms slithering out into the snow.

Monty just stood there shocked and speechless. He didn't know what else he could say to this guy. He was obviously deranged.

"Don't take this the wrong way," Monty said, taking a step back away from him, not sure how he would react to this next bit of wisdom. "But I think you may need some serious help. And I'm not talking about AA or religion or some bullshit twelve-step program, I'm talking about psychiatric counseling and a whole lot of medication."

Dave just laughed. "What the hell are you talking about? I don't need any medication. There's nothing wrong with me. I'm perfectly normal."

"No, you're not, Dave. You are definitely not normal. Look at you. Look at what you're doing."

"What?"

"You're stealing drugs from a detox trailer. You're getting high in rehab."

"Well, I can't help it. I have a condition."

"Yeah, no shit. You're an addict, just like everyone else in here."

"No, no, no, I am not an addict. I have a serious condition. I need it for my leg. I'm in serious pain."

This time it was Monty's turn to laugh. He tried to fight it, but he couldn't help it. This guy was utterly insane. "Yeah right," he said. "That's a good one. Your leg hurts, so that's why you get high. Have you ever listened to yourself? You sound like a lunatic. How can you honestly believe that you're not an addict? I mean, I hate myself, you know? I'm a fucking despicable person, but at least I have the balls to admit my own faults."

"What the hell, dude? Why are you being such an asshole? I thought we were cool. I thought we were friends."

"Friends? What do you mean? I just met you. We've only known each other for a few days."

"Fuck you, kid. You're an asshole."

"Yeah, maybe, but at least I can admit it."

"Go to hell." Dave reared his head back and hocked up a big loogie then sent it flying through the air. Monty had to jump out of the way so it wouldn't hit him. It landed only a few inches from his right shoe. "Jesus," Monty said. "Are you trying to spit on me? What are you, ten years old?"

"So what if I am?"

Dave bowed his shoulders and walked right up to Monty, his fists clenched together, his nostrils flared outward like a bull's. "What are you gonna do about it?" he said, then took a drag from his cigarette and blew the smoke right in Monty's face.

Monty stepped back, waving the smoke away from him. Was this guy trying to pick a fight with him? What was he, in the third grade?

Monty just shook his head in disgust then turned away from him. He didn't have time for this shit. He was getting out of here today.

As he trudged across the yard, he could hear Dave shouting out after him. He couldn't understand what he was saying, but he didn't really care. Only a few more hours and he'd be out of here. He couldn't wait to get back home. This place was a joke.

Chapter 27

One-on-One

When Monty got to the main house, he went right to Dexter's office, but Dexter wasn't there. Where the hell was he? He walked out of the foyer and into the main hallway then down the steps of the kitchen and out onto the back porch. He wasn't outside either. And he wasn't in the kitchen. He wasn't in the meeting hall. Where the hell was he?

Immediately, Monty began to feel the compression of panic coiling like a boa constrictor around his throat. What if he wasn't here today? What if this was his day off or something? No, no, no, that couldn't be possible. He had to be here. Who else was going to check him out?

He went back inside and sat down at one of the tables, his eyes glued to the patients coming in and out of the sliding patio doors. After about ten minutes of waiting, he decided to give up and retreat to the trailer. But, just as he stood up and made his way towards the patio, Dexter called out his name and came bouncing down from the kitchen. "Hey Monty. What's up buddy?"

Oh thank God. Monty was never so happy to see a rehab counselor. Now, he could get finally his wallet and keys and get the fuck out of here. "Hey Dexter," he said, trying to withhold his excitement. "How's it going? I was wondering where you were."

"Oh you were, were you?"

"Yep."

"Well, I was up front for our morning meeting. We were going over our new patient inventory...you know, trying to figure out who we got. Actually, it's a good thing we ran into one another. I needed to talk to you. We have some new patients coming in today and it looks like you're almost finished with your detox."

"I sure am."

"Oh so you know already?"

"Yep."

"You been keeping track?"

"Of course."

"That's good, good, I'm glad you're on top of things. Well, come on then, let's get you processed."

"Alright."

When they got into the office, Dexter flipped on the light switch then closed the door behind them and walked around to his desk. "Alright sir, go ahead and make yourself comfy. I just need to get myself oriented here."

Monty nodded and eased into the armchair, his eyes focused on the safe wedged up against the wall. There it was, just sitting there waiting for him. His keys, his debit card, his wallet...everything he needed to get home and drink himself into oblivion.

Dexter's head disappeared as he bent forward and started opening and closing his bottom desk drawers. "Where is it? Where is it? Ahaa! There it is." He reappeared with a fountain pen and pad of paper then he kicked off his dress shoes and let them clunk to the floor. "Ahh. That's better. You don't mind if I go shoeless, do you?"

"I don't care."

He lifted his foot and cradled it in his lap and started to massage the ends of his toes. "I hate those damn things. They kill my feet. I'd wear sneakers if I could, but you know me."

"No, not really."

Dexter chuckled and readjusted his posture, setting his foot back down on the floor. He straightened his tie, flipped to a fresh sheet of paper, picked up his pen, and narrowed his eyes. "Alright sir, let's get down to business. So, like I said, we have some more patients coming in tomorrow who are going to need to be detoxed, which means were going to need to utilize your bed."

Monty couldn't help but smile. He could barely contain his excitement. Here it comes. Finally, he was getting out.

"So, what do you think about moving into the main house? I was thinking about putting you up in Dave Bell's room."

For a moment, Monty just sat there as if he was paralyzed, afraid that if he moved he would confirm what was just said. "I'm sorry," he said, leaning forward slowly, his chin almost touching the top of Dexter's desk, "I don't think I heard you right. What did you just say?"

"Dave Bell. How'd you like to room with him? His roommate's leaving tomorrow and I was thinking you guys would be a good fit."

Monty looked around the room. Was this some kind of prank? Any moment now, he expected a dozen people to walk out from behind that cherry armoire with balloons and cameras and a big *Gotcha!* cake. "Wait a minute," he said, "I thought I was leaving. Today's my last day. Today's the fifth day."

Dexter cracked a smile. "What are you talking about, Monty? You just got here. You're not leaving yet."

"No, no, no, no, no, now wait a minute, just wait a god damn minute"—Monty dug into his pocket and fished out the commitment papers and laid them flat on Dexter's desk—"I have the commitment forms right here. It says five days…five days detox. That's the maximum amount of time you can keep me here."

"Unless a petition for involuntary commitment has been filed with the court."

"What?"

"A petition for involuntary commitment. Your parents and Robby filed one with the court."

"What the hell are you talking about?"

"It's right here," Dexter said, pointing to the commitment form, "at the very bottom, in the last paragraph. In no event may you be held for a period longer than five days *unless* a petition for involuntary commitment has been filed with the court."

Monty looked at the form then back up at Dexter. The son of a bitch was right. It was right there in plain ink. No, this couldn't be happening. Something had to be wrong. This had to be a mistake.

Dexter reached into his drawer and pulled out a bulky stack of papers. "Now, this was just faxed to me yesterday. It's the petition for involuntary commitment, and as you can see, it's already been approved by the judge."

Monty looked at the stack of papers, but everything was all blurry. He couldn't see straight. He was having some kind of stroke.

"This gives me, your primary counselor, the final say as to when you can be released from the program. And to be quite honest with you, you haven't given me any reason as to why I should release you yet. You have not been cooperative, you've refused to tell me anything about your history, and when you first got here, you even admitted to wanting to kill yourself. How can I release someone who is suicidal? If you hurt yourself, who do you think will be called into court? Me. That's who."

Monty sat there paralyzed, cemented to the armchair, his heart beating faster, his stomach closing in on itself. "You can't do this to me," he said, as he clenched the fabric of the armchair, the blood from his stomach flushing to his face. "You can't keep me here."

"I'm sorry, but I'm afraid I can."

"No. This isn't right. I don't want to be here. I want to go home. I want to…"

"What?"

Monty looked at Dexter, his mouth wide open, the tears of frustration streaking across his eyes.

"What do you want to do, Monty?"

"Drink! I want to drink!"

"Well, that's exactly why I can't let you leave here. Not until you show me that you're *ready* to leave."

"Well, what if I just leave? Huh? What if I just walk out of here?"

"Where you gonna go? You don't have your wallet, you don't have any money. How will you get home?"

"I'll hitch."

Dexter laughed and reclined backwards, folding his hands behind his head. "Well, good luck. We're out here in the middle of nowhere. The closest town is forty miles away."

Monty clenched his fists. He wanted to hit him. He wanted to wipe that stupid smirk right off his fucking face.

"Come on," Dexter said, his voice softening. "Talk to me, Monty. Tell me what's wrong. Help me get you out of here."

"I don't have to tell you a god damn thing."

Dexter's expression immediately hardened. It looked as if Monty had just slapped him in the face. He took a deep breath and shut his eyelids then began to breathe deeply in and out through his nose. When he opened his eyes back up, he seemed calmer, like the breathing had somehow pushed the anger down. "You know what?" he said, as he leaned in toward Monty, "you're absolutely right. You don't have to tell me anything, because I already know."

"What the hell are you talking about? You know what?"

Dexter let out a long sigh then folded his hands in front of him, bringing his fingertips just underneath his nose. "I spoke with Robby last night. We had a very long chat about your resistance to this program."

The name hit Monty like a baseball bat to the forehead. He had to swallow his spit just to keep from throwing up. "What? You called Robby?"

Dexter nodded. "Yep."

"I didn't say you could that."

"I don't need your permission. I'm your counselor, remember? My job is to do whatever it takes to help you get better."

"Oh really? Is that what you're doing now—helping me get better?"

"You're damn right it is."

Monty leaned forward and clutched both sides of the armchair. Every muscle in his body was twitching. He could barely hold himself still.

"It was a good talk," Dexter said, reclining backward, trying as best he could to look like a real therapist. "He told me a lot about you."

"Oh, I see. So, you think you know me now? Is that it?"

"I know enough." Dexter smirked and took off his glasses. He breathed on the lens then began to clean them with the tail of his shirt.

"That's bullshit," Monty said. "You don't know me. You don't know a god damn thing about me."

"I know why you never got to your fourth step, your moral inventory."

"Oh this oughta be good."

"It's because you're scared, Monty; scared of what you might uncover; scared of what you might find out."

Monty started laughing. Where'd he come up with that one? He probably read it in his intro to counseling handbook. "That's ridiculous."

"Is it?"

"Yes. It is."

"Well then tell me this, Monty, out of all the good schools around the country, why did you choose to go to CU?"

"What?"

"Well, there are plenty of good schools back home in Florida, but you chose to move all the way out here, where you have no family, no friends, no relatives, nothing. Why? Why is that?"

"Well, CU's a good school. I mean, it's one of the best in the nation for chemical engine—"

"Don't give me that crap. You know damn well that's not why you moved out here."

"Of course it is."

"No, it's not. You moved out here because you were ashamed—ashamed of all the shit you put your family through—ashamed of all the terrible things you did and said. You thought that if you moved out here, you could escape from all those memories, all that shame, all that guilt. But you couldn't escape, could you? No matter where you went, no matter how far you ran, your disease was always right there with you, taunting you, teasing you, reminding you of just how inadequate you are. So, what did you do?"

"I don't know."

"Yes you do, Monty. You know damn well. You did what any alcoholic would do. You drank. You drank to try and drown those feelings. You drank to try and numb that pain. But it was never enough. No matter what you did, no matter how much you drank, you could never consume enough to fill that hole. But then something happened, didn't it? You met someone. You met Vicky. And somehow her friendship was enough to fill that emptiness…to choke those memories…to plug up that hole. You *used* her, Monty."

"No."

"You *used* her to fill that hole inside of you, to keep that shame buried deep down inside your soul."

"Shut up, Dexter. You don't know what the fuck you're talking about."

"Oh yes I do. I know, because I see people doing it here every day. I see people swapping out their addictions with what they think is love. But it's not love. It's not even anything remotely close to it. It's the *disease*, Monty. It's the disease playing tricks on them, distracting them from their recovery when they should be focusing on themselves. You didn't really love her, Monty. You only thought you did because she made you feel worthy…she made you feel safe…she made you feel loved. But it wasn't love. It was dependence. It was swapping one addiction out for another."

"That's bullshit."

"No, it's not, Monty. You didn't really love her."

"Yes, I did."

"No, you didn't."

"Yes I did god damnit!" Monty slammed his fists down against the desk so hard that it nearly shook the entire room. "I loved her more than anything you could possibly imagine! I loved her more than anyone I've ever known!"

"Then why are you doing this!?"

"What!?"

"Quitting! Why are you quitting now after everything that's happened? Why are you running away and just giving up? If you really loved her then you'd fight to stay sober. You'd try and live your life the way that she lived hers—with courage and strength, love and commitment, never backing down, never giving up." Dexter came around the desk and crouched in front of Monty, one hand on the armrest, the other on his knee. "What do you think Vicky would say if she saw you doing this? What do you think she'd say if she saw you just giving up?"

Monty looked away and stared down at the carpet, clenching his jaw and squeezing his fists. His hands were shaking, his legs were shaking, and everything inside him wanted to get up and run. But he couldn't run. He was completely frozen—frozen to the carpet, frozen to the chair, frozen with anger, frozen with fear. What was he doing? What was he waiting for? Why didn't he just get up and run for the fucking door?

"Monty?" Dexter said, inching in closer, his voice a rumble from deep within his lungs. "Monty, look at me."

Monty straightened his back and looked up slowly. His head felt like it weighed a thousand pounds. "What?"

"What would Vicky say?"

"I don't know."

"Yes you do. You know damn well what she'd say. She'd tell you to forgive yourself and move forward. She'd tell you to go give yourself a second chance!"

"And what if I don't deserve it? Huh? What if I don't deserve to be forgiven? What if I don't deserve a second chance?"

"But you do, Monty. Everyone does. Everyone here deserves to be forgiven. Everyone here deserves a second chance. Even you—especially you."

"No."

"Yes, Monty. You have to forgive yourself for what happened. You have to give yourself a second chance."

"I can't."

"Yes, you can."

"No, I can't."

"Why?"

"Because I killed her, alright? Can't you understand that? Can't you get that through your thick fucking skull? I'm the reason she drowned in that reservoir. I'm the reason she's fucking dead."

"But someone hit you. Someone crashed into the side of you and forced you off the road."

"Maybe."

"What do you mean maybe?"

"Maybe it didn't happen. Maybe I just imagined it. Maybe it was just my headlights reflecting off a fucking sign in the road."

"Come on Monty, you don't really believe that."

"I don't know."

"Bullshit. You know that's not what happened. You're just looking for an excuse to blame yourself."

"And why would I do that?"

"Because you're sick, Monty. You're trying to make sense of a senseless situation and the only defense you have is to blame yourself. You think that if you take responsibility for everything bad that happens, then you can justify crawling in a hole somewhere and killing yourself. But guess what? It's not your fault, Monty. There's nothing you could've done to stop it from happening. There's nothing you could've done to avoid that car."

"Yes, there is."

"No, there isn't."

"I could've stopped and pulled over. I could've waited for that fucking storm to pass."

"Monty—"

"If I would've just listened to Vicky and stayed the night in Boulder, we never would've gone up there and we never would've crashed."

"Monty, stop it, just stop it."

"I did this. I'm responsible. I'm the reason she's fucking dead."

"Stop it. Stop doing this to yourself."

"God hates me. He wants to see me suffer. He wants to see me fall flat on my face."

"Oh please, don't give me that pity bullshit. God does not hate you. He only wants what's best for you."

"Everything happens for a reason, right? Isn't that what you fucking people always say? Well what other reason is there? Why would he do this? Why would he kill her and take her away? She was the good one. Everybody loved her. It shouldn't have been her. It should've been me."

"But it wasn't you. You lived. You survived. You were the one who was strong."

"I'm not strong. Vicky was the one who was strong."

"No she wasn't, Monty. She was sick. She was dependent. She was struggling with this thing just like you."

"That's bullshit. Vicky wasn't sick. She was perfect. She could've been anything she wanted if I hadn't come along."

Dexter dropped his head and stood up from where he was kneeling then went around to his desk and eased back into his chair. "Monty," he said, as he reached beneath him and pulled out a manila file folder from his bottom desk drawer, "I didn't want to have to show you this. I didn't think it would really help. But now I'm convinced there's no other way." He opened the folder and pulled out a single sheet of paper then laid it flat on the desk and pushed it across. "Robby sent this to me. It's a toxicology report from the Boulder County Sheriff's Office. If you look under Vicky's name, you'll see what I'm talking about. She was sick, Monty. She was *using*. Traces of cocaine were found in her blood."

A cold chill descended upon Monty. He snatched up the paper and read down the left side. But he couldn't read it. The words were all jumbled together, like a jigsaw puzzle that he couldn't quite solve. The top of the form contained her name, age, sex, birth date, and social security number and the bottom contained a four tier table listing various types of medicinal and recreational drugs. There was a row for alcohol, THC, opiates, and barbiturates. And about half way down, right beneath methamphetamine was a space for cocaine, which had been checked off.

"No." Monty shook his head, set down the paper, and pushed it as far as he could away from his eyes. "This can't be right. It has to be an error. Someone must've made a mistake. They must've mixed up the blood."

"It's no mistake, Monty. Vicky *was* using. And judging by the concentration, it looks like she'd been using for a long time."

"I don't believe it. Vicky wouldn't have done that. She had everything under control. She seemed perfectly fine."

"But that's the insidiousness of this disease, Monty. It tricks you into believing that everything's perfect, when anyone could see that neither of you were fine." Dexter took the paper and put it back in the folder then opened the drawer and put in back in the file. "Now, do you see why I say you weren't really in love with one another—that you were just using each other as a means to cope? You were dependent, Monty, and so was Vicky, and you would've eventually found that out if she hadn't died."

Monty clenched his jaw and leaned as far as he could forward, holding his stomach like he was holding a child. He felt sick, like he was going to vomit, like something acidic was burning inside his lungs. He looked around the room for something to grab on to, but there was nothing there, so he held on to himself, squeezing his arms tighter and tighter around his abdomen, as if he was trying to keep something corrosive from spilling out, something white and hot burning inside him, eating his intestines, tearing at his lungs. He couldn't do this anymore. He had to get out of here. He had to go someplace where he could be alone. If he didn't leave now, he was going to vomit. He was going to lose his insides all over this fucking floor.

He gathered up his strength, pushed himself up slowly, and made his legs move towards the office door. But Dexter got up and moved out in front of him, positioning his body between him and the door. "Wait Monty, where are you going? You can't leave. We're not finished yet."

"I'm sorry, but I just can't do this right now. I have to get out of here. I have to be alone."

"But we're not finished yet, Monty."

"I know, but please, just…let me get out of here, just give me some space and leave me alone."

Monty squared his body and tried to move past Dexter, but Dexter reached out and grabbed his arm. "No Monty," he said pulling him towards him, his fingernails digging into the flesh of his forearm. "I will not leave you alone. I wanna help you. That's why I'm here. I'm here to help."

"Bullshit!" Monty spun around, jerking his elbow away from him. He bowed his shoulders and flexed his arms. "You're not here to help me. You're only here to help yourself—to feed your own fucking narcissism!"

"That's not true."

"Yes it is. The only reason you're here is because you think you owe something to this place for saving your ass. But I'm not like you Dexter. I can't be saved. I can't repent. I'm a walking, living, breathing ghost."

"That's just the disease talking. That's what it wants you to think. You *can* be saved. You *can* repent. I can show you how. I can help you find peace and understanding. I can help you live your life again."

Monty turned and walked away from him, across the room towards the door.

"Monty, if you walk out that door, I won't be able to help you. I won't be able to help you save yourself."

Monty stopped and turned towards Dexter, and said in a cold, flat, unaffected voice: "I don't need your fucking help."

Chapter 28

Sarah

About half the house was still inside finishing their hamburger dinners while the other half was outside braving the evening chill. The ones who were outside were all huddled together under the glow of the space heaters with those grey hospital-issued wool blankets pulled up to their necks. They were playing a new board game, not Monopoly. They must've exhausted that game and were now on to playing Trivial Pursuit.

Dave was among them, but off to the side in his own metal folding chair, his head down, his body hunched over, an unlit cigarette dangling from his wind-chapped lips. He was still pissed off about what Monty had said to him. The kid didn't know what the fuck he was talking about. What did he mean he needed therapy? He didn't need any bullshit therapy. He wasn't an addict. He was perfectly fine. He wasn't even supposed to be here. It was all a setup. Cheryl fucked him over. His own wife ratted him out. Why couldn't the kid understand that? It wasn't that difficult. Why was he having such a hard time grasping the facts? It was simple—Cheryl hated him. She was trying to get rid of him. He wouldn't give her another baby, so she decided to move on to someone else. But she couldn't just leave him. Oh no, that would be too civil of her. She had to take everything from him, so she could have it all to herself. Selfish bitch. She figured if she could get the courts to see that he was an unfit father then she could run off with everything—the kids, the money, the cars...hell, even the god damn house. And then what would he be left with? Nothing. Nothing but a bad leg and a shitty coaching gig.

But there was one thing Cheryl didn't count on, and that was his resilience. He wasn't just gonna lay down. He was gonna fight this thing. He was gonna prove his innocence. Cheryl wasn't the only one in this town who knew something about the law.

Dave smirked to himself and took a deep drag from his cigarette, and, as he expelled the smoke upward, the payphone began ringing its one note song. Aw fuck it. Let someone else answer it. He was tired of having to do everything around here all the time.

On the fourth ring, one of the girls from the picnic table got up and skipped towards it, scowling at Dave because he wouldn't move his legs. "Hello?" she said. "Who? Angie? Hold on a minute." She turned to the group and asked if Angie was around.

"No, she's not here," Dave said. "She's upstairs taking a shower. Why? Who is it? Who's calling?"

"Uh...hold on." The girl uncovered the phone. "Who may I ask is calling?" She turned back toward Dave. "It's someone named Sarah. I think it's her daughter?"

Dave jumped up from his chair. Holy shit. This was it. Finally, it was happening. "Give it to me," he said. "Give it to me now."

He tried to grab the phone, but the girl pulled it away from him. "But it's not for you," she said. "It's for Angie."

"I know, but I know her. I know Sarah. I'm her coach—I mean, I'm her dad."

"What?" The girl looked at Dave suspiciously. "You're not Angie's husband."

"Just give me the fucking phone." Dave ripped the phone away from her. The girl looked mortified like she'd just been raped. "Asshole," she said then gave Dave the finger and strutted back to her seat.

"Bitch," Dave replied, giving the finger right back to her, holding it up until she sat down.

After Dave composed himself, he stamped out his cigarette, then lifted the phone and said, "Hello? Sarah?"

"Yes? This is she."

"Sarah, it's me. It's coach, coach Dave."

"Coach?"

"Yeah. It's me. Where have you been, sweetie? Your mother and I have been trying to get a hold of you for like two days now."

Sarah's voice was barely audible. It sounded like she was crying, like she was sniffling into the phone. "Coach? What are you doing? Why are you doing this to me?"

"What? I'm sorry, Sarah, I can barely hear you. Hold on a minute. I'm outside. It's really noisy out here." Dave put his hand over the phone and turned to the people sitting at the picnic tables. "Can you guys please keep it down? I'm trying to have an important conversation."

The patients looked up at him like he was a gnat on the wall buzzing around their group. They dismissed him with the wave of their hands. The same bitch who answered the phone even gave him the finger again. Dave gave her the finger right back and even stuck out his tongue. Cunt. Didn't she have any courtesy? Couldn't she see he was on the god damn phone?

He let out a deep sigh then moved his hand away from the mouthpiece. "Hello? Sarah? Are you still there?"

"Yeah, I'm still here."

"I'm sorry, what did you say earlier? I didn't quite catch it. It's really noisy out here. These people are JERKS!"

"I said why are you doing this to me?"

"Uh…what…what do you mean?"

"Why are you harassing me and my mom?"

"What?" Dave turned his back to the group so no one could hear him. He covered his mouth and whispered into the phone: "Wait a minute, I'm not harassing anybody. I've just been trying to get a hold of you. I need you to come testify for me. I need you to tell the courts what really happened on the way up to Estes Park."

"What are you talking about?"

"Well, you remember the other week, don't you? Our trip up to Estes?"

"Of course, how could I forget? I've been having nightmares about it all week."

"Yeah, me too. But, that's why I need you to come testify. You can tell the judge what really happened—that the cops were acting inappropriately."

"What do you mean they were acting inappropriately?"

"You know what I mean. They pulled me over for no reason. They broke the law and then they attacked me."

"But you were out of control, coach. You were swerving all over the highway."

"What? No, I wasn't. I was driving perfectly fine."

"Are you crazy, coach? You almost got us killed. You almost drove us off the mountain."

"Wait a minute, wait a minute"—Dave squeezed his eyelids shut. What the hell was she saying? He wasn't swerving all over the highway. Why was she lying?

"Don't you remember, coach? I was trying to get you to stop, but you wouldn't listen. You just told me to go sit down and behave."

"Wait a minute, that's not right, that's not what happened. You and the girls were cheering. You were singing and dancing and having a great time."

"We weren't cheering, coach. We were screaming. We were screaming for you to slow down. We were scared for our lives. I *had* to call the police. I had no other option. You were about to get us killed. You were about to flip the bus."

Dave's throat began to close. It felt like he was choking. It felt like someone was stepping on his neck. What the hell did she mean she called the police? He thought Cheryl had called them. That's what Cheryl said, right? That's what she told him at the jail. "Wait a minute, what do you mean you called the police? I thought Cheryl called them."

"Who's Cheryl?"

"She's my wife."

"I don't know about that. All I know is that I called them, and some of the other girls did too."

"What!?"

"What were we supposed to do? We were frightened. You wouldn't listen to us. You wouldn't pull over."

Dave had to put his hand up against the wall to keep from falling over. He couldn't see straight. Everything was going dark. What the hell was going on? Why was this happening? Why was everything getting turned upside down? Did somebody get to Sarah? Could it have been Cheryl? Could she have somehow put Sarah up to saying all of this crap? She must have. Who else could've done it? She probably went to the girl's house. She probably talked to her dad.

"Please," Sarah begged him, "stop calling here. Stop harassing my mother. Leave her alone. She's sick. She needs help."

"I'm not harassing her. I'm just trying to—"

"I know what you're trying to do. You're trying to use her."

"What? No, I'm not."

"Then why did you tell her we were all going to move in together?"

"I didn't tell her that."

"Well, she seems to think so. You must've planted that idea in her head. You know she's not healthy, right? You know she tried to commit suicide."

"What?"

"Yeah. She tried to overdose on pills in front of our driveway. We were lucky my dad noticed her car out there and called an ambulance. She could've died that night. She could've killed herself."

Dave's legs became weak. He was about to fall over. He staggered over to his chair and carefully slunk down. "I didn't know that," he said, bowing his head forward, his voice lowering to barely a growl.

"Well, now you do, so please stop harassing her. She doesn't need to be messed with. She needs to get better."

"Wait Sarah, I told you I'm not—"

The phone went dead before Dave could finish his sentence. Sarah had hung up on him before he could say anything else. Almost immediately, the tightening in his stomach began to solidify like a vat of concrete had been poured down his throat. He slowly hung up the phone as if it was a ninety-pound dumbbell, the weight of the whole conversation suddenly shifting to his arm.

After he got it on the hook, he looked out across the patio at all the other patients laughing, talking, and playing their stupid little game. The bitch who originally answered the phone was standing right beside him, a Monopoly playing card resting in her outstretched palm. "Here," she said, "take it. We're done playing Monopoly. Besides, it sounds like you're going to need this a lot more than me." She handed Dave the card then smiled, flipped her hair outward, and strutted back to her table and started whispering to her friends and giggling at his expense.

Dave looked down at the card. It was pink with a picture of a man dressed in black and white striped prison scrubs. Dave recognized it right away. It was the *Get Out of Jail Free* card.

Chapter 29

Monty's Fourth Step

As Monty walked down the hall, he could hear Dexter shouting after him, his voice a pathetic plea penetrating through the paper-thin walls. But Monty didn't stop—he kept on going, down the kitchen steps, and across the meeting hall. Where was he going? What was he doing? He didn't know. All he knew was that he had to get away—away from all this bullshit about God and higher powers, away from Dexter, away from AA.

He slid open the door and stepped out onto the back patio, then put on his gloves and pulled up his hood. The patients were outside all bunched together, sitting under the orange glow of a tall umbrella-shaped space heater. They were laughing, talking, and sucking down cigarettes, playing some kind of board game that was spread out in the middle of the green picnic table. Monty kept his head down and his eyes forward and marched across the yard towards the trailer.

When he got back into his room, he shut the door behind him, then took a deep breath and leaned his head against the wall. He kicked off his shoes and unzipped his jacket, pulled off his gloves and pushed off his hood. He got in bed and buried his face underneath the pillows then pulled the covers up over his head. As he shut his eyes, he tried to focus on nothing—nothing but this room, nothing but this bed. But he couldn't focus. It felt like a weight was crushing down on top of him, like a fucking garbage truck was rolling over his chest. He wanted to get up and push the truck off of him, but he couldn't breathe, he couldn't scream. All he could do was lay there, staring up at the ceiling, hearing Dexter's words play over and over again in his head:

You didn't love her, Monty. You only thought you did because she made you feel worthy…she made you feel safe…she made you feel loved. But it wasn't love. It was only dependence. It was swapping one addiction out for another.

Was Dexter right? Was it just dependence? Was he just using Vicky as a way to cope without alcohol? So what if he was? He needed her. He needed Vicky. She was the only person in his life who still wanted to be around him. Everyone else was gone, because he'd turned his back on them. His parents, his friends, his sister, his brother—he pushed them all away, because he was too ashamed of all the horrible things he'd said and done. But Vicky was different, because she didn't really know him. She didn't know that he hit his mom in the face and sent her to the hospital. She didn't know that his dad called the cops and had him locked up in prison. She didn't know any of this, because he never told her, and, in exchange, Vicky never told him anything about herself. But, could you love someone you didn't know? No. But so what? That's the way they liked it. It gave them a chance to start over and be different people. They didn't have to face their shame and all those poisonous memories—they could just put them on a shelf somewhere and try to move on. So what if it wasn't real love? So what if they were codependent? They kept each other sober and that's all that mattered, right?

No, wait…that's not true. Vicky wasn't clean. She'd been using. Had she been using the whole time? Why didn't she tell him? Was she too ashamed? Was she afraid he'd be disappointed? Was their relationship that fragile that she couldn't even come and talk to him? But why? Didn't she know that he'd never judge her? Didn't she know that she could trust him?

"Fuck!"

Monty screamed as loud as he could into his pillow until his vocal chords felt like they'd been cut open with a saw. He shot up in bed and ripped off the covers and stood rigid and confused in the center of the room. He needed something to smash, something to grab on to, something to crush, something to rip. He paced back and forth beside the mattress, his fists clenched, his shoulders bowed outward, the adrenaline of self-hatred pumping through his muscles.

After a few paces, he stopped and squared his body then drove his fists into the wall, one after the other, until his knuckles became bloody, one after the other, until the flesh from his hands stuck to the wall. Then, he screamed and threw his entire body forward, driving his forehead like a sledgehammer against the wall. It felt good, so he did it again, only harder, and harder and harder until all he could see was a wall smeared with red, the blood streaking down from the gash in his forehead, forming dark pools where the plaster had cracked. But he didn't stop, because he knew he deserved it—he knew that this fucking punishment was his. He kept going, driving his head harder and harder, the tips of his teeth grinding against the soft, fleshy part of his gums. Then, all of a sudden, he began to feel dizzy. His muscles gave out and his body went limp. He crashed face-first into the carpet, the cartilage in his nose pushing back into his throat. He lay there for a while, staring at the blood streaks forming small pools at the base of the wall. The light in the room began to tunnel and all he could see was blackness and all he could hear was a sharp metallic ringing inside his ears. His eyes rolled back, his breathing became shallow, and the heaviness on his chest finally disappeared.

Chapter 30

The Discovery

Dave sat like a gargoyle perched on top of the back yard balcony, watching all the patients going in and out of the sliding patio doors below. His toes were numb, his hands had turned purple, and his ears were tingling as if they'd been doused with ant poison. He couldn't stay up here much longer. In another half hour or so, it was gonna be nighttime and any warmth from the sun would be long gone from the sky. He wished he could to go downstairs and thaw out underneath those space heaters, but he knew he wasn't welcome. He knew all the other patients hated his guts. He was an outcast, now, an exile, a man alone, a man by himself. Everyone else had turned their back on him, including Monty and Sarah. For whatever reason, they were all plotting against him, trying to bring him down, trying to sell him out. Could Cheryl be behind it all? Was she really that manipulative? Did she have that much power, that much clout? Even if she did, how'd she even know about Sarah? How'd she know about his plans to get her to testify in court? He never told anyone. The only people who knew were Angie and his lawyer, Weinstein.

Wait a minute, what if it was Weinstein? What if he told Cheryl? What if the old son of a bitch had called her up? What if they were old friends, old lawyer buddies from college? What if they met to discuss the case and Cheryl somehow seduced him and got him to talk? He could've leaked the whole plan. He could've told Cheryl everything—that Sarah was gonna testify that the cops didn't have reasonable suspicion. No, that couldn't be it. That was impossible. But then why would Sarah lie? Why would she make up that ridiculous story? She didn't call the cops. She didn't try to get him to pull over. She was having a good time. She was singing and dancing. Hell, all the girls were, weren't they?

Dave shook his head and cupped his hands together then took a deep breath and tried to blow life back into them. But they were too numb, too solid. They felt like frozen fish heads against his knees. Christ—now, what was he gonna do? How was he gonna get out of here? Without Sarah, he had no case.

He reached into his pocket and pulled out the bottle of Suboxone, but there were only three pills left. Shit, that wasn't gonna be enough. He needed more. His knee was really throbbing, probably because of all this stress.

He tossed back the pills and swallowed them with whatever saliva he could conjure then peered over the balcony and checked his watch. There was still another forty minutes before dinner was officially over, which meant the nurses and counselors, who ate last, would just now be sitting down. That meant the detox trailer would be empty at least for another twenty minutes, which gave him just enough time to get in and get out.

He pulled up his hood then stomped out his cigarette and made his way down the spiral staircase and out across the frozen lawn. As he headed towards the back gate, he tried walking as softly as possible, which was difficult to do on account of the snow being so god damn crunchy.

When he got inside the trailer, he shut the door behind him then started stomping his feet to bring feeling back to his toes. The trailer was warm, nice and toasty, and just as he suspected, there appeared to be no one around. "Hello?" he said, loud enough such that anyone in the back could hear him. "Is anyone here? Hello?"

When no one answered, he quickly limped over to the sliding glass window then poked his head through and looked around. The computer monitor was on, but there was no one sitting behind it. Perfect. This was his chance. Time to shine.

He went head first, his belly flat against the check-in counter, squeezing through the window like a baby seal being born. When he got to the other side, he dropped like a sack of potatoes onto the carpet, flat on his back, his eyes staring up at the ceiling. He brushed himself off then went right for the medicine cabinets, flung the doors open, and began scanning the rows and rows of pill bottles. The Suboxone was on the top, next to something called Dilaudid, which sounded kinda familiar. Where had he heard it before? Didn't Cheryl use to take it after her C-section with Larry? She did, didn't she? That meant it was probably pretty strong.

He pulled down a bottle and stuffed it into his pocket then replaced his empty bottle of Suboxone with a brand new one that was completely full. He shut the cabinets then squeezed back through the window and was about to leave the trailer when he heard the sound of something banging against a wall. What the hell? It sounded like a hammer smashing against drywall. And it was close too, probably right down the hall.

He pivoted on his toes and pushed through the saloon-swinging doorway then made his way down the dark, narrow hall. "Hello?" he said, his heart beating faster, his right ear cocked towards the sound. "Is someone there? Hello?"

When he got to the end of the hall, he stopped in front of a doorway. The banging was coming from inside, but the door was shut. This was Monty's room, wasn't it? "Hello?" he said, as he lightly tapped with his middle knuckle. "Is somebody in there? Monty? Is that you? Hello?"

All of a sudden, the banging stopped and there was a loud thud against the carpet, like a clump of snow falling from the overhang of a house. Dave grabbed the knob and tried to push the door inward, but it wouldn't budge. There was something wedged between the wall and the door. "Hello?"

He got on his hands and knees and put his right cheek to the carpet, closed one eye and looked through the little space between the door and the floor. It looked like there was a body or something sprawled out near the bedposts. He strained his eyes, got in a little tighter, and could definitely make out the silhouette of a person lying on the floor. Who was that? Was that Monty? He got in tighter. Holy shit. It was. The blond hair was unmistakable and it looked like there was blood or something running down the cracks in the floor.

"What the fuck?" He pushed himself up and pressed his ear against the door. "Monty, can you hear me? Are you okay? Do you need help?"

He waited for a reply but there was no answer, so he lowered his shoulder and started ramming it against the door. But it wouldn't budge—the kid was too heavy, so he started looking around frantically for something to wedge between the frame and the door. "Oh fuck, oh fuck, oh fuck." He bit his nails as he paced up and down the hallway then ran into the bathroom and started opening and closing the counter drawers. What the fuck was he doing? What was he looking for? He needed something long and skinny that could fit through that god damn door. Then he saw it, in the mirror's reflection. Of course. The shower curtain rod. He did an about face and grabbed a hold of it, yanking it down from in between the white tiled walls. He tore off the curtain then ran it through the hallway and jammed it in the little slit between the frame and the door. He got it halfway through then pulled as hard as he could backwards like some kind of maniac rowing a two-ton rowboat. The wood on the frame began to splinter and the door slowly inched forward. He got it open just enough to stick his foot though the crevice then squeezed and pulled as hard as he could. He was almost there—halfway through the doorframe—his crippled leg bending like an overloaded diving board. In one final thrust, he pulled himself forward and rolled out like a red carpet onto the bedroom floor. He crawled on his hands and knees over to Monty, then rolled the kid over and started shaking his shoulders. There was a round, golf ball-sized lump protruding from his forehead and spatters of blood on his face and shirt collar. "Monty," he said, as he started slapping the kid's face gently. "Come on kid, wake up, wake up."

Dave held his forefinger just underneath the kid's nostrils. The kid was definitely breathing. He could feel a slight tremble blowing from the kid's nose. He stood up, moved behind him, and stuck his hands underneath his armpits. He dragged him like a corpse away from the splintered doorframe, across the floor, over to his bed. When he got him beside the bed, he set him down gently, like an infant, holding his hand underneath the kid's head. Just as he set him down, the kid's eyes came open and a pained groan rumbled from deep inside his chest.

"Monty?" Dave said, as he bent over him, his face hovering just above the kid's lips. "Are you alright? Do you need help? Should I go get help?"

The kid coughed and lurched forward, shaking his head and clutching his chest. "No, don't get anyone, I'm alright, I'm fine."

"Are you sure?"

"Yeah, I'm fine."

Dave sighed and helped the kid upward, one hand on his back, the other behind his head. "You don't look fine. Can you walk?"

The kid nodded, although the pain in his face said he probably couldn't—his eyes were shut and his jaw was tensed.

"Alright, here, let's get you over to the bathroom."

Dave took the kid's arm and draped it over his shoulder, then straightened his legs and guided him to his feet. The kid wobbled, as if made of rubber, most of his weight falling on Dave's bad leg. They took small steps through the doorway and out into the hall. When they got to the bathroom, Dave flipped on the light switch, and carefully eased Monty down onto the top of the porcelain bowl. He took a step back and surveyed the damage, looking at the bloody mess running down the kid's forehead. "Jesus, it looks pretty bad. Are you sure you don't want me to get the nurse?"

The kid shook his head adamantly. "No, please...it's not that bad...it's just a little blood. I'll be fine. I just need to lie down."

"Are you sure?"

"Yes."

"Alright, well let's at least get you cleaned up, okay?"

Dave crouched down and grabbed a washcloth from underneath the sink then turned on the faucet and waited for the water to get warm. When it was warm enough, he ran the cloth underneath the water then brought it over to Monty and sat on the edge of the tub. As he raised the cloth, the water trickled down his forearms, dripping softly against the linoleum floor. He dabbed away carefully at the loose skin torn in the middle of the kid's forehead and wiped away the blood that was dried to his jaw. The kid flinched and let out a whimper each time the cloth took away a piece of his skin. Dave apologized but kept dabbing, assuring the kid that it would only be a few more minutes. He took the cloth and stuck it back under the faucet and, as he wrung it out, the sink turned a shade of pink. When he sat back down, he noticed that the kid's knuckles were also bleeding, the flesh hanging off the bone like dead leaves on a tree. Jesus Christ—what the hell happened? Did the kid beat his head and fists against the fucking wall?

He looked up at Monty. A cold chill ran through him, as he began to realize the disturbing severity of it all. What could have happened to make the kid so angry that he'd knock himself senselessly against a load-bearing wall? It wasn't because of what he'd said to him earlier, was it?

Dave bit his lower lip as he lowered the washcloth then finished wiping away the last of the dried blood. "Alright kid," he said, patting his hand against the kid's knee, "I think I got most of it. You wanna go lay down?"

The kid nodded, without lifting his head upward, as if his chin was super-glued to the base of his neck.

"Alright, come on."

Dave took the kid's arm and draped it again over his shoulder then carefully helped him off of the toilet seat. They walked in parallel down the hallway, like a pair of soldiers returning from a hellish war. The kid had all his weight leaned against Dave's shoulder and he let out a soft groan each time they took a step that was too wide apart.

When they got back into the bedroom, Dave eased Monty onto the edge of the mattress then helped him with his shoes and pulled his feet up onto the bed.

"Can I get you anything?" Dave asked, standing over him, not really too sure what to do or say next. "You want like some water or something?"

The kid didn't respond and just rolled over, pulling the sheets up over his head.

Dave sighed then straightened his bad leg out in front of him and gently eased himself down onto the edge of the bed. He sat there for a moment, staring down at the carpet, his palms clamming up with heat and sweat. How did this work? What was he supposed to say to him? What in God's name was he supposed to do next?

He cleared his throat and turned towards Monty. The silence was suffocating and unbearably thick. "I'm sorry about what happened earlier," he said in more of a stutter, his mouth dry and his vocal chords ripped. "I shouldn't have tried to spit on you. I was just pissed off and—"

"I'm not mad about that," Monty said from underneath the covers.

"You're not?"

"No. It's your life. You can do whatever you want with it."

"Oh." Dave let out a sigh of relief. Thank God. The kid wasn't mad at him. But then what would possess him to drive his head against a wall? "So, what are you so upset about? Did something else happen?"

The kid didn't respond and just lay underneath the covers, his shoulders rising and falling with each shallow breath.

"You know," Dave said, contemplating his knuckles, looking down at his dry, cold-cracked skin. "Sometimes it's good to talk about stuff…get whatever you got bottled up inside there off your chest. I know I felt a whole lot better when I told you all of my shit—about Larry and Cheryl, Angie and Sarah, the cops, the bus, the pod, the crack." Dave shook his head in disgust. "Actually, I'm probably not gonna be getting out of here as soon as I expected. In fact, I might be stuck here for the three whole fucking months. Remember that chick's daughter I was telling you about, Sarah? Well, for whatever reason, she's not gonna help me out. I don't know if my wife got to her or if she's just being skittish. Either way, it looks like I'm stuck here for a few more months. You should feel lucky, kid. Whatever shit you're going through, it can't be half as bad as the shit I'm dealing with."

"You think I'm lucky?" Monty said from underneath the covers.

Dave was caught off guard. He didn't think the kid was actually listening. He turned away and shook his head. "Well no, I didn't mean that…I mean, I know you got problems, but, shit, so do I. Hell, I mean, look at me. I'm fucked. I'm probably never gonna get out of here. I bet I'll be stuck here as long as you, maybe even longer. But I guess that's why we gotta stick together, you know? Because, honestly, I don't think I can get through three months of this shit on my own. You know what I mean?"

For a moment there was nothing but an awful silence, a silence so thick it seemed to throb inside Dave's brain.

After a few seconds, the kid sat up and pulled off the covers. His face was as pale and lifeless as a mannequin. "You got problems, Dave? Is that what you're telling me?"

"Well yeah. I mean, I'm in here, aren't I?"

The kid nodded and looked towards the windows, a pained expression on his bruised and bloodied face. His eyes were glazed over with a cold, simmering anger, but also weighted down with a much deeper pain. It looked like he wanted to say something, but was afraid to say it, like the words were flies buzzing inside his mouth.

"What is it?" Dave said, sitting perfectly rigid, afraid that any movement at all would scare the kid off. "You look like you got something you wanna say. It's alright, you can tell me. Whatever it is, I'm sure I'll understand."

"I doubt it."

"Try me."

The kid turned away and looked over towards the windows. The lines from the blinds threw shadows on his face.

"Come on Monty, what is it? You can tell me."

"I killed her," Monty said in a flat, low whisper, the flies finally spitting out from his mouth.

It took a few seconds for the words to register. Dave waited for Monty to say a little bit more. But when the kid didn't say anything, Dave edged closer to him on the mattress, his eyes wide open, his feet tapping nervously on the floor. "What? What are you talking about? Who? Who'd you kill?"

"Vicky. My fiancé."

"What?"

"I watched her drown as the water poured in through the windows. I listened to her scream as she died in my arms." Monty took a deep breath and slumped forward, burying his head into his arms. "It happened on the night of my one year sober anniversary. We were on our way up to the mountains for some time alone. I had just proposed to her at our Sunday night speaker meeting and I wanted to do something special, you know, like a romantic, little honeymoon." The kid smiled weakly for only a brief second, then turned and buried his head back into his arms. "We were driving just north of Boulder when it all happened, up around that big reservoir near Nederland. You know where that is?"

Dave nodded. He knew exactly the spot where the kid was talking about. He'd driven up and down that road at least a million times. Most of the time to get away from Cheryl and her constant bickering, to just drive and think and smoke in his car.

The kid continued, his voice barely audible, like something had been stolen from inside his lungs: "I swear to God, I thought I saw headlights, but maybe it was nothing, you know, maybe it was just something I saw. It all happened so fucking sudden. One minute she was smiling, holding my hand, looking out the window…the next minute she was screaming, the blood from her head all over the car. I tried to get her out, but I just couldn't pull hard enough, the dashboard was too twisted and I just wasn't strong enough. I lost her," he said, looking upward, the tears from his eyes dripping onto the sheets. "I watched her take her last breath of oxygen. I watched her die. I watched her drown."

A cold, dense chill descended into Dave's body, like a dead, petrified hand reaching into his soul. He sat there frozen, his legs glued to the mattress, unable to blink, unable to move. Something wasn't right…something was missing…something about the kid's story seemed to be off. Nederland…the canyon…the frozen reservoir…something about it all seemed to be horribly wrong. Wasn't that the same spot he'd dreamt about in his nightmares? The spot where he fell out of the car and lost his legs in the water? It was, wasn't it? But it wasn't real…it was just a nightmare…a horrible, terrible, God-awful dream.

Then, all of a sudden, the nightmare came back to him, like the pieces of a puzzle assembling in his brain—Larry's chubby face, blown up like a blowfish, his lips moving along to that same god damn song—*Magic Bus*, the kid's absolute favorite, a song he played on the way to every god damn volleyball game. The lyrics were like a scalpel scraping the inside of Dave's eardrums, the same horrible words repeating over and over and over again: *Too much, the Magic Bus…Too much, the Magic Bus…Too much, the Magic Bus.*

He slumped forward and stuck his head in between his kneecaps, sucking for breath like he was sucking his own dick. He felt cold and vacant, like something had been taken out of him, like all the air had been sucked from his chest. As he looked up at the wall, his mind flashed to images of the blue

Volkswagen and big gouge of metal just above the right headlamp. But when was that? When did that happen? Wasn't that the night before he got arrested on the bus? He stood up from the bed and looked down at Monty, the lyrics of that damn song still ringing in his head: *Too much, the Magic Bus...Too much, the Magic Bus...Too much, the Magic Bus.*

"Are you okay?" Monty said, looking at him quizzically, the tears from his eyes still dripping onto the bed.

"Uh, yeah, I'm fine, I'm just"—Dave looked around the room. It seemed to be getting smaller, the walls of the bedroom closing in on his head. His hands shook and his bad leg was throbbing, as if someone had just taken a hacksaw to his knee.

"What?" Monty said. "What's the matter?"

"Oh, nothing, I was just"—His lips were dry, his tongue was twisted, and everything inside was being tied in one big knot—"I was just wondering when the accident happened."

"Oh." Monty looked away and back at the pillow, rubbing his eyes and rubbing his nose. "It was about, three weeks ago, on Sunday."

Jesus...the volleyball game was on Monday...that meant the car must've been wrecked the night before...Sunday...the night of the kid's accident...the night he was watching Larry...the night he was supposed to be in charge.

He turned away from the bed and took a step backward, across the room, towards the door. His hands were shaking, his legs were shaking, and he felt like his fucking heart was about to explode. He extended his hand and grabbed the doorknob, but just as he opened it, Monty stopped him and said, "Hey, Dave?"

Dave did an about-face, his hands pressed up behind him, like a prisoner about to face the execution squad. "Uh...yeah, kid?"

"Thanks."

"For what?"

"For listening."

Dave's heart split into two pieces, like a log on a stump being split by an axe. His hands became clammy and his stomach turned to liquid and all the blood from his brain seemed to drain down to his toes. Jesus Christ, he couldn't fucking do this. He had to get out of here. He had to find what the fuck was really going on. He swallowed his spit and pushed the sickness downward—down his throat and back into his gut. Then, he lifted his head and nodded at Monty and forced a smile and said, "You're welcome, kid."

Chapter 31

The Call Home

Dave cursed to himself as he stomped down the steps of the detox trailer, through the side yard, and around to the back gate. His heart was pounding, his skin was crawling, and his stomach felt like it was about to jump out of his fucking throat. But he had to hold it together…he couldn't afford to lose it…not here, not now, not in front of all these people. This wasn't real…it was just a coincidence…a stilly, stupid delusion he'd dreamt up in his head. There was no way in hell he could've been the one responsible. No way in hell he could've been the one who caused that girl's death. Christ, he would've remembered something like that, wouldn't he? Hitting a car, running 'em off the road into a fucking reservoir? Jesus Christ. He'd sure as hell better remember something like that. That kind of shit doesn't just happen every day. Well then where in God's name was he? Why the fuck couldn't he remember where he was that night? Come on, Dave, think, think, think. He had to be somewhere. But where? Was he at the store getting groceries? No. Was he at the park walking the dog? Hell no. Well what about the high school? Did they have practice that night in the gymnasium? No, of course not. Not on a Sunday. Not on the night before a god damn match. Then where? Where in God's name was he? And why the fuck couldn't he remember anything?

"God damnit!"

When he got to the patio, he went right for the payphones. But wait. There were a bunch of patients swarming around them, playing their stupid, god damn board game. He couldn't talk there. Everyone would hear him. Everyone and their mother would be able to hear every single word he'd say. Well then where else could he go? Were there any other payphones? How could he find out what was going on if he couldn't talk to Larry?

He swung his head around looking for anything that resembled a payphone, but quickly came to the realization that there weren't gonna be anymore out here. The only other one was inside in the front room foyer next to all the counselors' offices by the main staircase. But he wasn't allowed up there in the front foyer, was he? No, only the counselors were allowed in that room. Fuck it. This was a god damn emergency. If anyone gave him shit about it he'd tell 'em to just fuck off.

He took a deep breath and grabbed hold of the patio door handles, then slid them open and stepped into the meeting hall. He turned towards the kitchen and made his way up the staircase past the bathrooms and into the hall. When he got to the front foyer, he stopped and peeked his head over the saloon-swinging doorway, making sure no counselors were there to give him any shit. There weren't. Thank God. He pushed open the doors and staggered into the foyer, his eyes darting around looking for the phone. He saw it. It was sitting beside the couch on a glass coffee table underneath the shadow of an unlit lamp. He went to it quickly, planted himself on the sofa, picked up the receiver, and held it to his ear. As he punched in the numbers, he began to feel a sharp tingling, the pain from his leg piercing into his sciatic nerve.

The phone began ringing, but no one answered it. It rang once, twice, three times, four. Then, the machine picked up. "Shit!" He slammed it down into the cradle, then picked it up and dialed again. "Come on Cheryl...pick up the phone...pick up, pick up, pick up."

This time she picked up almost immediately. "Hello?"

"Hello? Cheryl?"

There was a slight pause then she recognized who it was: "Dave? Dave is that you?"

"Yeah Cheryl, it's me."

"Dave? What—what are you doing? Why are you calling here? Is something the matter? Are you okay?"

"No, Cheryl. I'm not okay. I'm pretty far from okay."

"What is it? What's the matter?"

"Look Cheryl, I need you to listen to me very carefully. Okay? Are you listening?"

"Yes, Dave, I'm here, I'm listening. What is it? What's going on?"

"I need you to go get Larry."

"What?"

"I need you to get him and put him on the phone. Can you do that for me? Can you go get Larry?"

"No Dave. Absolutely not."

"Cheryl."

"I'm not going to go get Larry. He's asleep for Christ's sake."

"Well then wake him up. This is important God damnit."

"No, I will not wake him up. He doesn't want to talk to you. He's afraid of you. He's afraid of his own dad."

"Don't say that, Cheryl. Please don't say that."

"Do you even realize what you're doing to him? Do you realize the hell you're putting him through? He had to sit there and watch as his own father got arrested in front of a busload of high school girls. Do you know how humiliating that was for him? Do you realize the irreversible damage that did?"

"I know, Cheryl, I'm sorry—"

"Bullshit. You do not know. You don't know a god damn thing. All you care about is your own self-centered ego...your own pride...your own vanity. Do you know what it's like for me to have to walk around in public after your picture's been posted all across the front page? And what about your daughters? Huh? Do you know what it's like for them to have to walk back into their middle school when everyone knows that their father is a god damn crack head?"

"Cheryl, please, I don't wanna do this with you right now. I just wanna talk to Larry."

"Well, you're not going to talk to him, Dave. You shouldn't even be calling here. Your counselors said you weren't supposed to use the phone for an entire week."

All of a sudden, Dave could hear someone's voice in the background, a sleepy whimper on the other end of the phone. "Mommy? What's going on? Why are you yelling?"

"Oh great," Cheryl said. "Now look what you've done."

"Who is that? Is that Larry?"

"Do you realize how long it took me to get him to bed?"

"Larry, is that you? Larry! Larry!"

"Mommy, who are you talking to?"

"Larry! Larry!"

"It's alright sweetie. Everything's okay. I'm just talking to your father."

"Daddy?"

"Yes, sweetie."

"I wanna talk. I wanna talk. Gimme, gimme, gimme."

"No sweetie, not now, it's bedtime."

"Gimme, gimme, gimme!"

Cheryl sighed and came back on the receiver, her voice trembling it was so full of rage. "He wants to talk to you."

"Okay, then put him on."

"Please, don't say anything that will upset him."

"I won't. Jesus Cheryl, just put him on. Please."

She sighed again, only this time longer, then finally surrendered and handed Larry the phone. "Hello? Daddy, is that you?"

"Yep, it's me, buddy. It's daddy."

"Daddy!" The kid shrieked so loud that Dave had to pull the phone away from his ear. "Daddy, Daddy, Daddy!"

"Whoa, calm down, buddy. Not so loud. You're gonna make me go deaf."

"Daddy, where are you? What are you doing?"

"Didn't mommy tell you?"

"Tell me what?"

Dave snarled. That figured. She didn't even tell him where his own father was. "Well," he said looking around the foyer, trying to find the right words to describe this place, "I'm in a sort of a hospital."

"A hospital?"

"Yeah."

"Wow! What's it like? Did they give you ice cream?"

"What?"

"Ice cream? Did you get ice cream?"

"No, buddy. No ice cream."

"Aw, that stinks."

"Yeah, it does. Listen,"—Dave took a deep breath and leaned forward, his hand on his forehead, his elbow on his knee—"I need to talk to you about something. It's pretty important."

"Okay."

"Do you remember that night, before the volleyball game, when we went up to that place in the mountains?"

"The mountains?"

"Yeah, the mountains. Do you remember?"

"Hmm…" The kid paused for just a moment. Dave could sense the wheels beginning to turn in the kid's head. "Um…no, not really."

"You sure? Think real hard now. I think it was snowing and there might've been a lake or something around there."

"Oh. You mean the chuckleboard place."

"The what?"

"The chuckleboard place."

Dave narrowed his eyes and looked out across the foyer, trying to figure out what the kid was trying to say. Shuffleboard? What was he talking about? He didn't remember taking the kid to any shuffleboard place. Then, all of a sudden the images came back to him, like a freight train smashing into his brain—the long, narrow board that looked like a miniature runway with the triangular patterns at each end inscribed in the wood…and those little, flat discs that were shaped like hockey pucks that would float down the runway with the slightest, little push. Of course, that's where they were, up in Nederland, at that bar near the reservoir, O'Reilley's, right? He'd taken the kid up there to show him how to play shuffleboard. It was the only bar around Boulder that had one of those long sand tables. Oh Christ—how could he have forgotten? He was up there all day drinking and playing. He must've blacked out from all of the crack and whiskey shots.

He covered his mouth and leaned forward, lowering the phone against his knee. Oh Jesus. What did he do? What the fuck happened? What time did they drive back? What time did they get back home?

"Daddy? Are you still there?"

He looked down at the phone—it was talking to him, the kid's voice a small, distant plea. He picked it up and shook off the images then pressed the receiver against his ear. "Uh…yeah I'm still here, buddy. I remember now. We were playing that game you like—that shuffleboard game."

"Yeah, I love that game."

"I know you do, buddy. Say, you wouldn't happen to remember how long we were there, would ya?"

"Hmm…" The kid paused again and room fell dead silent, as Dave tried to choke back the nausea from his throat. "I'd say we were there for a pretty long time."

"Was it dark when we left?"

"It sure was."

"Oh okay, good, good. Now, do you remember if anything happened on the ride home?"

"Like what?"

"Oh, I don't know like maybe we a hit a tree or ran something over?"

"You mean bumper cars?"

"What?"

"Bumper cars. You said we were playing bumper cars."

"I did?"

"Yeah. Don't you remember?"

"No, buddy, I guess I forgot." Dave laughed nervously, rubbing the back of his neck. "Uh…who were we playing bumper cars with?"

"The pirate ship."

"The pirate ship."

"Yeah, the pirate ship. Don't tell me you forget about the pirate ship too, daddy."

"Yeah, I guess I did." He chuckled again. What the hell was he talking about? What pirate ship? "Uh, what pirate ship are you talking about, buddy?"

"The one that sank in the water…"

Oh Jesus.

"…They were trying to steal our treasure so we rammed it with our cannons."

No, no, no…this wasn't happening…this wasn't happening.

"…It sank really fast, and then you said that the British were coming so we had to get out of there quick or we'd be taken prisoner."

Immediately, Dave began to feel a tightening sensation, like a giant-sized wrench clasping around his throat. He couldn't breathe, he couldn't speak, and the wrench kept getting tighter, and tighter and tighter until it felt like his head was gonna explode. The images began to flash in frenetic succession like some kind of violent electrical storm going off in his head—the crack, the bar, the shuffleboard, the shots of whiskey, the snow on the windshield, the bend in the road. He could see it all now so very clearly, like a dark veil had just been lifted from his face.

They were going down Canyon road when it all happened, back towards Boulder, back towards the house. It was pitch black out and the snow was bombarding the windshield like a million cotton balls materializing from the dark. Larry was in the passenger seat, playing with the cassette player, singing along loudly to that same god damn song. But on this particular night, Dave was in no mood for any kind of singing, especially with the snow on the highway, the crack in his bloodstream, and the ungodly shots of liquor sloshing around in his gut. He had to concentrate. He was trashed beyond recognition. He had one eye that was barely open and the other was so bloodshot it looked like it had been stung by a wasp. He screamed at Larry to turn down the volume, but when the kid didn't do it, he reached over and punched out the tape. The only problem was...as he reached over to hit the eject button, the car slid across the centerline and ended up on the wrong side of the highway. When he looked back up, he saw a pair of headlights, like two giant flashlights shining into his face. He instinctively slammed down the brake pedal, but missed the brake and, instead, slammed on the gas. The Volkswagen shot out like a missile, colliding with the other car's front right headlight. There was a swirl of lights and a blast of thunder, metal on metal, glass on asphalt. The other car spun across the highway, rolled over the guardrail, slid down the ravine, and disappeared into the dark. His Volkswagen ended up on the other side of the highway, one tire on the road, the other on the snow. Dave sat there for a moment trying to regain his composure, his fingernails dug deep into the steering wheel's vinyl. He looked over at Larry—the little shit was enjoying it, laughing and nodding like he was at an amusement park. "Whoohoo!" he shouted, his hands raised above him. "Let's do it again."

"No," Dave said, "let's not."

He pushed open the door, stepped out onto the shoulder, and looked over the hood out at the reservoir. The other car was out there, upside down, sinking in the water, its headlights pointed up like two spotlights signaling for a rescue. He snapped his head around and peered down both ends of the highway, but there was no one coming, they were completely alone. When he turned back around, the other car was gone, swallowed up by the water, its headlights growing dim as it sunk beneath the ice. He stood there for a moment, debating his options, feeling as the fear crept into his heart. He had to leave…there was no other option…if he didn't leave now, they'd throw him in jail. He was probably more than ten times over the legal limit. He wouldn't be able to walk a straight line to save his ass. Besides, maybe someone would come by and see there was an accident and stop and help and pull them from the car. Or maybe they got out on their own already. Maybe they were already out and swimming towards the shore. Oh no—what if they were already walking up the embankment? What if they already saw him and spotted his car? Oh Jesus, he had to leave. He had to get out of here. He couldn't just wait around for them to call the cops. Panic set in like the jaws of a Rottweiler clamping down on the soft flesh of his arm. He spun around quickly and ducked into the Volkswagen, nearly crushing his bad leg as he slammed the door of the car. Larry asked him what was happening and he told him to just shut up, sit there, and be quiet, then gave him some line about pirates and bumper cars. Then, he checked his mirror and turned over the ignition, shifted into gear and sped off down the road.

He left them. He left them out there to die like road kill, trapped under the ice of the Barker reservoir. But why? Why didn't he try to help them? Why did he just leave them out there to die? He could've called someone. He could've gone in after them. What kind of fucking coward was he? A girl died and he killed her. He ran them off the road and left them there to drown.

An intense heat began to rise inside Dave's stomach, all knotted and twisted like a lump of smoldering coal. He looked down at his hand clutching the receiver—it was red, the blood swelling through his fingers, white on the knuckles, but red everywhere else. He went to hang it up, but it slipped from his fingers, bounced against the floor, and spun around like a top. As he tried to stand up, he fell back against the sofa, like a drunk trying to get up from an icy pond. He looked around the foyer—everything was spinning, like he was on a merry-go-round at the park. The walls were moving, the floor was spinning, and everything inside him was pushing up against his gut. He couldn't do this. He had to get out of here. He had to leave. He had to run. But where? Where could he go? If he left now, they'd throw him back in prison…they'd lock him up with those animals and throw away the key. But maybe that's what he deserved. Maybe that was his sentence. Maybe that was his fate. No. He couldn't do that. He couldn't allow that to happen. He'd rather be dead than have to go back to that place.

He took a deep breath and pressed his palms into the cushions, then straightened his back and straightened his legs. He got up from the sofa and walked out across the foyer, holding his stomach like he was nursing a knife wound.

When he got outside, he surveyed the patio, then zipped up his jacket and pulled on his hood. Everyone was outside, still sitting at those green picnic tables, laughing, smoking, and playing their silly board game. He kept his head down and tried not to make eye contact, his hands in his pockets, his eyes on the ground. Where was he going? What was he doing? He didn't know—all he knew was that he had to get away. He had to go some place where no one could follow him, some place quiet where he could just think and be alone.

He staggered across the yard and down the icy pathway, around the side of the house and towards the back gate. He grabbed the handle and pulled the gate open, but just as he did, he heard someone shouting his name. He looked over his shoulder. Oh fuck, it was Angie, yelling and waving at the top of her lungs. "Dave! Wait up! Wait for me!"

Angie caught up with him at the outer edge of the driveway and pulled him to a halt in front of the porch. She was out of breath and panting, snot bubbles like winter green bubble gum respiring from her nose. "Dave," she said, her hands on her knees, trying desperately to catch her breath. "What are you doing? Where are you going?"

"Angie, I am not in the mood right now. Please, just leave me alone."

"What? What do you mean you're not in the mood?"

"I mean, I can't deal with this right now, okay? I need to be alone. Please, just leave me alone."

Dave shrugged her off and went to march forward, but Angie reached out and grabbed the back of his hood. "Wait a minute Dave. What about Sarah? What about Larry? What about our plans to become a family and move away?"

Dave stopped and tilted his head backward, his breath spiraling up towards the full, yellow moon. He had to do something. He couldn't allow this to continue. He had to put a stop to this delusion before it got out of control. He took a deep breath then turned around to face her. He placed his hands on her shoulders and looked her dead in the eyes. "Angie," he said, as calmly as he could muster, "I need you to listen to me very carefully, okay?"

"What is it baby? What's the matter?"

Dave his clenched his teeth. "Don't call me that," he said. "I am not your baby. I will never be your baby. I will never be your anything. Do you understand me?"

"What?" Angie looked at him in utter confusion, her forehead wrinkled like a wet, polyester shirt. "Dave, what is the matter with you? Why are you acting like this?"

She reached out and tried to touch him, but Dave quickly swatted her hand away. "Don't do that."

"Ouch!" Angie pulled away in astonishment, holding her hand like she was holding a pet bird. "That hurt. Why'd you do that? What the hell has gotten into you?"

"Angie, I don't know where you got this crazy idea about me and Larry and your daughter all going off to live together. I mean, maybe it's my fault, maybe I put you onto it, but it's not real. Okay? It's just a delusion. It's some crazy, half-cocked fantasy that you got cooked up in your little head."

"Dave, what are you saying?"

"I'm saying, we are not a family, Angie. We never were and we never will be. Do you understand me?"

Angie just stood there completely frozen, like someone who'd just fallen into catatonic shock. Her chin was dropped open like a Christmas Nutcracker and her eyes were as black and glassy as a doll's.

"Look Angie," Dave said, stepping forward, touching his hand against her cheek. "I lied to you. I was the one who put your daughter in danger—not Cheryl, not the cops. It was me. I'm responsible. I was driving that bus under the influence. I was smoking crack and drinking all day."

"What!?"

"I used you, Angie. I used you to try and get to Sarah, but it didn't even matter, because I'm the one who fucked up. I'm sick, just like you are. I need help. We both need help."

Dave went to hug her, but Angie just pushed him away and let out a brain-piercing scream. "You bastard!" She came charging at him full throttle, flailing her fists against his face. "I'll kill you! I'll fucking kill you!"

Dave tried to jump back, but his left foot slipped out of his unlaced running shoe and he fell backwards into the snow. Angie pounced on him like a lioness going after her dinner, clawing her nails across his face. Her nails ripped deep just underneath his left eye socket, tearing the flesh away from his cheek. "Stop it!" Dave screamed, trying to block her punches. "Stop it, Angie. What are you doing?"

"I'm gonna kill you!"

Dave caught hold of her wrists and pinned them together to keep from getting scratched and cut to shreds. But Angie still didn't stop. She was furious, foaming at the mouth, trying to bite his face.

Dave had no choice but to thrust his head upward, catching her just below the bottom lip. She shrieked in pain and finally rolled off him, covering her lip with both hands. "You bastard," she cried, looking up at him, the blood from her lips pooling into her hands. "You hit me."

"I had no choice, Angie. You made me do it."

"I hate you," she screamed. "You're a fucking pig."

Dave stood up and knocked the snow off his jacket then hobbled over to his shoe and picked it up. He lifted his foot and wiped the snow off the bottom, then pulled back the tongue and slipped it back on. "I'm sorry," he said, as he looked back at Angie, rocking back and forth on her knees like she was a Muslim in prayer. "I didn't mean to hurt you. I didn't mean to hurt anybody, I just—"

"Screw you, you bastard. I hope you burn in hell."

Dave tried to think of something else he could say that would calm her, but couldn't think of anything, and so he just left. He spit the blood from his mouth then limped back towards the patio, leaving Angie crying in the snow, alone.

Chapter 32

Mother and Child Reunion

The phone began to ring. Angie could barely hold the receiver steady. She was shaking so bad, she had to clutch it with both hands. One ring, two rings, three rings, four. Sarah's voicemail picked up. The soft, teenage girl's voice was like a rusty nail being hammered into Angie's soul. "Shit." She jammed down the hook then shoved in another quarter, punched in the numbers, and waited for it to ring. Again, after four rings, it went right to Sarah's voicemail. She hung up the phone and tried again, then, again and again, until she only had one more quarter. After saying a quick prayer, she kissed the quarter and dropped it in. "Please, pick up Sarah. Please baby, I need you. I love you so much. Please pick up."

After two rings, Sarah finally answered. Her voice was soft and drowsy. She must've been asleep. "Hello?"

Angie's heart ricocheted against her ribcage. She wiped her tears and moved her hair from her face. "Sarah, is that you? Is that you, baby?"

"Yes. Who is this?"

"It's me, Sarah. It's me, mommy."

"Mom?"

"Yes. It's me, baby. I've been trying to get a hold of you. Where have you been? Why haven't you been answering?"

There was a long pause. Angie could hear Sarah crying, her sniffles like maggots worming their way through the phone. Were they tears of joy? Was she happy to hear from her? Or was something wrong? Did somebody hurt her?

"Sarah, is everything okay? What's the matter? Are you alright? What's wrong?"

"Mom, what are you doing?" Sarah's voice was rough and splintered like a broken broom handle that had been left out in the snow. "Why do you keep calling here?"

"What do you mean why do I keep calling? You're my daughter. I love you. I missed you so much."

"You can't keep doing this, mom."

"What?"

"You can't keep calling here."

"Why not?"

"Because it's just not right."

"But why?"

"Because you're sick, mom. Something's wrong with you. You're not healthy. I don't even know who you are anymore."

Angie gasped. "Sarah, don't say that. I'm your mother. That's who I am. I'm your mom."

"Then where have you been? Why did you just leave me?"

"I didn't leave you, baby."

"Yes, you did."

"No, it wasn't my fault. It was your father's. He did this. He drove us apart."

"That's a lie. Daddy only tried to help you. But you wouldn't take it. You were too busy getting high."

"That's not true. Is that what your father told you? He's lying to you. He's trying to turn you against me."

"He's not lying, mom. I saw you. I saw you out there in that trailer. I saw you with him. I saw you with Rick."

"What? What are you talking about? When did you see me? When, Sarah, when?"

"Two weeks ago, I drove out there to try and find you, and that's when I saw you. That's when I saw you doing those disgusting things."

"But that's all over with now, honey. Rick's history. He's gone now."

"Yeah and you killed him."

"No, honey. No, I didn't. Rick's a big boy. He did that to himself."

"Yeah right. You expect me to believe that? Rick was a sweet guy. He loved me. And I loved him too, and you fucked him."

"No, honey."

"Do you realize how twisted that is? How sick and perverted? You seduced him, mom. You fucked your daughter's boyfriend."

"No, baby."

"How could you do that? How could you be so selfish? I can't even talk to you anymore. You make me want to puke."

"I'm sorry, honey. I didn't mean to do it. It just sort of happened. It was beyond my control."

"You mean like my volleyball coach?"

"What?"

"I talked to him today. What? Are you fucking him too?"

"Please don't talk like that, Sarah. It's unbecoming."

Sarah laughed. "Unbecoming? You're a meth head, mom. Look who's talking."

"Sarah please. I said, I'm sorry."

"You're sorry? What about me? I'm the new school joke. Everyone knows about you and what you did with Rick in that trailer and now they're going to know about you and my coach."

"There's nothing to know about, sweetie. Nothing happened. We didn't do anything."

"Yeah right, you're full of bull. You're sick, mom…you're a sick person, and I don't want to have anything to do with you. You're not my mom anymore."

"Don't say that Sarah. Please don't say that."

"I hate you. Stop calling me. I never want to speak to you again. Get out of my life!"

"No, wait, please don't hang up. I love you, baby. I love you so much. Please don't hang up the phone."

But it was too late. The phone went dead and Sarah's voice vanished, replaced by a repulsively cheery operator speaking on the other end: "If you'd like to make a call, please hang up and try again. If you need assistance, please hang up and dial your operator." Angie's knees buckled and she sank down against the concrete patio, letting the receiver fall from her hands. She dropped her head in her hands and sobbed there quietly as the phone swayed back and forth in the cold, winter wind.

Chapter 33

Dave's First Step

The sun looked like a blister bubbling up from the earth's surface, its blood red beams oozing out across a bruised and cloud-swollen sky. Dave sat completely still on top of the backyard balcony, staring down at the dozens of cigarette butts scattered out by the legs of the metal folding chair. He'd been up there all night, hunched over in his green and gold Catholic High Crusader's warm-up jacket, thinking of his past, present, and future, going over his options, going over his life. The way he saw it, there were two alternatives and two alternatives only—either he could turn himself in and go to prison or he could keep his mouth shut and finish out this program. No one would ever know that he was the one responsible. No one would ever know that he was the one who ran those kids off the road. But what about Monty? What would happen to him if he never found out? He didn't even know there was another driver. Didn't he say he thought it was just a reflection off the guardrail? How could he let him go on living like that—blaming himself for the death of his fiancé, punishing himself for something that he didn't even do? He was a young kid, a good kid—he had his whole life ahead of him. Didn't Dave owe it to him to at least tell him the truth? What if it was his one of his own kids that this happened to? What if it were his daughters, Megan and Mary? What if it was Larry? What then? Wouldn't he want justice for the person responsible? Wouldn't he want them to be punished for the crime they committed?

But what good would it do if he turned himself in and went to prison? Wouldn't they just lock him behind bars and throw away the key? What would happen to Larry if he wasn't home to take care of him? Who would bathe him and take him to school in the mornings? Who would read him stories at night and put him to bed? Cheryl couldn't do that, could she? No. She'd be too busy, with court, with cases, with clients, with meetings— hell, she'd have to work overtime just to be able pay the premium on the kids' health bills. He couldn't do that to her, could he? Just abandon her and go to prison, leaving her to take care of three kids on her own? And what would that do to his kids knowing that their father was in prison? What would it do to Larry knowing that his father killed someone? The kid had enough strikes against him already—did he really need to grow up knowing that his father was nothing but some out-of-control, crack-addicted piece of scum?

How could he have let this all happen? How could he have let everything get so fucked up? He had everything any man could've ever wanted—a wife, a life, a family, a home. But he screwed it all up. He let it all slip away from him. He let that fucking rock define who he was. He forgot about the one thing in his life that actually gave him purpose—the one thing in his life that actually made him who he was. It wasn't the training or the races or the god damn medals—it was his wife, his daughters, his family, his son. They were the ones who made his life worth living. They were the ones who made him who he was. Who the hell was he if he didn't have his family? Who the hell was he if he didn't have someone to love? Without them, he had no purpose, no point, no function. Without them, he was just another beat-up, burned-out, cracked-out bum.

Dave sucked down the last of his cigarette then flicked it from his fingers and watched it fall to the ground. He checked his watch. It was nearly six-thirty. Another ten minutes and everyone would be getting up. He couldn't stay up here. He had to get out of here. He didn't want to have to talk to anyone or look them directly in the eye. How could he? He was a fucking criminal. He killed an innocent girl and left her alone to die. But where could he go? Where would it be quiet? Where could he just sit and think and be alone?

He turned in his chair and looked back toward the upper floor atrium, then down at the patio, and out across the lawn. Wait—he had an idea. What about the basement? Yeah. It was perfect. It was dark, empty, and probably even had a bathroom. He could hide down there forever until he figured this thing out.

He nodded his head as he got up from the folding chair then walked down the stairs and out across the lawn. When he got inside the house, he closed the sliding glass door behind him, then tip-toed up the kitchen steps and took a left at the end of the hall. He was lucky. The place was still quiet. Not even the sound of running water could be heard from the upstairs showers.

When he got to the foyer, he bent beneath the staircase and went to pull open the half-size basement door. But just as he opened the door, he was stunned by the piercing sound of a girl screaming, coming from somewhere on the woman's floor. The screaming was so loud that it caused Dave to flinch backward, knocking his bad knee against the basement door. He stepped away from the door and wandered out into the foyer, peering up the winding staircase, trying to see what the hell was going on. Some of the other patients, awoken by the screaming, began to wander out into the hallway from their rooms.

With one hand on the banister, Dave cautiously limped up the main staircase, the screaming so intense that he had to plug one ear. As he got closer to the fourth floor, some of the other female patients began screaming, some even running away and shouting for help. They stormed by Dave, knocking him against the banister then spilled out into the foyer like a stampede of elk. When he got to the top of the stairs, he approached a crowd of patients all gathered around the bathroom, looking inside. As Dave pushed his way to the front of the crowd, something appeared before him, something so horrific it looked like it belonged in a snuff film.

It was Angie. She was curled in the fetal position next to the toilet, lying in a puddle of her own vomit and drool. Her feet were bare, her legs uncovered, her breasts drooping from the neck of her fuzzy, pink bathrobe. And on the floor beside her outstretched fingers were two empty pill bottles with their caps screwed off. One was Suboxone and the other was Dilaudid— the same bottles that he had stolen from the detox trailer the night before.

Chapter 34

The Ninth Step

Something awoke him, shrill and intrusive, the sound of a siren wailing right outside of his room. Monty opened his eyes and let the light come to him, then turned on his elbow and looked towards the window. There was something bright red shining through the curtains whirling around the walls like some kind of hellish disco ball. He kicked off the sheets and swung his legs out over the mattress then planted his feet into the cold, trailer floor. He lumbered across the room and parted the curtains then looked across the yard towards the main house. There was an ambulance parked outside in the semi-circle driveway, its lights splashing red against the side of the house. He strained his eyes and pressed his forehead against the window and saw what appeared to be a stretcher being wheeled down the steps of the front porch. He couldn't tell who was in it, but it had to be a woman, because the only thing he could see was a head of wild, blond hair. It was sticking out of the top of a clean white hospital sheet, bouncing up and down as the stretcher was wheeled out across the cobblestone. There were two paramedics, one on either side of the gurney, bracing the rails to keep the woman from falling out. They said something to one another then lifted the gurney and, in one fluid motion, pushed it into the back of the swirling red ambulance. One medic stepped on the bumper and jumped into the back with the gurney, while the other shut the door behind him, and walked around to the front. A few seconds later, the engine started and the tires spun forward and the ambulance took off down the driveway wailing its frenetic, two-note song.

Monty crouched to the floor and pulled out his green gym bag then unzipped the zipper and pulled out his jeans and a fresh long-sleeve shirt. He pulled them all on and slid into his tennis shoes then grabbed his black snowboard jacket along with his gloves.

Once he got outside, he walked briskly towards the cobblestone driveway, the wailing of the ambulance now a distant murmur muffled by the insulation of the mountain snow. When he got to the front of the house, he noticed something perplexing—there appeared to be tiny droplets of what looked like vomit dribbled out across the boot-trampled lawn. He did his best to avoid stepping in any of it, by playing a game of hopscotch across the crunchy snow. Once he made it through, he ascended the steps of the front porch and walked into the main house through the front door.

As he walked through the foyer, he noticed something even more perplexing—a group of people, all huddled together in a tight little circle. They were embracing one another and talking very softly, as if they were at a funeral bereaving the dead.

"What's going on?" Monty said, as he approached them. "What happened? Who was in the ambulance?"

One of them looked up, a bald man with the earrings, an expression of sorrow worn into his face. He was about to speak when someone called out to Monty from the opposite end of the foyer. He turned and looked. It was Dexter, standing in the light of the kitchen doorway, his hand extended, waving him in. Oh great. What did he want? Thought he was done with all of his bullshit.

Monty reluctantly slid past the group of mourners and walked across the foyer towards the kitchen. "What do you want?" he said, as he approached the kitchen, his stomach beginning to turn at the sight of Dexter's face.

Dexter sighed and took off his glasses then began to rub his nose with his forefinger and thumb. Something was wrong. Dexter wasn't laughing, smiling, or even scowling. In fact, he seemed to have no emotion at all. "Hey Monty," he finally said, as he put back on his glasses, the bags under his eyes like they'd been stuffed with coins. "You got a minute? We need to talk."

"What's it about?"

Dexter hesitated, like he was about to answer, then shook his head and just said, "You'll find out."

When they got to his office, Dexter fished his keys from his pocket. "Monty?" he said, in barely a whisper, as if he didn't have the strength to use his vocal chords.

"Yeah?"

Dexter opened his mouth as if he was going to say something, but couldn't find the words and just dropped his head. "Never mind," he said, then turned away from him and pushed open the door. "Please come in. Have a seat."

Monty took a deep breath and stepped in through the doorway, hesitating when he saw Dave hunkered in the corner with his head in his hands. He was sitting on the green couch, slightly hunched over, his feet wide apart, his elbows on his knees. "Hey Dave," Monty said, as he stepped into the office, his heart beating faster, his hands starting to shake. "What's going on? Is everything alright?"

Dave looked up at Monty, for only a moment, then quickly dropped his head as if it was too heavy to hold up. He looked like shit. His eyes were drawn, all puffed up and haggard, and his hair looked like it had gone through a wind tunnel.

"Please have a seat, Monty," Dexter said, as he shut the door behind him then walked around the desk and slowly sat down.

Monty looked at Dave, then over at Dexter. Something was definitely going on. "What's this all about?" he said, standing by the doorway, preferring to stay there in case he needed to get out. "Is everything alright?"

"Just have a seat, please."

"Look, if this is about the damage to the trailer, I'm sorry, I'll pay for it. I was just pissed off—"

"No." Dexter cut him off. "This has nothing to do with that. Please, just, have a seat."

Monty conceded and scuffled towards the armchair that sat directly in front of Dexter's desk. His mind was swimming with questions about what was happening. If it wasn't the wall in the bedroom then what the hell was it? And why was Dave here? Why was he just sitting there and not saying anything, looking like a kid who'd been put in detention? What the hell was wrong with him? Did he do something last night that made him angry? Did he say something to him that pissed him off? And what was with the ambulance? Did somebody get injured? Why wouldn't they tell him what the hell was going on?

Dexter cleared his throat. "Monty," he said, folding his hands in front of him. "I'm sure you're wondering what this is all about."

"Yeah, no shit."

Dexter paused and looked down at his knuckles, as if the right words were somehow imprinted on the back of his fingers. His hands were shaking, his lips were trembling, and he had little beads of sweat forming just above his upper lip.

Immediately, Monty began to get that uneasy feeling, that feeling of nerves twisting deep inside his gut. Something was off, something was coming, something told him he should get up and run. But he didn't run. Not this time. Something told him to hold his ground. So, he sat up straight and squared his shoulders, his hands on his knees, his feet on the floor. "What's going on?" he asked, leaning forward, the twisting in his stomach now up in his throat.

"Monty"—Dexter's voice was a delicate whisper, like the exchange of condolences inside a funeral home. He glanced over at Dave, but Dave just sat there, chewing on his nails, staring down at the floor—"There's something we need to tell you."

"What is it?"

"It's about Vicky. It's about the accident."

The hairs on Monty's neck began to stand upward like the needles imbedded in a porcupine's fur. He clenched his jaw and dug his fingers into the armchair, so tight that his hands and arms began to quiver. "What about it?" he said, leaning so far forward, that it looked like his chin might touch the top of Dexter's skull.

"Well"—Dexter's eyes darted between Dave and the doorway, as if he was checking to make sure Monty couldn't escape—"It's a very fragile situation, and before we get into it, I just want to remind you what it says in the Big Book about forgiveness. Do you remember what it says?"

"What?"

"The Big Book, Monty. Do you remember what it says about forgiveness?"

"Look—cut the shit, Dexter, and just tell me what the fuck's going on."

Dexter stared at him for just a moment, then dropped his head and looked back down at his hands. "Alright, well, last night, you told Dave about the accident, about how you weren't sure whether or not another vehicle ran you off the road?"

"Yeah. So?"

"Well, Dave here has some information about it. He believes he might know who the other driver was."

"*What?*"

"Dave?" Dexter turned and looked over at him. "You wanna tell Monty what you know?"

Dave nodded and finally looked up at Monty—it looked like his head was attached to the floor. His eyes were dripping and his hands were convulsing. He was crying so hard, it sounded like he was choking, the words like something sharp lodged in his esophagus. "Monty," he said, looking up at him, the snot from his nostrils dripping down his chin. "I'm so sorry. I was fucked up and I didn't know what I was doing. I didn't even remember what happened until you told me last night. Please Monty, forgive me. I fucked up, I'm sorry. I'll turn myself in. I'll go to prison. Just tell me what to do. I'll do whatever you want—"

Monty's body went numb and he collapsed back into the armchair, watching as Dave's lips moved up and down. But he couldn't hear anything that the guy was saying, his words swallowed by a harsh, swilling sound—a sound like water flushing in through the windows, pouring in through the door, filling up the room. He looked down at his hands—they were shaking, his knuckles a trembling, bloodless rage. The sound of the water was getting louder and louder, its continuous drone drowning out all other sound. When he looked back up, Dave was still talking, his tobacco-stained gums flapping up and down. Then, something sharp swelled inside him, something white and hot pumping through his veins. It felt as if God himself had reached down and touched him and injected him with the fury of heaven and hell. He rose up from the armchair, as if lifted by something, his feet beneath him, but not touching the floor.

Then, all he could hear was Dave screaming, pleading with him to get the hell off of him. Monty had Dave's elbows pinned underneath his knees, his fists like cleavers dropping down on his jaw. He could hear the cartilage splitting beneath him like carrots getting chopped underneath the blade. The blood from Dave's mouth spilled out onto the carpet and his eyes began to roll into the back of his head, but Monty didn't stop—he kept on going, the flesh from his knuckles sticking to Dave's skin. But then something grabbed him and pulled him backward…away from the beating…away from Dave. It was Dexter. He had his skinny arms wrapped around Monty's shoulders and his hands locked just beneath his collarbone. He pulled Monty back across the office and threw him like a rag doll up against the wall. Then, he took his forearm and plunged it against Monty's adam's apple and locked it there just beneath his chin.

"Stop it!" Dexter screamed, as he leaned all his weight into Monty, the pressure from his forearm pinning Monty up against the wall. "Stop acting like this! How many times have you driven intoxicated? How many times have you gotten on that road drunk?"

"Get the fuck off me!" Monty screamed, writhing beneath him, the pressure from the forearm cutting off the air to his lungs.

"Can't you see, Monty? He's just like you! The only difference is, you haven't killed anyone yet. But he has. He admits it. He's accepted the blame and is ready to face himself. What have you done? Nothing. Nothing since you got here. Nothing but walk around, feeling sorry for yourself."

"Get the fuck off me. I can't breathe."

"No. Not until you tell me you're forgiven. Not until you tell me that you can forgive yourself."

Dexter took his forearm and plunged it further against Monty's adam's apple, the asphyxiating weight of it turning all light in the room to black. "Say it, Monty. Say you're forgiven. Say you can move forward. Say it wasn't your fault."

"I can't."

"Why not?"

"Because."

"Because why?"

"BECAUSE I DIDN'T LOVE HER, ALRIGHT!? IS THAT WHAT YOU WANNA FUCKING HEAR!?"

"IS IT THE TRUTH!?"

"YES! YES IT'S THE FUCKING TRUTH!"

Dexter finally released him, removing his forearm from Monty's throat. Monty collapsed to his knees while coughing, the oxygen in the air rushing back to his lungs. "I didn't love her," he said, as he sunk towards the carpet, the light in the room slowly coming back to his eyes. "I didn't love her, but I needed her. She was the only thing I fucking had."

"But she's gone now—"

"And I killed her."

"No."

"Yes. I'm the reason she's fucking dead."

"But it wasn't your fault. Dave just told you that. The guy over there just confessed."

"It doesn't matter."

"What do you mean it doesn't matter?"

Monty clenched his fists and slammed them against the carpet, his already chewed up knuckles further tearing against the floor. "Don't you see?" he said, as he looked up at Dexter, the tears in his eyes streaming down his cheeks. "If I hadn't met her, none of this would've happened. If I hadn't *used* her she'd still be here."

"That's bullshit Monty and you know it. You're just using that as an excuse so you don't have to recover. You're taking the blame so you can feel sorry for yourself."

"So what if I am?"

Dexter paused and took a step backward, his mouth wide open, his shoulders slumped forward.

"Well," he said, as he looked down at Monty, his eyes filled with deep disappointment. "I guess you're right back where you first started, hiding behind blame so you don't have to face yourself. Well go ahead. Keep blaming yourself. Keep pitying yourself and go crawl back inside your hole, because I can't do this with you anymore. I can't waste my time and my efforts trying to help someone who doesn't want to be helped. I have too many other patients in here to worry about—people who actually need and want my help—people like Dave over there, who are ready to recover, who are ready to face themselves. He didn't have to do this, Monty. But he did. He came forward. Because he knew that if he didn't, he could never recover. And now that he's told you, what are you doing? Just hiding behind the same cop-out that you were when you first got here. And that's pathetic. That's really pathetic. And I won't stand by anymore watching you do this to yourself."

Dexter dropped his head and drew a deep breath inward, then put his hand on his knee and pushed himself up. He walked to the floor safe and knelt down in front of it, pushed the code into the keypad and pulled open the safe. Reaching inside, he pulled out a little, plastic baggy that had Monty's name taped across. "Here," he said, as he stood up with the baggy and tossed it out onto the carpet, "it's all yours. Take it."

Monty clenched his teeth and put one hand into the carpet then, sliding the other hand against the wall for balance, he slowly pushed himself up. His head was spinning and his throat was throbbing, but somehow he was able to straighten his legs and regain his equilibrium. As he limped across the office, he held his stomach, the blood from his knuckles dripping out across the floor. When he got to the baggy, he stopped and looked down at it, then looked up at Dexter, then back at the baggy.

"What are you waiting for?" Dexter said. "Go on, take it. If you don't want to be here then get the fuck out."

Monty bent his knees and crouched next to the baggy then reached out his hand and scooped it up off of the floor. He opened it up and pulled out his wallet, pulled out his keys, and pulled out his phone. He shoved them all inside his jacket pocket and let the remaining contents fall to the floor—his cologne, his razor, his worn out shoelaces—he didn't really see a need to take them where he was going.

He cleared his throat and squared his shoulders then walked towards the door on the other side of the office. But before he could open it, Dexter walked out after him, grabbed his shoulder and pulled him back. "Just know, that this is it, Monty…this is your last opportunity. If you walk through that door, you can never come back. And you and I both know that you'll never make it. You'll eventually die a sad and lonely alcoholic death. It may not be today and it may not be tomorrow, but eventually, one day, you will die from this thing."

"I know," Monty said then pulled his arm away from him, opened the door, and walked out.

Chapter 35

The End

It was almost dark outside by the time they pulled into the Greyhound bus terminal, the last remnants of the day shooting like embers from behind the backdrop of the Rocky Mountains. It had taken him all day, but he finally made it. He was back in Denver. He was back home.

As the bus came to a stop, the driver pushed a button that popped the doors open. The passengers got up from their seats and scampered down the aisle. They brushed by Monty as he sat there waiting, his body turned towards the window, his forehead pressed up against the cold glass. Once the last guy had gotten up and walked by him, Monty grabbed the seat in front of him and slowly pulled himself up.

When he got to the front, he stepped down through the doorway then moved to the line of bags being stacked by the rear of the bus. He spotted his green gym bag by the right rear tire then carefully bent down and picked it up. He made his way through the sad, desolate terminal, past the succession of wooden benches and out the front door. When he got outside, he flagged down a taxi, threw his bag in the trunk and climbed in the backseat. The driver asked where he was going and Monty told him—back to his apartment in Capitol Hill.

The ride was short, about ten minutes, all the way down Colfax, a right onto Washington, and a left onto fourteenth. They stopped on the street in front of his building and Monty got out and paid the fare. Since he didn't have any cash, the driver took down his information, including the numbers on his health savings debit card. Then, Monty grabbed his gym bag, slung it over his shoulder, walked down the sidewalk, and up the two flights of stairs. When he got to his door, he reached into his pocket, pulled out his keys and shoved them into the lock. As he pushed the door open, he was nearly knocked over by the stench of puke, urine, and stale alcohol. It was like death greeting him, like something decaying, like pieces of human excrement that had been baked in the oven for too long. It was inside the walls, imbedded in the carpet, soaked in the furniture, and saturated in the air. He could taste it in his mouth and feel it on his body, like a hot bowl of pea soup sticking to his skin. The smell was so bad that it made him quiver, the sickness in his stomach rising up in his throat.

He shut the door behind him then pressed farther inward, trying not to step on the liquor bottles that were strewn across the living room floor. But that was easier said than done. The bottles were everywhere. It was almost as if someone had taken a trash bag and dumped it right in the middle of the room. They bounced off his shoes and rolled around on the carpet as he felt for the light switch that was mounted somewhere on the wall. He found it and flipped it upward, but nothing came on—the electricity was off.

He staggered into the kitchen then opened the window to let in some air. Standing on his tiptoes, he looked in the cupboard and saw the matches sitting on the top of the microwave. He grabbed the box and walked over to the window and lit the candle that was sitting on the sill. Then, he took the candle and placed it on the counter next to an old box of pizza. As he looked down at the candle, he noticed a pair of shadows, moving through the light that was dancing around from the flame. He lowered his head to get a little closer and saw a group of cockroaches scurrying back behind the stove. They were fat and hairy, the size of golf balls, bloated on a slice of pizza that was completely covered with a thick, black mold. He jumped back, the chills running through him, the hot bitterness rising up into his throat. He shut his eyes and stood completely stationary, concentrating on his stomach, trying to breathe through his nose. But it was too late. There was too much of it. The more he swallowed, the more it came up. He couldn't fight it. He had to get rid of it. It was coming up too fast. He couldn't keep up.

He covered his mouth and ran to the bathroom, then dropped to his knees and lifted the lid of the bowl. His stomach emptied like a winning slot machine, hot chunks of bile spewing from his throat. As it dropped into the toilet, the water splashed upward, hitting him in the eyes and dripping down his nose. But he didn't care, because it didn't matter. Nothing else mattered. Not anymore.

He finished puking then flushed the toilet and watched his entrails swirl around in the bowl. As he pulled himself up, he saw something sitting behind the toilet, wedged behind the drain pipe and the base of the bowl. It was a handle of Cutty Sark scotch, wading in a puddle of toilet water, cobwebs bridged between the base of the bottle and the wall. He quickly turned away and tried not to look at it, but it seemed to be watching him, as if it had eyes in its brown plastic cap.

He went over to the sink and opened up the medicine cabinet to see if his Trazadone bottles were all still there. They were—lined up together in straight, militant formation, like little red soldiers about to go to war. Four bottles times thirty, equaled one twenty, which was more than enough to send him to hell.

He nodded to himself as he shut the medicine cabinet, then reached behind the toilet and grabbed the handle of scotch. But before he opened it, he looked up into the mirror, at the pale, blue eyes that were sunk in his face. This was it, he thought. This was his moment. After tonight, he could never go back. Once he started, he had to finish. He couldn't wimp out. He couldn't quit. He had to pursue it to the gates of insanity, until his heart stopped beating, until he breathed his last breath. This was all he had left and so he had to embrace it. He had to turn his life and his will over to the care of his higher power—alcohol. It was his friend, his family, his life, his lover. Without it, he was nothing, he was nobody, he was lost. And so he drank, not out of gluttony or because he wanted to fulfill some kind of selfish indulgence—he drank because he had to. He drank because that's who he was. Alcohol was as much a part of him as was his genetic makeup. It was inside his body. It was inside his bones. It was his purpose, his destiny, his penance, his atonement. His name was Monty and he was an alcoholic.

Acknowledgements

I'd like to extend a special thank you to Cortney Rehnberg and her beautiful daughter, Eva, who gave me the love and support I needed to learn how to live life again. I love you both very much. I'd also like to thank my writing teacher, Doug Kurtz, whose brilliant insight helped me to sharpen this story. Finally, I'd like to thank the following people who contributed in one way or another to the writing of this novel: Randall, Patricia, Phil, Christine, Rupert, Taz, and Gigi Seaward, William McMechen, Stacy Garcia, Lisa Voltz, Dan & Elisabeth Wells, Dan Vade Bon Coeur (aka Dan Adams), Kevin Clark, Gus Carruth, Eric Johnson, Patrick Murillo, Matt Miller, Lisa Soderlind, Megan Zuchowski, Christian George, Keith Moodispaugh, Rachel Gillis, Matt Black, Robby Farina, Benson & Christina Ledbetter, Cliffe Umstead, Richard & Lark Fleming, Dave Wylde, Benjy Dobrin, James Scherrer, Tauna Rignall, Chris Cunningham, Cougar Littlefield, Rob McNeil, Nick Petraglia, Nathan Faber, Zeeshan Gull, Larry Hebert, John Jechura, Craig (the homeless guy), Still Kallil, Skip Francouer, Paul Minor, Tommy & Joey Knothe, Dion Awakian, Dr. Ronald Neuman, Dr. Chris Roberts, Dr. Robert Chambers, Dr. Jacobs (Houston), Ben Wong, Brian Vincente, Doug Wildemuth, Prasad Garimella, Brian Murphy, Suhki Kaur, Todd Frank, Mandy Schmiedlin, Jay White, Alan Brown, John Bryant, Paxton (*Oasis*), Dylan Ritter, Richard Bourgeau, Dennis (*Foundations*), and Josh (*Foundations*). I'd also like to thank Jessica Carter for helping me proofread this thing. Thank you all for your support.